Edward swung his legs back on the bed and closed his eyes. Enough of the chit-chat. He was terminating the interview. They would have to arrest and caution him before he said another word.

Andy recognised the stance. It was a familiar response to interrogation; but the law no longer recognised silence as a refuge for the suspect. Silence implied guilt; and Andy was damned if he would release Edward Jay so easily. He fired a warning shot.

"Tell me something. Are you still in contact with Samuel Tate?" Andy paused. There was no answer. "I suspect Tate had something to do with your troubles. It wouldn't surprise me if he got you out of Pakistan. Now you think you're indebted to him. I don't think you're so bad. A bit misguided. A fool, maybe. But Tate's a really nasty piece of work. We go back a long way. And I want you to know I'm following Tate; whatever he does and wherever he goes. If you're smart you'll steer clear of him." Edward continued to ignore Andy. "When you discover the truth about your mate, I want you to know I'll give you an ear. Remember that. I'll always give you an ear."

*About the Author*

Roderick Kalberer was born in Lagos, Nigeria, and brought up against a backdrop of post-colonial violence and corruption. Educated in England, he now lives on a small island off the East Coast. He races classic yachts and has sailed widely, from the Red Sea to the Grand Banks. He is currently writing his second novel.

**For Bob**

I would like to thank those who told their stories but must remain anonymous, as well as Alistair, Andrew, Caroline, Peter and Tony for their encouragement.

# Prologue

Andy finished hosing the deck of the fishing boat. He took off his oilskins and hung them in the wheelhouse. He lit a cigarette and watched the gathering clouds. He was glad to be in the harbour. It would be blowing a gale before midnight. Only a few dinghies from the Colne Yacht Club were still on the river, and they were racing against the ebbing tide to the clubhouse. He flicked his cigarette over the side; it was time to go ashore and see Rosa. As he stepped into the dory he caught sight of a yacht approaching the channel. The tide was already half out, and the mud banks were showing. The yacht would be lucky to find enough water. He watched as she nosed her way towards him, then drifted out of the channel. He waited for her to alter course, but she didn't. Her bow dipped, and she was aground.

Andy started the dory engines, and sped across. They'd have to be quick. The tide was ripping away. He pulled alongside and spotted the teak decks. She was an expensive toy and wouldn't like being stranded in a gale. If he towed her off he'd earn a drink.

Andy threw a line, waited until it was made fast around the anchor winch, and then started pulling. Slowly the yacht's bow swung towards the channel and she slipped free of the mud. Andy towed her to a vacant mooring. He noticed she was sitting low on her flotation marks. She was probably stocked with tons of cruising equipment for the summer holiday. He looked at the three crew. They were in their early twenties. They cast off the dory, gave brief smiles, raised their hands in acknowledgement and busied themselves squaring away the boat. Andy sped for the shore.

That night Andy saw the yacht's crew in the pub.

The one who fancied himself the captain approached him. 'My name's Samuel Tate,' he said. 'Let me buy you a drink.'

'Andy. Andy Ballot. I'll have a pint, thanks.'

'We're on holiday,' explained Tate. 'Bloody engine broke down. That's why we sailed in.'

1

Andy said nothing. He nodded.

'This is a quiet spot,' commented Tate. 'Does much ever happen here?'

'Depends what you're looking for,' replied Andy, reticently.

Tate nodded. Bloody yokels had no idea about the cut and thrust of conversation. 'What do you do?' he asked.

'Fishing.'

He made a last attempt at conversation. 'Any chance of buying some fish?'

'The next couple of days will be a bit windy for fishing.' Andy stood up. 'Thanks for the drink,' he said, and joined the pretty girl who had entered the bar.

Andy felt someone at his shoulder, turned, and found Tate standing there. 'That's for your trouble,' said Tate, putting a twenty-pound note on the bar.

It takes more than that to buy friendship, thought Andy, pocketing the money.

'Why don't you come for a sail when we've fixed the engine?' asked Tate.

'I'll be working,' said Andy.

'Is that your boat?' asked Rosa, looking at the yacht which dwarfed the other sailing boats in the harbour.

'Yes,' said Tate. 'Perhaps you'd like to come. We need someone with a little local knowledge. Andy had to pull us off the mud.' He darted a conspiratorial grin at Andy.

Andy shrugged it off. 'Staying long?' he asked pointedly.

'A couple of weeks. Maybe a month. We've no particular place to go,' said Tate, casually.

Plenty of time to sell you harbour mullet at bass prices, thought Andy.

'I'd love to sail on a proper yacht,' said Rosa, naïvely.

'My name's Samuel Tate.' He extended his hand. Rosa took it innocently.

Andy looked away. He didn't like Tate. 'Let's go, Rosa,' he ordered.

When they left Tate made the phone call. He'd got the feel of this place. There was nothing to worry about.

For the third and last time in his life Edward drove into Brightlingsea. He stopped the van by the wharf, got out, and stretched. He put on his overalls. He was in no hurry. He recognised every inch of the waterfront from the roll of photographs he took the first time. Behind him, The Anchor, to the right the Sail Loft, to the left the Yacht Club. In front of him the boats strained at their moorings as the wind lashed in from the sea. He went in search of a mug of tea. He'd let Tate track him down. After all, he wasn't supposed to know what the boat looked like. He stopped in front of the estate agent's window and looked at the price of the cottages. By nightfall he'd be able to buy one. In one day he could have what it took some people their whole lives to achieve. Momentarily the thought unsettled him. He turned back for the waterfront and caught sight of Tate standing by the van.

At lunchtime Andy was disappointed to find Tate ensconced in the bay window of The Anchor, with an audience of pensioners for whom he'd bought drinks. He couldn't help overhearing Tate's running commentary on the mechanic's progress. The yacht's engine hadn't seized after all. The problem was the fuel injectors. If Tate was so smart he should have hired a local engineer; but then people like him had more money than sense. Nice day out in the country for the mechanic, though. It was ten to two. The landlady turned up the radio for the shipping forecast.

In the early evening Tate and Edward played their little charade in the bar, loudly haggling over the price for fixing the yacht's engine, impressing the nature of their business upon the eavesdroppers. Tate complained about the cost, and the overtime. Edward told him he should have hired a local man and refused to accept a cheque. Tate ostentatiously paid Edward in cash. The locals nodded, sympathising with the mechanic. Yachtsmen were always the same: they expected everything to be free, just because they didn't pay for the wind.

Now it was time to go. Edward stood up and shook Tate's hand. As he returned his glass to the bar he overheard a conversation between two girls. He looked at them briefly. One was pretty with dark hair. She was upset because her boyfriend didn't want her to go sailing. Edward wanted to tell her to do it. Go for the adventure; it didn't matter what was right. There was always time to correct things in the future. 'Go for it,' he said to her, as he passed their table. 'You might never get another chance.' The girl looked up, surprised, and smiled hesitantly.

As he drove back to London, Edward thought about the girl who couldn't decide whether to go sailing. He envied her innocence and her caution. He wove a few dreams around her, and imagined a life with her in a cottage on the sea front. As he drove into the city he forgot about her. He had a job to do.

Rosa went sailing with Tate and his friends. The days turned into weeks. A high pressure system established itself over Eastern England. There was a heat wave followed by water shortages. The fishermen were busy catching bass. In early August, Tate left on the yacht. Three days later a man attracted by his whimpering spaniel on Clacton's beach found a young woman's naked body deposited by the ebbing tide. He realised she was dead when he was twenty feet away, but a morbid curiosity drew him closer. He stood for a moment, mesmerised in the face of death. She was young and had been beautiful. Her naked body, limbs askew on the sand, screamed 'murder'. The man hurried towards dry land and telephoned the police.

Rosa's body was quickly identified. Her capsized dinghy was later found on the other side of the river. There was no murder enquiry. The caressing action of the water and waves always stripped corpses of their clothes before returning them to the land.

After the inquest Andy sensed a conspiracy. Rosa's family no longer included him in their mourning. At the funeral he stood bewildered by the graveside; he felt some irrational responsibility for her death. Occasionally he intercepted an awkward glance. Afterwards he looked to see who had sent flowers. There were none from Tate, and that made him guilty. Tate knew about Rosa's death all right, because he'd been summoned to the inquest.

It was the two customs officers who inadvertently sent him searching for the answers. They interviewed him about the yacht. They asked if he was aware it had sailed from Holland. They warned him he could have committed an offence by helping, and not reporting its arrival. They said they were investigating rumours that the boat had been used to smuggle drugs and he had known about it.

Andy felt betrayed. He didn't care that someone had tried to implicate him. He wanted to know why Tate had left the morning Rosa disappeared. She would never have capsized her dinghy, and he wanted to know why the police didn't think her death was suspicious.

Finally he read the coroner's report and understood the conspiracy of silence which surrounded the village. Rosa had drowned, but high levels of hallucinogens and cannabis were found in her bloodstream. The coroner's verdict was 'Death by misadventure'. The autopsy revealed that Rosa was two months pregnant; and Andy knew that the child was his.

Andy didn't want to keep silent. He wasn't prepared to abandon Rosa. He didn't want to forget her. He was haunted by her ghost on the foreshore. Her eyes, once so invitingly curious, now stared back from the sea. He remembered too many things. The scent of freshly sawn oak reminded him of when he first kissed her in her father's wood yard. Even the wind conspired to keep her memory alive, conjuring the times they had sailed together and walked hand in hand along the foreshore.

Andy escaped from the claustrophobic village which had betrayed Rosa and enrolled at college. He spent long nights studying to make up for lost schooling. A year later he went to London University. His past ended with Rosa's death. His emotional development stopped because Rosa's death was never resolved. He changed. He didn't like people who cared about trivial things. He once told a girl about Rosa. She said his mourning was unhealthy, so he tried therapy. It didn't help. Feelings caused pain, and he cut them off.

When Andy graduated he joined Her Majesty's Customs and Excise Department. It was ten years before he ran into Samuel Tate again.

Revenge was a dish, best eaten cold.

# Chapter 1

## 1

For Julia, it began with a knock on the door. She stopped reading the book. As she stood up she knew that her life was about to change. The knocking had a particular quality; it was neither hesitant nor familiar. It had the air of authority and inevitability. She knew she had been waiting for that knock for a long time.

Julia opened the door and found an oddly lopsided man hidden in a black coat which seemed too large for him. He was thrusting some form of identification towards her. She didn't look at it. She heard him say, 'My name is Andy Ballot. I'm from Her Majesty's Customs and Excise Department. I have something to tell you.' His voice was not loud but seemed to silence the whole of London.

Julia stepped back into the room and smiled weakly. Andy Ballot followed her in. The two men accompanying him remained outside, and Julia closed the door. She knew the visit concerned Edward, but she didn't know why. Immediately she was convinced that he was dead. She didn't want to hear what Andy Ballot was going to say. 'Can I get you something to drink?' she asked stupidly.

'No thanks,' said Andy. 'Perhaps you should sit down,' he added, alarmed by Julia's pallid complexion. Julia sat down, now convinced that Edward had had an accident in Pakistan.

'You are Julia Crighton-Smith?' he asked. Julia nodded and bit her lip. 'And Edward Jay is your boyfriend?'

'Yes,' Julia whispered.

'I don't suppose you've heard that he's been arrested in Pakistan, in

7

possession of two tons of cannabis resin which he intended to import to this country?'

Julia sighed, and her shoulders shook with the relief. She closed her eyes tightly and offered a prayer of thanks. Two small tears formed in the corners of her eyes and rolled down her cheeks.

Andy looked away embarrassed. He was angry that someone like Edward Jay should have risked and squandered so much love. 'I'm sorry,' he said, not understanding the precise reason for her emotion, only knowing that he was somehow responsible.

'No, no, don't be sorry,' said Julia hurriedly. 'I expected . . .' she began, but then said nothing.

'We know you aren't involved, because we've had you under observation. However, I have a warrant to search this flat.'

'Of course,' said Julia. 'What's going to happen to Edward?'

'He'll go to prison.'

'For how long?'

'I don't know. I'm not an expert on the subject. Pakistan has strict sentencing. In the region of five to ten years.'

'Can't you extradite him to a prison in this country?'

'I'm afraid that isn't government policy.'

'Oh,' said Julia. The reality was beginning to take hold.

'Could you show me where Edward keeps his papers, address books and stuff like that? I'd like to have a look through them.'

Julia was helpful. There was no reason not to be. She knew that Edward kept no incriminating evidence. He kept names and telephone numbers in his head, and his bank accounts were meticulously in order. Edward had always been proud of that. He told her that Al Capone taught the criminal fraternity all they needed to know when he was indicted because he couldn't account for his expensive wardrobe. Edward owned nothing. He'd never been tempted to buy a house. He rented. If he needed money in the bank he bought something for cash at an auction and sold it elsewhere for a small loss if necessary. Julia's friends admired Edward's entrepreneurial skills. Julia had thought the charade ridiculous, until now.

The other two officers helped Andy Ballot search. They found little, and removed the bank statements which they promised to return.

'There don't seem to be many of his belongings here,' commented Andy. 'He wouldn't have another address, by any chance?'

'No,' said Julia.

Having carried out a discreet but thorough search, the customs officers left Julia alone to contemplate five or ten years without Edward. 'If you think of anything, or just want to talk,' said Andy, 'telephone me.'

He handed her a card, and grinned that hangdog, lopsided smile which she noticed when she first opened the door.

Two weeks later Julia heard from Samuel Tate that Edward had been sentenced to ten years. She was shocked. For years she had lived with the possibility that something might happen to him, but it hadn't prepared her for the reality. One or two of his business colleagues phoned nervously, fishing for information, trying to find out if there was an investigation which might jeopardise their own freedom. Once reassured, they all promptly forgot her. She never heard another word from Tate, who had called, that once, from a phone box. It was some time before her friends noticed Edward's prolonged absence. He'd always led a furtive life, appearing and disappearing without explanation. When they asked where he was, she lied and said he was setting up a business in the Far East. The lies distanced her from everyone and accentuated the loneliness. Only one or two of her closest friends knew the truth.

There weren't even letters from Edward. Surely he hadn't really meant she should forget him if he was ever caught? With Edward life had always been insecure; but it hadn't been like this, a life in limbo. She used to shudder every time she heard the phone ring because it might be summoning him to work. His unpredictable jobs meant that there were holidays to cancel, apologies to make for dates not kept, and friends left in the lurch. But, he had always been there to answer the questions, make up the lies, and provide explanations.

It had always been lonely. She was never able to tell the truth. People were always curious how Edward made his money. She told them he bought and sold things. Her parents remarked it was an insecure way to make a living. She pointed out that it was no more insecure than dealing in antiques. She was drawn into the lie, expanding on it; and eventually was corrupted by it. She explained how Edward researched his targets, looking to fill small pockets of demand. She said he flew by the seat of his pants. Her parents didn't understand. They wanted to know what sort of things he sold. As a result she was forced to create a romantic career for Edward, in which he was surrounded by forgotten Sickert watercolours, Fabergé eggs, and even containers of Levi jeans. Then, whenever they met friends or family, she reminded him to talk about his latest deal, and give some credence to the lie. Lying never bothered Edward. He said the lies never hurt people. But Julia knew they did. They were insidious. The illusion of his exciting life made others dissatisfied with their own lives.

Four months later Julia found she missed Edward more than ever. She forgot how insecure life had been with him. She forgot how frightened she felt every time he went out of the front door, scared that he would return in a Black Maria. She craved those experiences she resented so much before his disappearance; the sudden weekend trips to Paris, Venice or Berlin; expensive dinners; and first-class hotels.

Her yearning for Edward became uncontrollable. She wondered if she was going mad. She began to believe the lies she told others. She made herself believe that Edward was setting up some business in the Far East and would be returning soon. One day she saw him turning the aisle of a supermarket. She recognised him from the peculiar way he stalked through crowds; the slight hunch of his shoulders; his profile, the turn of his neck, the flare of his nostrils and the curl of lips beneath high cheekbones. She rushed towards him, heart beating faster, but he was gone. Suddenly she vividly recalled making love to him. She was annoyed to discover her body reacted uncontrollably to the memory. Her breasts ached. She longed to put a finger between her thighs, there, of all places, in a supermarket. She did not know whether to feel excited or disgusted at her feelings. There were so many days when he haunted her. Everyone seemed to have blue eyes. She stretched out a hand and chose a biodegradable washing powder and threw it on the supermarket trolley. She allowed her hand to graze her hardening nipples and reminded herself that she was a single woman again; a single woman who carried Edward's child. And because of that she would always belong to him. Ten years! Would he haunt her all that time?

It was the absence of any concrete information about Edward which made her make the telephone call. She wondered if there was any chance that he would be released before he completed his sentence. She was frightened about the future. She had never doubted that she was attractive, but would anyone want her now she was about to become a social pariah, an unmarried, single mother? Her body's curves were already being masked by her child. She wanted to talk to someone who understood her situation, knew about Edward's circumstances, and who would tell her what to do. She was desperate, and so she called Andy Ballot.

2

The customs officer taking a half hour break at London's Heathrow Airport could never explain why some passengers aroused his suspicions.

It was a question of having a nose for the job and an eye for detail. Gold watches and nylon shirts did not go together. The customs officer had been wandering around the departure check-in desks when he caught sight of the suspect. He watched the man change three large bundles of sterling into guilders and Swiss francs. Business men who exchanged sterling at the airport weren't exhibiting normal business acumen. Regular business men used gold credit cards or had their secretaries arrange their foreign exchange in advance. He watched the man deposit his baggage and then he had a word with the Home Office official on the passport desk. He waited while the suspect offered his passport for inspection, and the official memorised the name and number. Armed with the suspect's name, Samuel Tate, the officer made out a Suspicious Movement Report. He tapped the information into CEDRIC, acronym for the Customs and Excise Department Reference and Information Computer which contained over a quarter of a million suspect names. The computer referred him to the National Drugs Intelligence Unit, the joint police and customs unit at Scotland Yard, which would provide him with access to the Police National Computer. He read the information which appeared on the screen with interest. Tate had a criminal record.

The gate for the British Airways flight to Amsterdam had closed and the customs officer made his way to the departure gate to retrieve the flight coupon. The details would show where and how the ticket was bought, and whether there was a connecting flight. As he looked at the ticket details he was sure of one thing. Samuel Tate was still up to no good. He had bought the ticket for cash. That was not illegal, but business men usually bought tickets with credit cards or had accounts with travel agencies. Curiously, he noticed the ticket was made out to Mr Yate, and not Tate. It was probably a slip of the typist's finger, but it could also be an alias. There was also a flight connection to Geneva five days later. Cash and Switzerland suggested one thing. Dirty money. Someone, somewhere, would welcome this snippet of information about Samuel Tate.

Meanwhile, Samuel Tate sat in the aisle seat of the British Airways flight to Amsterdam, travelling Business Class, a *Financial Times* on his knee. Over the years he had worked hard to create the image of old money and blue blood. After all, policemen thought twice before they apprehended the upper classes. Only English gentlemen of the old school smelt a rat. His immaculate dress sense was the result of frequenting Savile Row tailors where obsequious salesmen offered advice. 'Oh no, sir. It's not done to wear a handkerchief in the top pocket of a town suit. Perhaps I could interest you in a pair of platinum cufflinks, sir? Not the gold ones in this instance, sir, if I may say so. Gold is correct for daytime

11

use, but it's very common in the evenings.' His sartorial elegance had been an expensive exercise, but it was the details which made all the difference.

Tate's family was nouveau riche and the blood was red, but who gave a shit about all that. He certainly didn't. He peered through the porthole of the plane, watched the grey tarmac speeding past, and imagined his silver Mercedes racing along under the wing tip. He felt the sudden lurch as the plane became airborne, and he relaxed. Despite his apparent ease, airports made him nervous. There was always the fear that he might be stopped as he boarded the plane. Always the fear that he had overlooked something. Perhaps they knew he carried another identity. Perhaps he hadn't spotted their surveillance.

He was tall and slim. His dark hair was turning grey at the temples. He wore spectacles with heavy frames, which on close inspection proved to contain lenses of clear glass. They rested on a bony Roman nose. He had a high forehead from which the hairline was receding, and on which the lines of age and worry were being slowly etched. His mouth was small and straight. He was wearing a double-breasted pinstripe suit. He looked fifty, ten years older than he really was.

Tate's thoughts were broken by something unpleasant. A man had changed seats and was now sitting across the aisle from him. He was wearing a shiny blue suit which could have done with cleaning. He was somewhat greasy. Thirty years old. Why did common people always lack style when they tried to look smart? Why did they bother to dress for flights? Then Tate noticed his footwear. The socks were nylon. The shoes were well used, but they had a thick composite sole. He always looked at a person's shoes. 'You can tell a gentleman by his shoes,' his mother once told him. Gentlemen and policemen, Tate had learned.

Tate felt a flutter in his stomach. He knew why. He was paranoid. He knew all about surveillance. There were those small incongruous signs; the builder's van parked opposite his flat all day, and not a builder in sight; the dry cleaner's van which no business could afford to leave idle; odd incidents at bars when he caught people looking at him.

The plane hit an air pocket. Tate looked up and realised the man was addressing him. 'What?' he said.

'I said, it's worrying how the wings flex in these planes.'

'They'd snap off if they were rigid,' Tate replied, curtly.

'Do you have a plane of your own?'

Some people have no idea about personal space, thought Tate. Especially the police. Again there was the little flutter in his stomach. 'No,' he replied.

'Oh! It sounded like you did. Do you often use the shuttle?'

'First time,' lied Tate. He hadn't once looked the man in the eye. He was definitely a member of the other firm. No one else would have the gall to pursue a conversation in the face of such taciturn resistance.

'It's my first time as well. I've a meeting in Amsterdam. Where are you going?'

'Amsterdam,' replied Tate, 'unless you're planning to hijack the flight.'

'Oh no. I'm going there on a business trip.' This one had absolutely no sense of humour.

'I might have guessed. You are travelling business class, after all.' Tate laboured the point.

'Yes, I'm in the textile industry. We're having a hard time in Europe. There's a lot of competition from Turkey, India and the Far East.'

Tate didn't reply. He hoped the man would shut up.

'What's your line of business, if you don't mind me asking?' The man chirped again.

Tate minded very much. 'Investment consultant,' he snapped, and wondered how to terminate the conversation. One thing was sure. He wasn't under surveillance. After all, if you could see the buggers then they weren't watching you. They'd have stopped him at the airport and asked him a question or two if they were interested. They weren't shy, but they were tenacious; and this little sod didn't look like giving up.

The flight was turning into a nightmare. He had some greaseball sitting next to him, who might or might not be a policeman. Next time he'd travel on a plane which had a First Class option. In the meantime he had to stop this conversation. He stood up and marched to the lavatory. When he returned, he opened the *Financial Times* and studied the market prices. It was hard to concentrate. He couldn't remember what was in his Swiss portfolio.

'Settling down to work?' chirped the voice.

Tate ignored him.

'I've not been to Amsterdam before, Mister Tate.'

Tate blinked. Had he introduced himself as 'Yate' or 'Tate'? He didn't know. Perhaps he'd misheard. No. He never gave the man his name. The bastard must have looked in his briefcase. Yes. He'd peered at his passport which was poking out of his briefcase. Or had he known the name before he embarked? Nasty, beady black, inquisitive eyes. 'Try the—' he was about to say, 'Amstel', but remembered he had a meeting there. 'Krasnapolsky.' That would set the little shit's bank balance back a bit. He'd have a job claiming that on expenses. It would probably send the whole textile industry spiralling into a slump.

'Could you write it down for me?'

Tate looked at the hand which proffered paper and pen. If the man thought he was getting a set of fingerprints on that scrap of paper he had another think coming. Samuel looked squarely at his fellow traveller. He stared into his eyes. He said very quietly and firmly, 'Go fuck yourself. I'm busy.' He turned back to his newspaper.

'That's nice. That's bloody charming,' commented the voice. 'It's my first time abroad and I ask some arsehole for a bit of advice...' He blushed. 'You're a jerk,' he finished lamely.

# 3

'What did I do?' thought Tate. 'He was only some pimply salesman and I pretended he was Pinkerton personified.' Tate had hopped in and out of taxis all over Amsterdam in case he was being followed. He had too much to lose through carelessness. 'I'm too old for this game.' It used to be fun but now it was business and he was tired of looking over his shoulder. However, a chance encounter wouldn't force him into retirement. He was at the pinnacle of his career. Even the smallest deal made a hundred thousand; and he wouldn't lift a finger for less. As the governments cracked down on drugs, the street prices soared to reflect the risks. At the same time the middle men demanded lower prices from the producers to reflect the marketing risks. The margins widened and the profits escalated. Things had never been better. So long as he didn't take chances there was no reason why it should ever end.

It had been stupid telling an innocent stranger to fuck himself. However, it wasn't surprising if he over-reacted sometimes. He was under pressure; and it wasn't helped by ill-informed drugs campaigns in England. They'd once advised the public that people with runny noses were cocaine addicts, and not suffering from flu. It was bad enough enduring inflamed sinuses half the year without that sort of insanity being broadcasted. Now, depositing a grand in cash at the bank meant giving explanations in triplicate. Soon they'd be saying that anyone paying with cash was a drug pusher. It was ridiculous.

At last, convinced that no one was following him, he made his way to the rendezvous. The Amstel is the finest hotel in Amsterdam. The best rooms have a view over the Amstel River, where barges still carry cargo and the bridges open for them giving precedence to navigators as opposed to car drivers. A hundred metres from the entrance to the hotel a small footpath leads to a tunnel running over the Singelgracht. It is now known as the Heineken Tunnel. It was through this tunnel that the men who kidnapped Freddy Heineken, the brewery magnate, escaped to an estimated million dollar ransom, outwitting the police. It was this route which Tate took to approach the Amstel. There was a time when he had admired the kidnappers for their crime without violence. Now he wasn't so sure. He was turning into a potential target himself.

Some six hours later Tate sat in a plush second-floor suite of the Amstel and tried not to think about his hidden agenda. He found it hard to act naturally with his Dutch partner, de Groote, now he knew the truth. The two men were sitting in near darkness, for which Tate was grateful. Now and then de Groote poured another flute from the champagne magnum. Outside, the street lights on the Sarphatistraat shone crisply in the icy autumnal dusk. Winter was coming. It was a time when criminals planned the next year's scams, and double-crossed their partners.

At last de Groote stood up and turned on the light. He was large rather than tall, and although his clothes were expensive they hung on him rather than fitted. He had once been good looking, but was turning to fat. The features which had made him attractive to women now tended to repel them. Hair pumped out of his chest. His skin had an unhealthy jaundiced pallor. Sweat stained the armpits of his silk shirt. Tate imagined him smelling of death. The size of his wallet was his most endearing feature. The heavy gold chain on his wrist bore the legend 'Jan', although everyone knew him as de Groote. A gold medallion hung around his neck. Tate didn't like to be seen in public with him any more; and he never said when he was arriving at the airport in case de Groote came to meet him. Nevertheless, de Groote was one of the few men he'd been forced to trust and who knew him by his real name. They had done business together from the very beginnings. He supplied the drugs when Tate had been a student and sailed the yacht from Vlissingen to Brightlingsea. Now, however, de Groote was careless. There was nothing more dangerous than a drugs baron exercising the last throes of power. De Groote knew too much about Tate and it made Tate nervous.

De Groote flopped in a chair. 'So what do you want, my friend?' he asked. He had obviously decided the pleasantries were over.

'I have a client ready to ship a ton of cannabis within the week.'

'This is no problem.'

'What's the country of origin?'

'Middle East,' said de Groote evasively. 'The one with the butterfly on the cloth.'

Akbar's product!

'What about the price?' asked Tate.

15

'We are partners,' said de Groote. 'We will share the profit.'

'Fifty per cent of nothing is nothing,' said Tate. 'What's the material costing you?' Tate knew what it cost; and now he knew how de Groote had ripped him off for years, he wanted to see how good an actor he was. He wanted to hear the figure from de Groote's lips.

'We have done business before. We don't need to talk prices.'

'I need to know the price now, not later. I'll make a firm commitment to one ton.'

'One ton is not such a big deal.' De Groote almost sneered. He had made his point. He was one of the biggest drug barons in Holland. In the early days he and Tate had only dreamed of moving a ton of cannabis.

Tate had to keep him sweet. 'This is a one-off deal. After that, I'll be looking for a metric ton each month. That's twelve tons this year.'

'So, you are in the air freight business,' said de Groote quickly, with a smile. He knew that when people bandied precise figures they were restricted to a schedule. Air freight was always calculated in metric tons.

'That's my business.'

'If you air freight, then it must be good. My supplier cannot afford to give you credit. The risks are too big.'

De Groote was talking shit; but then he didn't know that Tate had made contact with his supplier, Akbar, and already arranged a credit rating. 'I never said it was air freight. How I do it is my business, and I want to keep it that way for security reasons. But, no credit. No deal. No partnership. You're having trouble finding safe outlets in Britain. That's why I work with you. You have big options on the harvest in Pakistan but you've got a glut here in Holland. You need me, but you need Britain more because it's the biggest market in Europe.'

'Sure. But the pound is always weak. If your government devalues, I lose too much.'

'Right now the pound is stable. Your problem is the transport into Britain and I've solved that.'

'Things are not so bad. I can get the material out of Pakistan; especially now I have new methods.'

'But you can't land it in Britain, can you?' Sometimes Tate wondered if he was talking English. It was like talking to a five-year-old. 'Right now I want a credit price for the hash. Good quality, packed and ready to load.'

'Four thousand guilders a kilo,' said de Groote. Tate nearly gagged. De Groote liked to haggle over the figures, but that price was robbery. The Dutch Empire had obviously been built on more than fair trade and barter. Some things never died.

De Groote would never know that Tate was only feigning an interest in the deal to keep him quiet. That interest would die as soon as he took possession of the ton of cannabis which belonged to Akbar. De Groote's days in the business were numbered. He was too greedy. He had made himself too many enemies. He'd bought options on material he couldn't possibly sell; and now he was irritating genuine buyers who were forced to negotiate with him as a middle man. Ahmed Akbar in Pakistan was cutting up rough because de Groote had inflated the prices, and failed to pay on time. De Groote was slitting his own throat, and Tate was enjoying the show.

Tate had powerful contacts. He had Akbar on his side. He only had to pretend to agree the price with de Groote. The price was immaterial, because Tate was going to pay Akbar a fraction of what de Groote wanted. Tate had gone in through the back door and de Groote was being pushed out at the front. De Groote's last deal would be to pass Akbar's material, which he was holding on credit, to Tate. All Tate had to do was make sure de Groote didn't suspect anything.

The door from the adjoining suite opened and a girl walked into the room. She was scantily dressed in expensive underwear but nevertheless Tate stood up politely. De Groote waved him down. 'This is Monique,' he said. 'A friend from France.'

'Paul,' said Tate. 'My name's Paul,' he lied instinctively.

Monique cast a glance in Tate's direction and ignored him. She walked to the mini-bar, opened it, stared inside, closed it. She pouted, but she was past the bloom of youth and it had no effect. 'I'm hungry,' she complained.

'We are still talking,' said de Groote, carelessly. Monique left the room. 'She is good in bed. But I send her back to France. Hookers don't cost so much money as girlfriends. You can have her.' He laughed, but he wasn't joking.

Tate didn't comment. He didn't fancy Monique. Real bimbos were two a penny. He was calculating percentages. They were more rewarding. He reckoned the dollar would fall against the pound over the next six months. If he paid Akbar in dollars he could earn another twenty grand on the deal. If he offered to deliver the money to an account in Switzerland that would be worth another five per cent.

'Tell me,' asked de Groote curiously, 'why are you scared to make a real big deal? Why not take five tons? Why this business of one ton each time? All you do is increase your overheads.'

'After all this time, I'll let you into a secret. It's why I'm still in business after twenty years and my bigger competitors have been busted. The British market is the biggest in Europe but two tons is enough to saturate it for a month. After that, marketing slows down, which means the

17

material needs warehousing. Most busts occur because of storage. You
need people to look after warehouses. You keep visiting and collecting
the dope for distribution. After a while everyone, including the police,
knows the gear's in storage. Then you get busted. If you import one ton
at a time the whole lot is on the streets within three days. No warehouse.
No evidence.'

'I have people in England who say they can take five tons.'

'Fine. Work with them,' said Tate. De Groote was always a pain.
Always chipping away. If he knew the English market so bloody well he
should have been over there doing the business himself. But, the Dutch
were scared shitless of England; the trouble was the customs, the police
and the prison sentences. The Dutch had good reason to be scared,
thought Tate wryly.

Tate suddenly remembered he had to make the negotiations look
good. 'I want one more condition on this deal. I want an exclusive contract
with you. I don't want you to work with another outfit in Britain.'

'My business affairs are my own.'

'Not when you work with me. I have to market the material. If two
people have the same material we stand the danger of a price war. The
dealers start shopping around for the best prices. I hope you don't suffer
from the delusion that the material sells itself. It needs marketing, like
anything else. It's a business, with quality control and price points.
Sometimes you forget that. I don't want you complaining that my
competitor is selling quicker than me, and I have to give him my supplies.
The dope starts flying around the country going nowhere and not even
being sold. In those cases the only winners are the police.'

'You always drive a hard bargain, my friend.' De Groote stuck out a
fleshy palm for Tate to grasp. It was evidently a deal.

No way could de Groote suspect Tate of a double-cross now. 'I'm
paying you over the odds, and you know it,' said Tate. 'Otherwise, you
wouldn't do the deal.'

De Groote almost smirked.

'My client will collect on Wednesday, at midday, from the usual location
in Rotterdam. He will return the truck to you twenty-four hours later.'

'OK. But I want you to think about something else I have.'

'What is it?' asked Tate, his attention wandering.

'I want you to think boats.'

'I am not thinking about boats,' said Tate firmly, suddenly returning to
reality. There was no point wasting time, talking dreams, with a man at
the end of his career. 'Boats are a nightmare to organise. You send them
on a thousand-mile journey to pick up the dope. When they get back to
England they look exactly like they've been on a dope run. Their
waterline is six inches under. That's if the crew didn't get frightened and

jettison the cargo. Forget it. I've been there. I've tried that. I've lost a lot of money playing that game. I'm not doing it again.'

'OK, Samuel. Listen to me. This time is different. I have a fifteen thousand-ton ship. You know how big that is? It is a big ship. It is travelling all the time. All across Europe. To Rotterdam. Bilbao. All the time there is hash on board. You tell me when you are ready. You send some fishermen to meet it. Just one day from England. You can have six or ten tons.'

Tate knew he had to humour de Groote. Once upon a time he would have been interested. But times had changed. He'd lost Edward, the only person who could deal with the logistics of an operation like that. Now he was running back-to-back deals, instead of marketing, because Edward was locked away in a Pakistani jail for ten years.

'That's not very interesting for me,' said Samuel. 'And anyway Edward is not available.'

'So find someone else.'

'Not so easy. Edward has the contacts for an operation like that.'

'Everyone is available for a price.'

'Not him. He's doing ten years in Pakistan. They grabbed him when your friend Mir's import-export business was blown apart by the American Drug Enforcement Agency.' Tate watched de Groote's reaction closely.

'I did not know you lost someone important.' De Groote stared at Tate for a moment. 'Everyone is available for a price. Even your friend Edward. I have good contacts in Pakistan. Maybe they can get him free.'

'What's the price?'

De Groote thought for a moment. 'Thirty thousand. Sterling.'

'How long will it take?'

'The last time was very fast. Ten days maybe. If there are no complications. How long do they need to take one paper from the Justice Department to the prison?'

Tate's mind jumped ahead. Edward would be out of prison. Edward would be very useful at the moment. The new scam would be simplicity itself. He wouldn't have to recruit anyone else. He hoped de Groote stayed alive long enough to spring Edward.

'You have a deal,' said Tate. He smiled. He was almost forty and a cash millionaire several times over. The gravy train was rolling.

De Groote smiled. A gold tooth glinted among his teeth. 'So now we fix a price for my new deal?'

'Three thousand guilders a kilo,' offered Tate.

'OK,' said de Groote, after a moment's thought. 'This one time.'

Tate smiled. De Groote thought he'd made a bargain. It was almost pitiful.

# 4

'New Happy Year. English. Bloody Fucking New Happy Year,' shouted the Turk in Karachi Prison. There was a big smile on his fat sadistic face. It wasn't news to Edward, who was contemplating a New Year's resolution. 'Escape!' Unfortunately the signs weren't propitious, and the day began as any other. No guard came to summon him to the Governor's office. He looked around the prison yard. The walls were ten metres high, topped with broken bottles and barbed wire. A million shuffling feet had long since trodden the earth into concrete. There was no chance of digging a tunnel even if he could organise the lunatics, murderers, thieves, politicians, smugglers, filth and the innocent. On the face of it, the only quick escape was in a coffin.

The fat Turk punched the imbecile who gave him blow jobs in return for scraps of food. The other inmates grinned. It was entertainment of a sort. The Frenchman spat in disgust and walked away. The hot dust pounced avidly on the blob of mucus. The Turk registered the insult. The Frenchman had money which bought him protection. One day the Turk would break the Frenchman. One day the francs would run out, and then the Turk would have his day.

The Turk ruled the quarters by virtue of some heinous murder. Soon he would be bored of tormenting the imbecile boy and search for another victim. 'Hey English!' he shouted. He was too late.

Edward had slipped away to hide among the lesser criminals for the time being. Only six months of his ten-year sentence had elapsed. He thought incessantly of escape. Each day his escape plan moved forward. He only hoped he wasn't making a terrible miscalculation.

The guards relied on supplementing their wages from money the prisoners gave them in return for food. Foreign prisoners were the most valuable because they had money, and consequently they were nurtured and cherished so they could serve full sentences. Penniless foreigners were a problem. They appealed against their sentences but didn't have the funds available to pay for a proper lawyer. Worst of all, without family or friends they received visits from their Embassies who were invariably dismayed at the decaying condition of their nationals. The Frenchman would serve his time. He was arrogant. Edward had explained the workings of the Pakistani prison system to him but he wouldn't listen. He was not interested in suffering briefly in return for his freedom. The Frenchman optimistically expected a reprieve.

In the meantime Edward was sustaining himself with the belief that he would soon be free. Free or dead. Some kind of louse was burrowing beneath his skin. He could see the raised tracks under the skin of his stomach. He'd already lost twenty pounds. He was sure he had a tapeworm. There was something wrong with his liver. He didn't know how much longer he could survive without asking the Embassy to cable for money from . . . whom? . . . Julia? He'd rather not alarm her.

Samuel Tate knew where he was and what had happened. He was surprised he hadn't heard from him already. Samuel would be on the case. Edward was sure of that.

Of course he could write to Julia. He would have to borrow the money from the Frenchman to bribe a guard to post the letter. The guard would take the letter and steal the postage. Edward wondered what he would say in the letter. 'Greetings from Karachi. New Happy Year. Goodbye all.' They would have to admit him to hospital before they let him die. It would be easier to escape from hospital, assuming he had the strength.

Edward looked towards a corner of the prison compound, sectioned off for the New Year's festivities. The new year was a time of hope. New beginnings and better resolutions. It was coincidentally a day of escape. Fourteen gallows had been erected in that corner of the compound. There were to be executions. It was rumoured that there was a delicate refinement to the proceedings because there would be a reprieve for one man. Thirteen prisoners would escape into death. One man would remain behind. No one knew which prisoner would be reprieved, yet.

'Who cares? They are all murderers,' said the Frenchman phlegmatically, offering a cigarette, which Edward accepted in a moment of weakness. 'Every day we are all dying a little more.'

Fourteen prisoners were bundled up the scaffolding. Edward observed that none of them appeared to have been given any medication. Prayers babbled from their lips. There was an unnatural hush over the prison as the inmates contemplated their own mortality. The Prison Governor made a speech. Thirteen trap doors sprang open. One remained shut. One man remained standing. He twisted and turned, pirouetting on the boards. He screamed. He was the example of clemency. He couldn't stop screaming. His screams echoed across the compound. Thirteen men twisted and turned, delivering a spasm or two, at the end of the ropes. That day one man was reprieved. Edward knew that the reprieved prisoner would never be the same again. Now he knew that death by

21

hanging was not instantaneous. 'Pour encourager les autres,' said the Frenchman.

'Hey English,' shouted the Turk. 'You like?' The Turk laughed and punched Edward. It was a friendly gesture under the circumstances. Edward thought he was going to be sick. Suddenly he snapped, and all his bottled rage exploded.

'You fucking arseholes haven't got a clue.' The Frenchman vanished.

The Turk's smile froze. This was a moment he'd been waiting for. The English had made a mistake. He'd snap his bones like kindling.

'English!' shouted a voice.

Edward turned towards a guard. 'Governor waiting for you. Hurry.' The guard jabbed him with a stick. 'Hurry. Quick.'

# Chapter 2

## 1

They won't catch me again, thought Samuel Tate. He was more careful now than he had ever been. He was taking safety into another dimension. His plane flew into Zurich, but he hired a car and drove to his bank in Geneva. The British Customs or Interpol might know he was up to something, but they had to find out where it was going on. To do that they had to follow him, and he was keeping an eye on his rear-view mirror. That time he had done on remand had been worth it though. He'd cleaned up plenty of dirty money. If they asked him what he was living off he had over half a million pounds tax-paid. The Inland Revenue had agreed a ludicrously low figure as an income tax settlement after they investigated him. He then invested what he had left in England, and made it work for him. The dirty money? They would have to find it first and that would be hard, especially when he'd completed this trip.

The numbered accounts of the Swiss banking system were inadvertently instituted because of Hitler. When the Nazis came to power, many people transferred their Reichsmarks to Swiss banks. The Nazis decreed that this constituted economic sabotage of the German state and was punishable by the death penalty. German intelligence agents tried hard to obtain details of German citizens with Swiss bank accounts. The Swiss banks countered by introducing the numbered accounts. Hitler considered invading Switzerland but found it would require twenty-three crack divisions, and turned his attentions to Russia instead. Things didn't go well and by 1945 a large number of Germans had their own numbered bank accounts in Switzerland. The Swiss had made their major contribution to humanity, and it was far more important than the cuckoo clock.

Of course, things were changing. Soon the Swiss and British governments were going to sign a treaty concerning exchange of information with regard to accounts held by British citizens. In due course Switzerland would join the European Community, in which case they would have to conform to the Common Market banking regulations, and all those accounts might be compromised. That was why Tate was making this inconvenient journey.

One of Tate's acquaintances had recently been investigated by a joint Inland Revenue and customs team. They knew the man was smuggling drugs but had only managed to convict him on the relatively minor charge of 'possession with intent to supply'. They made a detailed study of his standard of living and discovered he was living beyond his means. They found he made frequent trips to Switzerland and deduced that he had secret bank accounts, but they didn't know where. They tried to make small deposits in his name at a number of banks, and when one bank accepted the deposit they knew they had struck gold. Customs then requested that the account details be divulged because they were the proceeds of crime. The transactions from that one account had led to other accounts, and a number of people were currently applying for legal aid to defend themselves at the Old Bailey.

There was no way that would happen to him, thought Tate as he pressed the bell above the discreet metal plaque in need of a polish. A manservant opened the door and admitted him. He was led to a familiar room which was sparsely furnished with a dark oak table, three chairs, and a silk Persian carpet no doubt presented by a grateful client. He stared at the carpet while he waited for Swantz. It looked like a Qum, depicting the Tree of Life. It was richly coloured with natural dyes. He flipped a corner over with the toe of his shoe, and peered at it. There were at least 500 knots to the inch. A few kids must have gone blind knotting that one, he thought.

The door opened. 'Good morning Mr Tate. Good morning.'

'Good morning Herr Swantz.' They exchanged a few pleasantries and then settled down to business. It had been like this for fifteen years. They never asked each other personal questions or used their Christian names. Swantz grew slightly older and became a little thicker round the waist.

'And what can I do for you?' Swantz produced an expansive smile, revealing perfectly capped teeth.

'I wish to rearrange my assets. I need to form a trust.'

'We have talked of this before. Very wise. And which of the options do you consider?'

'You mentioned Liechtenstein.'

'Ah yes, Liechtenstein.' That one name was enough for Swantz to know exactly what his client required. Of course, that was why he had clients. They didn't have to spell out their wishes. He was under few illusions. The kind of money which passed through his hands seldom originated from legitimate enterprises. He even had one or two eminent politicians on his books. 'I have a colleague who is a lawyer there. He will do this for us. If I might suggest the best way for this. I will open the company for you,' he paused and took out a gold-plated Montpelier pen. 'Is there perhaps a name you would prefer?'

Tate thought for a moment. 'How about Tapis Flottant Aveugle?'

'Very well. We will incorporate a Liechtenstein Company in the name of Tapis Flottant Aveugle. I must check first there is no company existing in this name, but I think this will not be the case.' Swantz had no sense of humour at all. That was the trouble with the Swiss. If they wanted to laugh they had to go to the bathroom. 'I will be the theoretical stockholder of this company. You see, there is nothing remaining to connect you with your company. And now we will make a secret trust agreement between us, which you will keep. I will arrange for your company to open a numbered account here, at my bank. Of course, it will not be the same number as before.'

'What would happen if, for example, the accounts of Tapis Flottant Aveugle are examined?'

'That is easy. It will show that Tapis Flottant Aveugle is a company operating from Liechtenstein. It will show that I am the officer, and I am above suspicion, I can assure you. The only proof of ownership of Tapis Flottant Aveugle is the Trust Agreement, which will be prepared for you tomorrow.'

'I have an appointment tomorrow. Perhaps I could meet you in four days?'

'At your convenience.'

'Is that all?'

'Yes, that is all. The rest will not be a problem. We must provide a minimum capital of twenty thousand Swiss francs, but once the company is formed this will be returned to you. Apart from that we must pay one thousand six hundred francs every year to the lawyer who is also the director of Tapis Flottant Aveugle. I hope that everything is clear.'

'Perfectly, Herr Swantz. So I will see you on Friday morning?'

'Certainly. At eleven o'clock.' Swantz stood up. Tate looked into his eyes and had a moment of panic. He wondered if he could really trust this man with his fortune. Swantz interpreted the look. 'Do not worry Mr Tate. This is all completely normal. You see, in Switzerland we rely on making arrangements like this. If anything went wrong we would no longer be the banking centre of Europe.'

'Of course. I wasn't doubting the arrangement for a moment.'

Swantz led him to the door, opened it, and bowed imperceptibly. The heavy door closed behind Tate. He was pleased. He had safeguarded his money and provided a comfortable home for the proceeds of the next scam.

Tate's European arrangements were not over. He had other meetings. After a quick lunch he was back in the hired Mercedes and heading for Italy. He'd stop the night at a five-star hotel on Lake Como to pamper himself. In the morning he'd catch a flight from Milan to Cyprus, where he had meetings with Ahmed Akbar and another man. This man, whose existence was unknown to all Tate's business associates, was the only person Tate feared; and discovery of their relationship would be dangerous for both of them.

This man had provided Tate with the details of Edward's arrest. He told Tate what had happened, and that Ahmed Akbar was reputed to be de Groote's source. He even told Tate how to contact Akbar; all for a price, of course. Most important of all, this man told Tate how de Groote had tipped off the Drug Enforcement Agency about the consignment. At last, the pieces fitted together. De Groote kept Tate's advance payment because Edward had taken possession of the material before the bust. Then, de Groote bought the material at a reduced price, and it never reached the incinerator on the outskirts of Karachi. De Groote's only insurance lay in a ton of cannabis he held in some warehouse outside Rotterdam; and when that was delivered, he was dead. Good riddance. It was good to be shot of shit.

# 2

Some mornings were better than others, but generally they were all bad. Andy Ballot consistently promised himself he would go to bed early one night. He'd stop smoking and drinking too. Somehow the habits kept interfering with the resolution. He pulled out a packet of cigarettes and lit the first one of the day. It was half past nine. The packet would be empty when he left the Customs and Excise offices in the evening.

The headache which would develop over the course of the day made a few tentative stabs. It had nothing to do with the habitual nightcaps, or his eyesight. Andy knew the open-plan office caused it, amplifying every sound, until the traffic outside on Fetter Lane, the whirring of the computer disks, and the urgent ringing of the telephones all merged into one wall of sound. The harsh fluorescent lighting blinded the eye after an hour or two. The ventilation was inadequate. Smog inside and smog outside. Andy stabbed his cigarette into the ashtray. Out there on the beaches of the Caribbean, breathing pure Atlantic air, were smugglers who'd made their fortunes out of drugs or gold, and long since retired. It was galling.

Andy flipped through the various sheets of paper which had appeared on his desk overnight. He was in his mid-thirties and the youngest officer to be leading a drugs investigation team. His promotion had caused resentment among the older officers, but he didn't lose any sleep over that. He opened a drawer and popped some painkillers into his system and washed them down with the dregs of lukewarm coffee from a plastic cup. It was best to deal with the headache before it dealt with him.

He was in charge of the Yankee team. The Yankees had been set up for targeting suspects and piecing together evidence. The intelligence reports landed on his desk first. It was the most interesting, if not the most rewarding job. Andy might not have a say in how customs deployed their resources, but at least he could doctor the information on which his superiors made their decisions. He had been promoted from the Hotel team six months previously. The Hotels dealt exclusively with referrals, which meant following up suspects after an arrest. That was rewarding because there was real contact with the suspects. Results were measured by the number of bodies in a cell. There was plenty of room for overtime and undercover work in the Hotels, which made it popular.

Andy attracted resentment from his peers, not only because of his age, but also because he put in substantial overtime which he didn't claim. His peers mistakenly believed he expected them to emulate him. He didn't give a damn. He worked overtime because he had long since forgotten what to do with his leisure time. His peers, from what he could gather, spent their off-duty hours between the football pitch, the pub and the shopping malls.

Andy's attention was suddenly caught by a fax among the papers. He carefully pulled it from beneath the mail and squinted at the blurred print. It came from the liaison officer in Pakistan. He wasn't working on anything remotely connected with Pakistan so he doubted it would provide a link in any of his cases. However, it might lead to a trip abroad, which would be no bad thing.

Gathering intelligence soon put paid to any belief in the probability of coincidence. Suspects who'd been flagged in the past and who suddenly reappeared usually indicated some new conspiracy in the making. The fax concerned Edward Jay. The Pakistanis had released him after he'd served a mere six months of the ten-year sentence for being in possession of two tons of cannabis. The fax gave the flight number and time of arrival at Heathrow. The information irritated Andy.

Andy's thoughts sped to Julia and the few drinks they had together after she called him.

'Thank you for meeting me,' said Julia, awkwardly.

'It's no problem,' said Andy. 'Is there something you want to tell me?'

'Oh no,' she said quickly. 'Nothing like that.' She paused.

'I understand,' said Andy. There was an uncomfortable silence. 'Look Julia, I'm not here officially. I'm here because you sounded distressed when you called.'

'It's just that I can't get used to what's happened. There's no one I can talk to. I can't seem to grasp the enormity of it all. Is there really no hope? No chance that Edward could be freed?'

'There's always a chance,' said Andy, cautiously. 'But it's slim. You'd best put Edward behind you. Start again. Put bluntly, he was willing to sacrifice you, and now you have to make a decision.'

'It's not as easy as that,' Julia said angrily.

'I know.'

She said quietly, 'I'm having his baby.'

Andy looked away. 'I'm sorry I said what I did. It must be awful for you.' He knew it was a mistake to become involved with the enemy. It affected judgements. They were on one side of the law and he was on the other. It was better to leave it like that. Except in this case. 'I wish there was something I could do.'

'Oh no. I didn't expect anything. I only wanted to talk. You see, there isn't anyone else who knows the whole truth.'

'What was it like with Edward?' Andy asked curiously. 'What do you find so hard to leave behind?'

'It was fun,' said Julia. 'We always enjoyed ourselves.'

Andy knew about that. Of course they enjoyed themselves. They had money. He saw it all the time when he was on surveillance. There was a rosy glow which ready money brought to the cheeks of criminals. 'You know,' he said, 'it's not unusual, in the world you've experienced, to find that relationships never progress beyond the honeymoon stage. All those dinners, all those hotels, all those holidays; neither of you had to face up to the humdrum world.'

Julia was silent, digesting what he said.

'I know I don't seem sympathetic. I think it's more honest to be realistic.'

Julia smiled weakly. 'What you say makes sense.'

'Forget him,' said Andy. 'You're young, you're beautiful. You still have a life ahead of you. You can pick up the pieces. Edward is not going to be released.' Inside, he wished he dared to say how happy he would be to look after her. He felt comfortable in her presence. Her black hair and dark eyes reminded him of Rosa. He was doing what the therapist had warned him against: repeating, and repeating without knowing why. The therapy had been a waste of time.

'If you're ever at a loose end in the evening give me a call,' he offered. 'We could go out.'

'That might be too much of a betrayal,' said Julia, as if coming to her senses.

Julia never called him back. Now he knew he ought to tell her the news of Edward's release. It was better she should hear it from him and not someone else, and jump to the wrong conclusions. He picked up the phone and dialled Julia's number. It was still early in the morning. He imagined her dark hair on white linen, and her red lips slightly parted in sleep. He heard her voice, 'Hello?'

'Julia, it's Andy Ballot here.'

'Oh?'

'I thought I should let you know I was wrong the night we met. Edward has just been released from prison.'

'I know,' said Julia. 'It's fantastic. I can't believe it.'

Andy hesitated a moment too long. 'How did you find out?' he asked, suspiciously.

The line crackled for a long second in response, before Julia's voice, a few degrees colder, replied, 'Someone told me.'

'Oh,' said Andy. 'Well, I'm very pleased for you.'

'Thank you,' said Julia. There was another brief silence.

Andy wanted to ask if they might meet again. He began to speak, but he heard Julia. 'Thank you for calling, it was good of you to think of me.'

'No problem,' said Andy quickly. 'Maybe we'll bump into each other one of these days.'

'Maybe,' replied Julia, doubtfully. 'Oh, the kettle's boiling. I must go,' she said.

'Goodbye,' said Andy, and replaced the receiver. Their friendship had come to an abrupt end.

He knew who had told Julia the news about Edward Jay. It was Samuel Tate.

Edward Jay was freed because someone knew where to place an accurate bribe. By no stretch of the imagination were six months a respectable proportion of his sentence, however tough the prison conditions. What irritated Andy more than anything else was a memory.

Edward Jay was Samuel Tate's right-hand man, and Andy wanted to nail Tate. No doubt Tate was responsible for springing Jay. If Tate was springing Jay then he was planning something. It fitted together. Tate, after months of inactivity, had suddenly appeared in a variety of reports, the most recent being a Suspicious Movement Report when he boarded a flight to Amsterdam.

Andy picked up a pencil and began sharpening it. He stared at the wood shavings falling on to the desk. For a moment he thought about Rosa. For a moment his heart ached. He wondered what had happened to her sailing boat after her death. He pictured its name, 'Joanne', carved into the transom. He briefly experienced the loneliness of not sharing his life with anyone in particular. Then he cut it out, and swept the pencil shavings on to the floor.

He had worked hard on that case against Samuel Tate, five years ago. It had been a pleasure to have Tate fall into his lap. He began to feel there was some divine justice in life. He built a strong case. He had the pleasure of a number of interviews with Tate, all of which had proved fruitless because the only information Tate furnished was his name and date of birth. In the final interview he found himself alone with Tate and reminded him of the past. 'I'm going to get you, Tate. I want you behind bars for a maximum seven years on this charge. Not because you're guilty. But for Rosa's sake.' He knew Tate hadn't recognised him from all those years ago. Tate reacted with shock to the name of Rosa. He remembered her somewhere in his warped mind. Andy relished the momentary alarm on Tate's face, but it hadn't elicited any response.

It had been downhill from then on. Tate walked free from the Old Bailey. Andy remembered Tate's words snarled in his ear as he left the courtroom. 'You're the one who made this personal, Mr Ballot. That's not professional. Remember that. You're the one who made it personal.' It was true. Andy had made it personal. He'd built the case brick by brick, savouring every twist and turn, toying with every new development. He hadn't known what Tate's defence was going to produce, nor had he been counting on a lousy, superannuated barrister from the Crown Prosecution Services to present his case. He'd nailed Tate all right, and Tate had known it. Tate hadn't even applied for bail; he was that guilty. He spent the year on remand knowing that it was worth double time off the sentence he was ultimately going to receive.

Tate had been under surveillance for a year. They knew he was importing drugs but the only evidence was circumstantial. He never touched the drugs himself. Finally he made a mistake by picking up a suitcase full of money and was arrested. The suitcase contained two hundred thousand pounds. He was charged with drug trafficking and handling the proceeds. He pleaded 'Not guilty'. In court he produced a

Lebanese businessman who provided documentation and argued the money was destined for a property deal. 'In used fivers and tenners?' asked Andy. Apparently the judge didn't think it unusual tender for a property deal, and decided to convict Tate for the lesser charge of Value Added Tax evasion, a charge which Andy had included so that they could pick at Tate's successful property empire. It was a hollow victory. They'd got him on one charge, but failed miserably on the ones that mattered. He was acquitted of trafficking in drugs.

Andy had retaliated to this defeat by putting the Inland Revenue's Special Office Ten on to Tate. This department specialised in the assessment and the taxation of earnings derived from illegal activities. They had managed to squeeze a hundred and fifty thousand pounds in back tax on his estimated earnings. It was a short-lived success. The action effectively legitimised all Tate's money and assets in Britain.

A few months later Andy received the photographs through the post. They left little to the imagination. They showed Andy in bed with a colleague's wife whom he'd been seeing for a year. Someone had spared little expense in obtaining them, and Andy knew who that person was. The message which accompanied them read, 'Nothing personal'. The covering letter delivered to his colleague was more detailed.

Andy let the fax fall from his fingers and decided he would make his way to Heathrow and take a look at Samuel Tate's lieutenant, Edward Jay, and welcome him back to the fold. He'd take a couple of surreptitious pictures of him as he came through immigration to bring the records up to date. He might stop him for a chat on his way through the Channels. Tate might even be at the airport to meet his lieutenant, but if not, perhaps Jay would provide a lead. One day Samuel Tate would make a mistake.

# 3

Julia had never really liked Tate. She'd met him when she first met Edward while she was at Art College, eight years ago. He'd always been distant and aloof. She thought he was emotionally retarded. She knew he resented her relationship with Edward and had competed for his attention in the early, days. When she had found out that he and Edward were involved in smuggling she made it clear that she didn't want Edward bringing his work home. That meant that Edward didn't bring Tate to the house. Consequently Tate drifted out of her life. They bumped into each other from time to time, but they seldom did more than exchange pleasantries. Over the years people had come to assume that they hated each other, though Julia thought that too strong a description for the indifference she felt.

When Tate phoned to give her the news that Edward would be released from prison he asked her if she wanted to dine with him. Her first impulse was to refuse the invitation; but she accepted. She wanted to know exactly what had happened to Edward. After she replaced the receiver she wondered why he had invited her. There were six months when she would gladly have welcomed dinner in the hope of knowing a little more about Edward's disappearance.

'I thought we'd celebrate Edward's release,' said Tate, luckily finding a parking space for his Mercedes outside Le Jardin des Gourmets in South Kensington. 'Have you dined here before?'

'No. I thought people only came here to be seen,' replied Julia.

'The food really is excellent,' said Tate.

Julia said nothing as they climbed the stairs. 'This is nice, very nice,' she thought. 'There's Edward on bread and water in some prison, and you've been dining out every night.' She bit her tongue.

Inside the restaurant, Tate was greeted with familiarity by the waiters, and was shown to a reserved table which was slightly distanced from the other ones, to afford some privacy.

'There are not many people with whom I care to be seen in public,' said Samuel. 'But you're one of them.' Tate squinted at the wine list.

Julia supposed the remark was meant to be flattering. Perhaps Tate had severe delusions of grandeur. 'Why didn't you call me for six months? You and Edward are supposed to be best friends. I think I might have deserved a call.'

Tate took off his glasses and laid them on the table and looked at Julia. 'Why do you suppose Edward is being released now? I've been working solidly on his case to find the right people to reverse his sentence. It took a lot of time, effort and money. I didn't want to call you and raise your hopes unnecessarily.'

'I'm sorry,' said Julia, quickly. 'That sounded churlish of me.'

'It doesn't matter,' said Samuel, graciously. 'You were entitled to an explanation.' He turned his attention to the menu. 'What have you chosen?' he demanded at last.

'Coquilles St Jacques, followed by the turbot.'

'Good,' said Tate. 'I like decisive women.' He closed his menu and the waiter arrived at his elbow. He ordered, while another waiter poured the Puligny Montrachet.

'I have some news for you,' said Julia. 'Edward is going to be a father.'

'Really?' said Tate, raising his eyebrows. 'I hadn't noticed.' He placed his hand on her's and left it a moment longer than their familiarity warranted. 'Does Edward know?'

'No.'

He nodded. 'Don't you think he has a right to know?'

'Of course. I wrote to him a few times. I don't know if he received my letters, and I didn't hear anything in return. I spoke to the British Embassy, but they weren't helpful. Actually, I was going to go to Pakistan and see him if I didn't hear anything soon.'

Tate nodded. 'I don't know if Edward is ready for children. He might not want it.'

Julia didn't react. They sat in silence until the first course arrived, and Tate tucked in. He smacked his lips. Julia winced. 'Delicious!' he commented. Julia thought her scallops were over-salted.

Tate embarked on a monologue about his property company. It didn't interest Julia in the slightest. She ploughed through her main course. Tate ordered another bottle of wine. Occasionally he tried to draw her into conversation. 'You ought to buy a house. You can't go on renting for the rest of your life.'

'Perhaps I will, one day,' said Julia. 'When I can afford it.'

'I could arrange a mortgage for you.'

'That's kind,' said Julia, and guessed it somehow helped him launder money. She wondered why he was going to all this trouble to pretend that he was a legitimate businessman.

'What happened to Edward in Pakistan? What went wrong?' asked Julia.

'I wouldn't know,' said Tate, blithely. 'I only look after his financial affairs these days. You see, I've retired. He was up to his old tricks. I heard about it through a third party and felt I should use my contacts to help him.'

'I'm not stupid,' said Julia.

'I know you're not,' replied Samuel. 'You're not stupid and you're very attractive.'

'You've drunk the best part of two bottles of wine.'

'That has nothing to do with it. I've always thought you were attractive. There's something about you I've always desired. You're radiant.'

'I'm pregnant.'

'It suits you.' He smiled. His leg encountered Julia's under the table. She moved her leg briskly. 'Would you like anything else?' he asked.

'No thank you,' said Julia. 'I should be getting home. I'm tired.'

'I think I'll have a brandy. Are you sure you won't join me?'

'No. Really, I have to be going.'

'Very well, then. I'll give you a lift home.' He raised his hand to the waiter and indicated he wished for the bill.

'Actually,' said Julia, 'I don't think it's very wise for you to visit me. I had a call from Customs and Excise this morning. They told me that Edward was on his way home.'

Tate's mouth tightened. 'Did they say anything else?'

'No.'

He looked at the bill and reached into his jacket for his wallet. He counted out the fifty pound notes, and laid them on the table. 'I always think its flash to pay with cash,' he said.

'I think it's common,' said Julia. 'But thank you for dinner.'

They stood up and Tate followed Julia out of the restaurant. On the street he didn't suggest driving Julia home again, before she hailed a taxi. As she opened the taxi's door, he leaned forward to try and kiss her. She moved her head at the last moment and avoided his lips.

'Goodbye Samuel,' she said.

He stared coldly at her as the taxi pulled away.

# 4

When the plane took off, Edward knew he was free and that the Pakistan authorities were not playing some malicious trick. He swore he would never gamble with his freedom again. Nothing on earth was worth the risk of doing time. One thing was certain. He would give up smuggling now. He had enough money, once he had collected it from Tate. He could buy a small house in the country. He might start an antiques business and try to launder some of the money. That would please Julia. He knew that his activities had increasingly perturbed her. She had long wanted him to retire. He hoped she had not taken him at his word when he told her to forget him if he ever went to prison.

He smiled at the stewardess as he took the lunch tray. She didn't smile back; she'd seen him handcuffed at the departure gate. Edward didn't care, though he'd have liked an excuse not to harbour racist thoughts. He turned his attention to the pre-packed food. It looked like a gourmet's feast after the shit he'd eaten for the past six months. He wondered if he could stomach it though. He had amoebic dysentery. He uncovered the prawn cocktail and picked up the spoon. The amoebae could sink their fangs into that. As soon as he was back in London he would see a doctor.

As Edward looked at his fellow passengers he realised the prison sentence had taken its toll. In the past he prided himself on his physical anonymity. He was a shade under six feet tall with a slim build. No Arnold Schwarzenegger. He had brown hair and blue eyes. He could melt into a crowd within seconds. Now he stood out like a sore thumb. People looked uncomfortably at his emaciated body. They avoided his blue eyes which couldn't help but stare from their black sunken sockets. He barely recognised himself from the polished steel mirror in the plane's lavatory. He never remembered his nose being so long, or his ears so big. His head was close shaven to prevent the lice from gaining a foothold. No doubt about it, he looked like a dangerous escapee from some madhouse or a fanatic from a religious sect.

After a month of good living he would put on some flesh. His hair would grow. The past would be a nightmare. He began to picture the life ahead. A new start. He'd tried retirement from the business once before, but hadn't really believed it would last. He found he drank too much. The money slipped away. He gambled recklessly searching for excitement and sensation to replace the life which he had given up. He finally recognised that he was suffering from the same symptoms as soldiers who had been under fire. Nothing in the real world could replace the rush of adrenaline or the thrill of survival. He came out of retirement and succumbed to what he believed was his fate.

Now, things had changed. He was discovering what others had told him was true. No amount of money made prison acceptable. He tried to remember what ambitions he had when he went to university, before he started smuggling. He couldn't remember. Smuggling had been fun. It had been exciting. It had provided the means to travel, support himself through university and earn a second-class degree in English. His ambitions always seemed to have been to escape. University had provided escape. Escape, from his background. Escape, from the terraced cottages and the Essex suburbia of his childhood. Once upon a time there must have been something else. Now he envied the rest of humanity. He wanted to fill out a tax return. He wanted to buy a Cabriolet on the never-never. He wanted to stand a round at the pub and know what it really cost. By the time the plane reached England he had grown used to the idea. He was about to join the real world at last.

When the plane landed Edward felt weaker. The prawn cocktail had been a mistake. He needed a doctor and a bed, fast. Over the past six months his weight had fallen from twelve to eight stones.

The spasm hit him as he handed his passport to the immigration officer.

'Is something the matter, sir?'

'Dysentery,' Edward groaned.

The passport was returned swiftly, with a sympathetic puckering of the lips. Edward shuffled, buttocks clenched, in the direction of the lavatories.

Andy Ballot, hidden by the one-way glass partition, photographed the scene from the observation cubicle. The immigration official had alerted his attention to Edward Jay's arrival by pressing a button on the desk. 'That is not going to be a very good photograph for the records,' Andy thought, as he made his way to the baggage hall to speak to a duty officer in the Red and Green Channels. None of the passengers paid any attention to Andy. None would have guessed that he was a customs officer. His black curly hair always looked as if it needed cutting. His physique gave the impression that he was small, although he was of average height. His arms were slightly short and his midriff bulged. There was nothing he could do about it, and much of his childhood had been wasted trying to alter it through exercise. He always looked untidy because he could never buy clothes which would fit his awkward shape. His shirts slipped up to bunch above his trousers, and the cuffs of his jacket slid down to hide his hands. He bought oversize jackets because the regular size would fit his arms and then not close around his middle. However, he'd grown used to the problem over thirty odd years and developed a sense of humour to match. Indeed, if nothing else, this congenital affliction had made him an expert on the subject of dress. Undercover work was one of his specialities.

Fifteen minutes later Andy caught sight of Edward Jay standing by the baggage carousel. He wondered what sort of luggage Jay would have. Probably Samsonite. Smugglers liked Samsonite, whether they were on or off the job. He watched Jay lunge for a bag, and miss it. He waited for the luggage to come round again. This time Jay retrieved his bag and started walking unsteadily towards the Green Channel. It wasn't a Samsonite after all. Andy nodded at his uniformed colleague standing on duty and indicated Jay. 'Even if I didn't know Jay,' he thought, 'I'd stop him. He's wearing an expensive suit, carrying a leather suitcase, and he's sick. Rich people can afford doctors.' He watched as the colleague he'd briefed stepped forward to intercept Edward.

'Excuse me, sir. Can I have a word with you?' said the customs officer to Edward.

Edward shut his eyes, opened them, forced his lips into a smile, and said 'Certainly.'

'Where have you come from?'

'Karachi.'

'May I see your passport?'

He offered it without a word.

'What were you doing in Pakistan? I see you were there for quite some time.'

'I was in prison.'

The officer looked up sharply. Although Andy Ballot had briefed him, he hadn't expected a truthful answer. 'Oh dear,' he commented. He looked down at the passport again, flipping through the pages to see if Edward had visited any other suspicious places. There were plenty of them. 'What were you in prison for?' he asked at last. He stared at Edward.

Edward stared back. Inscrutable.

'A bloody Pakistani ran in front of my car. Could have happened to anybody. Broke his legs, so they stuck me in jail.'

The customs officer raised his eyebrows. 'How unfortunate,' he remarked. He tapped the suitcase with his hand. 'Can I look in your luggage, please sir?' he was being excessively polite. Playing his fish.

'Go ahead.' Edward's eyes had narrowed.

'Perhaps you would open it for me.'

Edward sighed. Exasperation. He leaned forward. His head was just beneath the officer's mouth. The officer said, quite softly 'Did you know that a lot of drugs are smuggled out of Pakistan, sir?'

Edward jerked up. Stood straight. Blinked. 'No,' he answered.

The officer put a hand into the open suitcase and his fingers ferreted around looking for packages. 'You haven't brought any presents home, have you?'

'No.'

The officer looked carefully at the lining of the suitcase. He picked at the corners to see if someone had tampered with them. He was playing for time. He didn't know whether Andy Ballot wanted to interview Jay. 'You aren't trying to smuggle any drugs are you sir?'

'No. Of course not.' Rapid eye movement. The suspect was uncomfortable. Not surprising under the circumstances.

'You don't look very well, sir.'

'I'm not. I need a doctor.'

In the background the officer could see Andy Ballot. He decided that he would let Andy conclude the interrogation. 'If you don't mind me saying it, you do look as if you've been taking drugs.'

'I've got dysentery,' Edward snapped between clenched teeth.

'Oh dear. In that case we'll not take too much of your time. Would you step this way with me?' Jay started to repack his suitcase. 'Don't worry about that, sir. We'll bring it along for you.'

'Well, make sure you don't slip anything inside.'

'I can assure you that Her Majesty's Customs and Excise do not find it necessary to resort to such tactics.'

'Where are you taking me?' asked Edward.

'To what we call the Stuffers and Swallowers room. It is my opinion that you may well have swallowed some dangerous drugs in order to smuggle them into the country.'

'Jesus Christ,' muttered Edward. 'This is a set up, isn't it?'

'I don't know what you mean.'

'I want to see a doctor, immediately.'

'If you are concerned that the drugs may have leaked out of the container into your stomach, then we'll summon medical aid immediately.'

'No. That is not what I mean. I have a particularly vicious bout of dysentery.'

'In that case we won't take up too much of your time. We only require two bowel movements, sir. If you want some food we're only too happy to provide some. In our experience, beans produce the swiftest results.'

'You're enjoying this, aren't you?' snarled Jay.

'Not in the slightest. I am not looking forward to examining your faeces. I can say that with a clear conscience. However, if people insist on smuggling drugs then we have to do our duty.'

'I can assure you that I am not smuggling drugs.'

'That's what they all say. Then what happens? The chaps excrete three pounds of cannabis. Can you believe it? Some of them even claim they never saw it before, let alone ate it. It beggars belief.'

The officer opened a door and ushered Edward inside. There was a simple bed covered with a blanket.

'The more determined smugglers hold out. The record is nineteen days, if a competition interests you. You only have to press the button beside the bed if you want to visit the throne room. An officer will accompany you.'

The door closed behind Edward Jay and he heard the key turn in the lock. He lay on the bed, looked at the remote video camera briefly, and closed his eyes. He was almost home. Only two bowel movements. Well, that wouldn't take long considering the state of his stomach. He wondered what other surprises freedom had in store for him.

Meanwhile Andy Ballot waited in the Arrivals Hall hoping to catch sight of Samuel Tate, but after half an hour he knew it was a waste of time. He went backstage to take a look at Jay on the video screen, and decide whether to interview him.

Jay looked older than thirty-five. Perhaps it was the effect of prison. Andy shook his head involuntarily. Jay had wasted his life. He could probably have been successful in any field he had chosen, but he had chosen crime. He had a university degree, a lovely girlfriend and was more gifted than the average person, but something was missing in his make-up. He seemed to have no interest in the things which motivated other people. He lived on the edge of life. He enjoyed taking risks. Andy recognised the symptoms. He was sympathetic to characters like that. Risk-takers, from gamblers to prostitutes, lived outside society. They took chances every day and it distorted their view of reality. Unfortunately, luck tended to run out with youth; and there was nothing more pathetic than an old criminal.

Five years ago Andy had put Jay under surveillance when he was working on Tate's case. He gained a grudging respect for him during that time, and came to understand him. He learned that Jay was generous; he didn't lend money, he gave it. He was also very professional. He was impossible to follow if he thought that he was being watched. Customs once used a fourteen-man team with a five-car back up and still lost him. Andy couldn't resist the temptation to talk face to face with Jay for what might be the first and last time.

As Andy put his hand to the door he reminded himself, 'Interrogation is a game of poker. The game starts when you walk into the room.' If Jay was interested, he had the chance of finding out as much as Andy about their respective businesses.

Edward looked with disinterest at Andy when he entered the cell. Finally he swung his legs off the bed and on to the floor, and waited for Andy to introduce himself. Even then he said nothing, waiting for Andy to explain himself. Andy sat at the table. Edward glanced at the chains which attached the table and chairs to the floor.

Andy grinned. 'Our suspects sometimes get a little upset.'

'It's not surprising,' replied Edward.

'I wonder if there's anything you'd like to tell me, Edward, about your time in Pakistan?' asked Andy.

Edward thought for a moment. He contemplated saying nothing, but there was little point in antagonising the opposition. Ballot appeared to be a cut above the usual gloating officer. Besides, he might learn something useful from the conversation. 'It wasn't pleasant. The sooner Pakistan subscribes to some human rights programme, the better.'

'Perhaps you'd like to tell me about your arrest?'

'I told your colleague the story.'

'That wasn't the truth.'

'If you know the truth there's little point asking me.' Edward smiled.

'There's a small matter to clear up. You probably know that conspiracy to import drugs into the United Kingdom, even when committed on foreign soil, is an offence.'

Edward said nothing. They'd have a job proving it. The case in Pakistan would never have reached the courts in England.

'Is your silence an acceptance or a denial of your conspiracy?'

Edward chose his words carefully. 'It's the first time I've heard of this conspiracy. I was convicted on a trumped-up charge. You'll see for yourself when you investigate the facts. I don't know what you mean by conspiracy. Where are my fellow conspirators? Perhaps you'd like to elucidate. Then I'll decide if I should speak to a lawyer.'

'You haven't answered any questions so far.'

'I would be grateful if you'd release me so I can see a doctor. As you can see, I'm not in the best of health.'

'I'm sorry to hear that, Edward. Think of it like this, the narcotics trade does not leave many people in the best of health.'

Edward swung his legs back on the bed and closed his eyes. Enough of the chit-chat. He was terminating the interview. They would have to arrest and caution him before he said another word.

Andy recognised the stance. It was a familiar response to interrogation; but the law no longer recognised silence as a refuge for the suspect. Silence implied guilt; and Andy was damned if he would release Jay so easily. He fired a warning shot.

'Tell me something. Are you still in contact with Samuel Tate?' Andy paused. There was no answer. 'I suspect Tate had something to do with your troubles. It wouldn't surprise me if he got you out of Pakistan. Now you think you're indebted to him. I don't think you're so bad. A bit misguided. A fool, maybe. But Tate's a real nasty piece of work. We go back a long way. And I want you to know I'm following Tate; whatever he does and wherever he goes. If you're smart you'll steer clear of him.' Edward continued to ignore Andy. 'When you discover the truth about your mate, I want you to know I'll give you an ear. Remember that. I'll always give you an ear.'

Edward resisted the temptation to tell Andy he'd be lucky. That would be an admission. Anyway he had no plans of becoming an informer.

'Now you're free to go,' said Andy. 'I haven't completed my enquiries. I may bring charges against you sometime in the near future. In the meantime your girlfriend, Julia, must be looking forward to seeing you.'

Edward Jay opened his eyes. 'Julia has nothing to do with this,' he said. He stared at Andy.

Andy smiled. He'd made his point. 'I'll give you a lift into London, if you like. After all, I only made the trip out here to see you.'

Edward suddenly felt uncomfortable. He didn't warrant that much attention. He looked suspiciously at Andy. 'No thanks. I'd prefer to make my own way.'

'I thought you probably would,' said Andy, and grinned.

# Chapter 3

## 1

De Groote replaced the phone in the Amstel Hotel suite which he now regarded as his home. Ahmed Akbar's courier was waiting downstairs. He put on his leather jacket and turned for the door. He looked at Monique contemptuously. She had dressed up for the evening. He threw a thousand guilder note on to the bed. 'That is for your dinner. I have to do work now.' Monique snatched the note, stuffed it into her purse and followed him out of the room.

They'd barely spoken a word all day. The writing was on the wall; but Monique wanted paying off before she left for good. She had given a year of her life to de Groote. The next time he left a bag full of cash lying around she was taking it back to France; and from the nature of de Groote's phone calls, she thought this might be the night.

Monique reached the lift first and pressed the button to summon it. De Groote hesitated for the briefest of seconds, then took the stairs. He reflected that he found Monique most attractive when she was rebellious. He'd fuck her up the arse later. She didn't like that.

In the foyer de Groote expected to see an Arab face. The only man waiting had a pale round face, and was short, stocky, and wearing a cashmere coat. Englishmen were always identifiable by their clothes. De Groote stretched his hand out. 'You are Ahmed Akbar's friend?' he asked.

'That's right,' said the man, returning a limp handshake.

'I am Jan,' de Groote introduced himself.

'I know,' the man nodded. There were freckles scattered across his cheeks. His eyes were brown and darted nervously around the foyer, deserted but for the receptionist and doorman. One of his eyes was lazy, and focused a second later than the other. The lift announced its arrival with a chime, and Monique emerged. She stared pointedly at de Groote as she left the hotel.

'Who's she?' asked Akbar's friend.

'No one,' said de Groote. 'Let's go for a drink.'

The two men left the hotel, turned right in the dusk and walked through the Heineken Tunnel over the Singelgracht.

'What name did you say?' asked de Groote.

'I didn't,' said the man.

Englishmen were all the same, thought de Groote. They didn't trust anyone. Cold fish. This one was no exception. He walked with his shoulders hunched and he didn't look people in the eye; he probably couldn't with that lazy eye.

'People call me Spider,' said Akbar's friend, suddenly.

'A strange name,' commented de Groote. He looked down at Spider's round face and long nose. He realised that the cashmere coat hid a muscular body.

'It's cold,' commented Spider. 'Don't you have no car?' He took his gloves out of his pocket and put them on.

'Of course,' said de Groote. 'But Amsterdam is so small I don't need it. I can walk everywhere.'

'I don't have the money with me. We have to go get it.' Spider talked with an accent. De Groote found it hard to decipher the words.

'That is OK. We can take our time.'

Normally de Groote wouldn't bother to meet a courier for the money. He'd send one of his men. This time Akbar said he was sending a trusted friend and asked de Groote to show him a good time.

De Groote wanted to know more about Akbar's plans. What sort of business was Akbar doing in England? Who was he working with? Why was he employing English couriers? He'd banked money for Akbar before, but not when they were the direct result of an operation. De Groote hoped Spider would let something slip.

De Groote stopped abruptly outside a door and rang the bell. 'What's going on?' asked Spider. He looked up at the tall narrow houses with black windows looming over the street.

'This is a private club,' replied de Groote.

This wasn't how Spider planned it. He thought they'd hop into de Groote's car and drive out to the airport for the suitcase. He hated working outside the British Isles. He hated abroad. It felt like he was in a fog. Even making a telephone call was a problem because he couldn't recognise the coin denominations. It had taken him an hour to realise he couldn't hail a taxi on the street, and another half hour to find a taxi rank. Now he was being dragged into some strange club.

'No,' he said. 'I don't feel like it.'

Spider turned away and looked at the glassy water of the canal. He didn't like water and he couldn't swim. He wondered if it was deep. He guessed the police picked a good few drunks out of there every week.

De Groote grabbed his shoulder as the door opened, 'This is Tam Pobo. The most famous brothel in Amsterdam. This is where I come with your friend Akbar. I pay for everything.'

Spider followed de Groote inside. It wasn't curiosity which made him follow. He had lost control of the situation.

They walked into the bar opposite the reception desk and sat on the stools. De Groote ordered champagne. In a recess at one end of the room three men in suits dozed. Two girls approached Spider. 'We drink champagne,' they said.

'Better ask him,' said Spider, and pointed at de Groote, who ordered two more glasses.

The girls paired off. 'My name is Tami,' said the one with Indonesian blood, to Spider. She rubbed her body suggestively against him.

'Very nice,' he replied.

'You don't drink?' asked Tami.

'No,' said Spider. He wanted to get out, get the business finished, get home. De Groote looked like he was settling in.

'Where you from?' Tami stabbed for conversation.

Spider thought for a moment. 'Canada,' he replied.

'Canada Dry,' she said mindlessly, and giggled.

Spider was nonplussed.

'You like me?' asked Tami.

'Yes,' said Spider, perfunctorily. If he didn't pay attention to the girl, he would be forced to talk to de Groote.

'You like to come upstairs with my friend? We can show you very nice time. We do nice speciality.'

'What's that?'

'You must pay four hundred guilders for upstairs then you see our speciality.'

'It must be good,' said Spider, curious at last.

'You watch me and my friend make love. Then maybe you can join us. It will be very exciting. Then we have extras if you like them. Afterwards we can take bath all together. With your friend also, one thousand guilders.'

'Leave him out of it,' Spider said sharply. He cast a look at de Groote who was deep in conversation. 'What about you and me?'

'I like,' said Tami, holding Spider's hands and pressing them to her breasts.

43

'Let's go,' he said, standing. De Groote looked up from his conversation and smiled. He picked up the champagne bottle and poured the remainder into the ice bucket. Spider watched mesmerised. No way de Groote was joining him and Tami for a foursome.

'What you do that for?' he asked.

'Marnie makes her wages with the champagne. I must buy another bottle. If not, she stops talking.' De Groote kissed Marnie. She giggled.

Spider nodded, relieved. 'I'm going upstairs.'

De Groote smiled.

Spider followed Tami into the room. He turned and locked the door. He didn't want de Groote and that girl creeping in. He sat on the bed. He wasn't going to do anything. He just wanted to be alone. He didn't want to have to talk.

Tami turned up the music and dimmed the red light. She wasn't in a hurry. Time was money. Spider watched her remove her clothes. She had shaved off her pubic hair. He'd never seen a hairless beaver on a grown woman before. He couldn't take his eyes off that pale empty patch. The memories came flooding back. He should have guessed she would be thinking of him tonight. He watched her thighs as she undressed him. It had been a long time. She began massaging his penis with oil. Her hand slipped up and down. He closed his eyes. The transition to that other world was complete.

He was looking at his little sister again; her smooth thighs, and that tight crack between her legs. He was mesmerised, as she stepped out of the bath. He dropped the towel. It hung for a moment on his erection, before falling to the floor. He remembered bending her over the toilet, spitting in his hand, wetting his penis and forcing himself into her.

He never heard his mother creeping up on him. He felt the blow on the side of his head, and his eardrum burst. In the distance, his mother shouted, 'You filthy little bastard.' She kicked him again and again while he lay on the floor, and his sister cried. He wasn't left alone with his sister for a long time, but when he was, he did it again.

Now he felt his sister straddling him. He felt the tip of his penis slipping into that smooth tight hole between her legs. He closed his eyes and recalled those thin white hips. Seconds later, an explosion ripped through his abdomen. There was a hollow echo in his ears.

Inadvertently Spider turned his head to the door to make sure no one was creeping up on him. The tart didn't use a condom, but he didn't care. He used to watch the gism dripping between his sister's legs.

In the adjacent room de Groote sat on a chair, spread his legs, and let Marnie nestle between his knees. He cupped her breasts and watched Spider through the mirror. He had learned a lot about his business partners by watching them in bed. The thing about Tami was that she had a trick.

Spider would leave that room and never know he hadn't been fucked. She'd smother his penis in baby oil and guide it between her buttocks and hold it in place with her hand. It was an old whore's trick, but Tami was good at it. Not many men could tell it wasn't the real thing. De Groote smiled.

Spider had parked his hired car in a dark corner of Schipol Airport's long-term car park. He directed de Groote towards it. They had not spoken on the journey since Spider reacted angrily to de Groote's questions.

'You like Tami, huh?' asked de Groote. 'She shaves her pussy.' Spider didn't react. 'Like a little girl?' teased de Groote.

'Mind your own fucking business,' said Spider. It was a long time since he'd felt like this. He was confused, but at the same time he felt secure. He'd rediscovered his childhood.

'We're here,' said Spider. 'Stop the car.'

'You left the money in this car?' asked de Groote aghast.

'Yes,' replied Spider.

'You are crazy. This town is full of junks and Moroccans. They break into all the cars.'

'We're lucky, then. They missed the jackpot this time.'

De Groote turned off the engine, and they both stepped out. They walked to the other car. Spider looked around. There was no one watching. He opened the boot and reached inside. De Groote peered in. He didn't see a suitcase.

De Groote felt a crushing blow at the base of his neck. He staggered and covered the back of his head with his hands. The blow had knocked the breath out of him. His legs were knocked away and he landed on the tarmac.

Spider kicked de Groote in the ribs, then seeing his neck undefended he dropped on to the Dutchman's chest and placed the jack handle across his throat and pressed down.

De Groote was stronger than he looked. Spider knew he should have got the handle across the windpipe from behind, then he'd have had some leverage. Right now they were in a no-win situation. Spider leaned forward and nutted de Groote savagely, then stood up.

This was messier than Spider had expected. That was the trouble with working abroad. You couldn't take the gun on the plane. He swung the jack handle at de Groote's head with all his strength. The handle wasn't heavy enough. It just opened up the skin and bounced off the skull. He swung again, and again, until the head lolled on the ground. A flap of skin flopped over de Groote eye. He kicked at the base of de Groote's skull. Blood sprayed in an arc, lashing at the cashmere coat.

'Shit,' Spider muttered under his breath. He hadn't wanted any blood, and now he had a contract with head wounds, and they bled worst of all. At least de Groote was quiet. Maybe he was unconscious. He ought to be. Spider watched and listened for a moment. He slipped the jack handle across the Dutchman's throat and balanced his feet on the ends. He bounced up and down, crushing the windpipe.

It was time to clean up. Spider opened the boot of de Groote's car, dragged him across and hauled him into it. There was some bloody frothing around de Groote's mouth as the body settled in the boot. He wondered if the bugger was still breathing. He had heard tales of victims recovering when they should have been dead. He couldn't afford a mistake with this one. He took the penknife out of his pocket and opened it. He cut deeply into the right side of de Groote's neck; and sawed through the jugular vein.

He slammed the lid of the boot closed. Now they'd need to find de Groote quickly, if they wanted to talk to him.

Spider fastidiously inspected himself. He wrapped up his coat and placed it in a plastic bag. He placed the jack handle in newspaper so he could clean it later. Finally he started his hired car, and drove back to the hotel in Rotterdam. He was flying out in the morning. Working abroad had its advantages. By the time they found the body he'd be long gone. He'd left no clues and he had no form in Holland. They'd be looking for a needle in a haystack.

# 2

After hearing that Edward was about to be released from prison, Julia phoned the airport every day to find out when the flights from Pakistan were due to arrive. She waited by the phone. Excitement flooded, then ebbed as each flight came and still she heard nothing.

It was three hours after the last flight from Karachi had landed when Julia received a reverse charge call from Edward, checking she was at home and able to pay for the taxi fare from the airport. She waited impatiently at the window for him to arrive.

When a taxi pulled up in the street and someone emerged, Julia had to look twice to check it was Edward. He had wasted away. His skeleton looked too large for him. He seemed unsteady on his feet. She rushed out of the front door and threw her arms around him, before paying the taxi, and leading him indoors.

Once inside, Edward clung to Julia for a long time without saying anything. At last he spoke. 'I was frightened you wouldn't be here when I came back.'

'Why wouldn't I be?'

'Do you remember I once told you to forget me if anything happened?'

'Yes, but I didn't take you seriously.'

'I meant it when I said it.'

'It wasn't that easy to forget you.'

'You didn't try hard enough,' he said, and laughed for the first time in a long while.

'Did you receive any of the letters I wrote you?'

'No.'

'Was it ghastly?'

'Yes,' he nodded. 'But I don't want to talk about it now. It's too depressing. Later maybe.' He hugged her again, and then pulled back. 'You feel different,' he said, and looked at her.

'I have something to tell you,' she said, cautiously.

'I can see,' he answered. He experienced a moment's panic.

'I'm pregnant,' Julia said, searching his face for a reaction. It suddenly occurred to her he might not think he was the father. 'It's your baby, and she's due in June.'

'How do you know it's a girl?'

'I have a feeling.'

'Well, I hope you won't be disappointed if it isn't.'

'Are you pleased?'

'I'm ecstatic,' he said. 'I can't think of anything better to come home to. We'll start a new life. I'm through with the past. The only thing that matters is that I love you. I've thought about you endlessly for six months. I was scared to death you might have been practical. You would have been right to decide that ten years was too long to wait.' He paused to kiss her. 'I don't deserve you,' he said.

'Don't be silly.'

'No. Really. You're so brave. A lot of people in your situation would have had an abortion.'

'I won't pretend I didn't consider it. But I had a premonition that things would turn out all right.'

'And things will. I promise you. I'm owed a lot of money. If I invest it, the interest should keep us in baby clothes.'

'Don't start worrying now, Edward. And remember, money isn't everything.'

'You're right. But I need to know that I can look after you.'

'We'll look after each other,' she said.

'Is that a promise?'

\* \* \*

Two hours later Julia took Edward to University College Hospital. He was delirious and running a high fever. He was admitted immediately and put on an intravenous drip. She realised how lucky they both were to be together. Another few months in prison, and a fever like that would have killed him. The thought made her shiver.

Now that Edward was back, Julia felt whole again. She looked forward to sharing her life with him again, and remembered how lonely she had been while he was incarcerated. She wondered if Edward would be willing to move out of London. A city was no place to bring up a child. She decided to start looking for a property in the countryside.

# 3

Andy didn't care for Vince, his second-in-command. Vince was everything that he was not. He was tall, good-looking and blond. When he entered a room it suddenly seemed crowded. His voice was pitched somewhat louder than average. Not loud enough to suggest that he was hard of hearing, but loud enough for people to notice that he was there. He had a mouth full of white teeth and a smile to boost them. His appearance suggested an uncomplicated personality. He wore fashionable clothes which were a few years too young for him. The jackets were always too small for his big frame, and emphasised the broad shoulders and toned muscles. He was self-confident and body happy.

Andy knew Vince was back from Cyprus because he could hear his voice in the reception area. He pushed the applications he was completing for mail intercepts and telephone taps to one side for the moment, and waited for Vince's entrance. Had it been any other officer Andy would probably have left his office and joined the conversation, but for some inexplicable reason Vince brought out the worst in him. Perhaps it was because Vince had no idea about personal space.

'How's it going Andy?' said Vince, barely glancing at him as he walked past. He placed a new aluminium Rimowa briefcase on the desk and noisily opened it. He was back.

'Fine,' answered Andy, but Vince didn't react. 'Looks like you had a

good time. Plenty of sunbathing?' He was referring to the suntan which
had an artificial glint. Vince probably used a sun lotion which dyed the
skin.

'I only took one day off. Things were busy.'

'So, how did it go?'

The American Drug Enforcement Agency had asked for a Customs and
Excise representative from London to be present at the planning of an
operation. Andy had recommended Vince.

'It's all happening in Cyprus. That island's like a transit lounge for the
underworld. You'd think they'd all have more sense than to meet there for
their deals. They pop over from Lebanon and Pakistan for business
meetings. If the person next to you isn't some criminal, then he's a spook.
It's a good feeling. Everyone pulls together, and cuts through the red tape.
Our intelligence monitoring stations couldn't be more helpful with signal
interceptions. You remember how secretive they used to be? Now they
can't do enough.'

'That's because the Cold War's over. They're having to justify their
wages all of a sudden,' said Andy, somewhat cynically.

'Yeah, but even MOSSAD's come out of the closet, giving us the names
of people they suspect in arms for drugs deals.'

'So what did the Americans want?'

'They're setting up a sting operation. They're sending some heroin
through Heathrow with a courier. They want to make sure we don't
intercept the consignment.'

'That sort of thing really pisses me off,' said Andy. 'Why don't they take
preventative action as soon as they find out about some smuggling
operation? If you know about a terrorist operation you don't let them blow
up a cinema before you arrest them.'

'That's your opinion, Andy. This way they get their man and they'll put
him behind bars. Your way, there's only conspiracy; and you know how
hard it is to win a conviction on conspiracy.'

'Just make sure that American consignment doesn't accidentally drop off
the plane when it gets to England. These stings have a nasty habit of going
wrong.'

'No way, Andy. There's a lot more than you imagine riding on this
operation. The CIA are involved. It's part of a secret operation to get back
one of the SAM guided-missile systems which the Americans lent to the
Afghan warlords to fight the Russians. It's turned up on the black market in
the Bekaa Valley.'

Andy sensed Vince's defences were up. He'd obviously been admitted a
glimpse of the murky world of the secret agencies and liked what he'd seen.
Andy's view was more pragmatic. 'The Americans shouldn't have lost
control of their missile launching systems in the first place.'

'If the Russian invasion of Afghanistan had been successful then Glasnost might not have happened.'

Andy wondered if that was the official CIA line. 'Sure,' he said, 'but that's a big "if".' He was bored with the conversation. Their discussions always ended with the adoption of opposite viewpoints. Andy changed the subject. 'The latest passenger manifests came through the computer, and flagged up our old friend Samuel Tate.'

'Yeah?' said Vince, looking up.

'He took a flight from Milan to Cyprus while you were there.'

'I wish I'd known,' said Vince. 'I'll have a word with the people out there and see if they saw him knocking on any doors.'

'Good,' said Andy. 'I want to nail that bastard.'

'Yeah,' agreed Vince.

At least they had something in common.

# 4

Samuel Tate stepped out of his silver Mercedes. His face looked more drawn than usual. The skin over his cheekbones was taut and his lips were pale. He looked up at the sky, then stooped to retrieve his umbrella. Gentlemen never wore macintoshes. He then locked and alarmed the car. He strode down the road, umbrella hooked over his arm.

He had not contacted Edward for three weeks after his return. It was a tactical decision. He knew from his own experience that it took time to adjust from prison, and to make plans about the future. He also knew that he had to let the dust settle after that disastrous dinner with Julia. He didn't want her poisoning Edward's mind. He hoped that Edward would be on time.

'It's a windy day,' he said on the phone, 'how about flying our kites at noon?' He had a moment's panic that Edward might have forgotten the coded location, but then reminded himself that Edward hadn't been away for such a long time. They would have to establish some new codes before they went back to work.

The wind grabbed at his jacket as he crossed the Bayswater Road and entered Kensington Gardens. He felt apprehensive about this meeting. He had a suspicion that Edward might be contemplating retirement, and he had to draw him back into the fold. People he could trust were thin on the ground. Suddenly he felt incredibly tired. It was hard work continually persuading people to do things the way he wanted. What was wrong with everyone? He gave them a chance to earn money and all they contributed were problems. He had to take things easy or he'd give himself an ulcer. He'd taken a dozen plane flights in the last month and had innumerable meetings. He was running a tougher schedule than Kissinger in his heyday. He'd stopped using his dodgy passport and was travelling on his own until he could arrange a new identity. He needed to keep Martin Sheehan, citizen of the Irish Republic, under wraps in case things went wrong.

He caught sight of Edward standing by the Round Pond and hurried to join him.

'Good to have you back,' he said, putting his arm around Edward's shoulders.

'It's good to be back,' replied Edward.

'You're not looking too bad. We'll soon fatten you up.'

'I'm doing OK. I spent a week in hospital. I can now keep food down.'

'Sounds like I got you out just in time.'

'You did. I'm really grateful.'

'Don't mention it. You'd do the same for me.'

'How did you manage it?'

'I'll tell you later. I want to hear what it was like.' It would be best to let Edward get things off his chest.

They started walking towards Hyde Park. Their jacket collars were turned up to protect them from the wind. An old man's kite crashed into a tree and hung, flapping grotesquely. Even the noise of traffic was muted by the wind. There was no possibility of anyone eavesdropping, even if they had directional microphones. Tate listened somewhat impatiently to Edward's description of life in a Pakistani jail. He wasn't really interested. He wanted to get down to business. He watched an inbred Afghan hound crumple to its knees in a sudden gust of wind.

'See that?' asked Tate, interrupting Edward.

'What?' said Edward, looking around.

'It doesn't matter,' said Tate. He'd grabbed the initiative. 'It's good to see you've put Pakistan behind you. You don't know it, but you've come back at the right time. I've been busy since you've been away.'

Edward took Tate by the arm and stopped him. 'Before you go on there's something I've got to tell you.'

'Oh,' said Tate, looking innocent. He guessed what was coming.

'I've retired. I've decided it's not worth the risk any more. I want out.'

'You can't be serious. It was only six months. I did a year.'

'You did a year on remand. Not six months in hell. Anyway, this is not a competition. I've decided that enough is enough. Julia and I are going to get married. We're having a baby. We're moving out of London. I've promised her that I'll quit, and that's that.'

'I see,' said Samuel. He hadn't counted on Julia's role in this. Women could be tiresome. 'That's a bit of a blow. I don't suppose there's much I can do if your mind's really made up.'

'You'll manage,' said Edward. 'You always do. But, I think you're taking one hell of a risk. Times have changed. I did a lot of thinking in those six months.' Tate began to interrupt but Edward carried on. 'No. Hear me out. Take a look at what's going on around you. I've only been back a month or so. There's a drug bust or a feature in the newspaper every day. You're trying to ignore it all. Don't! Since Russia collapsed all the intelligence services have been desperately lending their facilities to the law enforcement agencies. They're trying to justify their existence. Without spies their jobs are on the line. The public enemy isn't a Commie any more. It's a drug smuggler.'

'You're talking about hard drugs,' interjected Tate irritably.

'Sure. Hard drugs, in particular. If they come across some cannabis at the same time they're not exactly going to turn a blind eye. Get real, Samuel. You can't fight off the multinational resources. You've earned enough to live off for the rest of your life.'

'Hold on a minute,' said Tate. 'There have been developments since you've been away. Things have changed. I've made new connections. How else do you think I managed to spring you from prison? I'm a big player now, and I've got protection.'

'You're deluding yourself.'

'No, I'm not. Drugs are here to stay. The farmers in the Middle East are controlled by warlords. The warlords need the money for arms. Why do you think the warlords are tolerated?'

'I don't care why.'

'Because America wants them. They destabilise the governments around them.'

'Come on, Samuel. That's just a convenient interpretation.'

'No, it's fact,' said Samuel, emphatically.

Edward shook his head. 'We started this business for a bit of fun, Samuel. Christ, I was a student when we did the first one. It paid the bills and the holidays. It was never meant to be a way of life. You've been in the business longer than me. Don't you remember what it was like in those days? It was easy, and it was fun. I'm very grateful to you for including me. It's time to quit now. You've done better than me. At least you have a property business. You've done all right. Don't push your luck.'

'You might be right under different circumstances,' said Tate finally.

'You might be right, except for one thing. I wish I could quit, but I can't. The money has gone.'

'What money?'

'When you went down, I lost all my savings. I bought that whole consignment in advance.'

'Why on earth did you do that? You've never done it before.'

'Percentages. They needed cash for arms, in a hurry. They offered a fifty per cent discount.'

'Of course you lost!' Edward was aghast. 'You broke one of the oldest rules. If you buy in advance you lose your insurance policy. The supplier no longer has to keep his mouth shut. Come on. You know that. That's what credit is all about. I don't have to give you this lecture.' Then the truth began to dawn on Edward. He looked more closely at Tate. 'I wondered what went wrong. I was very careful, Samuel. That consignment was popped because you got greedy.'

'No,' said Tate quickly. He certainly hadn't meant Edward to jump to that conclusion. 'I had to put down a deposit. I was about to be gazumped. I had to put my money on the table. We were not double-crossed. Believe me. I held a full investigation afterwards. I had to. I lost over a million.'

'Perhaps you should hold another investigation. There is plenty which doesn't add up.'

'I don't need to. I know what happened. The Pakistan organisation was infiltrated. They found out who was responsible, and executed him.'

Edward rolled his eyes. 'I don't want to be involved in things like that, or with people like that,' he said. He was putting the business behind him. 'Forget it,' he reiterated. 'I'm not interested any more. It's all history as far as I'm concerned.' He struggled to light a cigarette, but the wind kept blowing out the flame. He was rattled by what Tate had told him. 'There's something else you should know,' he said, at last. 'A word of warning. I was stopped on my way back into the country and interviewed by a customs officer called Andy Ballot. He told me he was going to make it his business to put you inside.'

Tate looked thoughtful for a moment. 'Him again. Funny how he seems to pop up from time to time.'

'What's he got against you?'

'He was the one who tried to put me away five years ago. Took it badly when I got off. I guess it damaged his promotion prospects.'

'Well, I wouldn't take his warning too lightly,' said Edward.

Tate said nothing. He appeared to be thinking about it. He wasn't. He didn't give a shit about some spiteful customs officer, whom he'd put in his place a few years ago. Anyway, he had that angle covered. There were more important things to deal with. 'I don't want you thinking I'm to blame for what happened in Pakistan.'

'It doesn't matter whose fault it was. I had a good run for my money. And talking of money, I'm going to need some soon.'

Tate stared at the ground. He didn't want to look Edward in the eye. 'I'm afraid there's a problem, Ned.'

'Problem?' echoed Edward. He didn't like the sound of that. And when Tate called him Ned, there was always something unpleasant in the background. He had a hundred and fifty thousand which Tate had banked for him. When Tate mentioned problems, they were invariably financial.

'Springing you from Pakistan wasn't cheap. It cost fifty thousand by the time everyone was paid off. That leaves about ninety thousand, but it's tied up with what I lost. You've still got the boat we bought a couple of years ago for that scam. That's worth sixty thousand. You can take that off the bill.'

'Hold on a minute, that's what it cost to buy and convert the boat. It's not what it's worth.'

'What's it worth?'

'I should say twenty-five thousand.'

'Well, there you are. Twenty-five thousand.'

'No, Samuel. The boat is a joint asset. Half is mine. So we're talking about twelve and a half grand off the bill.'

Tate thought for a moment. 'Expensive business, boating,' he commented. 'We should take a look at our investment. We could go for a sail when the weather picks up.' He suddenly hesitated. He'd remembered something. 'No. Don't sell it. I'll buy your share.' Edward raised his eyebrows, but Tate didn't explain his change of heart, and Edward didn't want to know the reason for it. Tate had a feeling that the freighter de Groote had mentioned was connected to Akbar, and it was worth holding on to it for a while. In a high risk business he needed to keep as many options open as possible. 'Where is the boat?' Tate asked.

'Tucked away somewhere it won't catch any attention.'

'Good,' said Tate.

'Let's get back to business,' said Edward. 'The money you owe me?'

'You don't need to worry about that. It's guaranteed by the property I own. It may take a little time, but I've put the whole lot up for auction. I've put a low reserve on most of it, so it should sell, even in these straitened times.'

Edward shivered. He had barely enough money to buy a house; let alone start a business. His plans for retirement were already beginning to crumble.

Tate read Edward's expression. 'Let's have some lunch. I've booked a table somewhere special to celebrate your freedom,' he paused. 'I want to talk to you about something. It could solve all our problems.' He wondered if he'd said enough, then added, 'I'm sure we can work things out.'

# Chapter 4

## 1

Andy Ballot steeled himself for the Monday morning meeting with his chief, Simon Patterson. He had come to various conclusions over the past few weeks. Samuel Tate was planning something new, but this time his modus operandi was different. Andy had received a photograph from a Metropolitan Police surveillance unit which was watching two former bank robbers who were known to have been involved in smuggling gold. The police supplied the picture hoping that the third man, whom they did not know, would be identified. The first two men were Patrick Phillips, known as Ginger, and James Kelly, known as Spider. The third man was Samuel Tate. However the police, with their traditional suspicion of customs procedures, were unwilling to tell Andy the nature of their own investigation, only imparting that the picture was taken within the previous ten days.

So far as Andy knew, this was the first time Tate had been in contact with the hard-boiled criminal fraternity. Judging from the expressions on their faces, it wasn't a coincidence that the three men were photographed together.

It was time to catch up with Tate again. Andy wanted a surveillance team on him. He wanted phone taps. He wanted the works. He knew he would have to fight for the resources and hoped Simon Patterson would be in a good mood. He prayed no strange requests had filtered down from the Home Office requesting new priorities, because they were always guaranteed to irritate Simon.

He knocked on Patterson's door at precisely ten. He opened the door in response to the grunt from within. Simon Patterson was approaching retirement. He reminded Andy of a moth-eaten bear he had once seen in a zoo, appearing good-humoured, behaving gruffly, but always dangerous. He appeared placid, but he was cantankerous if disturbed from his routines. The pint of strong coffee he drank daily had little effect on his drowsy demeanour. After thirty-five years in the service, little surprised him. Andy refused the offered coffee because he'd once accepted a mug and regretted it when his cigarette intake doubled. He noticed the packets of Douwe Egberts beside the cafetière and remembered that Patterson had been to Amsterdam at the end of the previous week.

'How was Holland, sir?' he asked brightly.

'Same old rubbish. Investigate means of controlling freight travelling through Italy and the Balkans. Check shippers and consignees to confirm they're bona fide importers and exporters. Assess the effect of the single market on smuggling operations. Ignore the problems we have at ports of entry. Mention the lax attitude of the Dutch government at your peril. Request more funds from Brussels. Then it's off for a weekend in the red light district for most of the delinquent delegates. Yours sincerely made it home on the last flight, Friday night.'

'A washout?'

'As usual.'

'Did you do anything else?' Andy asked.

'Like what?'

'I don't know. The van Gogh museum?'

'Not really my kind of thing. I went to the Rijksmuseum once. Too much to look at.'

'How about the coffeeshops?' Andy grinned at the thought of Patterson sipping a coffee, surrounded by hippy types smoking marijuana.

Patterson didn't respond directly. 'Funny lot, the Dutch. Impossible bloody language. When you listen to them talking it sounds like they've all got a bad throat infection.'

'They're pretty switched on though,' said Andy.

'Don't get me wrong,' said Patterson hastily. 'I like them. I've got a lot of respect for them.'

'Yes,' agreed Andy; but he was somewhat baffled as to why Patterson respected a country which had legalised cannabis. If Holland didn't act as a drugs warehouse for the rest of Europe then his job would be a lot easier. 'I want to open a case,' he said at last.

'What is it?'

'Samuel Tate. I want him under observation.'

'No resources available,' responded Patterson, brusquely.

'He's up to something. He's been seen with known criminals. He's been flying around Europe like a blue-arsed fly.'

'We don't have the manpower to chase him on the basis of a hunch. We need more than that.'

'We'll never get more than that if we don't follow it up,' persisted Andy.

'The last time we investigated him it cost half a million pounds of the taxpayers' money.'

'So? At least we found out that he was worth chasing. That was our investment. This time we could get a pay-off.'

'We need guaranteed results. You've got something personal against Tate. A good officer should never let personal grievances affect his decisions. If you come up with something concrete, I'll make sure you're the first to have the available resources.'

'I'm not talking about a total surveillance job. I think we should put someone on to him for a week. Bring our records up to date.'

'Listen, Andy, I need results. So do you. I want to retire having nailed some big bad guys. Who is this Tate after all? Some small-time cannabis smuggler. Sure, he used to be big five years ago. When big was a ton of cannabis. The world's moved on since then. The word from on high is crack. That means we concentrate on cocaine. We have three big investigations on the go right now. I want one of those to come up trumps. If we can get Tate then I'm happy, but he isn't in that league and he's not a priority when it comes to chasing a hunch.'

'I'm not so sure. The level of Tate's activities has escalated over the last ten years.'

'Perhaps the proof will drop on your desk, and then we can re-evaluate the situation. In the meantime, forget it.'

'Perhaps you could issue me with some guidelines, sir? Up to half a ton, not worth pursuing. One or two tons, keep your eyes open. Over three tons, make a phone call. That sort of thing.'

Simon Patterson stared at Andy. He didn't like the sound of that at all. Of course, he wasn't meant to like it. 'I don't think you've found quite the right tone there, Andy. You're a good officer, but don't fuck it up,' he said in a tired voice.

Andy didn't pursue the matter. There wasn't any point. The writing was on the wall. He would have to wait. The silence in the room made him feel awkward. He felt like a schoolboy who had been reproached. He stood up to leave.

'One more thing,' said Patterson, 'Your team's going to be looking after a Dutch officer for the next few weeks.'

Andy's heart sank. 'Is this part of an exchange programme?' he asked. The exchange programmes were a disaster. Foreigners tended to regard the seconding as a holiday and behaved like tourists.

'Not exactly. The Dutch are taking advantage of the programme to pursue some leads. There was a particularly gruesome drug-related murder in Amsterdam. They think that someone this side of the North Sea was involved. I expect you to be as helpful as possible.'

'Any idea what sort of bloke they're sending over?'

'No. I didn't meet him. He's arriving sometime Thursday. They'll fax the details. You better make arrangements for accommodation. Nothing too smart. The Barbican Arms probably fits the bill.'

'You know how much I hate a secondment, sir.'

'Yes. They're distracting. But do try to be hospitable, Andy. From now on we'll be working more closely with our Continental counterparts. They need insights into how we operate. It's also important for us to build personal relationships with our opposite numbers there.'

'I'll try,' said Andy. 'Do you have any good news for me?'

'It's a Monday morning,' said Patterson.

Andy waited until he was outside the door before he hissed 'Shit!'

It didn't make him feel any better. He jabbed his foot angrily at the bottom drawer of a filing cabinet. It scuffed the leather toecap.

# 2

Edward and Julia stepped out of the car and looked at the farmhouse. This was the third one they had viewed. Julia was surprised at how willingly Edward had agreed to move to the country. This property was the best prospect yet. It lay on the outskirts of a village in north Essex, a little beyond the London commuting belt. It was part weather-board and part brick; and not quite what Edward had expected. Julia put her hand on his shoulder and said, 'It's perfect.'

'We better take a closer look,' he replied.

The estate agent had given them the keys and told them they could show themselves around. They peered in through the windows at the distressed plaster and the low ceilings. No one had lived there for some time. A few sticks of furniture decorated the rooms. 'There's plenty for you to do,' smiled Julia.

Edward looked at the old farmyard. There were six sheds in need of some attention, and an old barn. 'There's a lifetime's work,' said Edward, thinking what a good place it would be to stash dope. He reminded himself that he wouldn't be doing that any more.

Julia put the key in the lock and opened the door. They breathed in the musty atmosphere. She looked around, her eyes taking in all the details. 'It's wonderful,' she said. 'Look at that fireplace. If we take it out we'll find the original behind. We can pull down the ceiling and expose the beams.'

Edward found it hard to visualise. He bounced on the balls of his feet and felt the floor springing. 'I think most of the floor joists have gone,' he said.

'I'd expect that,' said Julia, her enthusiasm undiminished. 'I think we'll have a total restoration on our hands.'

'It's a bit expensive considering the condition.'

'We'll make an offer,' said Julia confidently. Edward followed her through the kitchen and the sitting room. He watched and listened to her with a growing admiration. He never realised how much she knew, or how good she was as an interior designer. She had to be good. She was never out of work.

Julia looked under the stairs. 'You can usually tell from the construction of the staircase how old a house is. This is older than it looks. Probably mid-eighteenth century. Let's go upstairs.'

They wandered though the rooms, imagining how it might look when restored. 'It's unusual to find shutters in a house like this. It was probably a later addition.' Julia opened the shutters in the master bedroom. The view spread across the orchard to the fields beyond.

It wouldn't be easy for anyone to creep up on the house without being seen, thought Edward.

Julia leaned against the old dressing table tentatively. She undid the top buttons of her dress. 'I want you, Edward,' she said. 'Now!' she ordered.

Edward turned and looked at her, startled for a moment. With growing excitement he watched her uncup her breasts. His hands fell to his belt buckle. They stood apart from each other, each eyeing the other. Julia pulled her dress upwards revealing her stockings. With a sudden rush of excitement Edward realised that she was not wearing knickers. He took a step towards her, releasing himself from his jeans and underpants. He lifted her gently on to the dressing table and she guided him into her.

'Now this room is our own,' she whispered in his ear. She moaned as he thrust himself in and out of her.

'Don't wait for me,' she said. 'Don't wait for me,' she repeated. 'I want to feel you come.' She pulled up his shirt and pressed her breasts against his chest.

He gripped her tightly, pulling himself deeper into her. The dressing table creaked and swayed. 'Christ,' thought Edward, 'don't let it give way now.' Then he came, shuddering slowly until the room was silent again. He clung to Julia for a moment. When he opened his eyes he looked beyond the flaking green paint, out to the orchard.

'Yes,' he said. 'This house will do.' He kissed Julia's ear.

'Do you think our relationship is just sexual?' asked Julia.

He smiled. 'No. But it's a good starting point.'

Edward withdrew from her. He pulled up his trousers from around his ankles.

'Why do you always dress so quickly?' she asked.

'Because it's hard to run with your trousers around your knees.'

Julia slipped a finger between her thighs and then put it in her mouth. 'Mmmm,' she moaned.

'So, we'll make an offer?' asked Edward.

'Yes.'

'If you can manage the mortgage then I can pay for the restoration in cash.'

'You've got a deal,' said Julia. She buttoned her dress and stood up. No one would ever have guessed she had been making love.

'I love you,' said Edward.

'You're not going soft on me, are you?' laughed Julia, reaching out for his hand.

On the way back to London Julia began to have her doubts about Edward's commitment. He seemed to be distant. She tried to find out what was wrong.

'I'm worried about the finances,' he said finally.

'Don't be,' said Julia. 'My business is doing well. I can afford the mortgage. Now you're going straight you'll realise what a good thing it was that I started my company.'

'Yes,' he replied, unenthusiastically.

Julia remembered how quarrelsome he had been when she first suggested it. He thought she was being ridiculous. He earned more than enough money for both of them. She told him it was not just a matter of money; her self-respect was at stake. She didn't want his money. She didn't want to be a bimbo. She didn't want to be owned by him and his money. She wanted independence and security and if they separated, or something happened to him, she wanted to be able to continue with a life. He finally accepted that she was determined and offered to finance her, but she refused; if she wanted money she would go to the bank. She knew that for some time he felt an irrational jealousy. She was no longer available to go out and play whenever he felt like it.

Perhaps, in some curious way, his pride was hurt. But that was ridiculous. Life was too short, and she was lucky to have him back again.

# 3

Andy Ballot was late arriving for the KLM flight at Terminal Two. He had intended to collect the Dutch customs officer as he passed through Immigration and escort him through customs, but he had been in Terminal Three helping apply the finishing touches to an intelligence operation which had been running for a year. He lost track of time, and now he was almost an hour late. He searched his pockets for the crumpled fax which contained the Dutchman's name, and then found it in the first pocket he'd searched. He scanned it quickly and went to the Information Desk to request an announcement for Mr Jansen arriving from Amsterdam. He waited for Jansen to materialise. Andy was keen to return to the operation in Terminal Three, which would start reaping rewards with the arrival of the United Airlines flight from Orlando.

Andy gradually became aware that the woman at the Information Desk was attracting his attention. He noticed a slender blonde woman smiling at him somewhat quizzically. He found himself smiling back as he stepped forward, and he realised that Jansen was a woman. She was probably twenty-five years old. She was slightly taller than him, and he looked down to confirm that she was wearing heels. 'This might just change my attitude to exchange programmes,' he thought, immediately disappointed in himself for thinking along such lines.

She spoke with a slight accent, the ubiquitous American tinge that so many continentals seem to acquire. 'Hello. I am Annelies Jansen.'

'I'm Andy Ballot. How do you do?' He extended his arm. Her hand felt cool in his. 'I'm sorry I'm late. It's very rude of me.'

'It does not matter.'

Andy picked up her luggage. He noticed that it was Samsonite. 'Anna-lees?' he questioned. He wasn't sure he had heard correctly. Foreign names always sounded awkward.

'Yes. Annelies. But do not call me Anna. I do not like it.' After a brief silence she said, 'You know, they searched me.'

'What?'

'Your customs. Your men searched me. They searched everything.'

61

'Didn't you tell them who you were?'

'No. I wanted to see how you do it here. I thought it would be good for my research. But I think I would tell them when they wanted to take off my clothes.'

'I'm sorry about that. I should have organised the red-carpet treatment for you.'

'I was thinking maybe you already did so.' She laughed.

'No. Please believe me, I wouldn't have done that. Did you have a good flight?'

'It was not so long.'

'You're not too tired then?'

'No,' said Annelies, somewhat perplexed by this line of questioning.

'Would you mind if we stayed at the airport for a while longer. I've been involved in an operation and I want to see how it turns out.'

'Naturally,' said Annelies.

Andy led her outside to the courtesy buses which operated between the terminals.

'Where are we going?' asked Annelies.

'Terminal Three. You've arrived in time to watch the climax of an intelligence operation.' The bus lumbered off. There was no one else on board.

'So please tell me something of this operation.'

His first impression of Annelies was that she was disappointingly plain; neither ugly nor beautiful. She had a good figure though. Blondes always aroused high expectations. He reminded himself that Annelies was not a blind date. 'We've been on to this team for some time. They're what we call mules, carrying cocaine for a big syndicate in Peru. They fly from Bogota to Dutch St Martin in the Caribbean. You know St Martin has no customs controls?' He hesitated for a moment to see if Annelies would comment, but she ignored it. 'The suitcase is forwarded to Florida, and avoiding customs there, it is put on to a flight for London. The couriers pick up the suitcase at this end and walk straight through customs.'

'Where you stop them because you have some information?'

'Not quite. They are operating the scuffed suitcase scam.' Andy waited for her to nod. She didn't. 'Never heard of that one?'

'No.' Annelies was attractive. It was often the same with attractive people. The very features which stood out and initially spoilt the beauty were the attraction. Annelies's crooked front teeth rested on her bottom lip, making it seem as if she was always on the point of breaking into laughter.

Andy consciously glanced away from her lips. 'The scuffed suitcase scam. There are two couriers involved. One of them boards the plane in St Martin. The other joins the flight in Florida. They both have identical suitcases. But the cocaine is in the suitcase which originated in St Martin.

On the flight they swap keys. They arrive in London. One of the couriers takes the suitcase without the cocaine . . .'

Annelies interrupted. 'How does he know which suitcase? They are both identical.'

'They are both identical, except the one which has a noticeable mark. Now, he takes the suitcase through customs. No problems if he is stopped. There's nothing in the suitcase. The important thing is for him to get the suitcase and pass through customs quickly. Then get lost. The second courier picks up the remaining suitcase and walks through customs. If he's stopped and asked to open it, he finds his key doesn't fit. He looks closely at the suitcase and says, "This isn't my suitcase. My suitcase is scuffed here." He'll look at the airline tag and point out that he boarded in Florida. We open the suitcase and find the cocaine, but unless we catch both people together it's hard to make the charge stick. It's a clever little trick and more often than not the couriers get through.'

'This is very strange,' Annelies's eyes seemed to twinkle when she smiled. 'You are telling me that this suitcase is a big operation?' There was the note of disbelief in her voice.

'This is intelligence work. This is the tip of the iceberg.'

'You know, I do not think we have this kind of problem in Holland. Our problems are different. The operations there are more big.'

'When does an operation become big enough to warrant investigation? When there are ten, or twenty, couriers? If it's one operation then twenty couriers can be very big,' Andy retorted irritably. It wasn't a competition between England and Holland. He didn't have to spell things out. 'Our couriers are often pathetic people taking chances. We had one who surgically implanted kilo tablets of cocaine beneath the skin of his calves.'

Annelies winced and closed her eyes. She shivered. It was quite delicious.

The bus stopped at Terminal Three. 'Let's go,' Andy said, grabbing her suitcase from the rack by the door. Inside the terminal he looked at the information screen and saw the flight was on schedule. Andy opened a door marked 'Customs and Excise Only' and led Annelies through. He showed his identification to the officer on duty, then he led Annelies into the officers' common room. 'Would you like a coffee?'

'Yes please.'

Andy picked up two plastic cups and started pouring from the lukewarm pot.

'I have changed my mind,' said Annelies suddenly. 'I will not take a coffee. Now I remember how English coffee is.'

'Oh,' said Andy. The coffee always tasted fine to him. He recognised the machine. It was the same as the one in the offices at Fetter Lane. He was suddenly irritated by the fussiness. He drank his cup, deliberately enjoying it.

'We can leave your suitcase here,' he said. He tapped it. 'Samsonite,' he added. 'Smugglers like Samsonite. That's why they searched you. A pretty woman carrying a Samsonite.'

'Why do they like this Samsonite?'

'They're expensive but bulky. They're made of tough plastic, and it's relatively easy to build a false bottom into them.'

'In Holland the smugglers like containers. The kind they put on ships.'

Annelies seemed to be proud of her country's reputation. He ignored the remark. 'Take your coat with you,' he said, 'it's cold in the baggage halls.'

For the next half hour they watched the baggage handlers lining up the luggage. They watched the dogs clambering over the suitcases, sniffing them. The dogs were only effective against the chancers who didn't vacuum pack the drugs in clinical conditions. Professional couriers had their drugs packed so there were no telltale traces, and no scent for the dogs. Suspicious suitcases were deftly opened by officers and gently rummaged before being locked again.

It turned out that the couriers were not on the flight manifesto. It was thought that they were catching the next flight. 'Sorry about that,' he turned to Annelies. 'It ends up like this half the time.'

'I know,' said Annelies. 'Don't worry. They will arrive here one day and then you will catch them. In our work we have time on our side.'

They drove to London and by the time they had negotiated the rush hour traffic it was six o'clock. There was little point in going to the office so Andy delivered Annelies to her hotel. He stopped for a quick drink with her. He was glad of the opportunity to speak to her away from the office. There were things he wanted to say which would be difficult with the other officers around. He felt resentful that an outsider had been thrust upon him, and while he wanted her to be aware of that, he didn't want her to feel that she was being excluded. Above all, he didn't want her to get in the way.

It was some time before they settled down in the bar with their drinks. Annelies ordered an orange juice, and rejected it when it turned out to be bottled. She discovered that freshly squeezed orange juice was a luxury on an English menu. She opted for a mineral water. Andy hoped this fussy attention to her drinks was not characteristic, because otherwise she'd be better off with the Excise department.

There was an awkward silence. Annelies crossed her legs. She had neat ankles. Andy looked away.

'I understand you have your own agenda,' said Andy bluntly.

'Agenda?' questioned Annelies.

'There is a case you are working on in Holland. You want to do some investigation here.'

'Yes.'

'I hope we will be able to help you. Apart from that I understand you expect to work alongside us on our own investigations so you can learn how we operate.'

'That is correct.'

'I think it would be a good thing if we discussed how we're going to work,' said Andy.

Annelies guessed what was coming. It was a busy department. They were all busy. Not much time for explanations. She'd be running errands. Making coffee. Of course they were busy. There was a drugs war in progress.

'Yes,' she answered with an innocent smile.

'I do not expect anyone in my team to do anything which I'm not prepared to do. That includes any boring mundane work like checking through records. We all take our fair share of it. Nor do I subscribe to what has been a departmental failing in thinking that women are only useful behind a desk.'

Annelies said nothing. She was staring at him. He wondered if she was a feminist.

'If you ever think that I'm discriminating against you in any way, please tell me. I'm new to this job too, and I have enough trouble dealing with men. Let alone women.' He smiled self-consciously after that remark, and darted a quick glance at her. He had dark eyes. They were almost black.

Annelies nodded. She was thinking he was stupid. He didn't understand what he was saying. Perhaps he oughtn't to be in charge of the department if he had trouble dealing with men. To differentiate between men and women was ignorant.

Annelies nodded. She was about to say something but he continued.

'If you do think I'm discriminating against you in any way, I hope it will be a mistake or, at the very worst, a piece of male chauvinism which needs pointing out.'

'I understand,' said Annelies. Andy Ballot was a loser. She wondered if he had a girlfriend. She doubted it. 'I will try to keep out of your way. You should know that this is a very good thing for me to come here. It was not easy. I had to fight very hard for this assignment. It is not easy for women to have a fair treatment. Not even in Holland. I want to be good. I want to learn. I want to help you.' Her blue eyes seemed to have turned a steely grey. He looked away.

Andy felt guilty. Perhaps he had been a little heavy-handed. 'I didn't mean to sound so negative,' he said. 'I'm not good at working with people, that's all. You'll get on fine with the other guys. I guess you'll have to tag along for a while, and see how things go.'

'I understand,' said Annelies. She understood only too well. She felt the anger rising up. 'Just tell me one thing. Do you think you would speak like this if I was a man?'

'I hope so,' said Andy.

'I do not think so.' Annelies stood up. 'Thank you for the drink.' She picked her room key off the table and walked towards the lifts.

Andy followed her. They weren't getting off to a great start. 'Hey Annelies,' he said. She turned and glared at him. 'You've deliberately misunderstood.'

'I do not think so. I will see you tomorrow.' The lift doors opened.

'I'll pick you up.'

'It will not be necessary.' Annelies stepped into the lift and the doors closed.

Andy sighed. 'Fuck that.' All of a sudden he felt tired. He'd been dumped with someone who had something to prove.

# 4

Nearly six weeks had passed since Edward had returned, and Julia was growing impatient with him. She knew he had problems. She knew he was still owed money by Tate. He didn't seem to have turned over a new leaf though. He still had frequent meetings with old associates, although he claimed they were to clear up business matters. She didn't give a damn whether Tate had put all his properties on the market to pay back Edward. She had her own life to lead and she wanted to lead it with Edward. She didn't want Tate hovering in the background. The first time she went to ante-natal classes Edward hadn't accompanied her because he had a meeting with Tate. She didn't bother to ask him again. She didn't want to force him to do anything he didn't want, and she didn't want to risk the rejection.

'I have to sort out my finances,' he said. 'I think that's more important, don't you?'

'If you're worrying about buying the house, let's not do it,' retorted Julia.

'I'm owed a lot of money and I want it back,' replied Edward irritably.

Julia guessed that wasn't the whole reason for his listlessness. She asked him what was wrong, but he fobbed her off with vague answers.

Edward had a dilemma. At first he hoped Julia would guess the agonising decision he was making. He didn't dare tell her. He knew what her answer would be. He'd promised her that he would stop smuggling, but that was before he discovered he didn't have enough money to support a wife and child. That was before he looked realistically at his limited potential for employment. That was before he became involved in some dilapidated farmhouse. He had precious few options and now Tate was offering him a solution. It would solve his problems for a lifetime. The operation would be over in a couple of weeks, before the baby was born. He would earn almost a quarter of a million pounds without taking any undue risks. He couldn't refuse Tate. When it was over he could tell Julia. If he told her before that, she would never believe it was really the last time.

He looked back over the past ten years and hated himself. He estimated he had squandered over a million pounds, but there wasn't any point in harbouring regrets. He'd spent the money on too many things to worry about it now. He should have saved it for a rainy day. Like a spoilt child he did things impatiently. He learned to fly and bought a half share in an aeroplane; though he soon abandoned the idea of dropping dope into a field at low level. He bought a Morgan and raced it for a year. It was race-tuned professionally before each event; and all he had to show for that folly was a tin cup he won at Brands Hatch. It wasn't hard to shred a hundred grand a year with a few holidays in the Caribbean and the Far East. He never wanted to be an old man living in a cold room saying, 'If only I had done that. If only.'

The moment the offer on the farmhouse was accepted Edward knew he was going back to work again. As soon as he made the decision he felt as if a weight had been lifted off his shoulders. He felt the adrenaline rushing. He was back in a world he understood. He was whole again, in a world where survival was freedom and failure was imprisonment. It was a world where luck didn't exist. All that knowledge, earned over fifteen years, came flooding back. He was good because he'd never stopped learning. He studied criminals as well as the police. He didn't make the same mistakes as most criminals. They were creatures of habit. That's how they were usually caught. They always went to the same pubs. They were lazy because they were human. They always bought their airline tickets from the same travel agents. They drove their cars to meetings instead of taking the bus or underground. They wore the same clothes. Drank the same drinks. They even used their home phones instead of walking down the road to public ones. They bought flash cars which policemen envied and then complained when they were stopped and questioned. When transporting money and dope they worked at night, instead of driving in the rush hour. Reducing the odds was what success was all about. Most criminals were gamblers, but they never looked at the odds on a roulette wheel. Most criminals were lucky if they didn't get caught.

When Edward took Julia out to dinner to celebrate the acceptance of their offer on the farmhouse, he told her of his plans to start an antique business. She didn't guess that he was up to his old tricks. The business would provide him with the necessary cover for his meetings. Of course he would go to the auctions. He would rent storage for the furniture. She would accompany him to some of the auctions because she could use the items in her work. They'd even need things for their new house. He wondered why he hadn't thought of the possibility long before; interior decoration and antiques made a perfect business marriage. Most important of all, however, was that he would not have to keep telling her where he was going.

Julia responded to Edward's change in mood. He was positive again. He was his old self. 'Let's go to bed,' she said, prising the brandy bottle from his hand and putting it away. She felt this was a new beginning.

They turned out the lights and undressed each other in the silvery dusk thrown through the windows by the street lamps. She pushed him gently on to the bed and then sat on top of him. 'I think you'll have to let me make love to you.' She felt his hands stroking their child, and her breasts ached. She wanted to put them into his mouth. She pulled his head up, and he anticipated her needs. His mouth opened and his tongue searched out her hard nipples. She moaned. She felt his fingers teasing her, slipping into her. She stretched her arm behind her, and found his hard penis. She felt his body straining towards her, upwards. 'I want you so much,' she said, and she guided him into her. She moved gently, feeling him inside her. He stretched his arms up and framed her face in his hands and said, 'I love you.'

'I love you too,' she answered, quietly. 'I love you for what you are, not what you pretend to be.' He tensed for a moment and wondered how she could have guessed. She misinterpreted his body's sudden reaction and moved more quickly. 'I love you. Not for what's strong in you, or weak. I love you because we need each other, and because our baby needs us.'

'Sshhh,' he whispered and silenced her with a kiss which lasted until they both came.

Afterwards he remembered the silence in the room. He could hear the booming of his heart. There was the slight chill of the aftermath, resting like dew in the dawn, before he pulled the covers over their bodies. He imagined a poignant sadness in the shadows. His hand gently stroked her collar bone and glided over her full breasts, and the tight skin of her stomach to the softness of her thighs. He moved towards her and hid his face in the warmth of her. He was ashamed. The sadness he felt was the lie he was telling her. He hadn't the strength to tell her the truth. He did not know if he was frightened because he might lose her. He clung tightly to her. In the middle of the night he woke and kissed her, but she didn't stir. He felt a loneliness envelope him.

# Chapter 5

## 1

It was the beginning of February, and London was transformed by the first warm sunshine of the new year which seemed to herald spring. Samuel Tate did not care for spring and the sudden appearance of buds, bees, and flower stalls on the pavements. He skirted the flower display outside a florist, irritably avoiding the old lady smelling the imported freesias. He had no interest in flowers, trees, or mowing lawns. He would pretend to savour such pleasures momentarily, when they were pointed out by some girl on his arm. When he walked down the road he noticed things like the number of pedestrians. How many cars were parked. How many people were in the cars. Three people in a car suggested an undercover police operation. How many taxis. How many curtains were half-drawn in the upstairs windows, and whether the net curtains were twitching. He wondered if he had told anyone he would be at that particular spot at that precise time. There were other reasons why he didn't care for the spring. He suffered from hayfever, inflamed sinuses and an allergy to bee stings.

Nevertheless Tate was more cheerful than usual that morning. He was on his way to lunch with Edward and he guessed he was about to hear some good news. After all, Edward wouldn't have called him if he didn't have something to tell him. He had booked a table at one of the most expensive restaurants. It was important to remind Edward of those pleasures he might be relinquishing if he was thinking of retirement. He was looking forward to the 1953 premier cru Margaux which he'd ordered. There wouldn't be much change from a grand. He'd pay in cash, as always, because it left no traces.

He wouldn't tell Edward he had liquidated his property company for a little over two million in case Edward took what he was owed and decided not to work after all. Things were falling into place perfectly. In view of the sluggish property market no one would suspect the real reasons for the sale of the company. Least of all, Edward. No one would guess he was pulling out of England because it was too hot, and heading for the big time. From now on he'd work out of hotel rooms and live in the Cayman Islands. He'd fly into England to arrange the scams, and fly out when they began.

Tate found Edward waiting for him at the restaurant. They were shown to their table, and as a matter of course Tate requested another table on the other side of the room; there was always the slender possibility that the table was bugged. They sat down. Tate put his briefcase beneath the table where it snuggled against his legs. He took out his handkerchief, blew his nose, and asked the waiter to remove the fresh flowers. He looked around to satisfy himself that everything else was to his liking, ordered half a bottle of champagne as an aperitif, and turned to Edward. 'Have you made up your mind?' he asked.

'Yes.'

'And what's the answer?'

'I'll do it, but there are a few conditions.'

Tate smiled. 'I'm sure we can accommodate those.' He paused and felt a warm glow of satisfaction. 'It's good to have you on board again, Edward.' He meant what he said. Planning a smuggling operation was a lonely affair when there was no one with whom to talk it over. 'I always have the feeling nothing's going to go wrong when you're working with me.'

'I'm surprised you still think that way after the shambles in Pakistan.'

'Ah yes,' said Tate. 'That doesn't count.' They both smiled. It was like old times, making light of adversity. 'I guess we could put that down to experience.'

'Experience is the name everyone gives to their mistakes,' said Edward bitterly. The memory of prison remained vivid. Rich food still made him queasy. 'Going to Pakistan was a mistake. I broke one of my own rules. Never work abroad because you don't know the landscape. You don't know what the policemen look like. You don't know where danger's lurking. I should never have gone there. We should have left all the arrangements to the supplier.'

'It's all very well saying that now,' said Tate. 'At the time we thought we needed someone on quality control, otherwise we might have ended up with a couple of tons of cow cake at this end.'

'You'd still have lost a million pounds because the problem came from another quarter.'

'What?' said Tate, suddenly baffled. He'd only lost two hundred thousand.

'You'd still have lost all your money,' elaborated Edward.

Then Tate remembered. 'Oh yes. Yes I would, wouldn't I?' He finished his champagne quickly. That was the trouble with telling a lie. You had to be on your toes for ever afterwards. He had to remember that as far as Edward was concerned he was broke. Relatively broke. The bill for this lunch would rather stymie the suggestion of bankruptcy. 'Sorry. I was thinking about something else. Let's order. Have you chosen?' He glossed over the indiscretion.

They summoned the waiter and ordered. They worked their way through the dégustation menu while they discussed the mechanics of the latest operation.

'This scam is going to make us more money than all the others,' said Tate.

'I don't see how, Samuel. We've done some big ones in the past. The only way we'd make more money was if we moved into the white powders; and you know I'm not willing to touch them.'

'Nor am I,' agreed Tate. 'But just listen to this.' He began his explanation.

Finally Tate ordered a champagne cognac. Edward had to admit he was impressed by Samuel's planning. Despite his previous reservations he already felt excited. Once again he was being seduced by the thrill of danger. He felt a certain admiration for Tate's dedication to the pursuit of riches.

'When are you going to stop, Samuel?' he asked.

Tate nestled the brandy balloon in his palms. 'When I have an island in the Caribbean.' He sniffed the brandy. 'This bears no resemblance to a Remy Martin, you know. The Remy's caramelised. In comparison its attack on the mouth is quite vicious. Like being kicked in the teeth.'

Edward didn't like to say that he tended to prefer the bite of a Remy at a tenth of the price.

'We've come a long way since those early days,' said Tate.

'I'm not sure whether we're much better off.'

'We weren't paid enough for the risks we took.'

'The money was worth more in those days.'

'No it wasn't,' said Tate. 'We didn't have so much of it. Speaking of money, by the way, I've scraped together twenty grand in the briefcase. That should keep you going for a week or two, and pay for a few expenses.'

'Thank you,' said Edward, wondering why he was thanking Samuel for returning a portion of the money he was owed.

They lapsed into silence, each of them thinking about the past. Edward remembered sitting up for nights with the 'ABC' World Airway Guide which listed every scheduled flight. They tracked planes flying from Thailand to Toronto, or Karachi to New York, and so long as they stopped in Basle at the same time as a flight destined for London they were on to a winner. They did a lot of trade, meeting each other in the transit lounge at Basle. The Swiss made a mistake at Basle, allowing transit passengers to collect their suitcases and then mingle and swap luggage with direct-flight passengers in the departure lounge. The British Customs and Excise never suspected passengers arriving from Switzerland to be smuggling a suitcase full of Thai sticks or best quality black Pakistani hashish. 'I'm running a bit short of cash,' Tate would say and a week later they'd be ten thousand pounds richer.

Finally airport security tightened and the flight schedules changed. Someone at Basle got wise. Anyway, Samuel was fed up with pocket money, and turned to bigger things. He thought cannabis would be legalised one day so he planned to make as much as he could while the sun shone. 'Why import twenty kilos when you can import two hundred?' said Tate. They learned about haulage, freight, trucks, coasters and fishing boats.

'By the way,' said Tate suddenly, 'I've changed my mind about the boat. I want you to sell it after all.'

'Why?'

'I had an idea, but it's not going to work out.'

'Fine,' said Edward. He hadn't been to see the boat yet. He wondered what sort of shape it was in. The batteries would certainly be dead. He hoped it wasn't full of water. They'd learned their lesson with boats. They were hard on the nerves and the weather was never reliable. Air freight made a lot more sense now they had the right connections. In any event he could do with the cash if Julia's offer for the farmhouse was accepted.

Finally the waiter produced the bill. 'That's extravagant,' commented Edward, 'if you're so hard up.'

Tate smiled. 'I anticipated a celebration,' he replied blandly.

# 2

Annelies arrived at the Fetter Lane offices punctually at nine on her first morning. Neither she nor Andy referred to the previous night and their abrupt parting. Andy decided that they had reached a convenient stand-off, and he was no longer under an obligation to be more than courteous and friendly. If she wanted someone to show her the sights of London then he was off the hook. Nevertheless, she did waft some fresh air into the department. No one had ever worn Lycra leggings, a mini skirt and a baggy jumper to work before. The women in the department sniffed disdainfully, and the men showed more interest than their usual indifference. Andy enjoyed showing her around and introducing her. Vince made no secret of looking her up and down. He liked what he saw, and smiled. Annelies ignored him, and Vince bristled. Andy was gratified.

The three of them stood awkwardly in the office after the tour of the department. Andy lit a cigarette. Vince opened a window pointedly. Andy ignored him. It was a long-term battle which would only be resolved when smoking in the office was outlawed and then Andy would quit the service.

'So where do we go from here?' asked Andy. 'Do you have any questions, Annelies?'

'No,' she answered. 'Perhaps you can tell me what you are working on at this moment. I do not want to cause you problems.'

'It's a pity she didn't turn up when we were opening a new investigation. That's the best way to find out how we work,' said Vince.

Annelies stared at Vince. She didn't like being talked about as if she was not present.

Vince wondered if he might suggest she worked through the expense receipts he'd accumulated in Cyprus. That would give her an insight or two. Every now and again he saw the outline of her breasts beneath the baggy jumper; they weren't too small and they certainly weren't supported.

'It's difficult,' said Andy. 'Our investigations are complex and require a

73

thorough understanding of the background. Our options are usually limited by what is and isn't possible. That is dictated by a working knowledge of the law in this country. But, we could open a new case?' The question was aimed at Vince. Andy wanted to see how Vince would respond. He needed help for what he had in mind, and he had it in the form of Annelies. It would mean working behind Simon Patterson's back, and to do that Vince would have to be a party to the conspiracy.

'What are you thinking of?' asked Vince.

'The Chief's against it,' warned Andy.

'We have to go by our instincts. If we always did things his way we'd never get a breakthrough,' encouraged Vince.

'Remember Samuel Tate?'

Vince frowned. 'Sorry, Andy,' he said, 'I promised to see if he was clocked in Cyprus. I forgot. I'll get on to it.'

'Thanks,' said Andy.

'Are you thinking of looking at him?' asked Vince.

Andy nodded. He turned to Annelies, and explained. 'For fifteen years Samuel Tate has been smuggling drugs. We managed to catch him five years ago in possession of a large sum of money. The case went to trial, but the jury cleared him. He has continued smuggling but we don't have any hard evidence against him. Now, a number of incidents have brought him back into focus. His second-in-command, Edward Jay, was imprisoned in Pakistan for ten years, but was released six weeks ago. I'm willing to bet that Tate paid a large bribe to spring him.'

Andy retrieved an unmarked folder from the bottom drawer of his desk. He removed a photograph and passed it to Annelies. 'This is Edward Jay. I took the picture at Heathrow on his return. Meanwhile, Tate was spotted travelling to Holland, Switzerland and Cyprus. He's been seen with a couple of bank robbers who are under surveillance by the police.'

'How do you know about the movements of this man, Tate?' asked Annelies.

'Passenger manifests from all airlines are made available to us by an agreement between the European Customs Co-operation Council and the International Airlines Association. I'm surprised you didn't know that,' said Vince.

'I know that,' snapped Annelies. 'I asked to know if you found this information from some different observation.'

'If we had Tate under surveillance then we wouldn't be having this conversation, would we?' said Vince, superciliously.

Annelies controlled her irritation.

'No,' Andy said to Annelies. 'There has been no other agency involved.'

# The Scam

'How did you find out about the blaggers?' asked Vince.

Andy turned to Annelies. 'He means the bank robbers.' Although he enjoyed Vince's thrusts at Annelies, he felt he should remain studiously impartial. She might realise how unreasonable she had been the previous night. He turned back to Vince. 'The Metropolitan Police thought we might know who he is. They sent a picture across. It shows Tate with the two men they've identified. They wondered if we could identify Tate and suggest what the three of them have in common.' Andy pulled the photograph out of the folder and passed it to Vince.

Vince looked at it quickly. It showed three men standing by a BMW. It was a typical surveillance photograph, a high angle shot, indicating that the police photographer was staked out in a first-floor room. The three men looked furtive. One was opening the car door. The other was walking around the bonnet. Tate was talking to the first man, but his attention was caught by something out of shot. That was what made Tate look suspicious. A criminal's eyes wandered, watching in case he was being observed, when he told his secrets.

'It's circumstantial,' said Vince finally. 'Nothing definite to go on. I don't want to get caught out by Patterson because we headed up some investigation into small time hoodlums.'

For a moment Andy was baffled. Vince had apparently encouraged him to ignore the chief's advice, and now he was pulling back. He still thought that there were reasonable grounds to initiate an investigation.

'I'd still like to run it for a while,' he said.

Annelies leaned forward and retrieved the photograph which Vince had failed to pass to her.

'I think you've got something personal against Tate,' said Vince. 'I know he got away from you. We all have our crosses to bear, but you've no proof against this guy. We know Tate's a dodgy character. I don't know why you're so surprised to see him talking with a couple of villains. It's par for the course.'

Andy wondered whether Vince might be right. It was possible to interpret evidence in a myriad of ways.

'I am sure I know this man, Samuel Tate,' said Annelies. The room was suddenly silent. They could hear voices down in the street, three storeys below. At that moment Andy forgave Annelies everything. He turned his attention to her. 'I have seen a photograph of this man. Maybe two weeks ago.'

'How can you be sure?' said Vince, for no good reason.

Annelies ignored him. She was excited. 'Andy, you remember I was telling you how there was a murder in Amsterdam of a drug baron called de Groote?' Andy nodded. 'The Central Detective Agency was making enquiries in Holland. The police have been watching de Groote for many

75

months. They have pictures of many people he was meeting. This man you call Samuel Tate was meeting de Groote. We do not know his name, but the department will be pleased to know this. They have a witness. It is de Groote's girlfriend. She has been identifying these people for us. De Groote was meeting a man the same night he was killed, and his girlfriend saw this man. We are paying for her to stay in Hotel Vermeer until our enquiries finish. You see, we take this murder importantly.'

'What do you think about it now?' Andy asked Vince.

'We should check it was Tate,' said Vince.

'I will make a copy of this picture and send it to my department in Holland. They will confirm it. Afterwards we can make a formal request for more information.'

'Great,' said Andy.

'I'll run off a copy in a minute,' said Vince. 'I've got some copying to do. I'll see if I can enlarge it.'

'So, we're agreed?' said Andy. Vince nodded. 'We'll do a little investigating of our own for the next couple of days, until we hear from the Dutch. We'll keep it between ourselves. No official records at the moment.' Andy turned to Annelies. 'Can you request the whole file on de Groote? We might find some leads in there.'

'Yes.'

'Next, we've got to find out what Tate was doing with a couple of East End hoods.'

'I don't think Annelies will be much help there. She wouldn't understand how the villains fit into this game,' said Vince.

Andy winced, and darted a glance at Annelies. Vince had finally attracted her attention. 'This is too much,' said Annelies. 'You are deliberately rude to me.'

Vince raised his eyebrows, and turned to look at her. He smiled. 'Not at all. I was only being realistic.'

'Then, explain this to me.'

'OK,' said Vince. He sat on the edge of his desk. 'I don't know how it is where you come from, but here we have two different types of drug smugglers. The first were the hippie types. Middle-class kids who felt they were on some kind of crusade. They were chancers, smuggling small amounts of cannabis. The organised criminals kept clear of the drug traffic. Then came the first big heroin explosion. It was caused by the fall of the Shah of Iran. Many of his supporters, particularly the secret police, took their wealth out of Iran in the form of heroin. Until the late seventies English criminals kept away from the drug trade. They were still emerging from the days of the protection rackets. You'll find that our criminals are not very imaginative. They tend to emulate the American crime patterns. Anyway, they thought that drugs were a dirty business;

it's kind of touching that there should have been a morality in their criminal activities. They soon discovered that there was money to be made out of drugs. They muscled their way into the industry using organised crime methods. We now had a second type of smuggler. By the middle of the seventies things were changing, and the scene was becoming more violent.' Vince stopped abruptly. 'So, there you are. The history lesson is over. Unfortunately, you probably won't be here long enough to learn anything useful about the underworld.'

'Thank you,' replied Annelies. 'It is not so different in Holland, I have to tell you. We have organised crime too. We also have hippies. So let me ask you something. You want to know why this man Tate is talking with two bank robbers?'

'That's right,' said Andy.

'These bank robbers are doing business with him. They have money from a robbery and they must invest it. No? Do I miss something?'

'No. I think you're right on target,' said Andy.

'Good. I was thinking maybe Vince has some problem to make this connection.' Andy looked at Vince, who smiled, and scratched his head. He was beginning to enjoy this relationship. Annelies opened the door. 'I will fax my request to Holland and ask them for information about de Groote.'

'Do you remember where to find the fax machine?' asked Andy.

'Of course,' replied Annelies. She had seen it in communications room down the corridor.

'Any chance of a cup of tea, love?' asked Vince. She looked at him, and then ignored the remark. She closed the door behind her.

'Think she'll be much good?' asked Vince.

'She might give us a surprise.'

'Seems a bit hard of hearing.' Vince grinned.

'The Dutch don't drink much tea,' said Andy grimly.

'OK,' said Vince. 'I'll give her a chance.' He picked up the folder lying on Andy's desk. 'The most important thing is to find out where Tate is hanging out. I'll run through what we have on file.'

Half an hour later Annelies returned to the office. In one hand she held a fax. In the other was a mug of what was unmistakably Dutch coffee. There was only one place she could have found it, and that was in Simon Patterson's office. Andy looked askance. He wondered if she had said anything to Patterson about the investigation. Annelies interpreted his look, and smiled. 'No. I did not say anything to him. I was waiting for the reply to my question, and I am smelling this coffee in Simon's office. He gave me this cup. We had a good conversation. He welcomes me to the department and tells me you are good officers to be working with.' She looked directly at Andy, and smiled. It was a private joke. He grinned

77

back. He guessed he was forgiven. 'So here I have the answer to my question already.' She rustled the fax.

The reply was in Dutch and Annelies translated. There was no further information on Tate, but there was plenty on de Groote, and the Dutch were interested in anything more they could find out. De Groote was killed by an unknown assassin. It was assumed that it was a drug-related killing. He was found in the boot of his car in the long-term car park at Schipol Airport. In 1988 de Groote was suspected of killing an associate, and ordering the assassination of two rivals. He had been under sporadic surveillance since that time. It was possible that his own death had taken place as a reprisal for the killings he had ordered. Tate had been seen leaving the Amstel Hotel after a meeting some three weeks previously. It was not known what had been discussed at the time nor had Tate been identified. De Groote's operations were large and he was known to have imported at least fifteen tons of cannabis a year into Holland.

'Do you think that Samuel Tate was involved with de Groote?' asked Annelies.

'Definitely, if they were seen together,' said Andy. 'He didn't fly to Amsterdam for a cup of tea with an old chum. We know he flew to Switzerland shortly after that meeting. I'll bet that means he went there to perform some kind of banking operation. Perhaps he had struck a deal with de Groote.'

'Do you think Tate is having something to do with this killing?' asked Annelies.

'It's not his form,' said Vince. 'There's no evidence that he is violent. On one occasion we heard he was ripped off and he actually chose not to retaliate. Violence attracts the attention of the police. The smart offenders like Tate know that. It's the criminals who are violent.' Vince paused. 'No. It's not Tate's game at all.'

'You've got a good memory,' commented Andy.

'It's all coming back to me. It was one of my first cases. I helped you try to make that case against him. I was in Romeo at the time,' said Vince.

'You're wrong about him,' said Andy, sharply. 'He's capable of it. He's ruthless.'

Vince looked at Andy. There was an awkward silence. Annelies broke it. 'I do not know what you mean. You make a difference between these words, offender and criminal.'

'I know. It's a class distinction. In England it's hard to see anything outside a class context which is very much alive. We never had a social revolution in this country. For the record I am, what the French like to call, a Republican. Among the middle classes of this country there is no dishonour in breaking the law. The only dishonour is in being caught. For criminals it is an honour to be caught. They take pride in serving time. Consequently, crime is a habitual occupation,' said Andy.

'It is very strange for me to hear you talk like this,' commented Annelies. 'So what can you tell me about these two people, or criminals, who are friends of Tate?'

'The men are convicted bank robbers,' said Andy, picking up the photograph. 'They are hardened criminals. The one opening the car door is called Patrick Phillips, apparently known as Ginger because he has red hair, except that he has dyed it. The small one is James Kelly, known as Spider.'

'Why is he called Spider?' asked Annelies.

'For some reason people with the surname Kelly get called Spider,' said Andy.

'That's what I mean about our villains,' said Vince. 'If your surname's Harris you're known as Bomber. It's Chalky for White. Charlie for Peace. It's a whole new language, Annelies.'

'So what about Spider?' asked Andy.

'Incomprehensible,' said Vince, grinning. 'Doesn't it tell us on his record?'

'No. In fact, it says precious little on their records. And I have a feeling the Metropolitan Police will be reluctant to tell us much more.'

'Why? You must know what they are doing if it is connected to your case,' said Annelies.

'There's a lot of competition between customs and the police. If the police have spent four weeks watching someone and then we suddenly arrest him the police don't get any credit for the work they've done. When we work with the police it happens because there have been high level discussions, and only afterwards is there a complete exchange of information. Frankly I have to admit that we don't like co-operating with the police. Their security is not as good as ours, and operations mysteriously go wrong when they're involved.'

'You know what I am thinking?' asked Annelies rhetorically. 'Putting this body of de Groote in the back of the car. It's unusual for that to happen in Amsterdam. Normally there is the sea or the canals.'

'It's not unusual here,' said Andy. 'England is the home of the murder. We have the most imaginative ways of hiding dead bodies. They say the bridges over the motorways hide corpses from the gangland wars of the sixties.'

'Maybe that is what I am thinking. Perhaps de Groote was not killed by a Dutchman.'

'I still can't see Tate being involved,' repeated Vince, looking up from the expense accounts he was now sorting.

'We'll find out soon enough,' said Andy confidently.

# 3

It was time for Tate to introduce Edward to Spider and Ginger. He was apprehensive about the meeting, anticipating Edward's reluctance to work with unknown partners; and consequently he was unusually jocular. 'Make sure you aren't seen with them, Ned. They're not our sort. They wear cashmere coats and smoke Castellas when they celebrate. There are some things you can't buy, however much money you have.'

'Samuel, you're a snob,' responded Edward.

Tate felt reassured by the remark. Perhaps Edward wouldn't react to them. 'Their bark is much worse than their bite,' he concluded.

But even Samuel was beginning to have his doubts about Ginger's ability to fix things. It was too late to start looking for someone else, and, anyway, Ginger was too involved now. He was a linchpin of the operation. Tate was learning to his dismay that Ginger's attention to detail left much to be desired. When Akbar wanted someone to deal with de Groote, Tate only had one contact, who was in America. He mentioned it to Ginger who took the problem off his hands. In retrospect, Tate realised it was a mistake; he was beginning to hear rumours that de Groote's death had left some messy details which needed further attention. He would have to give Ginger a lecture.

Tate had arranged to meet them in an art gallery on Sloane Street, and therefore took the psychological advantage by placing them on unfamiliar territory. Spider and Ginger looked insecure as they waited for Tate to arrive, surrounded by middle-class affectation, and incomprehensible chit-chat.

Tate watched them through the plate-glass window from the relative safety of the street. 'The one on the left is Ginger. The other's Spider.'

'It was a bit ostentatious meeting them at a place like this,' commented Edward.

'We're not going to discuss anything here. The idea was to encourage them to become a little more discreet. Widen their horizons. Make them security conscious. Right now they probably think they're in the middle of a police convention.'

Edward looked at them. Ginger wore a black leather jacket. He had a wiry build, and stood with knees slightly bent, perpetually waiting to repel some assault. He had a scar on his left cheek, and when he spoke it was from the side of his mouth. He appeared to be the dominant personality, but Spider looked more sinister. Ginger was obviously nervous whereas Spider betrayed no discomfort.

It was Spider who absorbed Edward's attention. There was a menacing air about him. His face was pale and almost round, without colour, tone or expression. The features were all there, a thin nose, freckles on the cheeks, limp brown hair; but it was a childlike representation of a face, a Hallowe'en pumpkin, without feeling. His eyes darted, devoid of reaction. He wore a camel hair coat, and kept his hands firmly in the pockets. Ginger knocked back the champagne, but Spider drank nothing.

'We better save them,' said Tate. He opened the door and picked up a complimentary glass of champagne from the table inside.

Ginger immediately registered Samuel's arrival and barged through the guests towards him. Their presence was spreading dismay and consternation among the art fanciers, especially as they had now monopolised the complimentary champagne.

'When you say six I understand six. Sharp!' Ginger was evidently not pleased. 'Next time. Five seconds late I'll be gone. Want to synchronise watches?' He pulled up his sleeve and flashed his gold Rolex.

Tate glanced at Edward. There was the hint of a smile. 'I don't think that will be necessary. I usually synchronise my watch with the BBC time signals. By the way, this is the friend I was telling you about. Ernie.'

'All right, Ernie?' said Ginger by way of greeting, ignoring Edward's outstretched arm. 'Don't worry, I won't be calling you nothing because I know that ain't your real name. But I know Sam here. We did time together in Pentonville. Didn't we, my old mate?' Tate winced at the remark.

As Ginger spoke, his torso wove from side to side and his head ducked like a boxer.

'Excuse me,' said a red-faced man in cavalry twill, butting into their conversation, 'do you have invitations or are you friends of the artist?'

Tate produced invitations from his pocket, and waved them nonchalantly.

'This lot want to take the lollipops out of their cake-holes before they speak,' commented Ginger. The red face disappeared.

'The things you see when you haven't got the gun,' commented Spider, coldly.

Edward looked at Spider, and realised he was serious.

'You pulled a bleeding stroke on me,' growled Ginger. 'I'll choose the tearoom next time we meet. Let's evaporate. This place gives me the creeps. Fancy meeting us in the middle of this lot.' He started for the door and they followed. One or two of the art fanciers stared after them as they left.

They wandered around Knightsbridge for ten minutes and poked their noses into a pub which proved completely unsuitable for conducting a conversation about a criminal venture. Everyone in the bar turned to look at them. 'I don't like this place,' said Ginger and walked out. 'What were they looking at? Someone should teach them some manners. Don't you have no decent boozers round here,' he complained. 'Next time we meet on our manor.'

Finally they tried the Carlton Arms Hotel where they found a table in the corner. Ginger looked round while they waited for the drinks to arrive. 'Don't mind this place,' Ginger commented at last. 'Some nice girls in here. No scrubbers. Know what I mean. Look at her!' He pointed.

Edward turned and looked politely at the pretty leggy blonde. Breeding oozed out of her. The taxes had been paid on the Cartier jewellery.

'I bet her shit don't smell,' remarked Ginger.

'And she don't shave her cunt,' said Spider. They all turned curiously towards Spider, but he didn't provide an explanation for the remark.

'Let's talk business,' said Ginger, and leaned forward conspiratorially. 'The first consignment comes the end of next week. We don't have the day yet, but soon as I know I give the word to Sam here,' he jerked a thumb towards Tate. 'Then he tells you, Ernie.' Edward nodded. 'Now! Where we going to meet?'

There was a moment's silence. Edward suggested, 'There's a sandwich bar down Wandsworth Bridge Road, about a hundred yards from the bridge. Vans are always parked there.'

'Fair enough,' said Ginger. 'I'll check it out. You get there half eight in the morning with the van and give me the keys. I fetch the gear. I'm gone an hour. I come back and give you the van. You got any problems with that?'

'No,' replied Edward.

'The van!' said Spider, turning his eyes on Edward. 'I don't want some scrap heap. Got to be clean and unmarked. No van hire. Nothing written on it. Don't want it more than three years old in case the Bill stops me for the papers. You got that?'

'Yes,' said Edward, dutifully. At least they understood the importance of the vehicle's appearance. Spider kept staring at Edward. One of his eyes was lazy. It was hard to hold the stare.

'We meet you one week later for our dosh,' said Ginger. 'Make that nine in the evening at some boozer.'

'No,' said Edward. 'Meet at lunch time or at six. I don't drive outside the rush hour or daylight hours.'

'What's your problem? Bit windy? This is ain't a bottle job you know.'

'It's your money,' said Edward. 'If you want to take chances with it that's your problem.'

'I don't give a monkey when we meet. Make it six if you want.' Ginger glared at Edward.

'Where?' said Edward.

'Liverpool Street Station,' said Spider. 'Plenty of people around.'

'Plenty of police around too, especially if there's a bomb warning.'

'So what do you reckon? You got all the ideas. Mind you, we don't want you standing out like a sore thumb with the suitcase.' Ginger was becoming irritable.

'Victoria Bus Station. Plenty of car parks nearby. We meet there and go to my car. I drive you to your car. You get out with the suitcase.'

'No problem. Just be on time,' said Ginger.

'I will be,' said Edward.

'Why don't you beetle off to the john? I want a quiet word with your mate,' ordered Ginger.

Edward left the bar and wandered around the hotel. Fifteen minutes later he saw Ginger and Spider leaving and returned.

'What do you think of my two little jailbirds?' asked Tate cheerfully.

'They're a liability,' answered Edward.

'Yes,' said Tate thoughtfully. 'We really don't want to be seen with them. They've got form as long as your arm. I'm not joking. If the Bill sees you with them you can kiss goodbye to your private life. They're not our sort. They drive cars with personalised number plates, for God's sake. I think they even use mobile phones.'

'I can see that. I thought we had a rule. We don't work with anyone who's been inside prison.'

'Well, that counts us out,' Samuel chuckled. 'This is different. We need these guys for the air freight. You let me handle them. I know what carrots they like, and which stick works.'

'Samuel, we've always tried to avoid working with firms like this. These guys carry guns, don't they?'

Tate thought he'd defuse the atmosphere. He didn't want Edward to be alarmed. 'They're all front. Listen, I'll tell you a story someone told me about Ginger when he was still doing bank jobs. He used to go into a bank and shoot a sawn-off shotgun into the ceiling to show he was serious. One time he did it a piece of plaster fell down and knocked him unconscious. His mates had to carry him out and abandon the raid.'

'That's exactly what I mean,' said Edward. 'Do you really want to work with people like that?'

'Don't worry about it. They're voices on the edge of the action. They think they're hard. Sure they have connections, but then they don't have the expertise to put things together. They couldn't smuggle a tube of toothpaste into the country without my help or contacts.'

'So long as you're happy, Samuel.'

'I wouldn't say I was happy. After all, they know my real name. I'm taking all the risks. At least I didn't waste my time in prison. I made some links.'

'You know what they say, Samuel? Prison's only a finishing school for public schoolboys.'

'Bollocks,' retorted Tate. He didn't like to be reminded he had gone to a minor public school. He counted himself amongst the self-made men.

'Listen, I've got to fly,' said Edward. 'Julia's waiting for me.'

'I thought we could have dinner together,' said Samuel, feeling somewhat rejected.

'I don't want to meet you again until this scam is over.' Edward delved in his pocket for a scrap of paper which he passed to Tate.

'These are the numbers of two adjacent public phone boxes. I'll be waiting for a call there every morning at half past nine. I'll give you some other times and numbers when you call me.'

Edward stood up to leave. Tate accompanied him as far as the bar where he ordered another drink.

# 4

It was seven thirty in the evening. There was a bitter north wind and the weather forecast even hinted at the possibility of snow. In a side street off Knightsbridge, an unmarked police car was parked on double yellow lines. Detective Sergeant Bill Davidson of the Metropolitan Police was on surveillance and had an excellent view of the Carlton Arms Hotel. He was looking forward to some traffic constable trying to ticket him for a parking violation. Even better if the constable tried to clamp the Rover. He fancied a little confrontation to liven things up. He was huddled in the passenger seat wrapped in a nylon quilted jacket feeling cold and irritable. He was fifty years old and it had taken him thirty-four years of work to get where he was that evening. He had a ruddy face, fair hair, bad circulation and he was still a bachelor. A variety of unwelcome thoughts drifted through his head, uppermost of which was that Customs and Excise were showing an interest in his suspects. He was buggered if he was going to let them into his case. He'd been following Spider and Ginger for six weeks.

Sooner or later he'd catch them in a bank raid.

Davidson wiped the condensation off the inside of the windscreen and peered at the hotel entrance. Customs knew sweet fuck-all. That he knew. They didn't even know where Tate lived. They'd asked him earlier in the day. He wouldn't tell them even if he knew. If they wanted involvement they ought to have turned their information over to him. Tate had nothing to do with bank raids; he didn't have the form and anyway, the computer said that he'd only done some time on remand suspected of drug dealing. Well, as far as Davidson was concerned armed robbery was a damn sight more important than that. Right now Ginger and Spider were meeting some new bloke whom he hadn't yet identified, but he'd find out before the night was over. Best thing would be if Ginger and Spider went back to planning bank jobs and customs could get on with following Tate.

Davidson knew a few things after thirty-four years in this game. Ginger wasn't about to commit some crime. This kind of thing was social. Since when did Ginger go to art galleries? Fencing old Masters wasn't his game. Since when did he have meetings in smart hotels? Bloody Ginger was getting ideas above his station. He'd have to work on his vocabulary if he was going to join the cocktail set. Davidson knew how Ginger and Spider worked all right, and it wasn't like this. He'd been about to knock off for the night when Tate turned up with the new bloke who looked like he worked in some bank. Maybe Ginger was working an inside job.

Davidson had a keen young detective in the foyer of the hotel keeping an eye on the suspects. He could afford to close his eyes for a mere two minutes of shuteye. Years of surveillance had developed this catnap into an art. He closed his eyes. He dreamed away. Two minutes later he sprang awake. It was like that some nights in his bed. Then he would reach for the sleeping pills, wobbly eggs they were called by the junkie from whom he confiscated them.

He jolted awake. Stared at the hotel. Nothing. He remembered the breasts he had conjured a moment ago. His hand had been warm down the white knickers. He snuggled into his nylon jacket and closed his eyes again and tried to splice the dream together. She was still wearing white knickers, high-heeled shoes and black suspenders. He pressed his face against her thighs and continued to pull down her stockings with his teeth. He jolted awake. He'd give himself a heart attack one of these days playing with that fantasy.

There they were. Spider and Ginger were walking towards their BMW. He let them go. He wasn't interested in them for the rest of the night. He could follow them any day of the week. They were as easy to follow as a three legged dog. What he wanted was a little more information about Tate's friend. He opened the car door and got out. He stretched and felt his blood circulating again. He locked the door and made his way to the hotel.

As Davidson entered the hotel he passed Tate's friend leaving. He cursed. He caught sight of his sidekick in the foyer and nodded his head in the direction of the unknown suspect. The detective followed. Davidson waited for a couple of minutes before hurrying outside.

# Chapter 6

## 1

Julia was furious. Edward couldn't expect her to believe that he was not up to his old tricks when he was out all day and came back late in the evenings. She'd suspected it for the past week and hoped it wasn't true. She felt used, and she didn't like the feeling. She looked at her watch. It was nine. She was letting her life be ruined by him. She had been better off when he was away. At least she had been in control of her social life. Now all she did was wait for Edward to come home. She went to work and she did the shopping. Meanwhile he treated their home like a hotel.

Edward returned at nine thirty. 'You told me you were going to be back at seven thirty. I've cooked your dinner,' said Julia.

Edward followed Julia into the kitchen, innocently. 'What is it?' he asked.

'A few tiger prawns gently tossed in fresh chillis on a bed of spinach, which is now congealing on the plate. That was for starters. And I want to see you eat it,' she said. She picked up the plate. 'On second thoughts, I think it would make me sick.' She hurled the plate into the sink where it smashed.

'What's wrong?' asked Edward, alarmed.

'You are. I want the truth. Will you tell me the truth?'

'Yes,' said Edward. He knew what was coming.

'Are you involved with Samuel again?' Julia stared at him. Edward held her gaze, but hesitated a fraction too long before replying. 'Give me a straight answer. Yes. Or no.'

'It's not as simple as that,' said Edward.

'Then the answer is yes. You've lied to me. You said you were retiring.'

'I am. But it's not that easy. There are unfinished matters to clear up.'

'Don't hedge. It's quite simple. You quit.' Then she added. 'Or I quit.'

'Please listen, Julia.'

Julia interrupted. 'To more lies?'

'Not lies. Give me a break. I'm trying to pick up my life. I haven't done anything yet. Sure, Samuel would like me to do a few things.'

'Oh, so you're thinking about it?'

'I don't have much choice. I have to get the money I'm owed.'

'Forget the money, Edward. Grow up. Can't you see what Samuel is? He's self-centred. He doesn't give a damn about anyone else. And he never has done. What did he do for you in prison?'

'He got me out.'

'He got you out!' Julia said sarcastically. 'He got you out because he needed to get you out. It was convenient. You didn't hear from him before then. You didn't have a decent lawyer arranged, did you? Why not? Did you ever stop to think it out? Either he forgot you, or he was too bloody scared he might find himself implicated.'

'Julia, you don't understand.'

'Why don't you open your eyes for once? Your friend Samuel isn't the nice safe Biggles you knew fifteen years ago. He's turned into a stark raving megalomaniac. He's got about as much respect for you as he has for the rest of the world and that isn't saying much. I know. Believe me. I know, because I'm a woman. I went out to dinner with him because I wanted to know what had happened to you. I told him I was pregnant. You know what he told me. He said he found pregnant women attractive. He didn't say a word all night about you in Pakistan. No. He was trying to get me into bed. That's your friend Samuel. Nice seamy Sammy who wants to fuck Julia because he wants to fuck Edward. Nice little Sammy who wants to fuck pregnant women because he knows he won't get involved in some paternity suit and lose some of his money. Or maybe it's nice little Sammy who doesn't like using condoms because he's too sensitive.'

'Julia, this isn't fair. I don't believe you. I think you've misinterpreted everything.'

'Fair!' shouted Julia. 'Don't you talk to me about fair. Is it fair that I have to share you with Samuel? Is it fair that I have to lie to everyone for you, waiting until they put you back in prison? It's not fair and I don't want you staying here until you feel capable of making some commitment to this relationship. It's me or Samuel.'

'I'm not prepared to make a trade-off like that.'

'Well, you know what you can do!'

'I'm tired Julia. My head's spinning with all this. I love you, but I can't bear all this vitriol. Please, bear with me a little longer.'

'No. You've run out of time. You go away and think about it. When you've made up your mind, come back and let me know.' Edward looked baffled. 'Now, you fuck off and think about it. Go and talk to Samuel. See what advice he gives you.'

Edward picked the car keys off the table, and walked to the door. He turned to look at Julia. Neither of them said anything. She didn't try to stop him. He walked out.

Davidson was surprised to see the suspect walk out of the flat on Leighton Road. He had just received details of the car which the suspect was driving. It was registered to Julia Crighton-Smith at the address opposite. She was probably the suspect's girlfriend. But the night wasn't over yet. The suspect was back in the car and was driving away.

'Follow him,' Davidson said to the detective constable behind the wheel. As the suspect doubled back on himself around a one-way system across the Camden Road, Davidson cautioned his constable. 'Back off a little. He might have sussed us.'

Edward stopped the car suddenly outside a pub. He'd been driving aimlessly for half an hour, feeling numb. Inside the pub he was relieved to find it was not crowded. He ordered a large whisky, drained it at once, and ordered another. He found an empty table in the corner and sat down. He felt hurt and rejected by Julia's reaction. She didn't understand. He was going to work for the both of them, and their future. Now she had given him an ultimatum.

He imagined a life without Julia. She would always be there, just as she was now, sitting at another table watching him; except that she would be with another man. She would be dressed in black. Always black. She would be talking too loudly, making exaggerated gestures to illustrate the importance of what she was saying. Her dark eyes would ignore him sitting in the corner, and she would lean forward to kiss the man across the table. Perhaps she would stretch her hand out and lead the man out of the pub, to take him home. Edward's imagination followed Julia until she was in bed with that other man. He imagined those intimate moments, savoured the pain he felt, and drained his whisky.

He went to the bar and ordered another drink. He was not going to lose Julia. They had been together for eight years. She had taught him how to feel, and not be afraid of those feelings. She had drawn him out of loneliness and given him something he was afraid of losing.

His thoughts turned to Samuel. It was strange how people changed. Especially old friends. They changed imperceptibly. Over the years their priorities shifted. Although Samuel behaved abominably at times, Edward kept an image of him from their early days. Friendships were based on memory, not on reality. Edward found it hard to put his finger on exactly when it was that his relationship with Samuel had altered. But Samuel had been there for him when it mattered. Samuel had got him out of jail. Whatever Julia said, if it hadn't been for Samuel he would still be in there.

All the same he was not prepared to dump someone he had known for sixteen years, on someone else's whim. He'd shared his formative years with Samuel. They were bonded by their experiences. They'd been a good team. Samuel had the ideas and he put them into practice. They'd had some great adventures. He wasn't going to throw all those memories away because he was having some argument with Julia. He felt calmer now. The pub was closing. He'd stay in a hotel for the night, and see if Julia was more reasonable in the morning. If necessary he'd tell her the truth, and then move out of the flat until the job was over. If not, he might introduce Samuel to someone who could do the work for him. He'd take a percentage for the introduction to keep a finger in the pie. Yes, that was the best solution.

Outside, the cold air sobered him immediately. He thought about catching a taxi and then remembered Julia would need the car in the morning. He got in the car and pulled away from the kerb. He waited for the man to cross the road in front of him. The man approached his window. He looked to his left. Another man was standing on the pavement. He wound down his window and heard the words 'Police officers'. He reversed the car back into the parking place, and stepped out.

'May I see your driving licence, sir?'

Edward took his licence out of his pocket and handed it over.

'I have reason to believe that you have been drinking, Mr Jay. Will you accompany me to my vehicle so I can give you a breath test?'

'That doesn't look like a police car,' said Edward. 'Would you show me your identification?' There was no point making things too easy for them.

'By all means,' said the policeman, pulling out his card.

'Thank you, Detective Sergeant Davidson,' said Edward.

He stood by the unmarked police car and blew into the machine, and saw the light turn predictably red. It came as no surprise to him. It had been that kind of day. 'We must ask you to accompany us to the police station, where we will take another reading.'

Edward got into the back of the police car. It was a short drive from Offord Road to the police station at Kentish Town. Edward guessed he had a long wait. It looked as if there had been a crime wave that night from the number of people waiting to be processed. The two policemen disappeared. In due course the desk sergeant asked him to blow into the breathalyser machine, and again the result was positive. He was asked whether he wanted to give a blood or urine sample. He opted for the latter; the sight of needles made him feel faint.

Davidson returned and escorted Edward downstairs and passed him a sample bottle. They were alone. Edward felt the wad of money inside his pocket. There were a thousand pounds. He looked at Davidson. He was about fifty. He had fair hair and a red complexion. There was a tapestry of broken blood vessels on his cheeks. His belly hung over his trousers. A man of that age and rank had few prospects and little money.

'Can I speak to you?' said Edward.

It was some time since Davidson had heard anyone use that expression. He knew what it meant. It meant that a bribe was on its way. 'Maybe,' he said.

'Have you been drinking, Sergeant Davidson?' asked Edward. He was taking a gamble.

'I've been on duty for twelve hours.'

Edward took out the wad of bank notes.

'What's that for?' asked Davidson. There was the smallest flicker of interest in his eyes. Things were taking a surprising turn.

'It's for you to piss in this bottle.'

'How much is there?' asked Davidson.

'Nearly a grand,' replied Edward.

Davidson looked at Edward. This was turning out to be a strange affair. He wanted to find out a bit more about this one, and now he was being paid for his trouble. There was a moment's hesitation before he stepped towards the urinal. He stretched out his hand for the money. Edward passed him the sample bottle. He took it, and then held out his hand for the money. Edward gave it to him. He looked at the notes, considering whether to count them. 'How much?'

'More than nine hundred pounds,' said Edward.

Davidson stuffed them into his jacket pocket.

Edward guessed he had a right to watch since he was paying. There was something indecorous about the way the policeman fumbled with his flies. Perhaps he was worried another officer would find them. The policeman spilled some urine down the side of the bottle and on to his shoes.

Davidson buttoned up and wiped his hand on the seat of his trousers. 'Never done that before,' he said.

'There's always a first time,' said Edward.

Cheeky fucker, thought Davidson, but what I'm going to tell you is going to cost a lot more than nine hundred quid.

'Mr Jay, this little charade was incidental. I wanted to have a quiet word with you in private. I've got a message for you to deliver to your friend Samuel Tate. I've got some information for him and it costs five grand.'

'Why don't you tell him yourself?'

'He's a bit difficult to find these days, and I wouldn't want to make him nervous by looking for him.'

Davidson opened the door. He turned round, and said, 'I'll meet you at that pub tomorrow night. Seven sharp.'

'I don't see much of Tate these days,' Edward covered himself. 'I don't know if I can contact him that quickly.'

'Make it the day after tomorrow. But make sure he's there, or I'll come knocking on your door,' threatened Davidson.

Edward followed Davidson to the desk sergeant and completed the formalities.

Outside the police station, Edward hailed a cab. It was midnight. He'd had too many surprises for one day. He decided not to stay at a hotel. Back at home, he found Julia in bed.

'I thought you'd gone,' she said, sleepily.

'No,' said Edward. 'Not yet.'

'I'm glad.'

'We'll talk about it,' said Edward. He squeezed her hand.

'In the morning,' said Julia. 'Come to bed now. I'm sorry about this evening.'

When Edward woke Julia was standing by the bed. She was dressed. She must have woken him. He scrabbled for the clock and saw that it was half past eight. She was on her way to work. There was an hour until he had to phone Samuel. He rolled over.

'Where's the car?' she asked.

The previous night came flooding back. 'It's across town. I had too much to drink. You'll have to take a taxi.'

'We'll meet for lunch,' ordered Julia.

'Phone to tell them you'll be late for work,' said Edward.

'I can't.'

He tugged at her skirt.

'Behave yourself,' said Julia sternly.

'That's not exactly what I had in mind,' answered Edward, playfully.

'It's not easy for me to perform on demand,' said Julia. 'There are some things we need to discuss. I'm booking a table for lunch at Lincontro. I'll see you there at one.'

Edward watched Julia leave the room. She was a long way from forgiving him.

# 2

Vince opened the door to the office and was unprepared for the chaos which confronted him. It looked as if the place had been ransacked. Andy stopped hunting through drawers and turned to face him.

'Where have you been?' he snapped.

'Heathrow,' replied Vince. 'Sorting out the American consignment, making sure it doesn't drop off here.'

'Where's that fucking picture?' Andy demanded.

'What picture?' replied Vince.

'The picture of Tate which you copied yesterday.'

'I left it on the desk. I thought Annelies took it.'

'She didn't,' snapped Andy.

'Did you check through the other stuff I had copied?' asked Vince, starting to tidy his desk. He looked with dismay at the receipts he had carefully arranged the previous day, and which now lay in chaos.

'Yes. And I've been to the copying room in case you left the original there.'

'Maybe someone picked it up by mistake,' suggested Vince.

'I've asked. No one's been in here.'

'Did you ask everyone?'

'Yes,' said Andy irritably.

'How about the Chief?'

'No. I didn't ask Patterson. It wouldn't have looked good after he explicitly told me that Tate wasn't a priority.' Andy thought for a moment. 'Anyway, what would he be doing in here?'

Vince didn't bother to answer that question. 'So what's your problem, Andy? Ask the Met for another print.'

'That'll take a week if they respond at all. I want to get things moving.

The Dutch are waiting for that picture. They've got de Groote's girlfriend waiting for a positive identification of Tate. As soon as they get the photograph and we receive an official request for information, we can get this show on the road.'

'You've got other pictures of Tate in the file. Send one of those instead.'

Andy said nothing. He looked with disgust at the mess around him. 'You're right,' he said, finally resigned to the loss of the picture.

'Where's Annelies?' asked Vince.

'Gone to the Dutch Embassy for something or other.'

'Any idea when she'll be back?' asked Vince.

'Before five, I hope. I want her to deal with this as soon as possible.'

'I might see if she wants a bite to eat tonight,' said Vince. 'Thought it might be a friendly gesture.'

'Good idea,' said Andy, brusquely; but he wasn't sure if he liked the idea of the two of them getting friendly.

Andy started clearing up the mess he had created. He was impatient to start the investigation into Tate. It was always the same with Tate. Things went wrong from the beginning. Now he was killing time, waiting for a photograph to be sent to Holland. He'd lost a day already. Tomorrow he'd spend waiting for their reaction. Tonight, he'd spend drinking. Waiting. Always waiting, for the letter, the phone call or the stroke of luck he needed; killing time until something happened.

'Next time,' said Vince, 'I'd be grateful if you didn't touch things on my desk.'

Andy glared at him.

# 3

Samuel Tate stamped his feet on the pavement. He was waiting until half past nine to make a call to the number Edward had given him. There were two telephone kiosks next to each other outside the Kensington Hilton, and neither had been vandalised. He was five minutes early. The wind was bitter. He went into the nearest kiosk, leaving the door ajar. The smell inside was rank. It smelt of cigarette smoke and urine. He once read that the telephone kiosk was the most infectious institution in the United Kingdom and that using one after major heart surgery was tantamount to suicide. However, he thought the telephone was more dangerous than that.

He knew that all international telephone calls were subject to monitoring. The monitoring was computerised and able to pick out key words from conversations played back at high speed. It was a long shot that any of his conversations would be intercepted, but his survival was based on reducing those odds at every conceivable opportunity. He made it his business to stay abreast of developments. He knew that there were three satellites over the Atlantic and each was capable of transmitting on 20,000 circuits. There were eight transatlantic cables with about five thousand circuits. They were all monitored. The National Security Agency computers covered eleven acres and could pick up a single key word, monitoring words at a speed of four million characters a second. They could read a book before a person could say the title.

Unfortunately the telephone was the only way in which he could ensure absolute security and still communicate with his colleagues. If international calls were dangerous, then domestic ones were worse. British Intelligence had only managed to catch the spy George Blake by tapping every phone in the King's Cross area. It had been a mammoth operation and only possible because Blake was a man of habit. Blake used a public phone in the same area every time and gave the police a fighting chance. Tate could choose any phone in London; but technology was reducing that advantage.

Nevertheless the British did make it easy. In Holland, public phones couldn't receive incoming calls. A telephone call could only be made to a subscriber's address, which made the surveillance a lot easier for the police. In Holland, de Groote habitually used his phone at home and consequently his security had been terrible. He should never have been in partnership with de Groote. Dutch dealers were surprisingly aggrieved when they were busted but they didn't have a right to complain. They only had their wrists slapped and a three-month suspended sentence for an offence which would put someone away for ten years without parole in England.

Tate never mentioned names, dates, times or places specifically over the phone. Cryptic remarks sufficed and he limited his calls to a maximum two-minute duration.

He looked at his watch. It was nine thirty. He dialled the number which Edward had given him the previous night. He was irritated Edward was being so safety-conscious this early in the scam. The problem with Edward was that he always insisted things were done his way. Hangover or no hangover, he would now have to be in a phone box by nine thirty every morning in case Edward wanted to talk. The phone barely rang before it was answered. 'Good morning,' said Tate.

'I need to meet you.' Edward's tone was brusque. Tate didn't like anyone dictating to him.

'I'm a bit busy,' said Tate. He had a number of phone calls to make. The air freight operation was a nightmare. He was having to send the crates through Bombay and Dubai to make them look innocent. He had crates drifting like flotsam around the world, being re-routed time and time again to disguise their origins. Each time they required re-routing he had to consult Ginger.

'Urgently,' he heard Edward say. He hoped Edward wasn't having a change of heart. He would be particularly annoyed if Edward dropped out of the operation at this point.

'I heard you,' he said. 'In an hour. How about breakfast?'

'See you there,' said Edward, and put down the receiver.

Breakfast was a hamburger joint called 'Tootsies' on Holland Park Avenue, which served late breakfasts for hungover nightclubbers. Tate left the phone kiosk. He walked to the Kensington Hilton. He had a few important calls to make and he wanted some warmth and quiet. He'd hardly been able to hear Edward over the noise of the traffic. It would have been impossible to conduct an international call.

There were moments when Tate looked on his life with a degree of self pity. This was a lonely job. There was no one in whom he could confide with safety. He always seemed to be wandering around the foyers of hotels waiting for a phone call or a man with a suitcase. It was lonelier than the life of a spy. Without glamour and without recognition. At least spies had a support group, with access to voices in high places who could arrange a trade-off. There were no heroes in this game, win or lose. Howard Marks, once the biggest smuggler in Britain, had made the connection between the two professions when he was acquitted of smuggling twenty tons of grass; he claimed to be an MI5 agent working undercover for the Mexican drug enforcement agency. His only witness was a seedy Mexican who claimed to be his chief, who couldn't give his name or provide any documentation because he too was working undercover. The judge at the Old Bailey didn't buy the story, but the jury did, thanks, it was rumoured, to some nobbling. Now look at Howard! He was serving twenty years in America for racketeering, just because he'd upset some Drug Enforcement Agent.

Tate shivered at the thought. Perhaps he should take Ballot a bit more seriously. Now he was standing in Howard's shoes. But with one big difference: he wasn't famous. Anyway, Edward would shield him from all that, and insulate him from the risks. If anything did go wrong, a few people in secret places would ensure things didn't get too hot because they wanted to be paid; half a million bought a lot of loyalty.

He looked around the Hilton's foyer. Everything looked normal. Hilton Hotels were similar the world over. Hilton Hotel customers didn't like surprises. Neither did Tate.

# 4

Edward could tell from the way Julia sat opposite him in the restaurant that she had made up her mind. He guessed she had worked out her terms and would not be side-tracked. That was how she worked. She liked certainties. She picked up the menu, looked at it briefly and laid it down.

'Have you chosen?' asked Edward.

'Yes,' she replied. Food was not on the agenda.

Edward spent longer deciding what to order and knew that his indecision was irritating her. Nevertheless, the menu provided a safe displacement activity. Finally he chose. He wondered if he heard a sigh of relief from Julia.

'So, have you thought about it?' asked Julia.

Edward assumed she was referring to her ultimatum of the previous night. Of course he had thought about it. They'd agreed to have lunch together to discuss it.

'Shall we order before we start talking?' he suggested.

Julia didn't reply. She recognised Edward's stalling tactics. She watched him signal the waiter. She waited patiently for the waiter to appear at the table. They ordered lunch. She declined wine. She waited until they were alone again. 'So have you thought about it?' she repeated.

'Of course,' said Edward. 'I suppose you want to know whether I've chosen you or Samuel?'

'Precisely.'

'It's not much of a competition. If you put it like that, I have to choose you.'

'So you won't see him again?' insisted Julia.

'That wasn't the deal. You can't expect me not to see my oldest friend.'

'If you see him, how do I know you're not working with him?'

'You have to trust me.'

'I already tried. You can't be trusted.'

There was a long pause. Edward perceived that the discussion wouldn't be fruitful if it continued along those lines.

'Do you still want to continue the relationship with me?' he asked.

'Yes.'

'At least we've found a starting point,' he said. He wondered in which direction to develop the conversation now.

Julia took the initiative. 'You don't seem to understand. If I'm living with you, then what you do affects me. Indirectly it will affect our child.'

'I understand that, Julia. Believe me. I'm not stupid. I'm concerned for all of us. I want to make money so we can have a secure life.'

'Bull shit,' said Julia with sudden vehemence.

'Why do you think I'm doing it?' asked Edward in an aggrieved voice.

'You're frightened of giving up because you'll have to rely on yourself. You'll have to stop taking your lead from Samuel.'

'You're not giving me much credit for self-determination. Why do you dislike him so much?'

'I've never met anyone who's so self-centred.'

'He's not as bad as you think. He's got a good heart.' Julia didn't comment. 'He's done some good things in his time. He paid for a child in the Caribbean to fly to the States for an operation on his eye. That's an altruistic gesture. He probably saved the child's sight.'

'One swallow doesn't make a summer,' commented Julia, intransigently. Then warming to a theme she continued. 'After all, he was only playing at God. It's a role he obviously likes.' Edward said nothing. Julia downed a glass of water. 'Yes, I remember now, you told me that rather endearing story once before. You were very impressed by the gesture. I was disappointed in you, if the truth be told. If he paid all the taxes he owes, then a lot of blind people might be able to see.'

'We're not getting anywhere, are we?' said Edward pragmatically. 'What if I say I won't work with Samuel? I'll see him from time to time, for a drink. But I won't work.'

'If you mean it.'

'Fine,' said Edward, 'I mean it. Now, so there are no misunderstandings, I'll have to see Samuel a few times to introduce him to people who can take over from me. I can't very well leave him in the lurch. It'll take a couple of meetings, and then it will be over.'

'I hope you're not taking me for a fool, Edward. This time I mean it. If you break your word that will be the end of us.'

'I won't, Julia, and for the record, I haven't broken it yet. I might have been tempted but I would have told you. I'm not guilty.' He smiled.

Julia looked stern. 'Good,' she said.

'Jesus!' thought Edward. He was shocked by his own perfidy. 'I'll speak to Samuel tonight,' he said.

# 5

Early on Wednesday morning the street cleaners were clearing rubbish in Amsterdam's Zee dijk, on the edge of the red light district. Despite the City Council's attempts to gentrify the street, the junkies tended to gravitate there to score deals and shoot up in the crumbling masonry of houses being refurbished.

In a corner of the street, rolled in an old carpet, the street cleaners found a body, and called the police.

The body turned out to be that of a healthy woman in her twenties. She was one point seven metres tall. She had brown hair. Her hands had been tied behind her back with stockings. She was wearing a dress which buttoned at the front. The top three buttons were undone. She was wearing leather ankle length boots with worn heels. Her white brassiere had been pulled above her breasts.

She had been strangled by a rope. There were cuts and abrasions to both knees. There was bruising to the forehead. There were rope burns around both ankles. She was wearing no underwear, and her pubic region had been inexpertly shaved just prior to death.

By the following day the body had been identified as that of Monique Hubert. She was the girlfriend of the murdered drug baron de Groote, and had been in the Dutch witness protection programme. There was a mass of forensic clues, but no indication of who her killer might be. It was assumed that the murder was connected to that of de Groote.

# Chapter 7

## 1

Twenty-four hours after Annelies finally sent a photograph of Samuel Tate to Holland, Simon Patterson summoned Andy into his office.

'I've had a request from the Dutch. They want to interview Tate,' said Patterson. 'Did you have anything to do with this?'

'Sir?' asked Andy, innocently.

'I hope this is a genuine enquiry, and not something you've put them up to through Miss Jansen.'

'No, sir,' said Andy. 'It was Annelies who saw a picture which the police had circulated and recognised Tate.'

'I'm glad to see you're on first name terms with Miss Jansen,' said Patterson, and nodded, suggesting he was reading something into the fact. Andy didn't react. Patterson continued. 'I suppose you better bring Tate in for an interview with Annelies.'

'It won't be as easy as that. If you remember, we don't know where Tate is living. If we pick him up I doubt he'll talk about anything before speaking to his solicitor. If he speaks to a solicitor he'll be out within minutes.'

'Is Tate really worth all this trouble, Andy?' asked Patterson, wearily.

'The Dutch seem to think so. There has been a murder, you know. He might be involved. We can't afford to ignore it.'

'Very well, then,' said Patterson. 'This is what I propose. We put a team on to locating Tate. We allow seventy-two hours. If we don't find him, then we drop it. If we do find him we review what we've discovered before we take any further action.'

'I think the approach is too cautious, sir. We need longer than that to produce anything worthwhile.'

'Seventy-two hours,' said Patterson firmly. 'Tell the team there will be a briefing at four. In the meanwhile I want you to tell me everything you know about Tate. I don't want any surprises later.'

'One more thing, sir.'

'What is it?'

'I would like to go out with the surveillance teams for a couple of days.'

'It's not your job.'

'I know, but I have good reasons. I know these suspects because I was on surveillance the last time. I might be able to provide a few pointers. I also think it would be useful for Annelies to see how we go about these things.'

'There's something you need to learn, Andy. If you're going to the top in this career, then you better get used to staying behind that desk. Delegation of responsibility is the most difficult task to master.' He stood up and indicated that the meeting was over.

'Is that an order, sir?'

'You're running the operation, Andy. It's up to you. It's your promotion which is on the line.'

'Thanks for the reminder, chief.' Andy left the room before Patterson started lecturing.

At four, there were sixteen officers waiting for Simon Patterson in the briefing room. The atmosphere was informal, as always within the department, but each member could feel the excitement spreading around the room. It was always like that when an investigation took off. At last the officers were getting to grips with the suspects after what might have been months of research.

The room fell silent as Patterson entered. Over the years the officers had learned that he tended to become short-tempered towards the end of the day. The blame was generally attached to the amount of coffee he had consumed during the previous eight hours.

'Good afternoon,' began Patterson. 'I apologise for holding this meeting so late in the day, but some of you were on another investigation. I'll try to make this as brief as possible. The operation is code named "Juniper". No doubt you'll want to know why I chose that name.' He paused. He always liked the team to know why he had chosen a particular code name. The names followed the letters of the alphabet. The last operation had been 'Indiana', because the prime suspect resembled Harrison Ford. 'It's quite simple. I believe that genever, Dutch gin, is made using juniper berries, and this operation has a Dutch connection.' He smiled benignly at Annelies. 'Now then, back to the nuts and bolts. We believe we are dealing with a conspiracy to import a large consignment of cannabis resin into this country. As some of you will know, this investigation has been proceeding on and off for some five years. All our information leads us to believe that things are coming to a head. We have received information from both Holland and the Metropolitan Police and now it's time for us to start filling in some of the gaps.'

Andy was surprised. He hadn't expected Patterson to give the operation such a high profile. He realised that he continually under-estimated him. The man was a communicator and he was conveying, on the basis of very little information, the impression that this was a major operation. On the other hand, Patterson had to account for the depart-ment's resources and this would read well if there was ever an enquiry.

'I want to emphasise that we must to be very careful. These guys are good at their trade. They've been in it for at least fifteen years. They are very hard to follow and they are alert. What we have on our side is the psychological factor. They will be very loath to give up an operation they may have been planning for a year or more. They will be only too happy to persuade themselves that they're not being watched. Nevertheless, any officer who makes the mistake of showing himself will be removed from this team. Do I make myself clear?'

There was a murmur of agreement from the room. Patterson continued. 'Do not underestimate this organisation. We have a report from Holland that at least one dealer has come to a sticky end, and this may be closely connected to this investigation. Furthermore, we are investigating what I call organised crime. If we take a look at the characters involved, that will become clear.'

He opened the folder in front of him and took out a photograph which he pinned to the board behind him. 'This is a photograph of Tango One. He is the reason for this operation. He's a very slippery customer. We've had him in court before but he got away. His name is Samuel Tate. He is known to use aliases, but we do not know them at present. He has been seen talking to a variety of suspects over the past year. He is certainly one of the few people in this country able to put together a big importation of cannabis. By big, we are talking a minimum of one ton upwards. He is unlikely to be interested in anything which would make less than a million pound profit.

'He's been a busy chap. Andy Ballot ran through the IATA passenger lists and found that he clocked up quite a few destinations, the Middle East, Holland, and Thailand, to mention a few of the sussy ones. What's a lot more sussy is that when he travels he employs a number of little tricks so the computer won't flag him. For instance, he will book his tickets under the name of Yate, or Rate, which might well be a slip of the typist's finger, but which serves to screen him from our enquiries.

'You will be given a file on the operation, but I want you to engrave the suspects' features on your memories. I don't want you going into action staring at the photos trying to make sure you're looking at the right person.'

Simon Patterson peered at his audience properly for the first time. He seemed to be taking stock of the individuals. He pulled a second photograph from the folder. 'Now, this is Tango Two. His name is Edward Jay. For six months he was imprisoned in Karachi having been caught in possession of two tons of cannabis resin. He is Tate's right-hand man. They have been in close association for many years. They came to our attention a little over five years ago, but the level of their activities was such that they must have spent some years building their contacts. Jay is a particularly tricky customer. He only speaks on public telephones when he communicates with Tango One and his other cronies. He is extremely difficult to follow, as you will find out. We believe he will be running the operation here, and for that reason he was sprung from prison in Pakistan by Tango One.'

He pinned the photograph on the board. He took two further pictures from the folder. 'Finally, Tango Three and Tango Four. These two convicted bank robbers have been seen in company with Tango One, as you will have deduced from the picture.'

Andy stared at the picture. He wanted to know how Patterson had obtained that picture. It was the one which had been mislaid.

'We do not know the precise nature of their involvement, however, they are presently under surveillance by the Metropolitan Police in connection with an investigation they are pursuing. Now! I want you to be particularly careful if you sight these two because they will have Metropolitan Police units in the vicinity. The last thing I want is a complaint that our units have in any way interfered with their operation. To date, the police have indicated that they are prepared to hand over any information which is pertinent our investigation. We will, of course, do the same for them.'

Patterson paused. 'Any questions?' he asked, but there were none. 'Good. You'll meet up at the garage tomorrow morning at six. It's an early start, I know, but it can't be helped.'

As the customs officers shuffled forward to collect the notes which were left on the desk, Simon Patterson slipped towards the door. He liked to be away from the office by five. His two little girls would be bathed and ready for their supper. They'd be waiting for him. He liked to talk to them about school and read a story to them in bed.

'Yes?' snapped Patterson, turning towards Andy.

'I wanted to know where you found that picture of Tate.'

'What picture?'

'The one with Phillips and Kelly,' explained Andy.

'It was in the file,' said Patterson without further explanation, and strode off.

'No,' thought Andy. He was sure it wasn't. He wondered where it had been and why it suddenly reappeared.

# 2

'Fuck Edward!' thought Tate. 'Why the hell can't he keep his bloody woman under control?' It was hard enough being in this business without having their lines of communication ruined. He looked with disgust at the radio paging contraption he'd been forced to hire and on which Edward would tell him what time to call a public phone box. Julia had to be bloody good in bed if Edward was willing to go to all that trouble for her. If any woman tried to put him under house arrest he'd show her the door.

Tate watched as people came into the pub. He assessed them to see if they might include Davidson. This appointment was a nasty little surprise, but it couldn't be all bad. A meeting at the pub was much more interesting than one in the interview room at the local police station. It was typical of Edward not to back him up. What if the policeman was wearing a wire? He'd have to be very careful of what he said. He'd find a way to check out if the policeman was on the level. He'd play it by ear. Something would come to him. It always did. The first thing he'd do was insist they left the pub to throw off any surveillance.

It didn't take any training to spot Davidson. He stood out like a sore thumb. With feet like that he had been born a copper. He wouldn't wear out the soles of those shoes if he lived to be a hundred. The unpleasant thing was that Davidson identified him straight away.

'Where's your mate?' asked Davidson.

'Keeping an eye on the back door,' replied Tate. There was no harm in pretending that he was taking a few precautions. He finished his drink. 'Let's go,' he said. Then elucidated. 'We'll find somewhere quiet we can talk.'

Outside Tate hailed a taxi. 'King Street, Hammersmith,' he instructed the driver. He sat on the jump-seat opposite Davidson and looked at the traffic behind. He couldn't see any signs of surveillance.

'I hear you have a car you want to sell.'

'Yeah,' replied Davidson.

'It's expensive,' remarked Tate.

'It's good,' replied Davidson. 'You'll be surprised how good it is.'

'We'll see.'

Half an hour later having crossed central London, the taxi entered King Street, and Tate ordered it to stop. They stepped out. Tate paid. He watched to see if any cars had followed, but he was confident they were alone. It was a one-way street. He quickly walked down a side road. Davidson followed, his rubber soles making no noise. The street ended in a subway which ran under the Great West Road. So far so good, thought Tate as they walked through the subway. There were no footsteps behind. No mobile units could follow them now. They emerged in a small park on the bank of the Thames. They quickly walked back towards the road and within seconds had hailed another taxi.

'Nice one,' said Davidson. He was impressed.

'That was for starters,' said Tate.

'Where are we going?' asked Davidson.

'We'll be there in a minute.'

'You're a suspicious bastard aren't you?' commented Davidson.

Tate nodded. When it came to doing deals like this he turned into a paranoid schizophrenic. The taxi stopped on Chiswick High Road. Again Tate paid the fare. He led Davidson to a small private health club, and signed him in. They were going to take a sauna together. He'd be damn sure Davidson wasn't wired then.

Once they were ensconced in the sauna Tate felt much safer. 'What are you selling?' he asked.

'A little information.'

'What is it?'

'The money?' asked Davidson.

'I've got it here in the building.' Davidson looked sceptical. 'You'll have to believe me.' Tate wasn't lying. He always kept a few grand in his locker in case of emergencies.

'You're connected with a couple called Phillips and Kelly?' Tate didn't answer. He didn't know if Davidson was ferreting for information. 'OK. Maybe you call them Ginger and Spider. But I know you're involved with them because they're under surveillance. I'm in charge of the surveillance. I've been watching them for six weeks.'

Tate was glad they were in the sauna. He felt faint. He could hardly bring himself to ask, 'Why are you watching them?'

'Don't you try and swindle me,' warned Davidson.

'Why should I?' replied Samuel.

'It's a bank job. We know they've been involved in a couple of robberies recently. We got a tip-off they were planning another.'

'So what's that got to do with me?' asked Tate. 'You must have checked me out. Blagging isn't my line.'

'I found out that Customs and Excise are very interested in you.'

'I'm afraid that's not news to me.'

'How?' asked Davidson, surprised.

'I've got my contacts.'

'As from tomorrow your friend Edward Jay is under surveillance and they're looking to get you.'

'Who's the officer in charge?' asked Tate unnecessarily. He'd be receiving the details soon enough.

'Simon Patterson. A bloke called Ballot's running their operation.'

'What's the basis for the investigation?'

'I don't know.'

Bad news, thought Tate. He felt that he was sweating somewhat profusely. 'Why are you telling me this, apart from the small matter of payment?'

'I want Ginger and Spider. I don't want the fucking customs messing up my case.'

'You're taking a chance, talking to me.'

'Not really. What are you going to do? Call up customs and tell them? It's your word against mine.'

Tate stood up and chucked some more water on the charcoal. It was time to turn up the heat. He had an idea. He settled back on the bench.

'Would you be interested in earning a little more than five grand?' It was a stupid question, but one had to observe the niceties.

'What sort of figures are you talking?' said Davidson, keeping what he hoped was a cautious note.

'Say twenty grand.'

'Maybe,' said Davidson. He squirmed on the bench. His white skin had turned raw with the heat. 'What's the deal?'

'I thought you might loosen up your surveillance on Ginger for a few days. Maybe you could make up a few reports. I'd let you know what I had in mind. There are one or two occasions when it might be useful to have people think Ginger was somewhere else. Do you follow my drift.'

'Couldn't be for too long. I've got to get a result on this one soon.' Davidson shifted his trotters uncomfortably.

'No. It wouldn't be for too long. Say the twenty grand was a retainer for four months. From time to time you could let something slip. Maybe I could give customs a lead on to something.' Tate thought about one or two old scores he would like to settle.

'I'm not going to queer my own pitch. But what you're suggesting is possible.' Davidson was thinking about the money. He had a moment's concern. 'What are you up to?'

'That would be telling,' said Tate. He threw more water on the coals.

'It's not a bank robbery, is it?'

'No,' said Tate. 'You know that's not my style.'

'Good,' said Davidson. His few reservations evaporated. 'It could be embarrassing for me if it was a bank job.'

# 3

Annelies lay on the bed in her hotel room and idly watched the television. The hotel was depressing, and she wondered if she could find somewhere more salubrious. She could stay in one of the best hotels in Amsterdam for what this one cost. Beneath the surface England was a worn-out country. No wonder there was a drug problem. The hotel staff took no pride in their work, but then there were little incentive. She was shocked when she heard how little the waiters were paid and how much they had to pay for rent. She hoped that Andy was not late. She contemplated waiting for him in the bar, but couldn't face the thought of any more businessmen engaging her in conversation and hoping for a one-night stand with a Dutch girl. Five minutes of conversation and they were talking about Amsterdam's red light district, and then there was no doubt what they had in their smutty minds.

Annelies wondered where Andy would take her to dinner. Two nights before Vince had taken her to an Italian bistro in Covent Garden. She thought it an inappropriate choice, and cringed as soon as she saw the candlelit tables. She realised that Vince planned to end the evening between the sheets. He even bought her a rose from the man who came round the tables selling flowers. She was embarrassed. Conversation was one-sided. He was not interested in her opinions and talked about himself.

'What do you think of Andy?' he asked at the end of dinner. She was already aware there were tensions in the office, but didn't want to be drawn into taking sides.

'I don't know,' said Annelies. 'It seems to me that he is a private kind of person.'

'I don't know about private,' said Vince. 'He doesn't have many friends.'

'Does he have a girlfriend?' asked Annelies.

'No,' said Vince. 'He's not interested in women. I guess they're not interested in him. He's not exactly good-looking. I don't know what he does for sex. He's probably not so good in bed.' Vince stretched back in his chair, suggesting a sexual athleticism. She wondered if she imagined a leer. 'Probably pays for tarts,' said Vince, completing his character assassination.

Annelies invented a headache in preparation for her escape when dinner was over. When the bill arrived Annelies insisted on paying for her share. He put up little objection. When they left the restaurant Annelies excused herself from the nightcap Vince suggested, and caught a taxi back to the hotel.

The phone rang at precisely seven thirty. Andy was waiting in the foyer. Annelies stood up and looked at herself in the mirror. She decided to apply some lipstick. She looked at herself again, pursed her lips irritably and took off her blouse and jeans. She rummaged in the wardrobe for a tight black dress. She chose a pair of simple gold earrings. She kicked off the court shoes and put on her high heels.

Annelies realised the high heels might have been a mistake as Andy stood up to greet her. She looked down at him. He smiled, and raised his eyebrows as if complimenting her on what she was wearing, but his eyes dropped and lingered on the high heels. His smile faded a little. He was wearing a suit, which should have looked smart, but only looked mediocre on him. 'Let's go,' he said. He seemed to be impatient.

He walked briskly down the pavement. A taxi passed and Annelies wondered why he didn't hail it. She guessed he had parked his car around the corner. She hoped it wasn't too far. Perhaps the heels weren't such a good idea. Suddenly he stopped. For a moment Annelies was baffled and then realised it was a bus stop. 'You didn't drive your car?' she asked.

'No,' said Andy. 'Drinking is a problem. So is parking.'

Annelies noticed the order in which he gave the priorities. 'Where are we going?' she asked.

'A casino called Savilles. I think you'll find it interesting. They have a good restaurant, and we can play some roulette.' He paused. 'Do you gamble?' he asked.

'No,' said Annelies.

'Oh,' he said, and the subsequent silence sounded like disappointment. The bus arrived and Annelies followed him on board. He paid the fares.

'And you?' asked Annelies. 'Do you gamble a lot?'

'Some,' replied Andy. 'When the mood takes me.'

'Like tonight?'

'I thought you might be interested in this club. It is one of the best. Eight years ago I was on a surveillance operation and I took out membership to it. Something went wrong with the casino computer and I was given a life membership. Normally I go to other clubs like the Victoria Sporting Club. The stakes are not so high, but then the food's not so good. Anyway, you'll find it interesting. Casinos are full of people with dirty money, or black money. You see them pulling out thousands of pounds in cash. That's why I was there in the first place. We were watching some smugglers whose bank accounts were continually being credited with large cheques from casinos. They were obviously laundering money, but we didn't know whether the casinos were involved. The team we were watching were working at all the casinos. They'd buy chips at various tables using cash. They'd gamble a bit, here and there, and then one of them would take all the chips and cash them for a cheque. It was a perfect method of cleaning dirty money. Gambling wins aren't taxed either. On a good night those guys were laundering fifteen to twenty thousand pounds.'

'Did the casino manager see what was happening?'

'These days the casinos are stricter. Even so it's hard to spot a discreet operation. They could afford to gamble a few thousand at a time, which made them look like big punters. Sometimes they won. If they lost it was still cheaper than paying taxes.'

'Did you catch the people?'

'Oh yes. We told the casinos and they gave evidence at the trial.'

When the bus stopped on Palace Gate, they alighted.

As soon as Annelies entered the casino she felt the cloying presence of a class-ridden society. Andy signed her in as his guest. Nowhere in Europe could she imagine such obsequious servility in the staff. She wanted to tell Andy that the Club was not for her, but curiosity kept her there. 'Let's have a drink at the bar before dinner,' said Andy. She followed him, her high heels sinking into the woollen carpet. She ordered a Martini. He ordered a large Vodka, gulped it down, and ordered another, with a dash of tonic this time. 'I'm feeling thirsty,' he said. He was either nervous, or he was an alcoholic, thought Annelies. They sat at the bar and watched the gamblers spread around the roulette and baccarat tables. She looked at the croupiers. They were all girls, chosen for their bodies, and decked out in low-cut velvet dresses; but no one looked at the soft furnishings.

'Have you always lived in Amsterdam?' Andy asked suddenly.

'No. I was born in a small town near The Hague. My father was a policeman. Holland is a small country. You have as many people in

London as we have in the whole of Holland. Amsterdam is very different from the rest of Holland. Some people hate it. I like it. I could not live anywhere else.'

'Why did you join customs?'

'I think because of my father. Also because the work is interesting. There are not so many women doing this in Holland.'

'I wouldn't enjoy the job in Holland. I'd be frustrated because your sentences are lenient. You work for three years to put someone behind bars, and they're free in a year.'

'We have a different attitude from the English. That's true. We are spending more money with intelligence. We know who are the big people. We want to keep this problem with drugs under control and the best way to do this is keep it above the ground. When we catch people we treat them very differently. You send criminals to prison for fifteen years. You are saying that you want to kill them and forget about them. They are being thrown out of society. That is not very human. We have a higher social conscience than you.'

'Society needs protecting from criminals. Especially drug dealers.'

'Yes. There are different ways of doing this. Here you are spending money to catch someone who is smuggling cannabis. There is no evidence that cannabis makes people take cocaine or heroin. When you make cannabis illegal, then the people and the dealers don't see the difference between drugs. I do not see why you spend all your time trying to get one man like this Samuel Tate into prison. Instead you could pass laws like Holland and Spain.'

Andy felt defensive. Annelies didn't understand the situation in England. 'We're enforcing the law. Not making it. How criminals are treated is not my department. Sure, I'm obsessed with Tate; but I know he's bad. Society needs protection from people like him.'

'OK. I did not mean for you to take this personally. I am talking about this country. You have here something like "prohibition" in America. In America now, ninety per cent of the big families who are still powerful have their money from making and selling alcohol when it was illegal.'

'So? There are problems with the system here, just as there are problems with your system. Tell me, what makes you happy about your job?'

'There was this time when we knew some ivories were coming into Rotterdam. We found the container and we caught the men. This made me very happy. There were all kinds of animal skins including cheetah.'

'Animals may be innocent, but so are the vast majority of people. They need protecting too. They have the illusion of choice and freedom, but

those things are worthless without dignity and education. Drugs deprive
people of dignity. Education is the only thing which can stop them from
taking drugs.'

'So you are in the wrong job. I read in the newspapers that the
education in England is not so good now.'

'No,' agreed Andy, shaking his head. 'It is not good.'

'So tell me about you. Why are you in this job?'

'I grew up in a small fishing village on the East coast of England. It was
very quiet and I left there as soon as I could. I don't really know why I
joined the customs. I've been thinking about that recently. I've been
thinking about my past.' He hesitated for a moment, then picked up his
train of thought. 'I remember my mother read this poem called "The
Smuggler's Song". It was my favourite.

> "If you wake at midnight and hear a horse's feet,
> Don't go drawing back the blinds or looking in the street,
> Them that asks no questions isn't told a lie,
> Watch the wall my darling, while the gentlemen go by."'

Andy waited a moment, searching Annelies's face for a reaction. He
guessed she didn't understand, or else poetry didn't translate well. 'I
never knew why I should watch the wall. I always wanted to look. It's not
in my nature to turn a blind eye. I shouldn't have become a customs
officer. I was betraying my past. In the old days much of the village's
wealth was based on smuggling things like tea, tobacco or gin.' Andy
laughed. 'All of it from Holland. When I told my mother I was joining the
Service she said my grandfather wouldn't have been pleased. He had two
fishing boats and he bought our house when there was a bad herring
season.'

A liveried flunkey appeared at the bar. 'Your table is ready, sir,' he
said. He was armed with a tray to carry their drinks. Annelies drained her
glass on principle, before being escorted to the table.

After dinner Annelies watched Andy gambling. She had no desire to join
him. 'Do you have a lucky number?' he asked.

'Eighteen,' she said.

He placed a bet for her. The wheel spun. He lost.

'Another number?' he asked.

'No,' she said. She didn't want to be a party to this.

She watched him playing for an hour. She could have felt annoyed that
he had invited her to dinner and was now ignoring her; but she was
fascinated by his addiction. He lost, and he cashed a cheque. He lost
again, and cashed another cheque.

'Do you not think it is time to go?' she asked, as they waited at the cashier's desk.

'Not yet,' he said.

'Why do you do this?' she asked.

'I like it,' he said.

'It has no point.'

'Gambling's like the job,' he said. 'You play. You concentrate. You try to make sense of the numbers. You think you see some system emerging. You place your bet, and wait for a win. When you win it bears no relationship to the effort invested. It's still only a matter of luck.'

Annelies said nothing. She was shocked by his self-destructiveness. He smoked too much. He obviously drank too much. He gambled without caution. He told her over dinner that he once had a girlfriend who had been drowned, and that he thought he knew who was responsible. He never forgave himself for not bringing that person to justice.

She watched Andy placing his bets. For the briefest moment she wanted to nurture him, and teach him to love himself. She checked herself. He was a loser, and he needed professional help if he was going to survive.

It was two in the morning before she was back at the hotel.

# 4

When Davidson reached home that night he was a changed man. He had suddenly acquired ambition and drive. Thirty-four years of protecting property and upholding the law, and all he had to show for it was a seedy one-bedroom flat in urgent need of modernisation. He had a pension fund but that wasn't exactly going to keep him warm and supplied with hookers during his old age. The rest of his savings bumped along the bottom of the stock exchange floor, thanks to some useless advice which had turned forty grand into eleven grand overnight. When he complained about the performance of his shares he was told that what went down had to come up. Yeah? Plenty of bodies went missing every year and never turned up. He put his faith in hard cash these days.

Now the tide was turning. He stared at the furniture and kicked off his shoes. He turned on the electric bar heater and went into the kitchen. He took the two bundles of money which Samuel had given him and fingered them for a moment. Ten grand. Next week another five grand. He might stay on the payroll a lot longer than a month or two. He opened the fridge and tried to stuff the money into the freezer compartment. He ripped wildly at a packet of frozen peas, and then gave up the struggle. The fridge needed defrosting. He slammed the fridge door. He stared around the kitchen in search of inspiration. Then he smiled. He opened the cupboard under the sink, swept aside a few ancient bottles of cleaning fluid, and the remains of a mouse. He pushed the bundles into a small hole where the woodwork had rotted. He rearranged the cleaning fluids, surveyed his handiwork, and was pleased. That would do for the moment, until he found himself a safety deposit box. He grabbed a can of beer and flopped down on the sitting room sofa.

He was going to put in some overtime tomorrow down at the station. He'd fire up the computer and do some research. He'd be careful. He'd have to key in his code to access the information. Some time in the future he'd be asked why he made those enquiries, especially if things went wrong. Sod it. He had a perfect right to find out all he could about Tate, because it touched on his investigation into Ginger and Spider. He wasn't so sure about checking out Edward Jay. Customs wouldn't want him snooping around their cabbage patch. The more he knew about Tate the more indispensable he would become, and the more money he'd make. He might find out another officer's private code for the computer. That wouldn't leave his fingerprints.

Davidson peeled open another can of beer and downed half of it in a gulp, then wiped the froth from his lips with the back of his hand. He'd looked at the membership rates for Tate's health club. Three grand a year. Tate wasn't short of the folding stuff, that was for sure. He might be turning over as much as a million quid a year. It would be worth trying for a percentage. He finished the beer and dropped the can behind the sofa. He levered himself upright and looked for his shoes. Tomorrow was another day and he was no longer happy with a two-week time share in the Costa Brava. He wanted a villa and a bank account. He thought of his two bundles. They weren't in such a good place. It would only take a rat a moment or two to shred those fifty pound notes. He padded back into the kitchen and scrabbled under the sink again.

# Chapter 8

## 1

'So how do you feel?' Annelies asked Andy. It was five in the morning. They had barely slept for three hours. Andy regretted having offered to pick her up from the hotel.

'I should have quit,' grumbled Andy. 'At least I didn't drink,' he added.

'Do you know how much you lost?' asked Annelies.

'I don't want to talk about it,' said Andy after a moment's thought.

As a result they drove in silence to the garage in Southwark where they met the rest of the team. The garage looked like any other, but an innocent member of the public breaking down and requesting help would find the proprietor unwilling to undertake any work. The proprietor was an ex-policeman who bought and sold a variety of vehicles for the sole use of the Customs and Excise department. There was a wide range of cars and vans, from Ford Transits and Renaults to small Japanese saloons and the ubiquitous Fords favoured by travelling salesmen. There were also a number of licensed black cabs which tended to be the most popular among the officers. The vehicles were uniformly anonymous, chosen by the practised eye of a policeman who had spent twenty years on traffic duty.

The officers knew which roles they were playing and had dressed accordingly so they wouldn't look out of place driving their allotted vehicles. Two taxis, four cars, a van and a motorcycle left the garage at half past six and made their way towards North London in the early morning rush hour. They would be in place around Tango Two, Edward Jay's flat, shortly after seven. The officers knew that it would probably be a two-hour wait until the suspect appeared at his front door. Criminals were seldom early risers.

The van had been carefully adapted for surveillance operations. Discreet peepholes had been made in the panels. There were two cameras, a variety of lenses and tape recorders with directional microphones. The van would be parked at a suitable vantage point and left for the day. The officers in the back would remain until a driver returned to pick it up later. They had bottles of water, sandwiches and a portable lavatory in case of emergency.

The use of the surveillance van was a short-term measure to establish the profitability of watching the suspect's premises. If Tango Two did not operate or entertain colleagues at home, then the van would be discarded. If it proved rewarding, customs would find an amenable person in a flat opposite, who'd let them set up a video camera in the front room. The camera had a special low-light lens which worked day and night and was set at one frame per second. The three-hour cassette would last for three days.

Andy parked the Ford around the corner from Edward Jay's flat and, having located and established radio contact with the other officers, walked to the nearest cafe. His portable radio was turned to 'stand by', and if there was a transmission it would vibrate in his jacket pocket instead of crackling noisily into life. He ordered an English breakfast and a coffee for Annelies. They sat down and waited. Andy looked at the morning's newspaper.

'I want to find another place to stay,' said Annelies.

'Oh?' said Andy. 'What's wrong with the hotel?'

'Maybe the hotel is fine. But the people are terrible. I cannot have dinner without all the men talking to me. What is wrong with the English? If they see a woman on her own they must try to talk to her. It is making me crazy.'

'I'm sorry,' said Andy. He thought for a moment or two. 'It should be possible for the department to find you a service flat. I'll try and organise it when we get back to the office.'

'You know, I think it is because the English woman is not so emancipated. On the Continent, and especially in Holland, because of the Second World War the women fought against the Germans, and they suffered at their hands. This made them realistic about their own men who could not protect them. In England you were never conquered so the men could always pretend that they were more strong, and keep their women weak.'

'You might have a point there,' said Andy. He didn't want to discuss the subject so early in the morning. A moment later he decided the remark deserved more consideration. 'I've never thought about it. It must be irritating.'

'Yes. It is,' said Annelies sternly. 'Worse than that. You have no time for your own thoughts, even in public places. Men are always trying to catch your attention.'

That's the price you have to pay for being attractive, thought Andy. He knew better than to say anything, though. 'Remind me to make some enquiries about accommodation when we get back to the office.' He turned back to the paper.

Andy's breakfast arrived. It did not look appetizing. He was embarrassed to be seen eating it. If one became what one ate, then he had cast himself in an unsavoury light. He compromised by leaving the sausages on the side of the plate. When he finished, he looked at his watch. It was a quarter to nine. He guessed Jay would be getting up.

He felt the vibration from the radio in his pocket. 'Let's go,' he said to Annelies. Outside, he pressed the button to transmit, and spoke. 'This is Hotel Two. Over.'

'This is Hotel One. Tango Two proceeding East, approaching Hotel Three. Do you eyeball, Hotel Three?'

Hotel Three was disguised as a telephone engineer. He was parked outside a telephone junction box. He said nothing over the radio. It was obvious the suspect was on top of him. Andy now had his bearings and would be able to pick up Jay at the end of the road. He slowed his pace. 'This is Hotel Two. I am on foot and will pick up,' he said. Meanwhile the other units would rearrange themselves attempting to anticipate the destination of the suspect.

'I hope this isn't going to be a waste of time,' said Andy. 'I hope Jay leads us to Tate. There was a time I thought computers would make it easier tracking people down, but they don't help. When people go to ground the only way to find them is still old-fashioned legwork.'

He saw Jay emerge at the end of the street and walk to a public telephone. He made a telephone call.

'He's definitely up to something,' said Andy. 'No one leaves home to make a telephone call. I bet this is his regular phone. We need to put a tap on it immediately.'

Jay finished his conversation and replaced the receiver. He looked at his watch. Andy checked the time. It was two minutes to nine. 'He's waiting for a call. It'll be at nine. We've struck gold with this phone box. I bet he uses it for all his calls.'

Andy and Annelies were too far away to hear the phone ring, but at nine exactly Jay span around and removed the receiver. It was a brief conversation. He emerged from the phone box and started to walk towards Andy and Annelies. Andy looked desperately for a street they could turn down. They were caught in the open. If they crossed the road it would be too noticeable. How had he found himself in this situation? He should have anticipated this.

'Jesus,' said Andy. 'He's going to recognise me. He knows me.' If they turned around it would be too suspicious. The distance between them was closing. They were less than a hundred yards apart. Jay would be able to discern his features within a few seconds.

'Look at me,' said Annelies. 'We are having an argument,' she said.

Andy turned and looked at her. She slapped his face. It stung. He was taken aback.

'Now, follow me,' she ordered, turning on her heel and walking quickly away from him.

Andy tried to grab her arm, but she shrugged it off and increased her pace. She turned the corner.

'Thanks,' said Andy. 'But you didn't have to hit me so hard.'

'I think it looks better if I hit you hard,' said Annelies. 'Better if he can hear it.'

They were still walking quickly. Andy felt Jay's eyes burning into his back. He didn't turn to see if he was right. He was impressed by how quickly Annelies had reacted to the risk of being recognised. As soon as he thought it safe Andy turned on the radio and listened to Jay's progress.

Jay was picked up by the mobile team on Kentish Town Road, tailed into a newsagent, watched making another phone call from the tube station, and finally observed drinking a coffee at a cafe. All seemed well.

It was ten thirty before Jay returned home. The officer impersonating the telephone engineer had departed, and his place had been taken by a motorcycle messenger who was tinkering with his engine. Half an hour later Jay emerged from his home, got into his car and sped off.

'It's a lift off. Lift off. Lift off,' barked Hotel One's voice over the radio. 'Tango Two in a red Vauxhall Astra. Registration. Echo two three golf papa victor.'

'OK. Eyeball,' said Andy, catching sight of the car. He started his car and set off in pursuit.

The six vehicles scattered around Jay's flat gradually organised themselves in a random pursuit. Sometimes a vehicle would be a long way in front of the suspect and then have to double back when he took an unpredictable turning. The drivers were good at their jobs, tailing and juggling their positions so they wouldn't be noticed. Andy monitored the operation from the rear, listening to the voices of his officers. Things were going well. For the first time he relaxed. 'I've been thinking,' he turned to Annelies, 'if you really can't stand your hotel you can use my spare room. I mean, my flat's fine. It's not great, but it's comfortable. It's central. I'm not around much and you can use it as your own. You can entertain there if you want. I won't get in your way. It might be quicker than trying to find a service flat in some red brick building.'

'You are very kind,' said Annelies. 'Are you sure?'

'I wouldn't have offered if I wasn't sure. Why don't you pop around one night this week and see what you think?' Suddenly he felt irritable. He'd have to clean the place up. Then he remembered why he was offering. He felt grateful to her. He felt he owed her something.

'Thank you,' said Annelies. She wasn't sure if she liked the idea. She liked her privacy. She was relieved when the radio suddenly crackled into life telling them that Jay had pulled into a multi-storey car park in Soho. Within seconds of trying to pursue him on foot they had lost him.

'Did he do this on purpose?' asked Annelies.

'I've no idea,' said Andy. 'He's a professional. When he goes to work he takes no chances.'

'Better watch his motor,' said one of the officers. 'Let's order a lump. It'll make our lives a lot easier.'

'Go ahead,' said Andy. Tailing Edward Jay was going to test them to their limits, and the electronic tracking device would help.

## 2

Edward expected a phone call from Samuel at a public phone box at nine. He hoped that Julia would go out so he wouldn't have to lie to her. He was increasingly self-conscious about his movements, knowing that she'd be suspicious. Fortunately Julia was in the middle of a call to a client at eight forty-five, so Edward put on his jacket nonchalantly and said he was going to buy a newspaper. Julia put her hand over the receiver and said, 'We need some milk.' Edward slipped out.

Once on the street, Edward heaved a sigh of relief. He had a lot of arrangements to make. He prayed that Jason was still at home. If it hadn't been for Julia he would have been up at eight, but then Julia's suspicions would definitely have been aroused. He dialled Jason's number. Jason recognised his voice immediately. 'Edward!' he said. 'It's good to hear you. I didn't know you were back.'

'Are you doing anything today?'

'What do you have in mind?' asked Jason.

'How about lunch?'

'Sure. Where?'

'Willy's still open?' asked Edward.

'Yes.'

'How about twelve thirty?'

'Great. See you there.'

Edward replaced the receiver and thought about Jason. He was dependable. Always cheerful. Scrupulously honest. He'd worked his way from being a builder's labourer to having his own building company specialising in restoration projects for English Heritage. He was one of the best distributors. He could be given a ton of cannabis and he would account for it to the nearest gram. He also worked quickly, distributing as far afield as Manchester and Glasgow. If things went well, he paid up within a week. The money arrived neatly bound up, sorted into the various denominations, with the queen's head to the right. He poured his profits back into the property market where they were quickly laundered. His apparent success had not spoiled him, and he had the charm of appearing baffled and humbled by the accident of success.

Edward looked at his watch. There was a minute until Samuel's call. He decided he would buy a van that afternoon as the first step of the antiques business. It would certainly help keep Julia from jumping to conclusions. It was a sound idea. He should have started a business a long time ago. It would have laundered the money, and he wouldn't now be in this predicament. He would have to decide in what area he wanted to specialise. He didn't want to end up with bric-à-brac.

The telephone rang. He answered it. 'Oh. There you are,' Tate said, as if he had been trying to make the connection for some time.

'Yes. I'm here,' said Edward.

'Listen carefully and don't react wildly to what I'm going to say.' Tate paused. 'Your affairs are under close scrutiny.' Edward's heart started pounding. He hadn't seen any signs of surveillance. He immediately calculated what the charges might be. Conspiracy at worst. That's all they had against him. It was enough, if they made it stick. Tate continued. 'There's something else. Your dog at home is very ill.' Dog? What was Samuel talking about? Suddenly Edward realised it meant his telephone. 'I think all the dogs you've adopted are going to come down with this canine fever very soon.'

'That figures,' said Edward, as calmly as he could. His telephone would certainly be bugged.

'Meet me in two hours. Same place as before,' said Tate.

'OK,' said Edward.

'Make sure you're not followed,' added Tate unnecessarily. The phone went dead. Edward replaced the receiver. His heart was pounding as he walked away from the phone box. He tried to walk normally; one moment it felt as if he was walking too quickly, and the next, too slowly. He noticed nothing out of the ordinary. He remembered a telephone engineer he had passed earlier. A couple were walking down the street towards him. They were too obvious. They were having an argument. The woman slapped the man and walked away, and he chased after her. He watched them turn up Lady Margaret Road, and stared after them for a moment.

He needed time to think about the development. He had to be rational and logical. The knowledge could possibly be to his advantage, although he didn't see how. If damage had been done, then it was limited. He bought a newspaper and walked to the tube station. He couldn't resist the temptation of seeing who was following him. He went to the telephones and dialled a number. He watched the entrance. A few moments later a man hurried in, flashed a rail pass, and disappeared in the direction of the trains. Edward returned to the street, went into the local cafe for a coffee, and tried to read the newspaper.

After half an hour he walked home. He saw no signs of surveillance, although a motorcycle messenger drew his attention. He confirmed that Julia did not need the car, and told her he was going to look for somewhere to rent to store the antiques. She looked at him dubiously. 'You've been gone almost an hour,' she said.

He wondered if it was an accusation. 'I had some coffee and read the newspaper.'

'You forgot to buy some milk,' she commented.

'I'm sorry. I'll pop out and get some.'

'It doesn't matter. I have to go to the post office.'

'I'll see you later,' said Edward, and leaned down to kiss her. She seemed cool, but he hoped he was just imagining it.

Edward drove slowly into central London. He had no intention of letting the observers know he was aware of their presence. From time to time he thought he had identified one of the cars, but it was hard to be certain in the weaving London traffic. He pulled into a multi-storey car park in Soho, off Wardour Street. There were three exits from the car park, and each led on to a separate street. It was child's play to lose surveillance, thought Edward. He hailed a taxi to Hyde Park, then caught the tube to South Kensington and finally a bus to Hammersmith, where an apprehensive Tate was waiting in a pub.

'Are you sure you weren't followed?' Tate greeted Edward.

'Quite sure,' said Edward. 'After all, if they saw me here with you it would be a prison sentence wouldn't it?'

'I think you're being melodramatic.'

'How did you find out about the surveillance?' asked Edward.

'That policeman, Davidson. I've got him on the payroll.'

'You trust him?'

'He sings like a bird when you show him the folding stuff. Did you spot the opposition?'

'Yes. I've no idea how many there are, but enough. It's a serious operation.'

'Bad news,' commented Tate.

'We'll have to knock it on the head,' surmised Edward.

'Can't do it,' said Tate. 'It's too late. The material's in transit. We can't abort.' It was true. Spider was in Switzerland dealing with the paperwork which would accompany the freight. There was no turning back now.

'You'll have to find someone to take over from me.'

'Why?' asked Tate. 'You can lose those guys any time you want. Far better to have them where you can see them. At least we know what they're up to.'

'You're living in a fantasy, Samuel. If this comes on top, and we get popped, there's no way we'll get out of prison.'

Tate looked at his shoes. He was worried, 'I can't lose this one, Ned. My neck's on the chopping block. I can't pay for the gear if it's caught. I'm out on a limb. I perjured myself to clinch this deal.' Tate hesitated. He waited for the information to sink. Then he played his trump. 'I think they'd shoot me for the stroke I pulled on them.'

'Who's they? Ginger and Spider?'

'Oh no. They're on a no-cure no-pay deal. It's the guys back in Pakistan.'

'What about de Groote?'

'He's been rowed out of the deal.'

'He was your partner.'

'He was being awkward. The Pakistani won't deal with him any more,' said Tate.

'Perhaps he knows something you don't.'

'Listen, Ned. It's one quick operation. We still have everything going for us. You know I can't market this without you. You've always done the marketing. They're your people.'

'I'll give you my people.'

'They won't work with me,' Tate complained.

'How do you know?' asked Edward suspiciously.

'While you were away, one or two possibilities came along. Your guys blanked me.'

'Whom did you try?'

'Jason and Whiz Billy. I hadn't seen them for years.'

Edward didn't comment. He was irritated to think that Samuel had the audacity to approach his contacts, but he was gratified to hear that some of them were still loyal.

'Come on, Ned. It's only a couple of hours out of your life. The law won't even know you're up to anything.'

'I'm not into kamikaze.'

'I'll make it worth your while. I'll give you two hundred a kilo. That's two hundred thousand.' Edward didn't say anything. There was nothing to say. He knew that he was going to do it. He didn't have any other options. 'I don't know what else I can say that will persuade you,' persisted Tate.

'Don't drive that bloody Mercedes and stay away from me until it's over,' said Edward.

Tate searched Edward's face to make sure that he had heard correctly, and then said 'Thank you' with sincerity. When this deal was over he wouldn't need Edward any more. The nature of the business was going to change. 'Now, let's deal with the agenda. The consignment's arriving the day after tomorrow. You meet Spider at nine in the morning with the van. Wait for him to return, and the rest is down to you. I've got the pager here if you need to talk to me. You can let me know when the paperwork is ready. I'm going to be using the same banker as before, so you can drop the money with him.'

'What about Ginger and Spider? Are they trustworthy?'

'Yes. I'd stake my life on it. They've invested in this as well. They won't want to see anything go wrong.'

'What do you mean invested? Are you in partnership with them?'

'No. They weren't prepared to provide the facility at the airport unless they could take some of the action. I gave them a twenty per cent stake. They paid cash in advance.'

'That was risky.'

'It didn't seem so at the time. It left me in a more fluid position.'

'I've got a bad feeling about those guys.'

Tate ignored the remark. 'Listen, there's something else. I nearly forgot. There will be twenty containers. They're well packaged. I specified it. The material was vacuum packed in one room, then taken to another to be soldered into the tea chests. Then they were hosed down with petrol and taken for wrapping. No chance of any traces.'

Edward wondered why Samuel was telling him this. It was normal procedure.

'Two of the containers are different. They're half the size of the others. You have to deliver them to a man you'll meet at St John's Wood tube station at six. You'll recognise him because he'll be carrying a copy of *Playboy* magazine.'

Edward's mouth dropped open. He didn't believe what he was hearing. Surely they'd grown out of that kind of madness ten years ago. No one met strangers in this game any more, and certainly not strangers who were carrying copies of *Playboy*. He looked intently at Samuel, but there was no indication on his face that he was joking.

'Wait a minute Samuel. I don't know about this. I think maybe you've gone a little crazy. Then on the other hand perhaps you're trying to find out if I'm too crazy to do this whole thing. Maybe that's it.'

Tate looked baffled by the remark. 'You don't seem to understand. It wasn't that easy to set this up. The deals aren't getting any easier to negotiate. I had to make some concessions. This was one of them. The supplier insisted I pass some samples of the consignment to another interested party.'

'I don't care what deals you've made, Samuel. Right now my problem is that I am about to meet someone who could be an undercover policeman carrying a magazine. I'm going to give him a couple of boxes and I'm not going to get paid for doing that. In fact, I'm taking twice the risk now because every time I deliver dope it's a risk. Except that this time it's worse because I don't know the man. I don't even get to make money on it. If my calculations are right, it means that I'm losing twenty grand.'

'Put it on the bill, Edward, but do stop complaining. I thought you wanted to do this.' Tate was irritated. Here he was, doing Edward a favour, paying him over the odds, and all he did was find fault with the arrangements. If Edward complained any more he had a good mind to leave everything up to Ginger with all the risks that incurred.

'Thank God this is the last one,' said Edward. 'I don't think our partnership could take much more of this.'

'Let's try not to end on a sour note,' said Tate, tight-lipped. 'We'll go somewhere like Venice and celebrate when it's over.'

Edward gave the thinnest of smiles. 'I have to be off. We probably won't speak until it's over.' He left Tate sitting in the pub hunched over the remains of a drink.

Edward had half an hour before his meeting with Jason.

# 3

As Jason drove his pickup truck to the building site he thought about the meeting with Edward. Things were going well in the building trade. He had contracts which would keep him busy for the next year. He'd made a name for himself restoring old houses. He didn't need the money from this deal with Edward. He didn't know why he'd accepted it. By doing so he was breaking one of his rules. Never work with anyone who had been busted. He justified his actions by telling himself that a bust in Pakistan didn't really count, and that his past dealings with Edward had always been trouble-free. Nevertheless, aspects of Edward's explanation about his release were a little too cosy. If people were released it was usually because they'd made a deal. Not that Jason thought that Edward would make a deal with the authorities. However, it did leave a few questions unanswered.

Edward's proposal was good. Too good to turn down. He'd have to be careful, but he always had been with Edward. He didn't socialise with him, but then he never socialised with villains. One never knew where they had come from or where they were going. It was all too easy to find oneself on the police computer as a known associate of someone who'd been arrested. Jason never wanted to hear that knock on the door in the early hours.

Edward had been in the black market for over ten years without any legitimate explanation for his money. It didn't take much to open a shop or start a business with plenty of loose money. That was the first thing anyone had to do if they were going to be professional in the game. The Edwards of this world were opportunists. They were grossly overpaid for their short piece of work. They didn't know what it was like at the sharp end of the market. Jason used four or five dealers. Each of them would use four or five. It was pyramid selling. Somewhere down that line there was a policeman trying to work his way up, infiltrating the system. Somewhere down that line there was someone who might get caught and who might talk. That was the sharp end of the marketing business.

He knew Edward had other dealers, but he also knew that he was the best. He knew his credentials were good, which was why Edward had worked almost exclusively with him for the past five years. Jason had been shocked when Tate had approached him to do some marketing while Edward was incarcerated in Pakistan. It wasn't the kind of loyalty he expected from a partner, and he refused on principle. He hadn't liked Tate from the start. They'd been introduced a long time ago so that Tate could make his own judgement about granting a credit facility. He had started small in those days, with a credit facility of ten kilos. Over the following years he worked up to a thousand kilos. He had not seen Tate again until Edward's trouble, nor had he wanted to. Now and again he'd been reminded of Tate's presence in the background. He was suspicious of him. He'd read about Tate's arrest five years ago, and his subsequent acquittal. As far as he was concerned, Tate was a marked man. Jason was only working with Edward because he trusted him to be careful.

Nevertheless there were aspects of Edward's arrangements which he didn't like and which didn't make sense. Edward had insisted that he should be at a public phone box every evening. A reference to the evening newspapers would indicate that the operation was going ahead the following day. Any other instructions should be completely ignored, even if Edward changed the meeting places. It was as if he expected the call to be overheard. Jason shrugged mentally. Perhaps Edward had become overly paranoid.

For the first time he was tempted to ask Edward to supply a few details to put his mind at ease. This operation was different to previous ones. He had gleaned that. All the same, he didn't want to know about details. If things went wrong no one could suspect him of leaking information. If, heaven forbid, he was ever interrogated then he wanted to be able to deny knowledge of events with a clear conscience.

Providing a van wasn't a problem. Every couple of years Jason took a driving test under a different name. He opened building society accounts in those names, and by massaging the accounts he would find he was offered a credit card after a while. Accessories like that were worth a couple of thousand pounds. They were invaluable for hiring vans and they didn't leave fingerprints. It was his care for the fine detail which made him indispensable to the importers, and naturally they favoured him, not his competitors who balked at providing a van which might be traceable.

As soon as he took possession of the material he'd take it to his yard. He'd unpack and weigh it. Only then would he contact his dealers. He didn't like to let people know there was something happening. The police relied on tips like that. It gave them a head start. As he thought through the motions of the deal his nervousness evaporated. This was another job and the price was very good. He hoped it was none of that blended stuff they imported from Holland; re-constituted hash with pieces of plastic wrapping in it; old dope which had been chopped, shredded and re-pressed with the addition of all sorts of chemicals, including, it was rumoured, bovine tranquillisers. The dope better be good. Bad dope never sold, whatever the price.

# 4

The Swissair stewardess suggested Spider gave her the large briefcase to put in the overhead locker.

'You'll be more comfortable,' she said.

'No,' he replied coldly; but he carefully folded his new camel hair coat and passed it to her. The businessman in the adjacent seat eyed him suspiciously. Spider sniffed deeply through his long thin nose, curled his lips in a grimace of indifference and sat down. He wrestled with the briefcase and finally retrieved a copy of *Playboy* magazine. He opened it on the centrefold and spent some moments nodding with appreciation. He didn't really care for soft focus photography. He preferred the detail. He finally turned the page.

When the plane landed, Spider dragged the briefcase from between his legs. It was so heavy it seemed glued to the floor. He raised it on to the seat where it sank deeply into the cushion. He slung his coat over one arm and nonchalantly picked up the briefcase with the other. It nearly ripped his shoulder out of the socket.

He wondered if he'd overdone it this time. Ten kilos of gold was the limit for this kind of transportation unless he started going to the gym. It was a good racket. Gold in Switzerland was over fifteen per cent cheaper than in England because it wasn't taxed. That meant there was a grand a kilo profit. Ten grand for an afternoon's work. Not bad at all.

He dumped the briefcase on a trolley and squinted at the luggage on the carousel. The next load of contraband would be coming through the airport in a couple of days. He'd made all the flight arrangements and freight bookings. The waybills were in order now. It was going to make him fifty times as much money.

As Spider entered the Green Channel a customs officer approached him. Spider fixed his eyes straight ahead. The lazy eye flickered at the officer; it had a mind of its own.

# 5

From the towpath the boat didn't look as bad as Edward had expected. She was listing slightly to starboard. There were no signs of vandalism, which was probably due to the other houseboats up the canal. Their owners were suspicious and hostile at the best of times, and consequently were ideal neighbours. He stepped on board. She was a solid motor sailor and if things hadn't gone wrong she'd easily have carried the three tons of dope from the meeting point off Brittany back up the English Channel. He slipped his fingers under the ventilator on the deck and felt for the keys. They were rusty after seven months in a damp atmosphere. He jiggled them in the padlock which locked the companionway hatch and after some persuasion the lock sprang open. The damp air rose out of the cabin. There was going to be a good day's work making the boat habitable. He clambered through the hatch and down the steps to the cabin where his foot disappeared in water up to his ankle. First things first, he thought, climbing back into the cockpit. He started pumping the bilges dry.

Half an hour later the last of the water was out of the boat. He guessed it had come through the stern gland. He went down below again and lit a paraffin lamp. He checked the acid levels in the batteries, primed the auxiliary generator and cranked it into life manually. He put the batteries on to charge. He turned on the lights and looked around. There was a dusting of mildew over the whole of the interior. He cursed himself for not having squared away the boat properly when he left her, but he hadn't expected to be gone for so long.

While he worked he thought about the risks he was taking. It was a shock to find he was already under surveillance. There could only be one reason. They must have clocked him when he met Spider and

Ginger with Samuel. The police investigation must have been far advanced. As he analysed his situation he became more confident. Knowing that he under surveillance gave him an advantage. It was certain that they would have tapped his phone as well as all the public phones he had used. It would be easy to plant a few red herrings down those taps.

He found a bag of coal and lit the stove, then opened all the ventilators and the fore hatch. Soon the air was circulating, being sucked in from the cockpit and expelled through the fo'c'sle. He boiled some water on the gas ring and started wiping down the surfaces. For the first time since he'd bought the boat he realised how big she was. Forty-five feet long didn't seem big. Ten feet wide didn't seem excessive. However, with over a thousand square feet of surface area to be wiped clean she had suddenly turned into a huge boat. He worked his way forward, through the galley into the main cabin, then through the watertight bulkhead into the forward accommodation and the fo'c'sle. Whoever built the boat had not wanted to take any chances. The two watertight bulkheads were made of steel and if one section of the hull was damaged the other two sections would provide adequate buoyancy to keep her afloat.

It was dusk by the time he had finished. He turned off the generator and closed the fore hatch, bolting it from the inside. He filled the stove and turned it down low. The boat would be more hospitable the next time he came.

# Chapter 9

## 1

Ginger was furious. He slammed down the phone, and paced the sitting room of his house in Stoke Newington. He hoped Tate got the message on the pager. They kept the messages on those computers for three days. He couldn't understand why Tate wouldn't buy a mobile phone. He'd given him a nice little Smith and Wesson handgun as a present when they first started working together, but the bloke seemed more afraid of a bleeding telephone. Mobile phones were the business. The Bill couldn't bug them because they didn't know where the mobile was; and if they didn't know that, they didn't know which aerial site it had accessed.

He sat down on the sofa and stared into the carpet. Bleeding Spider. Why couldn't he be like everyone else and leave his money in the bank? No. He had to keep moving it about, buying a bit of this, selling a bit of that, to make what? Chicken feed.

Spider hadn't been himself since he did that job in Holland. He'd never been much of a talker, but now he hardly spoke. It was like he had something on his mind. That wasn't the Spider of old. Maybe someone was putting the squeeze on him; that would explain why he had risked blowing their operation with this little number. Spider wasn't thinking straight, that was for sure.

He heard the bedroom door open and turned around. Tracy was out of the bath. She was eighteen years younger than him. Her skin was soft and rosy. She was wearing the silk knickers he'd bought her the last time he knocked her around. For a moment he felt excited, looked down at his suit and thought about removing it briefly. It was covered in fucking cat hairs. 'Shit!' he exclaimed.

'What's wrong, pet?' Tracy asked. She'd learned quickly there was only one way of calming him down when he was angry. She pouted and squeezed her breasts together. He liked to come between them.

'That fucking cat. My suit cost a grand and it looks moth-eaten. I should never have given you that cat.' He paused for thought. 'The cat goes,' he said finally.

'What's wrong?' Tracy repeated.

'I'm busy,' he said, grabbing his portable phone from the table.

'Not too busy for this, are you?' Tracy wiggled her pert bottom.

'Fucking right, I am. Busy as a one-armed paper hanger.' He opened the door.

'Where are you going?' asked Tracy. 'I thought we was going shopping.'

'Well, we're not. And cover those tits. I don't want you greeting no one like that.'

He slammed the door behind him. Outside the front door he looked right and left. He didn't see anyone watching him. That fucking Tate was making him nervous with all his talk of security. He rolled his shoulders and opened the door of the BMW.

He wasn't looking forward to meeting Tate. Things were not looking too good, and Tate was not going to be happy about it. Spider deserved a kick in the bollocks. Fancy getting pulled by customs trying to smuggle a few pounds of gold through Heathrow. In a couple of days he'd have been able to buy kilos of the fucking stuff. VAT or no VAT. Only God knew what Tate was going to say. It was too late to stop their consignment. It was on its way. He guessed Spider had made the final arrangements.

Ginger didn't have to wait long for Tate to show at the pub. 'Are you sure you weren't followed?' Tate greeted him.

'You think I was born yesterday,' countered Ginger.

'We must be careful at every stage,' said Tate. It was ironic. Davidson was watching Ginger and he hadn't got a clue. It was pathetic really. When he finally wanted them out of the way he only had to give Davidson the word.

Ginger glowered. Tate wasn't going to like what he was about to tell him.

'So why do you want to see me?' asked Tate. 'You said it was urgent.'

Ginger stuck his chin forward aggressively. 'Spider got nicked by customs at Heathrow. He went off to see his mate in Zurich to sort out the paperwork on this thing, and put the two shipments together, like. When he came back he got nicked.'

The blood drained from Tate's face. He couldn't believe it. He'd been promised nothing like this would happen. 'How did it happen?'

'Oh no,' said Ginger, realising that Tate had misunderstood. 'It wasn't nothing to do with us. Our thing's good. Spider was bringing a few ounces of gold back, as a present like. He got nicked.'

The relief surged through Tate's body. It was a brief respite before the rage. 'What a bloody moron! Has he got any brains at all?'

'Watch your lip,' said Ginger defensively. 'He's my mate and I'm not having you slag him off.'

'I don't care who's bloody friend he is. He's about to make a fortune and he's trying to dodge a couple of hundred quid's worth of duty. In a few days he'd have been trying to get gold out of the fucking country. It's pathetic. He's putting at stake a five million pound project. He doesn't need locking up. He needs his throat cutting. He needs putting out of his misery.'

'Yeah? Well, there ain't no deal until he's out.'

'What do you mean?'

'It's his blokes what are doing the dodge at Heathrow.'

'You mean to tell me if we don't get him out on bail this whole thing goes down?'

'No. I reckon the freight gets put in a warehouse. Then we got to figure some way of lifting it out of there.'

'Forget it,' said Tate. 'That was never mentioned when we planned this. You guys said you had your end covered. I don't call this organisation. You better pray Spider gets out on bail. It won't be me you've got on your back if something goes wrong.'

'You threatening me?' asked Ginger.

'Fucking right I am. I'm threatening you with the people who are going to jump on my back.'

'Well, they'll have to wait. Spider's got a problem with this bail thing. He's got a suspended sentence.'

'He's a bloody moron,' said Tate.

'You better show a bit more respect to Spider.'

'Oh really?' said Tate sarcastically.

'Yeah!'

'And why's that?'

'Because he did a little something for your mate in Holland. A little parking job in Holland at the airport.' Tate didn't react. 'At the air terminal. Remember? Terminal? Get it?' laboured Ginger.

'I don't know what you're talking about,' replied Tate.

'Don't come the innocent with me. You put that Pakki in touch with me so we could sort out this bloke Deroot. You owe Spider.'

'I don't owe him anything, and what he gets up to is his own lookout. If he did a job for someone I'm sure he was paid for it.' It goes from bad to worse, thought Tate. There was a way out of this mess, though, and

Spider and Ginger were going to pay through the nose if it worked. 'If I get Spider out on bail, what's it worth?'

'Few grand.'

'Twenty-five grand.'

'You must be joking,' responded Ginger, outraged. 'A brief don't cost that much.'

'You're the jokers if something goes wrong on this deal. I'm not talking about a lawyer here, I'm talking about a guarantee.'

Ginger thought about it. If Tate wasn't talking about a brief then he had someone on the take in customs. If things worked out it wasn't so much dosh. 'I don't reckon he has much choice.'

'You're right,' said Tate. 'I hope I can pull this off for your sake.' He stood up. He had work to do.


# 2


Davidson was in a good mood on Tuesday morning. He had something to look forward to. Every time he spoke to Tate he made a few grand. He was surprised when Tate told him that Spider had been out of the country, let alone that he had been arrested at Heathrow. Now he had to make sure Spider was released on bail, and then he'd earn another ten grand. No problem! He put a call through to Andy Ballot. Customs had promised to keep their noses out of his investigation but they'd broken their word. Now he held the moral high ground, and the longer he spoke to Ballot on the phone the more pleasurable it became.

'I thought we had an agreement,' he repeated.

'I can't help it if our officers arrest your suspect for smuggling. It's their job, after all.'

'Don't your officers check with the computer? They could have contacted me. They have probably fucked up eight months of investigation,' Davidson snarled. 'What are you going to do about it?'

'Frankly speaking, it's out of my hands,' said Andy.

'What are you proposing to charge him with?'

'He is being charged under Section 25 of the 1990 International Co-operation Act.'

'Do me a favour, save me the trouble of looking that one up.'

'We're seizing ten kilos of gold which we believe are the proceeds of drug trafficking.'

Davidson winced. 'You've got it wrong, sonny. I want Spider back on the streets. It might be a good idea to call your man at the Courts, and tell him not to put up any objections to bail. Your man better have a word with the beaks. I don't want any fuck-up here. I'm on the point of breaking this one.'

'No disrespect, Detective Davidson, but I don't work for the Metropolitan Police and I don't take my orders from you. Let's get that straight.'

There was a silence over the telephone. Andy heard something, perhaps it was a fist, smashed in rage. Then he heard Davidson's voice. 'You thick bastard. In a few moments from now your superior will probably be wishing that you didn't exist. But why don't you call your boss? Call Patterson and see what he has to say about all this. That gold was bought with the proceeds of a bank robbery. If Kelly had made it from the airport into London I could have wrapped up this whole investigation.'

Andy cursed under his breath. He didn't need this. Talk about bad luck. He could do without the Chief's involvement in this problem. He'd been reluctant enough to authorise the operation in the first place. 'I understand your concerns. I'm sorry our investigations have clashed. I'll have a word with the officers involved and see if I can do anything. I can't do more than that.'

'You can do more than that. You can give me a guarantee for a start,' demanded Davidson.

'I'm afraid I don't think I can get them to apologise to Kelly,' said Andy sarcastically.

'You think this is a fucking joke, don't you, Ballot? I've spent more than thirty years chasing criminals. You're just out of nappies. Catching these two may mean nothing to you, but it means a lot to me. You should keep on top of your own operation. You might be interested to know that Ginger was introducing Tate to some mate of his down Dover way yesterday, while you were fucking up my investigation.'

'Dover?' queried Andy.

'Yeah. Dover,' repeated Davidson. 'God knows why. I don't know who it was. Maybe it makes sense to you.' Tate had asked him to let slip that piece of information. Davidson reckoned he deserved an Oscar for this performance. He waited for the reply. There was a brief pause while Ballot assimilated that information and re-evaluated his relationship with Davidson.

'Listen, I'll make sure Kelly gets bail. Sorry about the mix-up. Let me know if you have any problems.'

'Thank you. Sorry about the harsh words. This investigation is close to my heart. Know what I mean? We should meet up for a drink one day.'

'Do you have an address for Tate?' asked Andy.

'Not at the moment. If I find one, I'll let you know.'

After a few more pleasantries Davidson replaced his receiver. Davidson leaned back in his chair and grinned at the wall. Spider wouldn't know what had happened. They'd be lighting cigarettes for him and bringing him cups of coffee. When he got bail, Detective Sergeant Davidson was another ten grand ahead. Roll on the good times.

# 3

Andy slammed the receiver down on the cradle. It bounced off and lay on the desk. Annelies and Vince looked at him. 'Shit!' he said. Annelies leaned across the desk and carefully placed the receiver on its cradle. Until that phone call with Davidson, Andy had been able to see light at the end of the tunnel. For the past two days he'd been running on a mixture of vodka and adrenaline. Sleep was an inconvenience he suffered for four hours a night.

'What's up?' asked Vince.

'That was Davidson. We've stumbled across the Metropolitan Police investigation into Ginger and Spider,' said Andy.

'How come?'

'Bad luck. The boys at Heathrow stopped Spider trying to smuggle some gold into the country.'

'That's not our fault,' said Vince.

'Davidson's cutting up rough. He says we're interfering with his investigation.'

'That's ridiculous,' said Vince.

'If Spider is central to Tate's plans, then it jeopardises our investigation as well.'

'So, Spider gets bail and everything's back to normal,' said Vince.

'No. He doesn't get bail. He's on a suspended sentence.'

'This Davidson? What do you know about him?' asked Vince.

'Next to nothing,' said Andy.

'He was responsible for putting Ginger in prison last time. Every time I check on Jay or Tate the last person to have accessed them is Davidson. His fingerprints are over everything. Do you think he knows more than he's telling?'

'I don't know,' said Andy thoughtfully. 'He doesn't want us near his investigation, nor has he been exactly been co-operative.'

'What's his game? He's keeping very close tabs on what we're doing. He's getting better results than us.'

'We better play things safe. I don't want any mention of the investigation to go back on the computer until we know where it's leading. We'll run this straight out of the office from now on. Let's see if that puts some blinkers on Davidson.'

'In the meantime, what do we do about Spider?' asked Vince.

'Get him out of there,' said Andy.

'Do you want me to go to Heathrow and speak to the officer on the case? I'll explain the problem and get him to tell the magistrate the computer's down when Spider applies for bail.'

'I don't understand,' said Annelies.

'When Spider comes before the Court the Magistrate will ask us if we have any objections to bail. We'll tell him the computer's out of order, and he'll understand that we want Spider on bail, although his record won't permit it,' explained Andy.

Simon Patterson let himself into the office. They looked up and fell silent. This was unusual. If he wanted to speak to them they invariably received a summons.

'Are you making any progress on Samuel Tate?' he asked.

'It looks good, chief,' said Andy. 'The telephone taps are starting to pay off. We're definitely on to something, and whatever it is, it's not far off. We've had the transcript of a conversation between Jay's girlfriend, Julia and another friend. She says Jay's up to something and she's thinking of leaving him because of it. True to form, Jay isn't using his own phone to make any arrangements. He's popping down the road to the public phone box.'

Patterson nodded. 'Nothing concrete on Tate yet?'

'Unfortunately not,' said Andy. 'Vince checked all his previous addresses, but he seems to have vanished. He's sold all his properties. We've looked at all the new owners, and as far as we can ascertain, they're all genuine. The next move is to find out where the funds are deposited.'

'I've had your people on the phone, Annelies,' said Patterson. 'They told me that de Groote's girlfriend has been killed. They think she saw de Groote's killer and had to be silenced. They're very keen to interview Tate. I'm going to speak to the police tomorrow. They were the last people to see Tate. I am tempted to pass this matter over to them. If it's a murder investigation then it falls under their jurisdiction.'

Andy's heart started pounding. 'Sir,' he said quickly. 'I'd rather you didn't act too hastily. I really believe we're on to something. Jay bought a van, and hired a lock-up garage in Maida Vale.'

'That's interesting,' Patterson nodded. 'And very careless of him. But, criminals get like that in their old age.' He smiled. 'I'll keep to my original agreement. This is a three-day operation. However, if you don't come up with anything definite I have no option but to pass it to the other side.' He opened the door to let himself out. 'Keep me informed,' he ordered, and closed the door behind him.

'Davidson's going to love it when the whole case drops on his desk,' commented Andy.

'Where is Davidson coming from?' asked Vince. 'He must be close to something if he's putting this much energy into keeping us off the scent.'

'Davidson was the officer in charge of Ginger's arrest,' said Andy.

'He got his result. He had Ginger put away. Did they ever recover the money from the robbery?' asked Vince.

'Must have, or he'd have done more than four years,' answered Andy, irritably.

'I'll check it out. Maybe something went missing. Maybe Davidson's got the hidden treasure syndrome,' said Vince.

'Forget it,' snapped Andy. 'I don't give a damn about Davidson. I don't want to waste time thinking about him. We're losing sight of the case. Five years ago Tate and Ginger were both on remand in "C" Wing at Pentonville. Their time there overlapped for six months. Tate was released. Ginger was transferred to Brixton and spent another four years inside. Now they're up to something, and we want to know what it is.'

'How did you . . . ?' Vince began asking, surprised. He thought better of it. 'That makes sense,' he said.

'I think you better get out to Heathrow and sort things out before everyone knocks off,' suggested Andy.

'I'll see you in the morning, then,' said Vince.

Andy looked at his watch. Vince wasn't planning to do any overtime. 'All right,' said Andy.

Andy and Annelies pored over the files for another four hours, cross-referencing information, trying to make sense of the facts. It was seven o'clock. They were thinking of leaving to grab something to eat when a tape was delivered. It was a recording made by Jay from the phone box. They listened to it in amazement. It gave them Jay's agenda for the following day. Times of meetings, places, and most important of all, confirmation that the operation was planned for the next day.

'I don't believe it,' said Andy. 'We've never had a scoop like this before. We put the tap on that phone in good time. He thought it was safe. Look,' he pointed to the details which accompanied the tape, 'it was a phone box to phone box call.'

Andy picked up the telephone and dialled Simon Patterson's home number. They would have to work through the night to organise the team.

# 4

It was Thursday morning, and Tate woke in the apartment he now rented from a German property speculator. This was the first apartment he'd bought, fifteen years ago, under a different name and now he was a sitting tenant. Later he bought the whole house under his own name, leaving the basement as a separate item. He knew it would be useful one day. Over the next few years he bought six more houses. Now he was back where he began, having sold all the properties. It was a curious feeling. It seemed as if the past years had been a dream. He felt cramped back in the basement, which wasn't surprising since he'd rattled around in a ten-room house until a month or so ago. Nevertheless, the basement made a good pied à terre, especially since no one knew he lived there.

Going to ground somewhat limited his social life, but since he planned to leave England for ever he had little need for social camouflage. 'Times are bad,' he told those who thought they were friends. 'I've had to sell the house.' Tate noticed how quickly they stopped inviting him to dinner, looking away awkwardly when they met him. He experienced a glow of self-satisfaction. He'd used the lot of them, and they never guessed he didn't give a damn for their conversation, their opinions, their homes or their wives. Yes, he'd fucked their wives in discreet hotels, pouring champagne over their breasts and licking caviar from their navels. The wives loved the extravagance and the frivolity of the affairs. He'd miss that part of it, although he might jet in from time to time and whisk one of them to some Caribbean island.

He padded into the kitchen and switched on the Gaggia machine which provided him with the endless cups of coffee he needed. He stared at the kitchen. It was a mystery to him. Perhaps he'd teach himself to cook sometime. He ate at restaurants twice a day. His annual bill was over twenty thousand, but at the moment he saw no need to economise.

He picked up his espresso and walked back to the bedroom. He looked in the wardrobe and surveyed the twenty odd suits. He carefully picked out an English country tweed suit with light brown checks. He laid it on the bed. He picked out a pair of hand-made brogues. He looked at his watch. There were two hours until his luncheon date with Oliver. He ran the bath, then padded into the kitchen to grapple with the Gaggia machine once again.

Tate had one more problem to solve. When the operation was under way he had to move around five million pounds out of England. A million pounds might fit into a large suitcase, but in this case that meant about five suitcases. It needed an army of porters to carry them, and anyway, in these security-conscious days, they couldn't be transported by air. Smaller sums could be accommodated by couriers taking weekend breaks on ferries, but in this case the sheer volume required some other method. It was too dangerous to risk such a large sum in the back of a truck. There were better ways.

Ginger and Spider had offered to deliver the money for a three per cent charge, but in view of Spider's latest escapade at Heathrow it was clear they weren't as organised as they claimed. Anyway, it would put Ginger into too powerful a position. Not only would he be investing in the material as well as importing it, he would also be dealing with the profits. When Ginger grasped that fact he'd be after much larger percentages.

Tate had better people than Ginger to handle the money. He had a genuine banker in the form of Oliver. He first met him at a society wedding, four years ago. They were standing outside the marquee, champagne in their glasses, looking down the lawn towards the river which lapped at the garden's banks on its way to Oxford. The dappled sunlight picked out the guests on the lush lawn. On the one hand Tate despised it all. On the other, he craved admission to this exclusive club.

'Only on days like this do I feel I'm still in the England of my childhood,' said the man standing beside Tate. 'I feel an overwhelming nostalgia. This scene suggests an impressionist painting by what's-his-name?'

'Seurat?' suggested Tate, remembering the name from a recent auction.

'Quite.'

'I know what you mean,' said Tate. There was safety in such gatherings. Here one was beyond the law, securely ensconced in the bosom of the class system. On days like this, and in places like this, police cars didn't exist. Samuel soon discovered that Oliver's family ran back to the Domesday Book.

'I'm afraid the old England's gone. We shall just have to accept it,' said Tate.

'What makes you say that?' asked Oliver, his eyes narrowing.

For the first time Tate took stock of Oliver. He identified him immediately as coming from the peculiar arena of the upper middle classes. He had been educated at vast expense to bring out the best of his limited talents. Physical prowess was not apparent. He was flat-footed. His open toothy mouth was framed by limp lips. He had abominable teeth. He was overweight and ageing fast. Oliver had connections, he worked in the City and his family shared a place in Debretts with the groom. Tate was only invited to the wedding because he had once fucked the bride when she was stoned, and had often gone out of his way to supply her with cocaine.

Tate decided it was worth taking a chance. 'Last year I did a property deal for an Arab who had half a million he wanted transferred to a Swiss account. I went off to my bank and they nearly confiscated the money. They weren't prepared to handle such sums outside the banking system. I had to return it to the client and tell him to make his own arrangements.'

Oliver laughed. 'That happens to people these days. It's only to make things difficult for the criminals. I'm surprised your client wanted to move his funds to Switzerland. If you're not English this is the best place to keep your money. If you're English, then Switzerland or the Cayman Islands are best.' Oliver turned to Tate, looked serious and added, 'If you find yourself in the same situation again, give me a call. Over fifty billion pounds of foreign currency changes hands in the City every day. My firm handles that much a year. We would be happy to accommodate you.'

Tate probed a little deeper. 'I hear things are tough in the City these days. What? Insider dealing and all that?'

'Things have always been rough in the City. It's just that the rags have started reporting things. There's always been a bit of dealing. It depends on whom you know. That's how all the bankers made their money in the old days. A word here and a word there. In the days before socialism there was never this ridiculous guilt about taking unfair advantage. Now it's against the law. Bloody stupid if you ask me. Anyway, we take a bit more care these days. Show me the plumber who doesn't take unfair advantage when your pipes burst in the middle of the night.'

Bingo! Tate had hit the jackpot. Tate had been introduced. Over the next two years he contacted Oliver at various times and found him as good as his word. They had become friends. They lunched together once a month, and every now and again Tate stayed with Oliver's family on their country estate. He resisted the temptation to sleep with Emma, Oliver's wife. She was bored with her husband, and Tate didn't blame her.

As Tate waited in the expensive Italian restaurant he wondered whether Oliver would balk at the sheer size of the deal which he was proposing this time. Oliver had never previously questioned the large sums in bank notes which Tate had delivered. He was either very trusting, or a gullible fool. Tate suspected the latter.

At last Oliver arrived and they were both shown to their table. They had ordered their lunch and were waiting for the waiters to bring the wine, the mineral water and the antipastos. In the meantime they watched the live shellfish in the ice-filled aquarium moving frozen claws. The two men shuddered.

'Can't say I give much for their chances of survival,' said Oliver. 'I doubt Darwin envisaged this.'

Tate didn't answer. His lips expressed distaste. He was wondering whether he really wanted to eat the lobster after all.

It was only while they were sipping their coffee that Tate brought up his proposition. Oliver didn't bat an eyelid. Tate wondered if Oliver understood the physical aspects of the proposition. 'Sterling's so bloody bulky. You'd think the Bank of England would print a hundred pound note at least. The Dutch have thousand guilder notes. The Swiss have five thousand franc notes. A million pounds in Swiss francs is the size of . . . of . . . of . . .' he cast about for inspiration. 'A volume of Boswell's *Life of Johnson*,' he finished lamely.

'Yes. I can see the problem,' replied Oliver. 'If I bump into the Chairman of the Bank of England I'll have a word with him.'

Tate looked at Oliver but couldn't tell if he was joking.

Out of the blue, Oliver said, 'You know, I heard the Mafia used to hire women to count the notes. They locked them in a warehouse and took off their clothes so they couldn't steal anything.'

'That sounds exciting,' said Samuel, who'd read the same thing.

'You wouldn't happen to use the same methods?' Oliver leered.

Tate smiled. So Oliver had guessed the source of the money. 'I'm afraid not.'

'A pity,' said Oliver, and chuckled.

'I know somewhere we could go one day and have the girls count some money. If you like?' said Tate. A few compromising photographs of Oliver might be useful.

'Yes. That could be amusing,' said Oliver.

It had been bound to happen, thought Tate. Oliver had to get greedy at some stage. It was human nature. So things were not so cosy chez Oliver. Perhaps Tate would be putting Oliver's wife to bed after all.

'By the way, I should remind you never to phone me at work. It's not a good thing. All our calls are taped. It's part of our self-regulatory policy. There used to be a time when your word was your bond. Now you sometimes have to prove it. It could be embarrassing if they wanted to know what I was up to with you,' said Oliver.

'Do you mean to tell me that all the banks are doing that?'

'I should think that most of them would be, by now.'

'How about the Swiss banks?'

'Well, especially the Swiss banks. They'll be taking instructions over the phone all the time.'

It was a sobering thought for Tate.

'You really don't need to worry,' continued Oliver blithely. 'Normally the tapes would only be for internal use.'

'All the same,' said Tate, 'it's not pleasant to know your private affairs are on record.'

# 5

It was Thursday, 12 March, 1700 hours. The Airbus 300 appeared for the briefest second above the clouds over Berkshire. The co-pilot made contact with Air Traffic Control. 'Good evening, London. LH 019, Airbus 300, approaching Lambourn, flight level eight zero.'

The air traffic controller picked out the Lufthansa flight on his radar screen. 'Good evening, LH 019, after Lambourn, turn left heading two one zero, speed two one zero.'

The co-pilot confirmed his controller's instructions, 'LH 019 heading and speed two one zero after Lambourn.'

The plane banked slowly, curling south-east. The co-pilot thought of a girl 5,000 feet below in a Berkshire village; she was a mother now. He always thought of her as he flew into Heathrow.

The controller broke into his thoughts, 'LH 019, descend four thousand feet on one zero three zero.'

The co-pilot repeated, 'LH 019 descending to four thousand feet. Flight level eight zero.'

The pilot and co-pilot adjusted their sea altimeters to 1030.

'Altimeter?' asked the pilot

'1030, 5000,' responded the co-pilot.

'1030, 5000,' confirmed the pilot.

'LH 019 turn right heading two three zero,' said the controller. 'Cleared JLS two seven right.'

'Heading two three zero, cleared JLS two seven right,' repeated the co-pilot. It would be another lonely night in a hotel room, an early start, and back to Frankfurt in the morning.

'Flaps one,' said the pilot.

'Flaps one,' repeated the co-pilot.

'Flaps two,' said the pilot.

'Flaps two,' repeated the co-pilot.

'Gear down,' said the pilot.

'Gear down,' confirmed the co-pilot. The black box recorded their automatic responses, so the air safety investigators could rule out pilot error, in case disaster occurred. Now the woman in Berkshire was married to a stranger.

'LH 019, outer marker,' said the co-pilot. But he would always remember her as a girl.

The controller responded, 'LH 019, Change to Tower one one eight, seven.'

The co-pilot repeated, 'LH 019, one one eight, seven. Goodbye.'

He switched frequencies and made contact with Heathrow Tower. 'Good evening Tower, LH 019, outer marker.'

'LH 019, continue number two to land,' acknowledged Heathrow Tower.

'Flaps three,' said the pilot.

'Flaps three.'

'Flaps full.'

'Flaps full.'

'LH 019 clear to land runway two seven right,' confirmed Heathrow Tower.

England was a cold and lonely place in March. Cold, any time of year. The girl would always be married to a stranger, because she had given her heart away, long before, to a pilot in Windsor Park.

'Landing check list,' said the pilot.

The co-pilot read through the check list. 'Landing all green,' he said.

The Airbus loomed out of the grey clouds suddenly, throttling back with a roar, hung over the tarmac and then dropped down. There was a shriek from the wheels as they spun into life, smoking for a second.

Five men watched the plane as it sped past, and out of sight. They looked at each other. The flight was right on time.

# *Chapter 10*

## 1

Edward stood outside the phone box. He knew that somewhere in the darkness a member of the customs surveillance team was watching him. He looked at his watch. There were only a couple more minutes to wait. Across London, in another phone box, Jason was waiting impatiently for the call which would tell him he could begin marketing. He had the van, and had checked his dealers were all available.

Edward rehearsed the diversions he was going to drop into the conversation and down the telephone tap. If things worked out, customs wouldn't bother to follow him in the morning, although he would still take counter-measures when he picked up Jason's van and met Ginger. He was pleased with himself. The customs operation would be completely sabotaged. The adrenaline was running. He stepped into the phone box and made the call. He felt a pang of guilt. Jason would be horrified if he knew what was going on. The telephone tap would automatically record the number being dialled, but Edward knew that Jason would disappear from the vicinity seconds after he'd replaced the receiver. Jason took no chances at all.

A few minutes later, and his conversation with Jason was over. The last pieces of the operation had been laid in place. Edward walked home to Julia. He'd taken care of everything, except for Julia. He could not keep lying to her. She must have guessed that he was more involved than he pretended. All he needed were a few more days, and then it would be over.

When he entered the flat he found Julia waiting for him. 'Where have you been?' she asked.

'Making a phone call.'

'That's what I thought,' she said, pausing for a moment. 'I don't want you to insult my intelligence any more. I know you're doing far more than helping Samuel. You promised me you would quit. Now, I've decided that I can't go on like this. It's over.'

'Listen Julia . . .' began Edward.

'No, Edward. I don't want to listen. Believe me. It hasn't been easy to make this decision. Don't make it harder. Leave me some dignity, please.'

Edward said nothing. He poured himself a drink. He looked at Julia. She was staring at a corner of the room. He wanted to take her in his arms, but he knew she would push him away. It was his fault it had come to this. Her patience had finally given out. He didn't believe she meant it. The best thing would be for him to suggest having a trial separation, and when the job was done he could see her again.

'I'm sorry,' he said. Tears started rolling down her cheeks. She made no attempt to brush them away. Edward went over to her, and put his arms around her. She did not push him away, but she didn't respond. 'I'm sorry,' Edward repeated. 'The last thing I wanted was to make you unhappy.'

Julia shook her head. 'It's over. You forced me to take this decision.'

'I didn't mean to. Things have got out of control. I'll move out until this is over. Then we can start again.'

'It's too late, Edward. It's too late. This afternoon I spoke to the solicitor and told him we weren't buying the house any more.' She pushed him away, suddenly.

Edward looked at her, startled. 'Don't do that Julia. Wait.'

'I don't want to wait. I don't want to live with you in some bloody farmhouse bought with dirty money. I want you to go. I can't bear this any more . . . this uncertainty.' She wiped the tears away. 'Please go away, now. If you don't, I will.'

Edward went into the bedroom and packed some clothes and a sleeping bag into two suitcases. He only needed enough for the next few days. It would all be over then. He'd take Julia for a holiday.

'Where are you going?' asked Julia when he returned to the sitting room.

'I don't know. A hotel probably. Why?'

'In case your cronies need to know where you are.'

'I doubt they will.'

'Don't leave it too long before you collect your things. I want to make a clean break.'

'I don't think it'll ever be a clean break,' replied Edward. 'You're forgetting the baby.'

Julia stared at him. 'No,' she said. 'It was you who forgot the baby.'

Edward sighed. It was time to go. 'We'll see,' he said. 'Goodbye.' He leaned forward to kiss her.

'Goodbye,' she said. She turned her head away.

Edward opened the door and stepped into the street and the darkness. He wondered if customs were working overtime. He couldn't take any chances, and it wasn't going to be easy to lose them carrying two suitcases. He took a taxi to Heathrow airport. The car hire firms were always open at the airports. Once he had a car it would be easy.

When he finally reached the boat, having made numerous detours in the hired car, he was sure that he had thrown off any surveillance.

The stove on the boat was still warm. He topped it up with fuel. He took the sleeping bag out of the suitcase and prepared for bed. He set the alarm clock; he had an early start and a busy day.

# 2

The freight handlers didn't always work together. There was a complicated shift system at the airport, designed to prevent conspiracy from occurring. However, on a couple of days each month these five men all worked together. They only had a week's notice of when the magic rota would operate, but that was all the time they needed. As soon as they knew the dates they informed Spider. He called Karachi and the crates were loaded on to an appropriate plane. The crates were destined for Toronto, but had to be transhipped through Frankfurt to Heathrow on another flight. Once the crates were safe in a neutral transit warehouse the freight agent in Switzerland assembled the paperwork for the shipment and was told when to book the flight.

When the plane landed in London, and the passengers had disembarked, the customs rummage crews went to work. They crawled through the hold to ensure that the containers all had the appropriate air waybills and that there was no other contraband. Once they'd finished their task the freight handlers removed the legitimate freight, including the crates ostensibly destined for Toronto.

The British Customs took little interest in cargoes destined for

Canada. Next, the freight handlers destroyed all the documentation for the crates they took. In Karachi the crates were marked as not having been loaded on to the plane. In Frankfurt, Akbar's Turkish contacts destroyed their documentation. The shipment had now disappeared from the system. All someone had to do was collect them at the right time.

If, for any reason, the contraband couldn't be removed from the plane it would fly on to Toronto, where new instructions forwarded the crates to South America or some other destination. The paperwork was always kept in order using fake companies and safe destinations.

Now the Lufthansa Airbus squatted on the runway outside the warehouses waiting for the rummage crew to search it. The freight handlers waited patiently in the tea room. They weren't in a hurry. It wasn't their problem if they weren't working because customs were taking their time. A couple of them played cards in a corner. Now and then one of them went out to see whether customs had arrived.

Finally two officers and an Alsatian dog walked to the plane. The wind whistled across the open tarmac and whipped at their clothes. There was the howl of a plane taking off from a nearby runway. The dog laid his ears flat on his head. They walked up the ramp into the maw of the aircraft and let the dog off the lead. One officer led the dog among the crates and boxes, encouraging him to sniff for traces of drugs. The other officer looked at the freight waiting to be unloaded. It was a cursory check. They did not expect contraband through Frankfurt. The dog was doing the hard work.

One of the freight handlers stood at the entrance to the warehouse. He was a study in indifference, but it belied the keenness with which he was watching the plane. He was looking for any sign of unusual activity as the customs officers emerged. He'd be alerted by something so insignificant as the Alsatian looking more perky, his ears pricked and his tail wagging, indicating that he'd been rewarded for his find. He watched for any hint of urgency in the officers' return. Bloody dogs! Of all the planes waiting to be rummaged, why choose to take the dog into this one?

If things looked bad, the handlers would have to take care. They would have to find out if the officers had suspicions. They'd have to make a decision. It might be another cargo which was under suspicion. They always had the choice of letting the freight continue to Toronto. Rain started to lash down. The customs officers were taking a long time in the plane. Half an hour was usually ample.

Suddenly the customs officers appeared at the top of the ramp. They ran through the rain, heads down, expressions hidden by the peaks of their caps. The freight handler started to pull on his yellow waterproofs. The officers burst through the door of the warehouse and brushed off the rain. The Alsatian shook himself. The freight handler stared at the dog and wished someone had the guts to poison it. In New York the sniffer-dogs didn't last long with five thousand dollar contracts on them. All of a sudden the Alsatian looked up and stared at him. Inadvertently he looked away.

'It's all yours,' said one of the officers. The freight handler nodded. He went to alert the rest of the team. The officers lit cigarettes, ignoring the 'No Smoking' sign, and waited for the rain to subside.

Once inside the plane, the team didn't take long to locate the crates and moved them along with the legitimate freight to the holding cage in the warehouse. There were two more things to do. The documentation in Pakistan had to be altered to confirm that the consignment had not been loaded. Then Spider had to collect the crates.

Nice one, thought the freight handler. The thirty grand was as good as in his pocket. He didn't care that Spider had said they shouldn't spend the money straight away. He'd earned it and was going to buy himself a decent motor. Maybe a Porsche 924.

# 3

The alarm clock rang at five thirty in the morning. It was still dark. For a moment Edward forgot where he was, then stretched out a hand to silence it. He lay in the warm sleeping bag for a few moments thinking about the day ahead, wondering if he had overlooked anything. He realised, with a jolt, that it was Friday the thirteenth. Scams were always planned for a Friday because the dealers went to work at weekends. On weekdays, people had jobs and no money. On weekends, police resources were usually over-stretched, dealing with football hooligans and demonstrations, and the constraints of overtime meant that they were less likely to be on normal duties. Dealers normally wanted two weekends of credit to sell the dope. Edward wondered if Samuel had even thought about the date. He doubted it. He struggled out of bed. There was no point in being superstitious; it was a luxury he couldn't afford. He barely felt the cold as he put on the kettle. He had other things on his mind.

By six he was on the towpath taking a short cut by sliding down the embankment and through a hedge to where he had left the car. Dawn was breaking. It was misty. Dew laden cobwebs hung in the still air. A cat stared at him and slunk into the bushes. There was the occasional cry of a bird waking too soon. He drove into London and parked the car outside a pub. He took out a sports bag and started walking towards the river. The city was waking up now and a cold breeze was dispersing the early morning mist.

He found Jason's van as arranged in Chiswick. He put his hand under the front offside wheel arch and pulled off the magnetic key holder. He put his gloves on, unlocked the door and jumped in. The vehicle documents lay under the seat. He opened the sports bag he had been carrying and took out a pair of blue overalls and struggled into them. He put a clipboard on the dash. He was behaving like a van driver about to make some deliveries; except his heart pumped faster as the minutes ticked away. He still had some time to kill. There was always time to kill because he made a point of being early for appointments in case something went wrong. If the van didn't start, then he needed that extra time to start it. If he was late then Ginger would be gone. If they had to make the arrangements a second time there would be twice the risk.

He drove the van through the early morning rush hour, doubling back on himself a couple of times to see if he was being followed. He listened to the engine. It sounded sweet. Finally it was time to make his way to the rendezvous with Ginger. He parked around the corner from the cafe and used the remaining few minutes to make a circuitous inspection of the other side roads. Ginger and Spider stood on the pavement outside the cafe. Spider still sported his camel hair coat. They stood out like a pair of sore thumbs, and Edward groaned inwardly. Ginger looked at his watch confirming that Edward was on time. Spider stretched out his hand. 'Keys,' he snapped, failing to observe the usual niceties.

'Good morning,' said Edward, shaking his hand before giving him the keys.

'Where's it parked?'

'White van round the corner. Registration number's on the fob.'

'Fob?' questioned Ginger.

'Another word for key ring,' Edward replied.

Ginger stared at him. 'Yeah? Well, speak fucking English.'

Edward looked at Spider. A man driving a van in that coat was certainly worth a second look. 'You ever done this before?' Edward asked Spider.

'What?' said Spider, taken aback.

'I'd remove the coat before driving the van.'

'You mind your own fucking business,' said Ginger. Edward shrugged. He doubted a policeman would believe anyone could be fool enough to drive a load of contraband in that outfit. It was probably safe after all.

Edward decided he would be circumspect about recovering the van when it returned. At least he had an hour to wander around and see if the terrain had been staked out. He watched Ginger jump into his BMW and pick up the mobile phone. Spider disappeared around the corner. Edward went into the cafe, ordered breakfast and memorised the features of the people at the tables. He didn't want to see any of them in the vicinity an hour later.

In six hours it would all be over. In the meantime he ignored what he was about to do, concentrating on his newspaper. He forced himself to read the sports pages to divert his mind from the operation. He had developed a theory in Pakistan that insanity was infectious, and on the same basis he was wary of telepathy. However, it seemed unlikely that the people eating sausage, eggs and chips were honing their psychic powers on that diet.

His stomach had still not recovered from his imprisonment and the breakfast made him bilious. He left the cafe and wandered down the street until he came to a chemist where he bought some indigestion tablets. There was no sign of surveillance. At ten o'clock he made a phone call, carefully reading the number from a scrap of paper. The call was answered immediately with the tones indicating that it was another public telephone. He recognised Jason's voice. He told him to be waiting across the river in an hour. He hung up. Jason would recognise the van, and tail him to make sure he wasn't being followed.

Edward surreptitiously dropped the scrap of paper with the phone number down a drain. He continued walking up Wandsworth Bridge Road, finally ending at the intersection with the Kings Road, which he guessed Spider would use on his return journey. In due course he found that his hunch was right, and he watched for five minutes to see if there were any signs of a tail.

Ginger and Spider were waiting impatiently outside the cafe when he finally returned. Ginger tapped his Rolex. 'Get yourself a bleeding watch,' he said. Spider tossed him the keys. Edward walked across the road to the van. He wondered what someone watching that little scene would have made of it. As he approached the van, he reached into his pocket for a handkerchief and pretended to sneeze. Still holding the handkerchief he opened the door and jumped into the driver's seat. He slammed the door behind him. He pulled the pair of gloves from his overalls and slipped them on. He hadn't left any fingerprints on the van. He watched Ginger and Spider drive away; their job was over. He started the engine and took possession of the consignment.

Edward knew he had a ton on board from the sluggish way the van responded to the throttle. He ground his way through the gears and drove up to the King's Road. He'd cross the Thames on Albert Bridge.

Jason would pick him up in Battersea. He swung into a one-way system. He went twice around the system before he saw the white Ford pull out behind him. Jason in the Ford followed for a while and then peeled away. Edward knew he was safe then, and headed North. As he cut through from Ladbroke Grove he avoided his normal short cut through St Anne's Villas. He knew that police cadets were often trained there, stopping innocent drivers who were only too pleased to be searched in the interests of law and order.

If Jason overtook him and threw a piece of paper out of the window it would be a different story. Then, Edward would know that he was being followed. He would drive to the pub where he had parked his car. The pub had two entrances. The police wouldn't stop him because they hoped to catch the person he was meeting as well. They wouldn't know the back door of the pub opened on to another street where Edward had parked his car. It took five minutes to drive from the front of the pub to the back, and by the time the police realised what had happened he would be long gone. The police would be welcome to the van and its contents.

Edward turned on the radio and pumped up the volume. He was a good driver, and had driven trucks much bigger than this one in the years gone by. At last he parked outside the builder's merchants in Harrow Road to let Jason climb on board.

'I'll drop you off around the corner,' said Jason.

'No,' said Edward. Jason wasn't going to like this. 'I've got to take a couple of the boxes. Drop me off at my car.'

'You said I was taking the whole lot.'

'I know. That's what I thought. This was sprung on me at the last moment. I had to agree to this condition.'

'This is a whole new deal now,' pointed out Jason.

'I don't like it any more than you do. The owners have pulled a stroke on me. They want a tenth of the material.'

'Come on, Edward. You know where this leads. I'm going to run into competition. If my dealers hear there's competitive material on the streets they're going to wait and see if there's a price fluctuation.'

'If you have any problems, I'll understand. If it takes you longer to sell I'll tell them why.'

'Promise me that there isn't another consignment being marketed simultaneously,' said Jason.

'There isn't,' answered Edward.

'OK,' said Jason grimly. 'Where to?' Edward directed him to the pub where he had left his car.

Jason grumbled. 'I don't provide a vehicle so you can do work for other people.'

'Look on it as a favour to me.'

'I've a good mind to refuse. Why should I expose myself to danger? How do I know they haven't been followed?'

'You're not going to meet them. We're only going to put a couple of chests into the back of a car.'

'How do I know the car wasn't followed?'

'It's my car, and I wasn't followed,' retorted Edward.

'Tell me something else. Why did you say all that stuff on the phone about meeting me in Dover?'

'I'm getting paranoid these days. I don't trust phones. How do you know they haven't got a tap on the phone for some other bugger?'

'So? All you had to do was say we were meeting for a drink. I'd have known what you meant.'

'I wanted to spread a bit of disinformation.'

'Well, don't do it next time,' commented Jason, severely.

Finally they reached the pub and Edward pulled up behind the hired car. 'I don't like this,' said Jason, shaking his head. Edward ignored him. He opened the van's rear doors and clambered inside. He looked at the boxes and identified the two he had to remove immediately. They were smaller. He noticed that the air freight labels were still attached. He started peeling them off. Ginger and Spider had a lot to learn. If the boxes fell into the wrong hands the labels would lead an investigation back to the airport.

'What are you doing?' asked Jason.

'I'll be finished in a moment,' said Edward.

He had reached the smaller boxes. He peeled off the labels and found older ones underneath. These boxes had originated in Turkey, not Pakistan. He stuffed the incriminating evidence into his pocket and moved the two chests to the rear. He jumped onto the road and joined Jason.

'What the hell are you playing at? We shouldn't be doing this on the street.'

'No one's going to guess what's in these boxes. No one gets suspicious if you do things on the street, in the open. Stop looking around. Relax.'

Jason grunted, and shook his head again. He didn't help Edward carry the boxes to the car. He slammed the van doors closed.

'Hold on!' said Edward, as Jason jumped behind the steering wheel. He picked up the clipboard and scribbled on a piece of paper, which he passed to Jason. 'There's your delivery ticket for the benefit of anyone who's watching.'

Jason looked at the meaningless piece of paper, then folded it slowly and put it in his top pocket. He'd had enough. 'Call me Friday. We'll meet at six, at the usual place.'

Edward watched him drive away. It was almost one o'clock. He went into the pub, ordered a drink and rang Tate's pager service giving his telephone number. Tate would call back in the next five minutes.

When the phone rang, he answered, 'Everything's complete.' He kept the conversation brief.

'Good,' said Tate. 'Just one problem. I'm afraid your next meeting's been postponed for twenty-four hours.'

Edward hesitated, before replying curtly. 'How come?'

'We were expecting a payment on this, and it hasn't been delivered,' said Tate.

If Samuel wanted advance payment for the consignment it meant he didn't trust the people. If Samuel didn't trust them then they were very dodgy. One thing was sure now. He wouldn't be making the delivery when it was arranged. Samuel would have to find someone else.

'Just put the stuff to sleep somewhere safe,' said Tate. 'Don't unpack it. I don't want any arguments with the owners about whether they've been short-changed or anything. If we don't disturb it, they can't complain.'

'Suits me,' said Edward. 'I'll call you about this later.'

'Call me this time tomorrow.'

'OK,' said Edward and put down the phone. He'd have to stash the crates on board the boat. He couldn't risk leaving them in the car. Samuel had pulled another stroke on him.

4

Andy felt the stigma of failure clinging to him. None of his fellow officers caught his eye as they returned their surveillance vehicles to the garage in Southwark. Back at the Fetter Lane Headquarters the team members busied themselves in their respective offices, looking at the time and waiting to knock off.

It was a far cry from the optimism Andy had felt that morning. He'd felt lucky then. Everything had fallen into place. He was sure that for once Samuel Tate had overlooked something. He'd been sure that things would go their way at long last. But things had gone wrong from the very beginning. Edward Jay had given them the slip during the night. The

154

information they'd gathered from the intercepted telephone calls had proved worthless. The surveillance on Jay's garage in North London had been a waste of time.

'What do you think, Vince?' he asked when they were back in the office.

'I reckon you read it wrong, mate.'

'Just me. You read it the same way,' insisted Andy. 'We were on to something last night. Where did it go?'

'Search me. You were leading this one. You picked out the pieces of information you wanted. I guess we could look through it again and come up with a different story.'

'Do you think we were deliberately misinformed?'

'No. I think we tried too hard to get a result.'

'I think it was a conspiracy. We were spoon-fed the information from all sides. We got it straight from the horse's mouth, so to speak. We even had confirmation through Davidson. How come it made so much sense then?'

'Because we wanted it to make sense.'

'Bollocks!' snapped Andy.

'It doesn't make any difference. Some you win and some you lose. Samuel Tate's your personal affair. I don't know why, but I don't want to get involved in this one. I'm washing my hands of it. I'm not going to start picking up the can for you on this. Why should I fuck up my chances of promotion over a cock-up?'

Annelies had been listening and was shocked by the lack of support for Andy. 'This is not a good attitude, Vince,' she said. 'You should support Andy. You were agreeing with him last night and this morning.'

'Stay out of this, Annelies. This is department politics,' said Vince.

'He's right,' agreed Andy.

'Look,' Vince said, 'I'll give you a bit of support. I'll admit things looked good on paper. That telephone tap appeared to be the business. On the other hand when we were staking out the motel in Dover things did not look good at all.'

'Jay must have changed his plans. The information we got from the phone tap was confirmed by Davidson who said he'd seen Ginger and Tate there two days ago.' Andy paused. 'I want to speak to Davidson. Maybe he's holding a little something back from us. Or that bastard Jay knew he was being tapped.' He pulled the telephone towards him, but before he could remove the receiver it rang. He picked it up. It was Simon Patterson summoning him to account for the failure of the operation. He stood up, put on his jacket and left the room.

Andy knocked on Simon Patterson's door. It was five thirty and it was unusual for him to be in the office so late. He heard the gruff command to enter and steeled himself for a difficult interview. He opened the door. Patterson was busying himself with a sheaf of papers. Andy said nothing, and sat down.

'Did I invite you to sit down?' said Patterson. Andy looked at him. He was still concentrating on his papers. He didn't look up.

'No sir,' replied Andy. He stood up again and carefully returned the chair to its original position.

Patterson straightened the papers and put them to one side. He looked up. 'Things are getting a bit slack around here. A little more discipline is what's needed, I think. We need tighter control of the reins, so we can avoid today's expensive time-wasting fiasco in future.'

'I don't know what went wrong. All our intelligence pointed to a successful operation.'

'No it didn't. I've looked over the facts you gave me in order to justify the operation and each one has been carefully doctored. Let's look at the matter of Tate and de Groote. The Dutch Central Detective Agency apparently wanted to interview Tate in connection with de Groote's murder. I've been on the phone to them. They told me they were still searching for his killer. The only lead they had was from Annelies, who told them that Tate may have been involved. They assumed that she had evidence on which to base her suggestion. You managed to involve Annelies Jansen in your scheme. You've now compromised her reputation and her future. The whole basis for your investigation has disappeared with one phone call. Worse than that. You deliberately misled me.'

'I resent that conclusion, sir. I believe that Tate's involvement with de Groote provides a valid premise for further investigation.'

'Don't play the innocent with me. You instigated the request for information from this side of the North Sea. You put Jansen up to it. What offends me personally is that I had specifically told you that Tate was not a priority target. We have other very good targets who could have done with the kind of resources we squandered today.'

'I'm sorry you think that. I know Tate and his cronies are up to something. We're at the start of something big. Tate is in some kind of partnership with organised criminals. Not only that, I think they may have contacts within the police force, if not the customs service.'

'I'm not interested in conspiracy theories. I'm not interested in circumstantial evidence. I'm interested in facts. Arrests and convictions come from facts!'

'Fair enough. But we can't—'

'I'm not interested in listening to you all night,' interrupted Patterson. 'The file on Tate is now closed. Starting from tomorrow, you and I will meet every morning to discuss the day's agenda.'

'Sir, if you remember, when I accepted this post we agreed that I would be allowed some freedom to follow my instincts.'

'The situation has changed. I think it's necessary to lay down some guidelines.'

Andy hesitated before replying. He chose his words carefully. 'I am considering tendering my resignation.'

'What's the point of that? You're a good officer. You shouldn't let one failure of judgement affect your whole career.'

'I don't regard it as a failure of judgement,' retorted Andy, tight-lipped.

'On occasions intellectual humility can be a virtue.'

'Not when it is inappropriate.' Andy and Patterson stared at each other. Neither looked away.

'This interview is over,' said Patterson finally.

'No sir,' responded Andy firmly. 'I am owed approximately two weeks of holiday. I would like to take advantage of it.'

'I think that's a good idea. I think you need a break.'

'Yes, it's very convenient for you to interpret it like that. You can write that in the operation report. That explains everything very nicely. Except of course, it isn't the truth.' Andy turned on his heel and left the room.

# 5

Edward dropped the tea chests down the fore hatch of the boat. He lit the stove, and then looked for the crowbar and some tin snips in the tool box. The chests were too unwieldy to transport and he wanted to re-pack the contents in sports bags, despite Samuel's instructions that he shouldn't open them. They would be easier to carry and not so obtrusive.

Anyway, he was curious. It was a long time since he had seen any hash come directly from Turkey or the Lebanon. It would be good quality. It would be too expensive to be commercially viable on the streets, and was probably destined for one dealer who specialised in exotic material at the top end of the market.

He manoeuvred the chests in the confined space of the cabin and prised off the plywood top to reveal the soldered tin box inside. He punched a hole through the tin with the crowbar, inserted the snips and started cutting. He could smell nothing, which meant that the packers had done their job well. At last the hole was big enough for him to put his hands inside and pull out the packages. They were covered in tape so he couldn't see the contents. They were also an unusual shape. Normally the hash came in rectangular or oval blocks, but these weren't hard.

He opened the other box and placed all the packages on the bunks. When it was dark he would sink the chests over the side of the boat. He placed the packages in the sports bags he had bought. Finally he took a knife and carefully cut the tape off the last one.

For a moment it did not register. He thought he had encountered some new type of wrapping material. Then he realised he was looking at traces of a white powder. He cut the bag open. He licked the tip of the knife, unnecessarily, for confirmation. He knew what it was before the bitter taste hit him. The powder didn't sparkle. It was dull and lifeless, like a chalk deposit. It was heroin. He carefully sealed the package. He walked to the end of the cabin, picked up a bottle of whisky and took a slug.

He didn't know what heroin was worth, but guessed that the eighty odd kilos were worth around three million at wholesale prices. They were worth a life sentence without parole or remission. They represented more misery than the ten million at street prices could pay for.

Samuel knew he wasn't prepared to handle hard drugs. They'd often agreed. Samuel would be as shocked as him to discover that someone had done this. He suspected Ginger and Spider. Samuel had told him how they demanded some of the action in return for the airport facility. Well, they were in for a surprise. They were going to have to wait for their delivery, and they might have to wait a long time.

Something gnawed at the back of his mind. A few moments later it became clear. Samuel had refused to postpone the operation even when he knew they were under surveillance. Edward cursed; he should have guessed there was something different about this deal. Samuel had been almost insistent that he should not open the boxes. That meant he knew what was inside them. Samuel was involved after all, and that changed everything.

Edward began packing the heroin into the chain locker in the fore peak. It was out of sight, but not out of mind.

# *Chapter 11*

## 1

It was nine o'clock and Andy Ballot lay stretched on the sofa in his sitting room. He had given up thinking about what had gone wrong during the day. From time to time he picked up a thought, had another swig of vodka, and turned over the scratched Neil Young record on the ageing deck. Good luck Vince, he thought. There had barely been a murmur of sympathy from him when Andy had cleared up his desk and announced he was taking a holiday. He imagined Vince nailing up the 'No Smoking' signs, and trying out the desk for size. There'd be speculation running through the department that he'd been fired. But tough luck, chaps. Vince might have been after his job for some time, but Simon Patterson wouldn't want to get caught in an unfair dismissal case.

So long as he didn't move there was little sensation that he had drunk too much. It was movement which made him feel unsteady. He fumbled with the lid and finally screwed it back on the vodka bottle. Of course, he wasn't going on holiday. He wasn't going to Benidorm for a couple of weeks, in the hope of some cheap holiday romance. No way. He was back on the case at nine in the morning, and this time he was running freelance. This time he was making his own rules.

'Tough luck Vince. I'm not retiring yet,' he said, and laughed. Retire? What would he do with the rest of his life? Get a job with some security firm? Do a little private investigation? He'd leave that to the likes of Davidson. Perhaps he'd hire himself out as a consultant to the criminals. His advice had to be worth a tidy sum. You could never be too sure what you'd end up doing these days.

His thoughts were interrupted by the ring of the doorbell. He looked at his watch. It was almost ten. 'Who the fuck was ringing his doorbell at this time of the night?' He stood up, staggered to the door and opened it.

'Hello,' said Annelies. She smiled and walked in. 'I thought maybe I would come and see your flat tonight.' Christ, she thought, the place looked like a bomb had hit it. She wished she hadn't considered accepting his offer of accommodation. He'd be offended if she backed out of renting the room now.

'It's a bit of a mess,' said Andy, defensively. 'I wasn't expecting you, otherwise I'd have made an effort to clear up.' He looked around the flat seeing it through her eyes. Why had he invited her to stay? It would take more than a couple of hours to sort out the place. He'd ignored it for the past five years. He'd have to call in one of those agencies which specialised in cleaning houses.

'I wouldn't look in there,' he said, as she opened a door. 'That's my bedroom.' Annelies looked all the same.

'You need some help to clean this place,' said Annelies.

'I guess so.' Andy opened the door to the spare bedroom. He hadn't looked in there for some time. 'I thought you could use this room.'

Annelies walked in and looked around. It was reasonable. It had more potential than Andy's bedroom. It had a window which looked out on to the street. It had character in the form of a small cast-iron fireplace, which was more than could be said for the hotel. She'd have to do something about the carpet; she wasn't going to put her bare feet on that. At least the hotel was clean.

'What do you think?' asked Andy.

Annelies knew that the room itself was not the real issue. She liked Andy and she knew that life in the Fetter Lane offices would not be the same without him there. She felt that he had been unfairly victimised. She knew about discrimination. She had more in common with him than the other officers. 'So, I take it,' she said.

'Well, let's drink to celebrate,' said Andy. 'What would you like?'

'Do you have white wine?'

'No.'

'What do you have?'

He hesitated, then grinned. 'Vodka. Vodka or vodka. It's the end of the week.'

'OK. So I take vodka.'

Andy opened the freezer and took out a fresh bottle. He caught sight of the empty bottles ranged against the far wall, and cringed. 'I must go to the bottle bank tomorrow,' he said unnecessarily.

'I think you drink too much,' said Annelies. She meant it kindly, not so much a criticism as an observation. He looked up sharply. She'd touched a nerve.

'That's my business,' he said, sharply. He poured the drink. 'I didn't mean to snap,' he said, and passed her the drink. 'Let's go next door.'

'Who lives there?' asked Annelies, surprised.

'No one. I meant, let's go into the sitting room.'

'Oh. Of course,' said Annelies, and laughed at her mistake. She followed him into the sitting room. 'I am sorry about today,' she said. 'I do not think they are fair in how they treat you.'

'I don't want to talk about it,' said Andy. 'It's politics and I'm fed up with them.'

'So what will you do?'

'Take a holiday. Sort this place out.' They lapsed into a brief silence. It might be useful having Annelies to stay. He'd get to know if there were any developments back at the office.

'You know you have some mice here,' said Annelies unexpectedly.

'No. I don't,' said Andy irritably. 'I got rid of them.' That was a couple of years ago, he remembered.

'I can hear them.'

'Well, I can't!'

'They are here,' said Annelies leaning over the edge of the chair and tapping the skirting.

'I've never heard them,' said Andy firmly.

'Women have better hearing than men.'

'I didn't know that.'

Annelies shrugged. 'All the companies who are making stereo equipment have women for testing.'

'Have the mice changed your mind about moving in?'

'No. But maybe you should find a cat.'

'No thanks.' Andy gave a quick smile. 'So, when do you want to move?'

'Maybe tomorrow. Or the day following.'

'Fine by me.'

There was an awkward silence. Annelies broke it. 'Maybe you should not give up this operation so easily.'

'Maybe I'm not going to,' said Andy after a long pause. He looked at Annelies to see if she understood.

'Good,' she said, and smiled.

He stood up and produced a pair of keys from a drawer and gave them to her. 'The one with the green tape is the outside door.'

'Thank you.' She put them in her bag. 'I shall give you some money.'

'Forget it,' said Andy. 'Another drink?'

'No. I must go back to the hotel.' She stood up. 'Until tomorrow.'

At the door she kissed him three times on alternate cheeks. He looked baffled. 'It is a Dutch custom with friends. When you greet them and when you say goodbye.'

'Why three times?' he asked.

'I don't know.' She laughed.

Andy closed the door behind her. He swayed back to the kitchen and poured another vodka to celebrate. He had a lodger, and it looked like she was on his side.

2

Tate expected to be marginally less bored at the dinner party than if he were dining alone at some restaurant. He was killing time. His host was an account executive in advertising and his hostess a television presenter; from time to time she donned an apron with the legend, 'Never trust a skinny cook.' There were eight guests: a Belgian diplomat and his wife; a couple from Hereford who kept rare sheep, whom Tate carefully avoided; a frumpy girl who worked in an estate agency, who had been inappropriately invited for his benefit. Henry was the most interesting person present although his American wife cast doubts on that epithet. He was the executive director of a tobacco company.

Henry proved himself to be a social liability over cocktails by arguing freedom for smokers in a room full of non-smokers. He denied that passive smoking contributed to cancer. Tate found the gaffe in such earnest company almost memorable. Unfortunately Henry was not impervious to the hostility of his fellow guests. He gulped his drink and plied nervously for conversation. He was shunned.

At the dining table Tate found himself seated between the frumpy estate agent and Henry. He quietly and politely informed the estate agent that he had moved out of property, and she wilted predictably in the direction of the sheep farmer. Henry seized upon a moment's silence to recapture lost ground. 'My company has just registered the names of the best known cannabis products.' Tate inadvertently coughed soup into his nasal passages and brought the napkin to his mouth. He dreaded this subject. 'Our experts predict legalisation within the next decade. We want to be ready with brands like Acapulco Gold, Durban Poison, Lebanese Red and Tibetan Temple Balls.' Henry delivered an expectant smile.

There was a stunned silence at the table. 'Do you mean to say that your company condones the legalisation of drugs?' asked the sheep farmer.

'We are merely considering the position should the law change, as it did with prohibition in America,' said Henry.

'Well, I think it's disgusting,' said the estate agent.

'The head of Interpol has suggested that drugs should be legalised,' said Henry, defending his position.

'His statement was made for quite different reasons. He believes that the war against drugs is lost,' stated the Belgian diplomat.

There was a murmur of agreement, followed by a silence. The ensuing conversation omitted Henry.

Tate bided his time. The opportunity was too good to miss. He turned to Henry and said, 'You know, I'm inclined to agree with you. I think drugs will be made legal.'

Henry turned to Tate with alacrity. He hadn't expected support from any quarter. 'I don't condone it, you understand,' Henry said. 'But the company has to plan for the future.'

'Quite,' agreed Tate. He wondered how he was going to put his suggestion. 'Apart from registering those names, have you taken any further action?'

'We've done some research. We've turned up some of the medicinal advantages of cannabis. For instance, it provides positive relief for multiple sclerosis sufferers. It's reputed to cure glaucoma.'

Tate could barely contain his enthusiasm. This would be a glorious stroke to play. There were millions to be made here. 'A funny thing happened to me a couple of years ago. I did a property deal for a Lebanese businessman. It became obvious that he derived his wealth from farming this cannabis. The thing is, he's politically very important and his farms are protected. It strikes me that you might find it beneficial to speak to him. You could get together on research.'

'Now that is very interesting,' said Henry. 'You see, we can square it with the governments to allow us to embark on a research programme.'

A sudden bleeping noise silenced the table. For a second Tate thought it came from the kitchen, then realised it was the radio pager he carried. 'Excuse me,' he apologised. Shocked faces turned towards him. He turned off the pager. 'I'm expecting a very important call.' Sod Edward! He looked at the number he had to dial in five minutes. How bloody embarrassing. 'I'm frightfully sorry, but I wonder if I could use your telephone to make a quick call.'

'Certainly,' said his host, stonily. 'You'll find the telephone in the hall.'

Tate turned to Henry. 'We'll finish that conversation in a minute.' He stood up and left the room, gently closing the door behind him.

He wondered what Edward wanted. They had an arrangement to

speak the following day. Why had Edward contacted him? He didn't like changes of plan. He hoped nothing had gone wrong. He picked up the receiver. It was a rare pleasure to make a business call from a safe house. He dialled the number and listened to what Edward had to say. It was not good news. The idiot had done precisely what he had been ordered not to do. He had opened the boxes.

'Why don't we discuss it tomorrow? You pass it on as arranged, then it won't be an issue any more,' said Tate quietly.

'No. I'm having nothing to do with it,' said Edward.

'I wouldn't recommend you adopt that attitude. You could jeopardise our arrangement.'

'Fuck your recommendations. Fuck your arrangements. You've stepped out of line.'

'What do you mean? Me? It's nothing to do with me. This is as big a shock for me as it is for you. I had no idea what was going on. De Groote and Ginger must have made a private arrangement.'

'Don't talk crap, Samuel.'

'I'd rather you didn't use my name,' said Tate controlling his anger and his voice.

'You knew it was heroin.'

'Don't use that word.'

'You deliberately told me not to unpack the boxes.'

'I think we should talk about that in the morning.' He wondered if he could be heard in the next room.

'You're joking. I'm not discussing it. Not now, and not in the morning. When I finish the marketing, my part of the deal will be over. Then I'll be in touch. I'll let you know where the material is hidden and you can pick it up.'

'I really wouldn't recommend that. You don't mess around with these guys. They don't listen to reason like you or me,' Tate whispered furiously.

'You should have thought about that before. I've told you what I'm going to do, and that's final. You'll be hearing from me,' said Edward.

'I think we should meet. Things will get really nasty if that attitude persists.' There was the hint of menace in Tate's voice.

'Things are already nasty. Goodbye.' Edward put down the receiver.

Tate stared at the telephone. Bad news. Tomorrow two million was being paid to Oliver. It would be wired to Switzerland immediately, minus expenses already incurred, which included two hundred and fifty grand for the airport facility, and the same again as an advance for Ginger. The buyer would not be amused to hear that it would be a week before he could have his goods. It was a bit embarrassing. It was going to be more than embarrassing.

The trouble with the white powder trade was that the money had to be paid in advance. The buggers couldn't be trusted once they'd got their noses or their needles into the gear. Really it was the buyer's fault. If the money had been ready in the afternoon then Edward would have made the delivery and been none the wiser about the contents. It was the warehousing which was the problem. Warehousing was always the problem. Unfortunately the buyer wasn't going to see it that way. Nevertheless, Edward was overdoing the moral angle, and he ought not to have talked about it over the phone.

Tate pondered the problem as he returned to dinner. He realised there was an answer. He would let Ginger and Spider off the leash and they'd find Edward soon enough.

Tate sat down at the dining table again, harbouring a contrite smile. 'I'm terribly sorry,' he said. 'It's to do with a very complicated deal in America. My lawyer needed to talk to me.'

He finished his cold soup quickly. 'Absolutely delicious,' he said to the hostess. He turned his attention to Henry once again.

# 3

Andy wouldn't have been surprised if Edward Jay had come to Julia's door in answer to the bell. He wouldn't put it past Jay to have returned home having accomplished what he set out to do when he evaded the surveillance teams. However, it was Julia who faced him, and when she saw who it was her face betrayed her fears.

'Hello, Julia,' said Andy.

'What's happened?' she asked, alarmed.

'I need to speak to you,' said Andy. She stood aside to let him through the door.

For Julia, events seemed to be repeating themselves. Andy's appearance made her aware that she could not control her feelings for Edward. She was more frightened than ever that something had happened to him.

Andy remembered the sitting room. Things hadn't changed since he'd been there over six months before. There was a Georgian table in the bay window; the three-piece Chesterfield with velvet upholstery; the discreet woollen fitted carpet; and the two Persian rugs. They were the kind of expensive but tasteful items dirty money could buy. Most people worked for years so they could afford to decorate a room like this. He wondered if Edward gave her an allowance.

But Julia had changed. She was now heavily pregnant. Her face seemed softer than before, and the concern at his sudden appearance was undisguised. The sneaking admiration he once felt towards Jay turned to anger. An anger, because he was proving himself to be so unworthy of Julia. An anger, because he was responsible for the failure of Operation Juniper. Andy determined not to let it show.

'What is it?' asked Julia. She had sat down on the sofa.

'It's about Edward,' began Andy, somewhat unnecessarily. He was hardly there to discuss his non-existent relationship with her. He hadn't rehearsed what he was going to say. 'Do you know where he is?'

'No,' said Julia, shaking her head. 'We've separated. Things haven't been going too well between us.'

'I'm sorry to hear that,' said Andy, sympathetically. 'You were so hopeful when I last spoke to you.'

'Yes, I was,' said Julia, simply.

'Have you any idea where he might be?' asked Andy.

'No. I asked him where he was going when he left. I don't think he knew himself.'

'I need to talk to him,' explained Andy. Julia said nothing. 'You see,' continued Andy, 'I think he's involved in something illegal with Samuel Tate.'

Julia looked at him. 'No,' she said. 'No, I don't think he is. He wouldn't do anything like that, especially after what happened to him,' she ''ed, defending Edward. She didn't blink or look away. Her stare was almost a challenge.

Andy admired her for defending Jay. 'Well, I'm worried about him. I had him under surveillance, but he's gone missing.' Julia reacted to this news, looking quickly away to a corner of the room. She realised he knew she was lying. 'Normally his disappearance would give us no cause for alarm. We'd assume that he was up to something he didn't want us to know about. But this time things are different. This time the game is different. One of Samuel Tate's partners in Holland, a man called de Groote, has been killed. I should say, murdered. Shortly afterwards his girlfriend was killed because she was able to identify the killer. Samuel Tate is implicated.'

'Edward wouldn't be involved in anything like that,' said Julia hastily.

'Oh no,' said Andy, 'I don't think he knows anything about it.' He hesitated, to add emphasis to this conclusion. 'I'm worried because something might have happened to him as well.'

Julia's eyes opened wide in horror. 'No,' she exclaimed. 'Why should it?'

'Don't be too alarmed,' cautioned Andy, pleased by her reaction. 'There's no reason to expect the worst. I have to consider all the possibilities. That's why I want to find Edward.' He knew he wasn't playing fair. The poor girl was expecting a baby. But there was no other way of finding out what he wanted to know. 'Are you expecting Edward to call you?' he asked.

'No,' said Julia, then corrected herself. 'Well, yes. I sort of expected him to call to collect some of his things. I think he'll call anyway. He didn't believe the relationship was irrevocable. I did, at the time. We've still got a lot to sort out.'

'Good,' said Andy. 'If he calls you, tell him he must speak to me. He won't want to. Tell him he's got nothing to lose. Tell him to call me at my home, so he knows it's unofficial.' Andy scribbled on a piece of paper. 'Here,' he said, passing it to Julia. 'Tell him not to call the office. If he refuses to call me, try to arrange a meeting with him and I'll be there. Trust me. I'm not acting in an official capacity.'

Julia nodded, though she looked a little dubious. 'All right. But you will tell me if you find out anything?'

'Of course,' said Andy. He stood up. By the way, you don't happen to know where Samuel Tate is living, do you?'

'No,' said Julia. 'But if I did, I'd tell you. I hate that bastard.'

The vehemence in her voice told him she wasn't lying. 'I'm so sorry that you're caught in the middle of all this,' he said.

'I'm not involved,' she said. 'I just had the misfortune to fall in love with Edward. Sometimes you don't get a choice.'

'It can't be easy for you at the moment. When is the baby due?'

'In four weeks.'

'Do you know if it's a girl or boy?'

'I don't want to know. It takes all the fun out of it.'

'It makes things a lot cheaper, so I'm told.'

'Money isn't everything,' replied Julia.

Andy smiled. 'No, it isn't,' he agreed. He opened the door to let himself out. 'Don't forget, if you hear from Edward you must call me.'

Julia nodded. She looked worried. 'Thank you,' she said, as she closed the door, leaving Andy feeling guilty for a moment.

The guilt didn't last long. It was replaced by elation that he had painted such a clever picture. When Julia told Edward what had happened to de Groote, it would be news to him; if it wasn't, then he was in the deep end with Tate.

And now, as always, it was a waiting game.

# 4

Edward woke in the damp air of the boat. He could see the fog swirling through the portholes. It was so thick it obliterated the trees on the bank. It emphasised his sense of isolation. He lay staring at the grey outside and looked back over his life. His life had always been like this, waiting for something to happen, waiting for someone to come into a room. And he was always alone. Even with Julia there was the loneliness, because he couldn't share the worry and decisions. Not that there was anything worth sharing, except for what the money could buy afterwards. Then there was never a shortage of people with whom to share the cash. There were always good-time girls ready to go out on the town, alive on a line of coke, who gave the brief illusion that he was a part of society. There had been plenty of them before Julia; and they had left him empty and alone.

He would phone Julia. He'd made a terrible mistake. She'd known what he couldn't see until now; that he was being used by people whom he trusted. He needed Julia. He loved her. She was the only solid thing in his life. She was his home. It was not as if things had been easy for her, but she fought for the small successes in her life. She never accepted refusal. It was the antithesis of his own life. Julia had a theme. Her life led somewhere. It led to a future.

Over the years he'd forgotten what scams he'd been involved in. He'd forgotten what had gone down. He'd forgotten the names and faces of people he'd worked with. He'd run from one thing to another. He'd been on an express train all his life, watching the scenery thundering past, going from one scam to the next. He never thought the train would stop. This time it had and he was stepping off.

He dressed quickly, skipped coffee and left the boat. He made his way down the towpath in the thick fog. He could feel the sunshine trying to burn through. Time seemed to be moving slowly and he wondered if he would catch Julia before she went out. When he reached the phone he realised he couldn't use it. Any trace to the number would lead customs directly into the vicinity of the boat. He trudged back to the car and drove for half an hour until he was in Blackheath.

'Julia,' he said, grateful to hear her voice. 'I need to see you.'

'I'm glad you phoned. I've got something to tell you. Are you coming round?'

He wished he could, but he couldn't take that risk. 'No. It's a bit difficult, but I want to see you.'

'Are you all right?'

'Yes. Could we meet somewhere?'

'Where?'

Edward thought for a moment. It had to be somewhere he could see if she was being followed. Then he wondered why he was being paranoid. He had nothing to fear from customs. They had nothing on him, so long as they didn't know about the boat. 'How about that place we had tea on your birthday?' Surveillance would stick out like a sore thumb there.

'OK.'

'Don't tell anyone where you're going,' he said unnecessarily.

'I won't. What time?'

'When can you be there?'

'Forty-five minutes.'

'OK. I'm looking forward to seeing you,' he said.

'Be careful, Edward,' she said, and put down the phone.

Edward was surprised that Julia was expressing concern for him. It was the first time he could remember her having done so. She had studiously ignored his activities in the past. He was disappointed she hadn't said she was looking forward to seeing him too. Suddenly he was curious to know what it was she had to tell him.

He flipped open the telephone directory and looked for the address of his car hire company. He found an office on the route. It was time to dump the car; he'd had it long enough and if customs checked his credit card transactions they would know he was driving it.

Julia was already waiting for him at the Ritz when he arrived. She was sitting in a corner at the rear of the room. It was the most private of the tables and he wondered if she chose it on purpose.

'I'm glad you called me, Edward,' she said. 'I had a visit from that customs officer, Andy Ballot, this morning.' Edward looked at her, surprised. He hadn't expected that. 'He says he wants to speak to you. He thinks you are in danger. He says that a man called de Groote was murdered. Do you know him?'

'I've met him a few times.'

'He says Samuel was involved.' Edward sighed. 'Do you know anything about it?' When Edward didn't answer, she asked. 'You're not involved, are you?'

169

This time Edward answered. 'No. But I think I know more than I want. And I wish I didn't. I think you were right about Samuel all along. I wish I'd listened to you. But, he did get me out of Pakistan. I was blinded by that.'

'Why do you think he might have had something to do with de Groote?'

'I can't tell you. I don't want you to get involved. If you know, then you're involved.'

'Why don't you speak to Andy Ballot?' Edward shook his head. 'He'll help you. I know he will. He's not acting in an official capacity, at least that's what he said.'

'There are unwritten rules in this game.'

'Even if Samuel breaks them?' asked Julia astutely. Edward didn't answer.

'It's not my business. You don't ask questions about other people's scams,' he said after a moment. 'It makes me very sad to think it's come to this. Samuel always wanted to be rich. It was something to do with his father. When I first met him he wanted to be a millionaire by the time he was thirty. He worked out the quickest way of getting there. He was cunning, inventive, diplomatic and charming. He could have gone into the Foreign Office. He could have done anything he wanted. The fact that he went into crime didn't change anything. He was determined to succeed at the expense of anyone who stood in his way. I thought I was an exception because I was a friend.'

'I never had any such illusions,' said Julia.

'I know you didn't. I used to think we were on some kind of crusade. It was fun. Twenty years ago it seemed inevitable that dope would be legalised. Sure we were breaking the law, but we didn't harm anyone. When we were ripped off a couple of times we let it go. We made sure the word got around and the guys never worked again. We didn't break legs or anything like that. I always thought we'd retire one day. We'd open a bar in Spain or something. Samuel never committed himself in those conversations. He's never acknowledged any responsibility to me or anyone else. If he had anything to do with de Groote's death then he's not a criminal. He's a psychopath. I hope to God he wasn't involved with de Groote's death. I find it hard to believe.'

'I don't want anything to happen to you, Edward,' said Julia. She put her hand on his.

'It won't. I promise. You know, when I came back from Pakistan I was so happy. I thought that for once everything was going to work out. I was going to retire. I was looking forward to having the baby. I used to have these funny ideas of being a grandfather, maybe with not so much money. I imagined saying to our grandchildren when we were collecting our meagre pensions, "It wasn't always like this, you know. There was a time

I once drove to Liechtenstein with a million pounds in the boot of the car."
They'd run and tell you I'd told another lie.'

'It could still be like that,' said Julia.

'Do you think so?'

'Maybe we can make things work out, Edward. I don't want to lose
you, but I can't go on like this. I love you, but I'm frightened.'

'Did you ever believe it was all over?'

'Yes. I couldn't see any more options. I couldn't go on like that.'

'Heartbroken?' asked Edward with a smile.

'I wouldn't go that far. You can't be heartbroken when things haven't
been going well for some time. When you feel betrayed and neglected,
you feel bad, but not heartbroken. You'd be a fool to have let it get that
far.' They sat in silence for a moment. 'I was sad though. I was frightened
that I was losing a friend. My best friend. We've shared a lot. And you?
How did you feel?'

'I couldn't believe it was going to happen.' Edward shook his head.

'And I suppose you were right, but for the wrong reasons.'

'Something always happens. That's the only thing I've found out in life.
I guess I'm lucky.'

'What are you going to do now?'

'I'm going to speak to Samuel. I want to know what happened to de
Groote. I have to know the truth. It affects what I do.'

Julia looked in her bag and pulled out a piece of paper and gave it to him.
'This is Andy Ballot's phone number. I think you should call him.'

'Maybe,' said Edward. He looked at the number, memorised it and
passed it back.

'When will it be over?'

'In a couple of days. We'll go away, if you want. Before we do that we'll
clinch the deal on the farmhouse.'

'Maybe,' said Julia. 'We'll see,' she said and smiled for the first time.

They lapsed into silence. A couple of American tourists arrived in the
lounge. They were wearing designer-labelled track suits and trainers.
They eyed the empty tables greedily. The head waiter glanced warily at
their footwear, and asked if they had booked a table. They shook their
heads, and he courteously but firmly showed them the door.

'Thank God for that,' said Edward.

'Are you turning into a snob?' asked Julia.

'Not at all. You might expect the Ritz to lend a you tie, but not to
provide a suit because you're not dressed.'

'I have to go,' said Julia. 'I have an appointment. Will you call me
tonight?'

'Yes.'

Julia stood up. 'Kiss?' she asked.

'Yes please,' said Edward. She kissed him.
'Be careful.'
Edward smiled, and watched her go. He lifted his hand for the bill.

# 5

Ginger was furious. He'd paged Tate for the past twenty-four hours, leaving numbers where he would be waiting for the return call. He'd done nothing but wait around street corners for the phone to ring. Next time they worked together Tate was going to have a mobile phone or there wouldn't be any deal. He wondered if Tate was ripping him off. Something was wrong. He had a quarter of a million in hard cash tied up in this deal, and no collateral security. He paced backwards and forwards in front of the telephones at Marylebone Station. He was a couple of minutes early.

The first payment was already late. He had problems with the baggage handlers. Spider had promised to pay them their whack within forty-eight hours.

Spider had problems. He wasn't concentrating on the business any more. They'd been talking about Tate, when Spider suddenly said, 'You know what my mum called freckles?'

'No,' said Ginger, baffled.

'Angel kisses,' said Spider.

'What's that got to do with Tate?' asked Ginger.

'See,' said Spider, turning to him. 'I've got freckles.' Then he stopped talking. Ginger wondered if Spider was hitting the bottle. He'd never mentioned his mum before.

Ginger suddenly spotted a man about to use one of the phones he was expecting to ring.

'Oi! You. Get off that phone. I'm waiting for a call.' The man ignored him. Ginger removed the receiver from his hand and replaced it on the hook. 'Get lost,' he said, 'I told you. I'm waiting for a call.' He looked ugly, and removed his sunglasses for emphasis.

The man shuffled away as the phone rang. Ginger glared at him, nodded righteously, and snatched at the receiver.

'Hello. Hello,' he shouted.

'Ah. There you are, Ginger. I've been trying to get hold of you.' He heard Tate's irritatingly patrician voice. It cut no ice with him.

'Yes? Well, you haven't tried too hard. Where's the fucking money?'

'That's what I wanted to talk to you about.' There was a pause. The line hummed.

'I'm listening.' Ginger looked grim.

'There's been a hold-up.'

'What kind of hold-up?' shouted Ginger, imagining men with guns making off with his money. His worst dreams were coming true. He should never have got involved with fucking yuppies.

'Relax Ginger. I'm sorting it out.'

'Don't you tell me to relax! I want the fucking money. I done my bit. You think I do this for fun? I'm not running some bleeding charity. I want my dosh, and I want it in twenty-four hours or I come looking for you. You know what I mean, don't you? You'll need more than a private fucking doctor!'

'We've got a problem.'

'What do you mean "we"? You have the problem!'

'Ernie decided he doesn't want to handle our consignment.'

'What?' Ginger was baffled. 'What do you mean handle? What's the fucking problem.'

'He's got some moral scruples. I must admit it caught me by surprise. I think he'll return the goods when he's finished marketing the other stuff.'

'You think?' said Ginger. 'You fucking think?' he repeated in amazement. Tate was out of his mind. Five million quid's worth of gear and he was only thinking. 'It's not a matter of thinking. The bastard isn't paid to think. You give me that cunt's address. I'll sort it out.'

'It's not that easy. He's disappeared. His girlfriend says he's moved out.'

'Give me the address all the same. I'll find him.'

'I don't know if he'd like that.'

'I don't give a fuck what he'd like.'

'Are you sure you want to deal with it? You could leave it to me.' Tate felt his conscience was clear. He would always be able to say he had tried to persuade Ginger to be patient.

'I did leave it to you, and look what fucking happened,' snarled Ginger. 'Give me his address.' Ginger groped in his pocket for a pen. 'Hang on,' he said.

'Oi!' Ginger accosted a girl walking past. 'Got a pen you could lend us, love?' The girl scrabbled in her handbag and handed him a biro. He scribbled Edward's address on a corner of his newspaper. He returned the pen, and smiled his thanks.

'What's Ernie's real name?' he asked.

'Edward.'

'Surname?'

'Jay.'

'What about his girl?'

'Julia.'

'Right,' said Ginger. 'Now get yourself a mobile phone. I want to stay in touch with you. Until then you keep calling me on my mobile. No more of this hanging about on street corners. Maybe I'll have some news for you. Got that?'

'Yes,' said Tate.

'Good.' Ginger replaced the receiver.

'You better pray I get some good news, Sammy,' he menaced under his breath. He walked back to the BMW where Spider was guarding it from the traffic wardens. He hoped Spider would snap out of his mood soon. All he did was stare, and get irritable if he was disturbed; that lazy eye of his would start jerking up and down like it was in spasm. Right now, though, they had work to do.

# Chapter 12

## 1

Julia heard the doorbell ring twice. Impatiently. She did not recognise the man when she opened the door. He was wearing an expensive black leather jacket and he had a scar on his left cheek which made his lip curl. 'Your name, Julia?' he asked, abruptly.

'Yes,' Julia answered.

'Have you had a call from Edward Jay?'

'No,' said Julia, about to add that she had seen him earlier, but then thought better of it. 'Who are you?' she asked.

'Friends of his. He said he was going to call you,' said the man irritably. 'He wants to see you. It's urgent, like. Said I was to pick you up and take you to him.'

Julia wondered what had happened. Edward had never asked her to do anything before. She guessed he needed her help; that was obvious. 'I'll just get my bag,' she said, and went back into the flat.

The man followed her.

She wondered if she should call Andy Ballot. She could give him a cryptic message which he would understand. 'I'm going to make a quick telephone call,' she said.

'No phone calls,' said the man, bluntly.

Julia looked at him, querulously. It sounded as if he was giving orders. 'I want to tell someone where I am going.'

'No,' said the man. 'We don't want no phone calls.'

'Where are we going?' asked Julia.

'You'll find out,' said the man. 'Now, let's go. We don't have time to mess about.'

175

'What's happened? Why does Edward want to see me?' asked Julia. She was unsure. Something was not right. She didn't like being hurried. Edward would have provided some explanation.

The man took a step towards her and took a gun out of his jacket pocket. He grabbed hold of her wrist. 'We could have done this the easy way. But I don't have time.'

He pulled her towards the window and looked out. He appeared satisfied by what he saw.

Julia was confused. She wondered why Edward was involved with someone like this. She felt nauseous.

'Come on,' said the man. He grabbed her bag and thrust it at her. 'We're going. I don't want no trouble from you on the street.' He still held her wrist firmly.

'No,' said Julia. 'I'm not going with you.'

The man stared at her. 'No?' he asked.

They stared at each other. The man slipped the gun into his pocket. He took his hand out, smiled, and slapped her sharply on the side of the head. Her head rocked back.

Julia stopped struggling. She was stunned. She realised resistance was foolish. She was too cumbersome to fight and she had to protect her baby. She stared at the man who pulled her towards the door. She followed him, concentrating on controlling her anxiety. Her baby would hear the quickening of her heartbeat, and she didn't want it to feel her fear.

She followed the man out of the flat and on to the street. She wished he would release her wrist from his grip. She looked down the street. The pedestrians were all too far away and the cars were travelling too fast to take any notice of what was happening. She wanted to put up a struggle, but it was pointless; people would think it a domestic argument. 'Don't even think about it,' said the man, stopping suddenly, and jerking her wrist. He opened the back doors of a van and twisted her around before pushing her. She landed heavily on the van. 'Get in,' he said.

She looked into the van. There was another man inside, sitting on an old mattress. She stared at him for a second. He didn't seem to be looking at her. He didn't react as she clambered in and sat as far from him as possible. She sat with her legs straight out ahead and her back against the panel sides of the van. The back doors closed and she heard them being locked. A moment later her abductor was in the driving seat and had started the engine. She looked at the man opposite again. He was looking at her legs.

'Shut your eyes,' said the driver. 'Make sure she don't look, Spider.'

Spider said nothing. He slowly looked up from her legs and stared at her. She thought he had a squint. He looked at her. She shut her eyes. She felt his eyes staring into her legs. She wished the driver had not mentioned Spider's name.

# 2

Tate switched off his radio pager for the night. He wasn't interested in negotiating with Edward. He was waiting to find out if Ginger had any success with Julia.

He phoned Ginger's mobile telephone in the morning from the Royal Court Hotel in Sloane Square where he had enjoyed breakfast. He wasn't going to hire a mobile phone despite Ginger's demands; they might be hard to tap, but the numbers were all recorded, and that was good enough to prove conspiracy. It was all the police had once needed to lock up a couple of Irish terrorists talking to each other down the motorway.

Tate was disappointed to hear that Julia hadn't told Ginger where Edward was hiding; but managed to calm him with some difficulty. Those guys had to learn the virtue of patience.

He wondered, with a morbid curiosity, how Edward would respond to the news that Ginger was holding Julia. He switched on the pager and waited for Edward's signal.

Tate began to have doubts about Ginger. He might turn into a liability. He would have to consider dumping him, and that would mean calling in some professional favours from the States. Twenty thousand pounds, and Ginger would be history. The man would fly in on Concorde, and fly out the next day. Ginger wouldn't know what hit him. It was worth considering. It might become necessary if he put Akbar in touch with Henry and his tobacco company, and they subsequently decided to collaborate. Tate didn't want people like Ginger in the background.

He should have put Akbar in touch with the American hitman in the first place. He hadn't, because Ginger offered the simplest solution; and anyway, negotiations with the American would have meant more phone calls and increased exposure to risk. As a result Akbar bought a messy hit and a few loose ends.

The pager sounded. It was Edward. Tate made his way to the

telephone. He was surprised to find Edward on the offensive. 'I've heard de Groote was killed.'

'What?' said Tate. He wondered how Edward had found out. He quickly feigned surprise. 'When did it happen? Who told you?'

'I'm surprised you don't know. You told me de Groote and Ginger hatched this heroin switch together. But they couldn't. Could they? Because de Groote's dead.'

'When was de Groote killed? Was it an accident?' Tate tried to buy time.

'You must have known about it, Samuel. I've phoned some friends of mine in Holland. They told me de Groote's luck was running out. They say he was rowed out of the deal with you before he was killed. You told me he was still involved to cover yourself. You're lying. You knew he was dead.'

'It's more complicated than that. We can't talk over the phone. Ginger's pulling stokes on me.'

'Were you involved in de Groote's murder?'

'For Christ's sake, Edward! No! I didn't know anything about it. You know that's not my style.'

'How can I trust you?'

'You have to trust me. We're in this together now. Ginger's fucked me up and now he's fucking you up. I warned you he was ruthless. I said you couldn't play games with these guys.'

'What do you mean?' asked Edward.

'He's got Julia.'

Tate was gratified by a stunned silence over the line. 'Jesus! Samuel! What's going on?' shouted Edward. 'What the fuck are you playing at?' His legs started shaking. His heart began pounding. He felt sick.

'Not me, Edward. Ginger! He was like a pit bull terrier. I couldn't control him. He went round to your place and couldn't find you. He took Julia as security.'

'What do you mean?'

'He's kidnapped her. That's what I mean. He's holding her to ransom until you give back the consignment.'

'You gave him my address?' asked Edward, incredulously.

'Of course not.' Tate thought of an answer quickly. 'He got it off that policeman, Davidson. Look, he's accusing me of ripping off the gear. He's an animal. We should have expected him to do something like this.' There was silence down the phone line. 'Edward? We should get together.'

'I don't want to see you. I want to see Ginger. Give me his number.'

'I don't know it. I have to wait for him to call me.'

'Don't give me that shit. You know his number. You told me he uses a mobile phone.'

'I don't know the number because I refuse to use it. I'd tell you if I knew it. I'll get in touch with you as soon as I hear from him. Tell me how I can contact you.'

'You can leave a message on Julia's answer phone. I can telephone in for the playback.'

'No. I don't think that's wise. It might be tapped.'

'OK. I'll call you. I'll call you on the pager every fucking hour, all day and night, until you've got hold of that bastard. All right?'

'Well, I hope he calls me before this evening.'

'So do I, Samuel.'

'Couldn't you deliver the material as planned?'

'I want a guarantee that Julia will be released unharmed.'

'If you'd only done your part of the deal this would never have happened.'

'I did my part of the deal. I'm doing the marketing. It was your deal which went wrong,' pointed out Edward angrily.

'No. Your part of the deal was to deliver those two boxes as well. You agreed at the time. Then you changed your mind. If you didn't want to do it you should have told me. I could have found someone else. If only you delivered them we'd never have known what was inside, and we wouldn't be where we are now.'

'That's not how it was. You can't twist it like that. You knew there was heroin in those boxes. You pulled a fast one over me,' retorted Edward.

'Think what you like. It's too late to start squabbling now. You have made things very awkward,' complained Tate.

'I'll speak to you in an hour.' Tate held the receiver away from his ear. Edward had hung up on him. He shrugged. He was in the driving seat.

Edward slammed down the phone and dialled Julia's number. There was always a chance Samuel was bluffing. He let the phone ring a long time before replacing the receiver. He wished he knew where Samuel was hiding out. He'd go round there and rip the bastard's balls off. He wondered if he should arrange to meet Samuel after all.

Edward knew it was over. This was the end. Julia would never forgive him. All his efforts to protect her from his activities had failed. He had no excuses to offer her. His only hope was that time would heal some of the betrayal. Every time he thought of the future his stomach turned and he felt sick. A yawning chasm of empty hours and days spread out in front of him. He'd come so close to piecing together his life with her, and now it had been destroyed. He didn't want to imagine how she felt.

But first, he had to get her out of there. He thought about the conversation with Samuel. It was possible Samuel had been double-crossed by Ginger. Samuel had sounded plausible; but there was only one way to find out if he was involved in de Groote's murder. He looked up Andy Ballot in the phone directory. He matched the phone number Julia had given him to the various listings until he had an address. If Samuel had lied to him then he was going to pay for it.

# 3

Julia cursed herself for opening the door without looking to see who it was. She hadn't expected anything like this, especially not in daylight. The journey in the back of the van was ghastly. After a short while she felt sick, and opened her eyes to try and control the sensation.

Spider stretched out his foot and kicked her on the shin, and pointed at her eyes. She shook her head, trying to force down the bile which formed in her throat. It was too difficult. She leaned to one side and was sick. She watched the pool of vomit spread along the floor of the van. It ebbed and flooded as the van turned the corners. The mattress soaked up a little. She stared at it for a moment and focused on a piece of tomato. She remembered what she ate for lunch. It seemed a long time ago. She was sick again.

Julia spent the remainder of the journey in a nauseous trance. Between the retches, her head lolled as the van twisted and turned through the London streets. She couldn't summon the interest to sneak a look out of the back windows to try and identify some landmark which might suggest their whereabouts.

She knew they had reached their destination because the van suddenly reversed and stopped. The driver got out and opened the doors.

'Out,' he ordered.

Julia crawled to the doors and gulped at the fresh air. Spider followed her. She was in a courtyard. The buildings which surrounded it were almost derelict. The rendering on the walls was blown. The guttering was shot. The site was ripe for redevelopment. She was pushed towards a door bolted with a huge padlock. The driver opened it. She followed him. Inside the building it was musty and dark. The windows were boarded with plywood shuttering. It was an old snooker hall. She could see three tables shedding tattered green felt in the gloom, before she was ushered up the stairs.

A thin layer of dust covered the surfaces. Their footsteps echoed along the corridor. Here and there floorboards had been prised up, as if a surveyor had been at work, and then abandoned the project as hopeless. She was pushed into a room and a low wattage light was turned on. There was a bed, some grey crumpled blankets which looked stained. On the lino-covered floor lay an old coffee cup and an ashtray with cigarette butts. She guessed this would be her cell. The windows were nailed shut and were boarded from the outside.

'I need to go to the bathroom,' she said weakly. The man with the scar opened a door and she went in. She started to close the door behind her, but Spider put his foot against it.

'No,' he said.

'Don't be stupid,' said Julia, irritated. She wasn't going to have them watch her. 'Do you really think I'm going to jump out? I'm pregnant, if you hadn't noticed.'

'What do you reckon, Ginger?' asked Spider.

'Shut the door, but don't lock it,' said Ginger.

Now she knew both their names.

She closed the door. She looked with disgust at the grimy toilet bowl. She used it quickly. She washed her face with cold water and felt marginally better. She looked at herself in the cracked mirror. She looked pale.

The door was rudely opened. 'All right, we want to ask you some questions,' said Ginger. She returned to the bedroom. She looked at Ginger more carefully, and realised that he dyed his hair. He had sandy-coloured eyebrows and eyelashes. It was an unpleasant combination. She wondered why he bothered with the hair dye.

Christ! If she'd known Edward was working with people like this she'd have ended the relationship a long time ago. He'd been astute to keep all the details in the background, dropping hints now and again, suggesting a nether-world romance to his activities. Well, he'd exploded that myth with the appearance of these two hobgoblins.

'We want to know where Edward Jay is hiding.'

'I don't know,' said Julia. 'I don't know because we are no longer living together. He moved out. If you happen to see him I would be grateful if you would tell him that any thoughts of a reconciliation disappeared when you introduced yourselves as friends of his.'

Spider stepped forward, looked at her, and grabbed a fistful of her hair.
'You don't know who you're talking to, you stuck-up tart.'

Julia didn't react. He tightened his grip on her hair. 'You're making a
terrible mistake,' said Julia. 'I don't know where he is, and if I did know I'd
tell you.'

'We'll see,' said Spider, releasing her hair. Julia's failure to react left
him feeling awkward. He stepped back, looked at her, and pinched her
left breast.

'Nice pair of knockers,' he commented. 'If your boyfriend don't turn up
soon, you and me will be getting to know one another. Intimate like.'

Julia slapped him.

Spider looked ugly. 'You don't want to play rough with me,' he said.
'Not when you're carrying that.' He poked her stomach harshly with a
finger.

'Don't mess her about now,' said Ginger. 'There could be a happy
ending to all this. We got to talk. I think Sammy could have pulled a stroke
on us.'

They left the room. She heard them lock the door. She looked around.
It was cold and she was miserable. She wondered how long this was going
to last. She sat on the bed. No way she was wrapping herself in those
blankets. They could get her some sheets, clean blankets and a book if
she was going to stay for any length of time. She stood up and began
beating on the door. She stopped and listened. She sat back on the bed
and stroked her baby, as if apologising for her tantrum. She heard
footsteps down the corridor.

4

The taxi dropped Edward outside a red brick block of apartments in
Bloomsbury. He found Andy Ballot's name beside one of the doorbells. A
sudden caution stopped him from pressing the bell. He didn't know what
Ballot knew. He couldn't afford to be arrested on suspicion of conspiracy.
It wouldn't help Julia if he were locked up for seventy-two hours. He went
to the telephone at the end of the street.

'Ballot speaking.'

'Mr Ballot, this is Edward Jay. I would like to talk to you.'

'I'm glad you called, Edward. When would you like to meet?'

'Are you free now?'

'Yes,' said Andy.

'Can you meet me in the Palm Court bar at the Waldorf Hotel?'

'I'll be there in fifteen minutes.'

'Good,' said Edward, and replaced the receiver.

Edward looked at the time and watched the front door. He wanted to see how long it took Ballot to leave the building. If he took too long it probably meant he was organising a reception committee at the Waldorf. In the event it only took Andy five minutes before he opened the door, and Edward intercepted him as he set off down the road. 'I changed my mind,' Edward said. 'Let's go for a drink at the Russell Hotel instead.'

Andy grinned. 'You needn't have worried. This is off the record. I gave Julia my word.'

'Good,' said Edward. He wondered whether the customs officer was that naïve. It was absurd to think that he was going to trust Ballot on the basis of a promise made to Julia. Edward wondered if he was talking to the wrong man.

'I want to do a deal,' said Edward.

Andy didn't respond at first. He waited until they'd crossed the road. 'I can't do a deal. Not if you've broken the law. In this country we don't plea bargain. You know that. However, I can probably ensure that you get off.'

'I know that. That's why I'm not telling you everything now. When I'm clear you can have all the details. Times, places and money. I'm sure about one thing. I'm not going to prison again. Right now I need your help.'

'Your position doesn't look strong, particularly if you're asking for my help.'

They reached the hotel, and stopped talking until they were seated in the bar.

'So why have you come to see me?' asked Andy.

'You spoke to Julia yesterday?' said Edward. Andy nodded. 'She's been abducted to apply pressure on me.'

'Samuel Tate?' guessed Andy.

'No. A couple of his partners called Ginger and Spider. I don't know their real names. They're in partnership with Samuel.'

'What do they want from you?'

'I've got something they want.'

'What is it?' asked Andy.

'I can't tell you at the moment.'

183

'Why have you fallen foul of your friends?'

'Let's say it's a question of morality.'

'Morality?' questioned Andy. 'Don't talk to me about morality. You're a drug smuggler. I didn't know you lot had so many scruples.'

Edward stared at Andy. He was definitely talking to the wrong person. However, there wasn't anyone else who could give him the answers. 'I take your point.'

'Why don't you go to the police? Abduction's one of their specialities.'

'I don't trust them and they wouldn't act quickly enough.'

'Why?'

Edward hesitated. He had to make every point score. 'I'm giving you the first piece of information and in return I'm entitled to something.'

Andy shrugged his shoulders. 'That depends.'

'A police officer called Davidson is on Samuel's payroll. I heard this morning that he is also tipping off Ginger.'

Edward watched Andy's reaction with interest. It was obvious the information had hit a nerve somewhere. Andy's face hardened. His lips whitened. A muscle in his cheek twitched as if he were wincing. 'I presume you have proof?'

'I set up the first meeting between Davidson and Tate.'

'What else?' asked Andy suspiciously.

'That comes later,' said Edward.

'No. That comes now,' said Andy, fiercely.

'Later,' said Edward calmly. 'You'll have to trust me. First you have to earn your information.' Andy looked at Edward, and thought what a clever little sod he was. 'You're the one who invited me to come and talk,' continued Edward. 'Or have you changed your mind?'

'No,' said Andy. 'I haven't changed my mind. But I'm going to need much more information than you've given before I help you.'

'Like what?' asked Edward.

'I need to know where Tate lives for a start.'

Edward frowned. 'It strikes me you don't know much at all.'

'I'm not going to tell you what I know, am I? You're going to have to learn to trust me too. Remember this. Without me you don't have a chance of finding Julia. So, let's start talking.'

Edward thought for a moment. Andy was right. He did need him. 'I don't know where Samuel lives.'

'How do you communicate with him?'

'Through a radio pager. I leave my number ten minutes before the hour, and he calls back on the hour.'

'What's the pager number?'

Edward wrote the number on a beer mat and passed it to Andy. 'Julia told me Samuel was involved with de Groote's murder. Is that true?'

'We have a lead which makes him the prime suspect,' Andy lied. It would do no harm to let Edward think the worst. He was going to be a lot more open if he was kept in that frame of mind. 'The Dutch are preparing Commission Rogataire papers.'

'What?' asked Edward, baffled.

'The Dutch are applying for permission to interrogate Tate over there, when we locate him.'

'They think he's involved?' queried Edward.

'They're sure,' emphasised Andy. 'Now, when do you next speak to Tate?'

'He hasn't replied to my last few calls. I want to contact Ginger to make a deal for Julia's release. I told him to arrange a meeting for us.'

'When did you find out that Julia had been abducted?'

'Three hours ago.'

'What have you said to Tate?'

'I told him I'd co-operate.'

'Good,' said Andy. 'I have to make a phone call now. I need someone at the office to run a check on Davidson and Ginger. I want the information as soon as possible.' Edward looked wary. 'You can come and stand next to me and make sure I'm not summoning assistance.'

'That's not really the problem. Samuel has intimated that he has another contact, apart from Davidson, who is well placed to protect him. I don't think it is a good idea to let anyone know you're in touch with me.'

'Are you telling me this person is in the customs service?' asked Andy suspiciously.

'I don't know, but I don't want to take chances.'

Andy reflected for a moment. 'No. I don't buy that. It's not feasible. Davidson, yes.'

'You don't realise what's at stake here. We're talking about three million pounds a month. With that kind of money Samuel can buy anyone. For half a million I could buy you.'

'Let's not get personal,' said Andy, coldly.

'Think about it,' said Edward. 'Go to sleep on it. Five hundred thousand pounds in a Swiss bank account. Are you really that principled?'

Andy said nothing. He dialled the office, and spoke to Annelies. He didn't mention Edward.

When they sat down again, Edward said 'Your phone call didn't make sense to me. You said you were on holiday. How come your assistant has to be so secretive?'

'The investigation was closed. I can't re-open it without a watertight case. I'm having to be somewhat circumspect.' He hesitated. 'I'm curious. Tell me how you managed to give us the slip.'

Edward couldn't resist smiling. 'We knew through Davidson that you had us pegged. It was easy to feed you the wrong information down the telephone taps, and back it up with confirmation through Davidson.'

Andy winced at the mention of Davidson. He would settle Davidson's hash soon enough. 'What would I have found out, if I'd stayed on the case?'

'Ginger and Spider have a team of freight handlers at Heathrow Airport. About once a month they can lift freight off the planes.'

'Do you have a flight number?'

'I'm holding on to that information a little longer.'

Andy decided not to comment. He looked at his watch. Ten minutes to the hour. 'You better make that call to Tate.'

Edward made the call. They waited in silence for Tate to phone back. As the hour approached Andy noticed Edward grew increasingly nervous. He shredded the coasters on the table. Andy caught the barman's disapproving glance. He swept the debris into an ashtray.

'I think Davidson is the quickest way to find out where Tate lives,' suggested Andy. 'If Davidson has done his job properly he should be able to tell us about Ginger. He might even know where Julia's being held.'

'Davidson's not going to volunteer the information. He doesn't know where Samuel is, because I had to arrange the meeting between the two of them. If you approach him, then Ginger and Samuel are going to know. I don't think that's a good idea.'

'It might force them to make a move,' said Andy. 'But I don't want to take chances. I think I'll arrange for Davidson to be taken out of circulation.'

'What do you mean?'

'I'll lock him up for a while. Preferably in isolation.' Edward felt reassured for the first time during their conversation. Andy was proposing action.

'Do you mind if we move on?' asked Edward. 'I don't like hanging around after giving my number. Davidson might be able to run a trace on it. I don't want Samuel to come looking for me.'

'Wise move,' commented Andy. They stood up. 'Why don't you come to my flat? We can talk there. There are more questions I want to ask you.'

'All right,' said Edward after a moment's hesitation. 'But I want to make something absolutely clear to you. If you arrest me I will give you no help at all. Your case will end as abruptly as it has re-opened. A solicitor will have me out in seconds, because you haven't a single piece of evidence at the moment.'

'Point taken,' said Andy.

For two hours they smoked cigarettes and drank cups of coffee in Andy's sitting room. Edward left twice to telephone Tate. Andy did not bother to follow him, and each time he returned, despondent that Tate had not returned the call. Tate was making him sweat. They barely spoke because Edward made it clear he was not answering any more questions.

Edward stood up quickly when he heard the key in the lock. He looked at Andy nervously. Andy shook his head calmly, and looked at his watch. It was Annelies arriving with the information he had requested on Davidson. She had brought her suitcase with her, as Andy had suggested earlier. He was pleased to notice how well she hid her surprise at seeing Edward Jay. He made the introductions and explained the recent developments to her.

'This is the plan of attack,' said Andy. 'From now on, Edward, you will be able to contact Annelies at all times, if I am not available. No one else in the department will know that we are in touch with you. Annelies is the only person I am prepared to trust until we find out if Samuel has a paid informer. Do you find that acceptable?' Andy looked at Edward. He nodded in reply. 'I am going to leave in a moment to speak to my Chief and let him know what's going on. I need his support because we will need to act quickly when the time comes, and then we'll need manpower.'

'What about Julia?' asked Edward. 'That's the most important priority.'

'I know,' answered Andy. 'I'm going to arrest Davidson, then interrogate him.'

Edward nodded.

'I want you to take my mobile phone number. Either Annelies or I will be manning it day and night.' He wrote the number on a piece of paper and passed it to Edward, who looked at it for a brief moment, memorised it, then dropped it in the ashtray. 'Annelies! I want you to keep this phone. If Edward's right, and there is someone bent in the department then I can't risk them being present when Edward calls. If anyone suspects I'm in contact with Edward then Tate will go to ground. And that will be the end of it all.'

As Andy left his flat he wondered whether Jay was setting him up. He wouldn't put it past Tate to have organised this. After all, they'd set him up two days previously. This might be Tate's parting shot. He'd feel a lot better if Jay had produced some concrete evidence.

For a moment Andy wondered if he was allowing his hatred of Tate to affect his judgement; but he was too far down the line to back off now.

# 5

'This better be important,' said Simon Patterson. 'Bloody important.' He looked at his watch, emphasising that it was long past office hours.

It was the first time Andy had been to Patterson's house and he had imagined something quite different from the pragmatic man he knew at the office. There was an unexpected elegance and comfort. He noticed Patterson's eyes dart at his feet as he entered and he made a show of wiping them on the doormat. He guessed Patterson didn't entertain much. He looked around the hall. A well-balanced choice of antiques were on show. There was an Axminster carpet. No wonder he liked to be out of the office early to come back and relax in this little womb. After a second or two, Andy began to find it unsettling. The house was too busy and claustrophobic. There were no signs of the two children. No signs of toys; only two little duffle coats hanging by the door. Patterson shut the door to the sitting room where he had obviously been watching the television with his wife, and led Andy down the hall to his study. As they went deeper into the house the baroque turned to rococo. The furniture belonged in some antique shop in Brighton.

'Yes?' asked Patterson.

Andy recovered from the shock of this revelation about Patterson. 'I've had some developments on the Tate case,' he said.

'I told you that the case was closed. In any event, you are on leave.'

'As I said, sir, there have been developments. I was approached by one of the principles involved, and he's prepared to blow the whistle on Tate.'

'I'm pleased to hear that, though I don't understand the urgency. It could have waited until the morning.'

'Two things have happened which make it imperative that we take action. The informant is Edward Jay, Tate's right-hand man. His girlfriend has been kidnapped by Ginger because Jay knows the whereabouts of the consignment that Tate wants.'

'I hope you haven't offered Jay a deal, or anything like that,' said Patterson, firing a warning shot.

'Of course not.'

'So you want a team to round them up?'

'It's not quite as easy as that. Whatever we do must be discreet. We still don't know where Tate is hiding. We don't know where Ginger is holding the girl. And we don't know where the consignment is being warehoused.'

Patterson stared at Andy. 'Is this a joke? You say you've got an informer and then you tell me you haven't got anything out of him.'

'I'll start again,' said Andy. If Patterson went on like that he'd get a kick in the bollocks. 'Edward Jay has given me the name of the policeman who is on Tate's books and who was responsible for our débâcle the other day.' Andy hesitated for a moment and then decided it was time to give Patterson a fright. 'He also said there was a source within customs who had been accepting money.' Edward Jay had intimated as much, after all.

Patterson turned round sharply. 'That's a serious allegation.'

Andy didn't say anything. The implications of what he had said were beginning to dawn on him. Something made him uneasy. He was thinking about the photograph of Tate and Ginger which had conveniently disappeared until de Groote's girlfriend had been killed. He was wondering how Patterson managed to keep a house in Kensington on his salary.

'Do you have any suspicions?' asked Patterson.

'No sir. Not at the moment. I know the consignments are brought in through Heathrow Airport, and that freight handlers are responsible. There might be a bent customs officer involved there.'

Andy decided that if Patterson didn't support him then he would become the prime suspect; and even if he did, he still wasn't in the clear.

'What course of action do you suggest?' asked Patterson.

'I want to pick a small team I can trust and I want to run the operation in absolute secrecy. We can't afford any more leaks. I've got some leads on Tate which need investigating. Hopefully, with Jay's help, we can arrest Ginger with the consignment.'

'What about Jay?'

'Everything depends on his co-operation. Without him, we have nothing.'

'Are you going to arrest Jay?'

'Not at the moment, sir. Ultimately it will depend on what sort of a case we have against him. At the moment it's all circumstantial. It might remain that way.'

'I know what you're telling me. I don't want anything that suggests a deal. In England we do not plea bargain.'

'No, sir.'

'OK. You're back on the case. Keep me informed.'

'Thank you, sir.'

Patterson showed him out of the study. 'Have you told anyone that we may have a security leak in the service?' he asked.

'Only you,' said Andy.

'I think you should keep it that way for the time being. We don't want to tip him off.'

As they walked past the sitting room, the door opened. A young woman came out. She smiled pleasantly when she saw Andy.

Patterson hesitated, then introduced them reluctantly. 'This is a colleague of mine, Andy Ballot.'

'How do you do?' she said, extending her hand.

'This is my wife, Elizabeth,' said Patterson.

'Good evening,' said Andy, politely. She was twenty years younger than Patterson. He wondered what attractions she found in such a plain man.

Patterson hurried Andy to the front door. As they stood on the doorstep Patterson said, 'It may be a bit premature to say this, but I think it's a good thing you're so tenacious.'

'What do you mean by that, sir?'

'If there is corruption in the department I want to get to the bottom of it.'

# Chapter 13

## 1

Andy made a call to Kentish Town police station and discovered that Davidson was on the night shift; then he told Vince to join him outside Davidson's flat. That was an hour ago, and Vince said he would be there in half an hour. He was late. Andy paced up and down the pavement.

Vince was the right man for this job. He had been irritated and suspicious of Davidson from the start. He didn't sound too pleased to hear Andy was back on the case though, and asked if it was sanctioned by the Chief. He wanted to know how Andy knew Davidson was bent but received no answer, and probably realised that Andy was holding out on him. He wouldn't like that; but Andy didn't care.

Andy was keen to break into the flat before Davidson returned. He looked at his watch irritably, and decided to give Vince a few more minutes.

He went to the telephone across the road and called Davidson's number. He looked at the windows opposite. No lights turned on. There was no answer. He replaced the receiver. He tried calling Annelies. He wanted to know how she was getting on with Edward. Again, there was no answer.

Andy wondered what was keeping Vince. He looked at the windows of the flats. Only a few were lit. There was no way of knowing which was Davidson's. He was tired of waiting. He was going in alone.

Andy crossed the road and rang the bell of Davidson's flat as a precaution. There was no answer. He tested the door with his shoulder unobtrusively. He put his hand into his pocket and pulled out his jigglers and twisters. He felt through the bunch for a moment and then slipped a

191

key into the lock. The door opened and he stepped into the hall. He shut the door behind him. He stood for a moment in the darkness listening to the sounds of the house. The old building smelt damp. Plastic bags of rubbish lined the wall. A television blared in one of the flats. No worries in that direction. The occupant was hard of hearing. He flashed his torch around the hall. It was grim with thirty-year-old wallpaper and rotten skirting boards. He decided to do without the courtesy light and started up the stairs keeping to the outside of the treads where they would creak the least. He found Davidson's flat on the top floor. He shone the light around the door frame. Nothing unpleasant. It looked straightforward. Policemen seldom worried about their own security. He took out the jigglers and turned the first lock, and then inserted another into the mortise lock. The door opened.

He closed the door behind him and stood in the darkness, acclimatising himself to the atmosphere of a strange house. He could hear the distant television. The sound-proofing was awful. The flat had been a cheap conversion. The sitting room had a view of the street, so he decided to leave that until last. It would only take him a short while to search the rooms. He started in the bathroom. It was a health hazard. He inadvertently held his breath as he levered away the bath panels. He looked inside the cistern, and checked the floorboards for loose ones. He drew a blank. He returned to the kitchen and started with the obvious. The fridge contained various decomposing foodstuffs. The ice in the freezer compartment had been recently hacked away. He removed a packet of frozen peas and found a plastic bag. He pulled it out and peered inside. There were four neat bundles of notes, each containing five thousand pounds. He took them into the bathroom and hid them behind the bath panel. He wanted an address book now. There was nothing else in the kitchen. He tried the bedroom. Davidson had run to form so far. He hoped to find something in his sock drawer, but there was nothing. Three pornographic magazines lay under the bed. He tipped up the mattress, but there was nothing underneath.

Andy suddenly froze. He heard heavy footsteps mounting the stairs. It wasn't Vince. They were too loud. He switched off the light and opened the bedroom door a fraction. He heard a key in the lock. There was a moment's hesitation. That would be Davidson wondering why the lower lock was open. His subconscious would be throwing out alarm signals and his conscious would be allaying the fears. He'd open the door, turn on the light, and look around. Then what? Search the flat maybe.

The front door opened and the light turned on. There was a moment's pause. The loud click of a switch being turned on. Probably the bar heater in the sitting room. The door to the kitchen was closed. It had been open. He probably never closed it. He was thinking. Probably confused. It was infuriating how slowly Davidson thought. What was the worst thing that could happen? The money. He was thinking about the money. He'd open the door cautiously. Turn on the light. He'd open the fridge.

The doorbell started ringing. Insistently. Urgently. It stopped for a moment before starting again. Something urgent. Davidson probably half turned and then his subconscious threw up the questions. If someone was in the flat that would be the warning signal from an accomplice in the street. The bell stopped ringing. Davidson opened the kitchen door. He turned on the light. Andy moved behind the bedroom door. Davidson looked in the bathroom. He approached the bedroom cautiously. There was only one place someone could be hiding now.

Andy flattened himself against the wall. He braced himself. The door opened. He could see Davidson's shadow on the wall over the bed. He was turning on the light. Andy propelled the door away from him as hard as he could. He heard Davidson grunt as it caught him on the shoulder. A moment earlier and it might have smashed his hand in the door jamb. Andy swung the door back and slammed it closed again on Davidson's advancing figure. There was a grunt from Davidson and a splintering of wood as the hinges gave way. He was a lot bigger than Andy had expected. He stood back as Davidson kicked the door out of the way. Andy reminded himself that he was dealing with a bent policeman. He wouldn't pull any punches. He lashed out with his left foot at Davidson's stomach. Davidson reacted quickly and managed to absorb some of the impact with his hands. Andy broke the grip on his ankle and stepped back as Davidson's momentum brought him into the room. He stood in the gloom for a brief second, back lit by the kitchen light, perhaps wondering if there were two intruders. He stood for a fraction of a second too long. Andy took the initiative. He stamped on Davidson's foot and as Davidson's head dropped Andy delivered an uppercut with all the strength he could summon. Davidson doubled up. Andy shouldered him backwards out of the bedroom on to the floor. Davidson covered his face with his hands. There was a trickle of blood between his fingers.

Andy's wrist was numb. He wondered if he had broken a bone in his hand with the punch. He stabbed Davidson warily with his foot. There might still be some fight left in the old boy. 'Come on, Davidson. Into the sitting room.'

Davidson groaned. He moved his hands painfully from his face and tried to focus on Andy for the first time. He was surprised to be called by his name. 'Who the fuck are you?' he asked, in a nasal voice.

'Come on. Into the sitting room,' ordered Andy, kicking him in the back.

Davidson tried getting to his feet. He made it to his knees before saying, 'You're making a big mistake.'

'Come on,' said Andy, kicking him again, so he was back on all fours. Davidson made a concerted effort to stand, finally balanced on his feet, and shuffled down the corridor. Andy pushed him into a chair. At the same time there was a knock on the door.

'Who is it?' asked Andy.

'Is that you, Andy?'

Andy recognised Vince's voice and opened the door.

'What are you doing here?' asked Davidson.

'Customs and Excise,' Andy answered.

'Well you have made one big fucking mistake breaking in here,' snuffled Davidson, undaunted.

'I don't think so,' said Andy. 'I've got my Writs of Assistance. You're forgetting I don't have to apply to a magistrate for a search warrant, if I believe you're involved in drug smuggling.'

'Fuck off,' said Davidson. 'You won't make that stick.'

'Things aren't looking good, Davidson. You're on Tate's payroll, and you've aided and abetted a kidnap.'

'What?' said Davidson. He was holding a dirty handkerchief to his nose. His eyes were beginning to swell from Andy's punch. 'You've got nothing on me.'

'Cuff him, Vince,' said Andy. He walked into the bathroom and retrieved the twenty thousand he'd previously removed from the freezer compartment. 'I found this little treasure trove earlier.' He stared at Davidson, now holding his bloody handkerchief with both his hands.

'Yeah? Well, they're my savings.'

'No way, Davidson. You're on the take.'

'You must be joking, Ballot. You're barking up the wrong fucking tree. Yeah, I did speak to Tate. He did make some propositions. It was my business to keep him on the hook because he's a known associate of two dangerous suspects.'

'I don't want to waste time discussing the complexity of your predicament. I want to know where Ginger might be keeping someone he's kidnapped.'

'I wouldn't know.'

'How about Tate? How do you contact him?'

'I met him once in a pub.'

'Where does he live?'

'I don't know.'

'Let's see if your memory comes back later. Vince, take him to Customs House. I want the money labelled as an exhibit. Charge him, and interview him again. Then, hand him over to his own people at the Met. They might like to investigate him. I'm going back to the office.'

Vince grabbed the chain of the handcuffs and pulled Davidson to his feet. Davidson shook his head. 'I wouldn't want to be in your shoes,' he said.

# 2

Edward stood up a few minutes after Andy had left the flat. 'I'm going out to make a phone call,' he said to Annelies. He was not hanging around to wait for Andy to change his mind and send his colleagues to arrest him.

'I will come with you,' said Annelies.

Edward shrugged.

She followed him to a phone box and watched him make the call to Tate. He waited impatiently for the return call. He gave up after five minutes and joined her. They walked towards Covent Garden. 'They have to phone me sometime,' he said. 'They can't afford to lose what I'm holding.'

'What is it?' asked Annelies.

She looked up at him, but he didn't look at her. He was preoccupied, and she knew better than to interrogate him. She sensed his dilemma. He would talk when he was ready. In the meantime her job was to make him talk about anything to gain his trust. The art of interrogation was to create a bond between interviewer and suspect. Dialogue had to be maintained. It didn't matter who asked questions or who gave answers because the process created the illusion of a relationship.

Annelies groped for subjects to talk about. She tried to remember what she had read in Edward's file. Nothing came to mind; only that he had been in prison.

'What was it like in prison?' she asked.

He didn't reply for a long time. She listened to their footsteps on the pavement. Just when she thought he had ignored the question he began speaking. 'It was terrible. Everyone tells you prison is bad. You don't believe it. At least, you don't expect it to be quite so bad. You're cut off from the world. Worse than that, you're cut off from civilisation and reduced to the state of an animal.' He hesitated. 'I won't do time again. Now I've lost the only person it was worth waiting for, I'd rather be dead.'

Annelies wondered if he realised he would receive a custodial sentence, whatever the outcome of this operation. 'I think you are doing the right thing talking to Andy. I think you have been betrayed by your friends,' she tried to reassure him.

He ignored her. 'The best way to protect yourself in prison is to let people think you're going mad. That way, they leave you in peace. That way, you gain some privacy. I spent a week walking in circles without speaking a word. Killing time. Thinking. I spent a week slapping the earth with the palm of my hand, pretending to kill flies. The other prisoners treated lunacy like a contagious disease. After you've been in a prison like that, you don't believe in humanity or morality any more. Some people deal in arms to make money. Those people aren't in prison. Compared to them the prisoners were decent.' He paused for a moment. 'In this country what percentage of the population have a criminal record?' asked Edward suddenly.

'I don't know.'

'Take a guess,' he said, irritably. 'Driving offences don't count,' he added.

'Maybe ten per cent.'

'No. Thirty per cent. Those guys are out there beating their wives, burgling houses or robbing banks. They're all voting for corporal punishment. They're polluting the planet to make money. Thirty per cent of the great British public are convicted criminals. Another thirty per cent are getting away with it but should be convicted.'

Annelies didn't get the point of what he was saying. 'You shouldn't be so bitter,' she said. She put her hand on his arm, trying to create a bond.

'I'm wheeling and dealing a drug that's been around for three thousand years and doesn't kill. What's so bad about it? It carries the death penalty in half a dozen countries, and it kills fewer people a year than alcohol.'

This was the moment, thought Annelies. This was the moment when the suspect unburdened himself and let everything out. At moments like this people blurted things they hadn't intended, or remembered things they thought they had forgotten. The key was to keep them talking.

'I do not think there is anything wrong with cannabis,' said Annelies, inveigling him into trusting her. He looked at her for a second, surprised. 'Only you do not pay your taxes. I am Dutch and we have different laws to the English.' Edward said nothing, and looked away. She had to keep him talking about himself. 'The only problem with cannabis is when people are hurt.'

'I was never involved in anything where people were hurt. We didn't go around breaking legs,' he replied, defensively.

'Yes, I understand. But now de Groote is killed. And his girlfriend, Monique. She was innocent.' Edward didn't respond. Annelies continued. 'Somewhere, sometimes there is always some person who is being hurt in this business. Maybe it is the small farmer in Pakistan or Afghanistan, where life is cheap. This is the problem. You are part of this system. You are responsible.'

'All right! I understand. I'm guilty,' retorted Edward angrily. 'But we are all guilty of something by association.'

'We can make a choice,' said Annelies. She wondered if she was pushing him too hard.

'You're missing the point,' said Edward. 'It's the intention which is important. You eat a hamburger but you don't want the rain forest destroyed to create grazing.'

'So you think you have a morality because you will not deal with heroin or cocaine?' said Annelies. Edward didn't reply. She had a flash of insight. 'It is this which is causing the problem? Tate is dealing with heroin?'

'Yes,' said Edward, bitterly.

'Now you have hidden it?'

'Yes.'

Annelies put her hand on Edward's arm again, and left it there. 'I think you are brave,' she said. There was something attractive about him. Stupid but attractive. So many criminals were naïve. They had no idea of the consequences of their actions. They were childlike in their innocence. They espoused causes like Greenpeace, believing they were good people, and never saw the contradiction in their lives. But, she knew what they needed. Encouragement and reassurance. 'So you have told me what it is. There is nothing more to frighten you. You are making the right decision. If you help Andy you will be free.'

'If I help him then I will be killed.'

'Why? He will protect you. There is the witness protection programme.'

'You know that's not true. If I go into the witness box someone will put a contract on me. I'll go to prison too, whatever you promise. The British don't make deals.'

'I think you should trust Andy,' said Annelies.

'I don't trust anyone.'

'What about your girlfriend, Julia? You do not trust her?'

'Love is not trust. Love makes you vulnerable. Love is a state of fear.'

Annelies looked at him sharply. He believed what he was saying. She was shocked. She hoped she never entered a world like that. She wondered what had happened to him in the past to make him feel like that. 'So what will you do about Julia?' She saw his face harden.

'I can't turn the clock back. I know that. My relationship with Julia is over unless I can rescue her quickly. But I'm going to salvage what I can. Make amends for her sake. Samuel has betrayed me, so I'm going to betray him. That's what I'm going to do about Julia. I'm going to tell you about Samuel Tate. Let's forget dinner for the moment. Let's have a drink here.' He turned into a pub abruptly. 'I'm going to tell you a story, and you can take out your pen and paper and make some notes.'

For the next two hours Annelies listened to stories about smuggling operations. She learned how money moved from one country to another. She made notes of where the money was banked over the years. He included the account numbers in Switzerland, Luxembourg and Austria. Edward had a memory for dates and numbers. People who never consigned anything to paper remembered details. Edward concentrated on the banking. He told her about Oliver Standon in the City. He hit Samuel Tate where it hurt. Without the money Tate would be nothing. Money always left a trail; and in the end people had to explain where it came from. Edward had opened the cell door for Tate.

When Edward had finished unburdening himself, he stood up and left Annelies, leaving her no opportunity to stop him.

'Please telephone me tomorrow,' she said.

He turned, looked at her, and said, 'Of course. Your part of the deal is to find Julia.'

## 3

It was nearly one in the morning before Andy was back in the office. He telephoned Annelies, waking her up, and discovered Edward had gone. He was irritated. He hoped Annelies would keep him at the flat. However, his irritation evaporated when he heard that Edward had given her details of Tate's banking operations and the name of his banker. He told her not to come to the office in the morning, but to stay at the flat and wait for Edward's call. Having done that he put his feet on the desk and slept in his chair for four hours.

The discomfort finally woke him. He lit a cigarette and poured a cup of lukewarm coffee from the machine, too impatient to let it heat up. He turned on the computer. It was six in the morning. The three or four hours before the office filled with noise and people were always the most productive. In the early hours the computer response time was quickest because no one else was trying to access it. He'd have done a day's work by ten, when the phones started ringing. He began by accessing the Police National Computer and acquainting himself with Davidson's investigation into Spider and Ginger. It didn't look like it would be too difficult to pick up their trail; but what he wanted to know was what Davidson had failed to log on the computer.

He would send a couple of officers impersonating gas men to Ginger and Spider's homes. They would ascertain if anyone was there, and if so, try and gain admittance to the houses and have a good look around. Under no circumstances were they to arouse suspicions.

The check on Tate's radio pager revealed it was rented by a man called Sheehan, and paid for by a standing order. All the messages for the past three days were retained as a matter of routine and were being retrieved and faxed by the telephone company. Andy had arranged an appointment with the bank manager at Sheehan's branch after lunch.

Vince arrived unusually early.

'Did you get anything out of Davidson?' asked Andy.

'No,' said Vince. 'The police are picking him up this morning.'

'Good. I want him out of the way. I don't want him fouling up this operation again.'

'Again?' questioned Vince.

'He tipped off Tate that we were on to him.'

'You don't know that for sure. A bundle of money which Davidson says represents his life savings is not exactly evidence.'

'I don't care what you think,' snapped Andy. 'I've got a witness.'

'Oh?' asked Vince, and waited for some explanation; but it never came. 'The police will want to know who it is.'

'I'll tell them in my own good time.'

'Well, I hope you can clear it with the Chief. He's not going to like this.'

'It's cleared. Anyway, he won't be in today,' said Andy. 'That's not a coincidence. He wants a New Year gong when he retires. He'll be around tomorrow. In the meantime he's giving me a free hand.'

'He's left you carrying the can,' said Vince, delivering an unnecessary warning. Andy guessed Vince was wondering where that left him on the whipping post.

'That's right,' said Andy, with a grim smile.

'How do you know Ginger kidnapped Jay's girlfriend?'

Andy thought quickly. He should have been ready for that question. 'I went round to see her. You know, after Jay gave us the slip. She wasn't there. Couple of people answering Ginger and Spiders's descriptions were seen helping her into a car. That, coupled with Jay's disappearance, leads me to believe things are not hunky dory in Tate's camp.'

Vince nodded. 'Pretty active imagination you have, Andy.'

'What do you mean?'

'It's not as if there's much in the way of facts to base it on.'

'Deduction,' commented Andy.

Vince grunted, 'Where's Annelies?' he asked.

'She's sick,' lied Andy.

'Best thing to be,' commented Vince. 'So, what's the plan?'

'We need two teams for a surveillance operation as soon as we locate Ginger. You organise them. Put them on stand-by. Have a look through the Tate file again and see if you can come up with something we've overlooked. Tate must slip up sometimes. If I decide to pull Ginger I want you to lead the team.'

'Sure,' said Vince. He didn't sound enthusiastic. Andy knew why. Vince wasn't the brightest of the officers, but he was a survivor. He knew that delegating responsibility was usually the surest way of having subordinates fired. Simon Patterson had hedged his bets and even Vince could see what was at stake. He wouldn't be making any suggestions which had his name attached to them. The last thing he wanted was to be in charge of the team in the front line. 'Where are you off to?' asked Vince, as Andy stood up and grabbed his jacket.

'A couple of meetings,' replied Andy enigmatically, leaving the room. He had an unofficial meeting with an acquaintance in the Fraud Squad to discover the best way of investigating Oliver Standon's laundering of Tate's money.

Andy finally returned home at midday. He was exhausted. When he opened the door he couldn't work out what was different. Annelies was lying on the sofa reading a book. Her long legs suddenly reminded him how long it had been since he'd curled up with a body. How inappropriate to think about that now, he thought. He looked around and realised the flat was spotless. Pieces of furniture had been moved. The windows were clean. For a moment he felt embarrassed. It provoked an irrational feeling that Annelies had been critical of him. He ignored it. 'Thank you Annelies,' he said. 'It looks wonderful. I feel embarrassed you did all this cleaning. I haven't had time. Did it take you long?'

Annelies put her book down. 'Me? I hope you do not think I did it. The bill is on the table there. When I woke this morning I thought it was time. So I found this cleaning company in the telephone book.'

Andy picked up the bill sheepishly. It was for a hundred and twenty-five pounds, plus VAT. He looked around the room again. It was worth every penny of it.

'Has Edward called?' he asked.

'Yes. Two times. He asks if you have found Julia yet.'

'What did you say?'

'I told him you are hopeful. He said to tell you that time is running out and he will telephone again.'

'How did he sound?'

'He was angry and something like nervous.'

'The next time he calls tell him I want to see him. Tell him I have something to say to him.'

Andy ran a bath and shaved. He spent fifteen minutes trying to find shoes, socks and handkerchiefs which were not where he had left them for the past five years. He put on his suit and departed for the appointment with Sheehan's bank manager in an irritable frame of mind. He wasn't sure if he liked strangers invading his privacy.

Bank managers weren't Andy's favourite people; he'd had his fair share of overdrafts in the past and the managers had done him few favours. Sheehan's bank manager immediately aroused Andy's prejudices. He was both arrogant and supercilious; no doubt mandatory assets for the incumbent of the Mayfair branch. He had kept Andy waiting for twenty minutes. He had evidently returned from luncheon with some client, having drunk too much free wine. With blatant distaste he invited Andy into his office.

'I must make it clear to you, Mr Ballot, before we begin this brief interview, that it is not my bank's policy to divulge any information concerning the accounts of our customers, unless you have evidence that . . .'

'I do not care to be kept waiting,' said Andy, looking at his watch. He didn't have time to fool around. 'I will make one thing clear from the start. I am a customs officer and that gives me more power than a police officer. I am investigating a serious drugs offence and I expect full co-operation. I believe the account of Michael Sheehan is used to launder the proceeds of criminal activities. Under the Criminal Justice Act of 1993, whether you know this or not, you have a legal duty to make yourself aware of the account you are managing. Furthermore, I shall want to know what actions you took to carry out these enquiries. Is that clear?'

There was a ponderous silence. Andy glared. The manager absorbed the threats with horror. He struggled to make a conciliatory gesture with his hands, found the top of his desk and sat unsteadily in his chair.

Andy continued. 'I would remind you that informing the account holder that his affairs are under scrutiny will make you personally liable for anything up to a five-year prison sentence under Section 26 of the 1986 Drug Trafficking Offences Act.'

The bank manager's greasy complexion turned sweaty. He took out a handkerchief and mopped his forehead. 'I'm sorry,' he said finally. 'I didn't realise the seriousness of the investigation. Let me assure you I checked Sheehan's files as soon as I finished speaking to you on the telephone. I can only say that my conscience is clear and that the bank has broken no rules.'

The denial immediately made Andy suspicious. Something about the account made the manager nervous.

'Do you know Martin Sheehan?'

'Not personally.'

'By sight? Have you ever met him?'

'Not that I remember. There are no notes in his file. I usually jot down a few reminders when I meet customers, so I know where to pick things up the next time we have an appointment.'

The manager shuffled through the file in front of him. 'Mr Sheehan opened the account in October—' he began but Andy interrupted him by stretching out for the papers. The bundle was passed across the table without question. Andy looked through the papers quickly.

'I want statements containing all transactions for this account, going back as far as you can, and as soon as possible. I want you to get in touch with the credit card company and ask them for details of all transactions over the past twelve months.'

'We should be able to provide you with those details in a very short time.'

'While I wait?' suggested Andy. The manager hurried out of the room. He couldn't be too helpful.

One of the references for Sheehan's account had been Samuel Tate. The account had been opened fifteen years ago. A credit card had been issued ten years ago. Five years ago Sheehan had apparently moved out of the country and requested that no mail be forwarded until he provided a permanent address.

The manager returned with a stack of statements which he passed to Andy. 'I assume these represent five years of mail which you were holding for Sheehan.' The manager nodded. 'Correct me if I'm wrong, but I thought that it was illegal for an account to operate in this way. You're required to have certain basic information about clients. An address? For instance?'

'Yes, of course. But we assumed that the client was now overseas. As you can see from the account transactions there was never any reason for the computer to flag us. The account was always kept in healthy credit. The credit card was paid through a direct debit.'

'Someone took advantage of the system's weakness?'

'That's the long and short of it.' The manager seemed relieved to find Andy so understanding.

After the briefest of silences Andy said, 'You would appear to have broken Section 93 C of the Criminal Justice Act in which you are required to maintain identification procedures and record-keeping procedures.'

He allowed the information to sink in. 'Do you have an account for a Samuel Tate at this branch? Or indeed, at any of your branches?'

'Let me check for you.' The manager tapped on the keyboard of his computer. Meanwhile Andy flipped through the bank statements. There were few standing orders. He was hoping to find one for rates, poll tax or council tax. He wanted an electricity or water bill, something which would lead to an address. Of course, Tate was too smart for that.

'There's no record of an account in that name,' said the manager.

'There's something else I want,' said Andy. 'I need to know when and where authorisation is requested for payment on Sheehan's credit card. I need that information quickly.'

'I'm not sure how to go about that. I'll have to make a phone call.' He picked up his telephone. Andy leaned back in the chair and waited. Soon the manager would open up the drinks cabinet in the corner and offer a drop of brandy. In due course Andy would contact the head office of the bank and tell them to tighten up the Mayfair branch.

# 4

The rain was relentless. Tate spent a tedious day making phone calls, attending to the intricacies of his business affairs. He had a notebook half-filled with numbers and the locations of phone boxes throughout the inner city. Oliver Standon finally confirmed that the down payment for the consignment Edward held was safe in a Swiss bank account.

There were clouds on the horizon though. Davidson's usefulness had been short-lived. Tate heard he had been arrested, and wondered how Ballot had made the connection so quickly. Davidson would be all right, so long as he didn't talk. Davidson would be more aware than most of the dangers of incriminating himself. The voice on the phone assured Tate that the trail ended there. Ginger would become the next problem, but he still had a job to do.

Tate looked at his watch. It was a quarter to six. At any moment a call would come through on his pager. He was becoming accustomed to the hourly reminders, though he'd finally turned off the sound. He scrolled through the last few messages. He relished the thought of Edward making those pathetic calls in the hope of rescuing Julia. Sod Edward. He deserved to suffer for the problems he was causing. Edward had been busily moving around town; the numbers bore few similar prefixes. Initially he had hoped Edward would make himself available at a single call box. It would have been simple to find out its location and pick him up. Unfortunately Edward was too cunning for that; but not cunning enough. Now, Edward would be desperate to make a deal for Julia.

The pager buzzed and Tate read the number off the screen. One of these days he was going to recognise a number as one of the phones he habitually used. He left the warmth of the pub and splashed his way through the puddles to a public phone, cursing Edward. His shoes were ruined. They'd been hand-made in Beauchamp Place and cost a grand. It was a bit late to think about buying some galoshes. It had been a miserable day and when it was over he was going to treat himself. If things went well he would be leaving England for ever within a week.

'That you, Edward?' he said, when the phone was answered.

'Yes. It's me.' He heard Edward's unusually resigned voice at the other end of the line.

'I'm sorry it's taken so long to get back to you. They've only just contacted me.'

'Is Julia OK?'

'Oh yes,' said Tate. He was going to keep this conversation short. He wasn't going to run the risk of the call being traced. Maybe Edward had recruited someone on to his side. 'I've arranged for you to meet Ginger tomorrow, at noon, at the Tower Hotel.'

'You release Julia first.'

'The Tower Hotel. You got that. Ginger holds the cards. You speak with him. You do what he says then you can go back to playing happy families with Julia.'

'I want a guarantee.'

'Come on, Edward. There are no guarantees in this game. You should know that.' He had an afterthought. 'Well, there is one certainty, but I hardly need mention it. Ginger was adamant that you turn up alone. Julia's health depends on it.' Tate put down the phone and walked away smartly.

The call only took half a minute, but it still made him nervous. He reassured himself with the thought that Edward would be a fool to make a deal with the police. He'd be lucky to escape a conviction even if he tried turning Queen's evidence. Anyway, he'd be risking Julia's life.

Edward didn't seem to realise he already had a guarantee, because there was still the money from the dope to hand over. Suspicious ungrateful bastard. Their partnership was definitely over. Maybe he could find out who was marketing for Edward. There weren't that many dealers who could handle a ton in such a short time. Probably only three or four. There was Shorty Mick, but he had supposedly retired. Maybe it was Jimmy the Scot. It was years since he'd spoken to those guys. Or Jason? Yes, Jason. He was the most likely. It wouldn't be too hard to check them out. He'd make a few calls in the morning. Then Edward's guarantee would expire. Now that was an interesting proposition.

When Tate finally made it back to his flat, he poured himself a stiff drink, took off his damp clothes and changed into something casual. He had one more phone call to make. He rang the agency in Knightsbridge. He'd used them before. He gave them the credit card number. After he put down the phone he waited impatiently for the door bell to ring.

He felt aggrieved. It had been like this throughout his life. Just when he thought he was about to realise his ambitions they were torn away from him. Now Edward had betrayed him. They'd been friends for over fifteen years. He'd given Edward every chance. He'd shared the good times with him, not to mention the bad times. Edward would have been nothing without him. There was no reason why he should suddenly become so unreasonable. Even if he had a moral standpoint he had a duty to be loyal. It wasn't a question of money. That was always negotiable. No. Edward had harboured resentment all those years, and was proving he wasn't trustworthy. It probably had something to do with the prison sentence in Pakistan. Some people couldn't do their time. Something cracked inside them. Well, Edward would still be inside if it wasn't for him. He deserved a few thanks for arranging his release, at the very least. It would probably have been different if Edward had gone to a public school. He might have learned loyalty and self-reliance. Now Edward was going to learn the hard way. Edward had fucked up a deal which would have been worth around twenty million a year.

Tate walked into the bedroom and tidied it. It didn't need much attention. He was meticulously fastidious anyway. He went back into the kitchen. It was a matter of time now. Things were under control. Ginger and Spider would ensure that Edward did what he was told. Abducting Julia was a drastic measure but it had produced results. Edward was co-operating.

Everything was such a battle. It always had been. Right from the start. He hadn't seen his parents for twenty years. But that was his father's fault. His father had always bullied him and made him feel worthless. Then there was his mother's ultimate betrayal. She found him training the shotgun out of the bedroom window at his father who was snoring in a deck chair. He wondered if he really would have pulled the trigger, after he released the safety catch. Her scream distracted him. She betrayed him. She didn't love him; she loved his father who humiliated her in every way. She called his father who thrashed him and tried to put him in the army. The school interceded. The psychiatrist didn't help. From then on,

Tate had been on his own. If he hadn't won the scholarship to university his father wouldn't have paid the fees. His father had been prepared to let him sink over the trouble in Brightlingsea when the girl drowned herself. It was only luck that his friends were well connected. Fuck his father. Now that little bastard Andy Ballot was turning up again. He was glad he fucked Ballot's girlfriend before she drowned.

The doorbell rang. He hoped they'd sent someone good.

Tate opened the door. The girl had big eyes which made her look innocent. They seemed to come young these days. Funnily enough she reminded him of that girl who drowned. He closed the door and took her coat. He looked at her legs. Stockings. At least she had some style. Well, she had no idea what he was going to do to her. She was going to do something for him she had never dreamed about. She was going to learn something about herself, and the power of money. Tate felt things stirring in his sports department.

'Let's have the champagne in the bedroom,' he said.

The tart smiled. He didn't care for the teeth, but then he wouldn't be looking at them.

'Do you like watersports?' he said, with a sly look.

The girl looked at him. 'That's extra,' she said boldly.

'Of course,' replied Tate. He looked forward to the negotiations.

There were plenty of ways to kill time, but this was one of the best. He switched off his pager. He didn't want any interruptions.

# 5

Jason gently eased himself out of bed at four in the morning. His wife stirred, turned over and continued dreaming. He slipped on his dressing gown and padded down the corridor to his study. He locked the door behind him. He didn't want his son bursting in on him. He knelt down beside the Victorian fireplace and depressed the wrought iron tail of an ornamental serpent. He pulled on the fireplace and it glided forward to reveal a secret chamber. He designed this little niche when he restored the house. No one, not even his wife, knew about it. He stooped to withdraw a bag and a small box. He placed them on his desk, opened the

The Scam

box and took out a money-counting machine. He opened the bag and looked at the jumbled notes inside. He settled down to work.

Things were going well. Good dope always sold. He'd be finished well before the weekend deadline he'd been given to market the consignment. There hadn't been a murmur of any competitive material in circulation. Edward had been truthful about that aspect of the deal.

There were three hundred and fifty thousand pounds in the bag. He put a handful of the bundled notes on to his desk and began arranging them into various denominations. When he had done that he put them into the machine. It whirred away. From time to time it faltered on a batch of new bank notes which it couldn't separate, and Jason counted them manually. By six he had counted all the money. It was sixty pounds short. There was one fake fifty pound note and one bundle was ten pounds short. He carefully put rubber bands around the now faced-up bundles and placed them in a wine box. He hid everything behind the fireplace again. He enjoyed counting money.

He went to bathroom and washed his hands. Dirty stuff, money. He congratulated himself on how well he did business. He operated through some of the best dealers and that was proved when the money came back so efficiently and precisely. These days he wouldn't take on new clients. There were too many stories of distributors being robbed of the cannabis or the proceeds. It was a tough world out there and there were too many people willing to kill to get ahead. The thought of the Yardies made him shudder.

He went downstairs to the kitchen, made a pot of tea, and returned to the bedroom. He woke his wife with a kiss on the cheek, then slipped into bed beside her and snuggled against her warm body. He liked his routines.

At a quarter to eight Jason backed his pickup van out of the double garage. He looked at his wife's Porsche 911, and smiled. He liked her to have the best in life. It made him feel good. He watched the garage doors close automatically. He did a three-point turn in the driveway and left for work.

He scowled when he saw an over-coated figure standing in front of his gates. His heart sank when he recognised who it was. By the time he had applied the brakes he was furious. He wound down the window. 'What the hell do you want?' he spat at Tate.

'I need a quick word with you,' said Tate.

'Get in,' ordered Jason. Tate obeyed. Jason turned out of his driveway and slipped into the rush hour traffic. He took a careful note of the cars behind him. He looked at Samuel. 'I don't care what you have to say to me, but never come to my house again. Do you understand?'

'What I have to say is very important,' insisted Tate.

207

'I don't care. My family is important to me. You are a danger. Do you understand that?'

'Of course I understand. I did take precautions, you know.'

' I should hope so. What do you want?'

'Edward has left the country. He's working on another scam like the one you're doing now. He told me to give you instructions for handing over the paperwork.'

'Why didn't you meet me at the rendezvous?'

So, thought Tate smugly, Jason *was* handling the job. 'You won't be meeting me.'

Jason looked grimly at the road ahead. He didn't like the sound of this. It was definitely the last time he worked with this lot.

Tate took out his wallet and passed Jason a business card. Jason looked at it and stuffed it in his shirt pocket. 'You should ring Mr Standon and make an appointment. He's a banker. Old school. Above board. Your name is Dieter Evans. He'll know what it's about. He will arrange to take the paperwork from you.'

Jason thought for a moment. He had a good mind to refuse. He didn't like changes in plan. He liked meeting new people even less; but refusal would result in a more complicated arrangement and mean meeting Tate again.

'No problem,' he said.

'Has everything gone well?' asked Tate. He wanted to know how much Jason was retailing it for.

'Everything's fine,' replied Jason curtly. He pulled the van over to the kerb, outside Baron's Court tube station. 'I'm turning off here,' he lied. 'You can catch the tube.'

'OK,' said Samuel, 'I'll see you later.'

I don't think so, thought Jason. A few minutes later he pulled over at a phone box. He didn't trust Tate. He dialled Edward's home. There was no reply.

# Chapter 14

## 1

It was Spider who should have been meeting Edward Jay at the Tower Hotel but he was proving to be unreliable. Ginger didn't know what was wrong with him. He was in a world of his own half the time. Whenever Ginger asked him what was wrong, he said he was thinking; that was if he answered at all. He'd always been a weird one, and when this business was over he needed to sort himself out.

Spider got nervous if he wasn't kept in the picture. He needed constant reassurance. Ginger knew he didn't like being left to watch the girl. 'Nothing to worry about. I'll give you a bell every few hours. You don't do nothing. Just let the girl go to the bathroom when she wants. Give her some food and drink. Don't make no phone calls. Keep away from the windows. Don't answer the door.'

'Yes,' said Spider. His eyes slowly swivelled towards Ginger. For a moment both eyes synchronised, before the left one peeled away.

'What if I want something from the shops?' asked Spider. 'I can't go outside?'

'Of course you can, Spider,' said Ginger, simply. 'You have to get food and stuff.'

'Maybe . . .' Spider began, but his imagination failed him.

Ginger shook his head. Maybe Spider was depressed. Ginger thought about his grandfather, before he died; he'd been like that until the doctor gave him some pills to perk him up.

'Catch you later,' said Ginger, cheerfully. 'You look after her, and everything will be fine.' Spider nodded.

Ginger took one last look at Spider. Spider smiled at him weakly.

209

Ginger convinced himself that everything would be alright.

That was twenty-four hours ago.

Ginger picked up his mobile phone and called Spider to check everything was fine. The phone rang for a long time. Ginger prayed Spider hadn't fucked up. If Spider did absolutely nothing it would be perfect. He wished he hadn't sent Tracy back to her mother's place because she would have been more reliable than Spider; but women couldn't keep their mouths shut.

The phone stopped ringing. There was no answering voice.

'Spider?' asked Ginger.

There was a long pause. 'Yeah.'

'You all right?'

'Yeah.'

'Good. You hang on there. It won't be long now. We'll be finished this afternoon. The girl? OK?'

'Yeah,' said Spider, and hung up.

Ginger picked up his mail on the way out of his house, and ripped open the envelopes. There was a letter from his solicitor. It looked like the property company was going to come across with the money for the Snooker Hall. That had been a nice little investment. He slipped the letters into a pocket of his leather jacket.

# 2

The phone woke Andy at seven. He looked at his clock as he answered it. He had overslept, and he still felt exhausted.

'Andy Ballot?'

'Yes.'

'This is Edward. Have you any news for me?'

'We had no luck with Davidson. We're still trying to locate Julia.'

'How about Ginger?'

'No leads yet?'

'I'm sorry, Andy,' said Edward. 'Time has run out.' He put down the phone.

Andy struggled out of bed, and pulled on his clothes. He guessed Jay was going to deal with Tate, and give him the consignment in return for Julia. There was nothing he could do to stop it. He didn't have grounds to arrest Ginger, and anyway, that would jeopardise everything.

He made a pot of tea and took a cup to Annelies, opening her door softly. He stood for a second looking at her. She was lying on her side. The covers were pulled down below her shoulders and he could see her breasts. The room was filled with the fresh, warm scent of sleep. He wondered if he ought to leave, but then placed the cup beside the bed, pulled up the covers, waking her.

'Annelies,' he said, 'I'm going now. Edward called me. I need you to stay here for another day in case he calls again.'

Annelies nodded, and closed her eyes again. He knew she was frustrated. He knew what it was like, waiting for something to happen, waiting for the phone to ring, waiting for the action to start. 'I'm sorry,' he said. 'It won't be for much longer.'

In the office Andy shuffled through Sheehan's bank statements, hoping to find something he had overlooked the day before. They had produced nothing worthwhile. The account was only used to pay off the credit card bills. The credit card had barely been used during the past six months, and most transactions had been carried out abroad, probably because Tate had no local currency. He had used the card in the odd restaurant, but never the same one twice; and the odds of some waiter remembering a customer were long. Investigating those transactions was prohibitively expensive and would take for ever.

As soon as Vince appeared, Andy despatched him to join the team watching Ginger. Vince was not happy about it. He wanted to be at the centre of the operation. 'It's a waste sending me out there,' he complained.

'I want someone I can trust on the case,' said Andy. 'I want someone who's good, and who won't lose Ginger when he hits the road. I know something is going to happen today.'

'Yeah?' said Vince. 'Nothing happened yesterday. Ginger made a couple of calls on his mobile, did some shopping and watched television. We're having problems tuning into that mobile frequency because he hardly uses it. Why don't I chase some leads on the bank statements?'

'I want you out there, Vince,' said Andy firmly. 'Take my word for it. Ginger is going to make a move today, and when he does I want you right on his tail.'

'How do you know?'

'I just know.'

Vince's eyes narrowed. 'It's no wonder this operation has been a shambles, right from the start. You haven't trusted us. Nor has it

improved since you started knobbing Annelies. Now you've blown everything because you only confided in your girlfriend.'

Andy stared at Vince. He didn't like the supercilious smile on his face.
He wanted to wipe it off. 'Just for the record, Annelies and I are not
having an affair. Not that it's any of your business.'

'What people think is what matters, Andy.'

'I don't give a fuck what people think.'

'Well, you should,' said Vince petulantly. He turned on his heel. 'I really
do hope I'm not wasting my time,' he muttered.

Andy watched him leave. He wondered if he should let Vince know he
was in contact with Jay. He might be more enthusiastic about the
operation if he knew it had a chance of success. Maybe he'd brief Vince
later.

He looked at his watch. The Chief would be in his office now. He
stood up wearily and made his way to deliver his report. He needed to
persuade Simon there was progress in order to keep the operation
alive. He wondered how long it would be before the Met started
demanding proof that Davidson had accepted bribes. They'd be busy
with the internal investigation at the moment, but that wouldn't last for
ever. Afterwards the shit would hit the fan; but by then he'd have
Tate and Jay. He hoped.

He stopped at the coffee machine and poured himself a cup. He
wandered into the communications room. It was empty. He concentrated
on the positive aspects of the operation, but they wouldn't stand up to
Patterson's criticisms. Andy was tempted to disappear for the rest of the
day, and lie low in the hope that something concrete would turn up. He
leafed through the fax tray.

There was a fax for him. It had arrived half an hour previously. He
looked around for someone to swear at; but there was no one. It
should have been delivered immediately. He grabbed it and ran back to
his office. Tate had used Sheehan's credit card the previous night. A
payment of one hundred pounds had been authorised to Contact
International Limited. Andy quickly found and dialled the number.
There was an answering machine. 'There is no one in the office at the
moment. Please call later.'

He looked at his watch. It was ten thirty. Three minutes later he dialled
again, with the same result. He paced the room. The phone rang. It was
Patterson.

'Good morning Andy. I was hoping you'd drop in to give me a progress
report.'

'Sir, I was on my way to do it, but I'm in the middle of making an
important call.'

'You are making some progress then?'

'Yes. I'm hopeful. It won't be long before we get a result.' Andy hoped he sounded confident.

'Good.'

'Sir, I'll pop in after lunch if that's all right. I've got a tight schedule this morning.'

'I'll expect you then.' Patterson replaced the receiver. Andy couldn't believe his luck. He had won a few more hours of grace.

He dialled Contact International again. This time the telephone was answered promptly. 'Contact International Limited. Dawn speaking. Can I help you?'

Andy realised he had not planned his attack. If he said the wrong thing it could ruin this last chance.

'Hello,' said Dawn again.

'Hello,' replied Andy. 'Your company was recommended to me.'

'Oh, I am glad to hear that,' said Dawn.

'I wondered if I could make an appointment with you.'

'By all means. We always recommend that new clients visit us personally. When would it be convenient for you?'

'Well, I'm not far away from you at the moment.' He glanced down at the fax. 'Are you still in Montpelier Square?'

'Yes.'

'In half an hour?' asked Andy, his heart thumping.

'Certainly,' said Dawn. 'And what name is it, sir?'

Andy hesitated. Better not give his own. That bastard Tate might recognise it if he was around. 'Wiltshire,' he said. 'Richard Wiltshire.'

'Thank you, Mr Wiltshire. I look forward to seeing you in half an hour.'

Andy slammed down the receiver. He grabbed his jacket, looked at the fax once again and stuffed it in his pocket. Despite a smart address in Knightsbridge, Contact International was probably not as grand as the name suggested, if Dawn was both answering the telephone and meeting the clients. He'd soon find out. He picked up his briefcase and raced out of the building.

The taxi dropped Andy in Montpelier Square. He passed a couple of polished brass plates advertising doctors' surgeries. Private and extremely expensive, he guessed. He rang the bell alongside Contact International's brushed steel plate. Four other businesses operated from the house. The door was opened remotely and Andy pushed his way inside. He entered the foyer and a woman whom he immediately identified as Dawn beckoned him into the office.

Andy looked round the reception room. He tried to ascertain what Contact International did. There was a black leather sofa, a white woollen rug and a glass coffee table. There were a few fashion magazines laid on the table.

He followed Dawn into the office. She closed the door behind him and gestured to a chair. He could tell she owned the business from the way she sat behind the desk. Her clothes were expensive. She wore too much make-up and it failed to soften her hard features. She looked fifty, but she was younger.

'As I said over the telephone, Mr Wiltshire, we do like our customers to peruse the photographs of our escorts in comfort.' So that was her game, thought Andy. 'If you make a note of the ones who interest you then we can ensure that you are well catered for when you call us in the future.' Dawn hesitated briefly, and licked her lips. 'Now, are you interested in the men or the women?'

'The women,' said Andy. The trail to Tate was getting warm. Dawn withdrew a worn photograph album from a drawer and passed it across the table. 'Could you tell me your terms?' asked Andy.

'We accept bookings over the telephone using all major credit cards. Escorts are available at all times, although some only work in the evenings. Our booking fee is one hundred pounds. The escorts make their own arrangements with the clients, but generally their rates start at fifty pounds excluding taxi fares.'

'I see,' said Andy. He flipped through the album as he spoke. The pages had been well-thumbed, as had some of the models; and there was no accounting for taste. Andy was shocked that some of the girls seemed so young; perhaps it was because he was getting older. 'Do you keep a record of your clients?'

Dawn misunderstood his question. 'Oh no. We're very discreet here. There is no way my clients' details could fall into the wrong hands. Absolutely no way.'

'How about their addresses?'

'We make a note of the client's address at the time of booking. The escort meets the client at that address. When the escort goes home she telephones to say she's finished the job, and then we destroy the address. We have to do it like that for the security of our escorts.' Dawn added, confidentially. 'There are some funny people out there.'

'I quite understand,' said Andy. 'So you record the addresses on your computer?'

'Not any more,' said Dawn. 'The girls didn't trust the computer in case it lost the addresses; and our clients didn't trust it in case their names and addresses stayed on it. Funny old world isn't it?' She chuckled. 'I'm not always here either, and some of the girls have never seen a computer before.'

'So how do you record the addresses?' insisted Andy.

Dawn looked at him suspiciously. The clients who asked the most questions were always the most difficult. 'You're not the first person to be worried about that, Mr Wiltshire.' She pointed a mauve fingernail to a corner of the office. 'That machine is a paper shredder. I put the addresses in there. That is the same machine as the Secret Service uses to destroy Top Secret papers, so I'm told. I think that's safe enough. Some of my clients are very important people, and they are satisfied.'

Andy was undeterred. There had to be some way of finding out Tate's address. If he kept asking the questions he'd find the answer; but Dawn didn't look like she was willing to answer many more questions.

'Anyway,' said Dawn, losing her patience, 'if we kept all our clients' addresses we'd end up looking like the bleeding tax office.'

'Andy smiled. Dawn had made a mistake at last. She'd given him an idea. 'You have a lot of clients?' he asked.

'Over one hundred a week,' she replied, proudly.

'How long have you been established?'

'Nearly two years.'

'Do you know all your clients?'

Dawn pursed her lips. 'If you don't mind me saying, you're asking a lot of questions.'

Andy nodded. 'Yes, I am. I'm sorry about that.' He snapped the photograph album closed and placed it on the desk. He leaned forward, opened his briefcase, took out his identity card, put it on the table and said, 'Customs and Excise. What is your VAT number?'

'We don't have to pay VAT,' retorted Dawn.

'You're mistaken,' said Andy grimly. 'Over a hundred clients a week at one hundred pounds a booking means you turn over a minimum of forty thousand pounds a month. That takes you well over the VAT threshold.'

'We don't charge VAT,' said Dawn.

'That doesn't matter,' said Andy affably. He took out his calculator and pressed the buttons. He looked at the results with interest. 'You seem to run a very lucrative business. I'll assume a half million pound turnover, rounding down. The VAT you owe for the past two years is, let's see . . .' Andy coughed, held the calculator up for emphasis, raised his eyebrows, and read off the figure. 'One hundred and sixty-eight thousand pounds.'

'You can't be serious,' said Dawn. She scrabbled in a drawer and produced a packet of menthol cigarettes. She lit one.

'I couldn't be more serious,' said Andy. 'By law I now demand that you hand over your accounts for the past two years.'

'But I don't charge VAT,' said Dawn desperately.

'No problem,' said Andy. 'You can write to all your clients and tell them that you made a mistake and should have charged VAT. It'll take some time, but you'll gather it all in the end.'

Dawn stared at him. 'What do you want?' She was used to paying off the police.

'I want some information.'

Dawn's eyes narrowed. 'What sort?'

'First, I'm going to caution you,' said Andy. Dawn's face hardened. 'You will be breaking the law if you tell anyone that there is an investigation in progress. Apart from being liable for tax avoidance you would face imprisonment for up to five years.'

Dawn nodded, relieved it was just a caution.

'I need the address of a client who saw one of your girls last night.'

'What was his name?' said Dawn. She was business-like. She had no qualms about indiscretion any more.

'Sheehan.'

Dawn flipped through a pile of credit card slips. 'If I tell you, will that be the end of it?' she asked.

'Yes,' said Andy. 'But I need the address where the girl went last night.'

'You need to talk to Dolores,' said Dawn.

'What's her real name?' asked Andy.

'Jane Boothby.'

'Call her up and tell her she has a client now.'

'She works in the morning. I don't know what she does. She's never free until one. I have to leave a message on her machine. She wouldn't get here until one thirty.'

'I want her address and phone number.'

'I only have her phone number,' said Dawn. She scribbled the number on a piece of paper.

'I want to meet her at one thirty, sharp. And make sure Jane Boothby is here. If she doesn't turn up for whatever reason I will make sure you are very, very sorry,' warned Andy. 'Is that understood?'

Dawn nodded. Dolores would be there. She'd make sure of that. She picked up the telephone and dialled the number. She left a message. 'Jane, this is Dawn. Pop in to see me at one thirty, soon as you can. I've got something perfect for you.' She replaced the receiver.

Andy stood up. He was short of officers, otherwise he would have taken the precaution of keeping an eye on Dawn. He gambled that she had too much to lose by making a sudden disappearance.

He showed himself out of the office.

# 3

An hour after Ginger called, Spider became conscious of a repeated knocking coming from upstairs. He got to his feet and climbed the stairs. He stood outside the bedroom door. 'Yes?' he asked.

'I want to go to the bathroom,' said the girl.

'Why?' asked Spider. She was always going. It irritated him and interrupted his thoughts.

'I'm carrying a baby, and that doesn't leave much room for anything else. Especially my bladder,' said Julia.

Spider unlocked the door and the girl walked past him into the toilet. She shut the door. Spider thought for a moment or two. She didn't speak to him. She didn't look at him. He knew the reason. It was his eyes. He listened, but he couldn't hear anything behind the door. Maybe she was opening the window. He opened the door.

'Get out!' screamed Julia.

Spider stepped back and shut the door. It was like a photograph. The girl was squatting above the toilet. Her dress was pulled up to her hips. Her legs were apart, and he couldn't quite see anything dark in the middle of everything. He wondered if they would shave it when she had the baby. He waited patiently in the corridor, and thought about his sister.

Something gnawed at the back of his mind. He couldn't put his finger on it. If only he could remember what it was. He walked back to the stairs, and stared at them. It seemed like he had been standing there for a long time when the girl came out.

'Where's Ginger?' she said.

'He's gone.'

The girl walked back into the bedroom and shut the door. He stared at the door. He imagined something dark in the middle of everything. 'Look after her and everything will be fine.' Spider walked down the corridor to his room and turned on the portable television. He watched the cartoons on the children's programme.

He remembered what it was he had forgotten. It came with a crystal clarity. They couldn't let the girl go. She knew too much. It didn't matter what he did now.

He hadn't seen his sister for a long time. Not since she had the baby.


# 4


Edward waited for Ginger in the foyer of the Tower Hotel at St Catherine's Dock. He was early for the meeting. Soon Julia would be free. He would try and persuade her to take a holiday with him to forget this nightmare. He regretted every decision he'd taken over the past week. If only he'd played along with Samuel. If only he'd listened to Julia in the beginning. Contacting customs had been a mistake. Ballot couldn't afford to spring Julia, even if he knew where she was being held, because it meant arresting Ginger and Spider; and that would result in Samuel's immediate disappearance. Ballot had been jerking him around, playing for time so he could locate Samuel.

Edward reviewed his options. He was still in a strong position. He'd hand the heroin to Ginger. They'd honour any deal while he still had the million and a half to collect from Jason. He looked at his watch. There were still thirty minutes until the meeting with Ginger. He looked around the foyer for signs of surveillance. There were none. The pace and atmosphere remained the same. He made a phone call to Annelies. He was giving Ballot a last chance. If Julia was free there was no need to meet with Ginger; but he was disappointed to find there were no developments on that front. He declined the offer of a meeting with Ballot, but told Annelies he would phone again. He didn't want Ballot to know he had an appointment with Ginger.


Edward saw Ginger's BMW arrive. He reached it before Ginger was out. He opened the passenger door and got in.

'Where's the gear?' Ginger asked.

'We'll go and fetch it,' responded Edward.

'You wouldn't be trying to pull a fast one, would you?'

'No.'

'Which way?' Ginger barked.

'Head towards Greenwich.' Edward looked out of the window. Ginger still failed to take basic precautions, the least of which would have been to hire a car for this transaction. It was only ten minutes before he noticed they were being tailed.

'You're being followed,' Edward pointed out. 'There are at least two cars, a blue Vauxhall and a red Ford.' He should have guessed that Ballot would be tailing Ginger.

'You must have attracted the bluebottles,' said Ginger. 'You were told to come alone.'

Edward ignored the remark. He wanted to be sure no one witnessed the transfer of the heroin. It was probably the only worry he had in common with Ginger.

Ginger pulled into a petrol station and filled the petrol tank. Then he set off in the opposite direction. After a few miles Ginger confirmed they were still being followed. 'I'll settle their hash,' he said finally. 'If you got unwanted company the best thing is tell them. That makes them buzz off.' He circled a roundabout three times and took off down a short section of dual carriageway at speed. He stopped in the middle of the carriageway causing chaos as cars were forced to weave past. He repeated the tactic a number of times until it was clear which cars were following them. In the end the customs abandoned the operation. 'That's taught them the lesson,' Ginger said, pleased with himself. 'Now let's get down to business.'

'What about Julia?' asked Edward.

'I get the gear, then I make a call to Spider. He lets her go some place, and you pick her up. That arrangement is not open to negotiation.'

'Pull the car over,' said Edward suddenly.

'What?' asked Ginger, unused to taking orders.

'I said, pull over!' repeated Edward.

Ginger stopped the car.

'Before you pick up the goods, I want to speak to Julia.'

Ginger stared at Edward for a long minute. He was evaluating the demand. Finally he nodded. He snatched the telephone off the dashboard and dialled a number.

'Put the girl on the line,' he snapped. He listened for a moment.

'I don't care,' he said. 'Put her on.'

Edward watched Ginger. He waited impatiently. Ginger stared out of the windscreen.

Finally Ginger awkwardly held the receiver to Edward's ear.

Edward heard muffled sobs.

'Julia,' he said. 'It's Edward.'

'Edward . . .' he heard her gasp. 'Please . . . I can't bear it any longer. Get me out of this. You . . .'

'Julia, I won't be long—'

Ginger snatched the phone away and hung up. He started the car. 'So let's get moving.'

Edward was frantic. He had never heard Julia so upset before. 'Tell Spider to let her go,' he said to Ginger.

'When we finish our business.'

'If anything happens to Julia I will kill you,' he said coldly.

'Yeah?' replied Ginger. He nodded as if assimilating the information.

The first doubts entered Edward's mind as he led Ginger along the tow path to the boat. They were the only people walking in the drizzle. 'Can't stand the country,' said Ginger.

Edward said nothing. The suburbs of London were hardly countryside.

'Makes you stand out like a sore thumb,' Ginger added.

His sudden friendliness aroused a sixth sense. Edward looked over his shoulder. Ginger's Italian shoes suffered as his feet slithered on the muddy path beside the canal basin. Away from the familiar camouflage of concrete walls he looked curiously vulnerable, staggering across an empty skyline awaiting development.

'Here we are,' said Edward, stepping on to the boat. Ginger looked at the boat with distrust. He looked at the gangplank which rested precariously on the edge of the deck. He looked at the black water between the side of the hull and the sheer concrete wall of the basin. He gripped his mobile phone firmly, stepped cautiously on to the gangplank, grabbed the lifeline, and finally stepped on to the deck.

Edward had unlocked the hatch in the cockpit and was already down in the cabin. He fumbled in the darkness by the chart table for the fuse box and the light switch. A collision flare dropped out of its holder and rolled on to the table. Ginger clambered down.

'So where is it?' Ginger asked, taking in his surroundings.

'Up forward,' said Edward, leading the way into the bows of the boat. He opened the chain locker, pulled aside the rusty anchor chain and retrieved the bags he had hidden. Ginger pulled them into the saloon, unzipped them and counted the packages. They were all there. He put the packages back in the bags and then carried them to the companion-way. He put them on the floor.

'Now my part of the deal,' said Edward. He stood by the chart table, between Ginger and the steps leading to the cockpit. He fiddled with the collision flare. 'Where is Julia?'

'We've got a problem,' said Ginger. He reached into his coat and pulled out the gun. He smiled.

'No,' said Edward. 'You're forgetting I have to collect the money for the cannabis.'

'Yeah? I forgot to tell you. Your mate Sammy is picking it up himself. He found out who was handling it.'

'What about Julia?' asked Edward. When the gun had first appeared he'd frozen, but now he could feel his heart pumping. He was being forced to do what he had anticipated, but dreaded.

'Who gives a fuck about some tart when there's five million at stake?' said Ginger.

'What strikes me about you Ginger, is that you're not a cold-blooded killer. You're probably quite a nice person deep inside. I mean, you're not a hit man. You've got to have something personal against your victim, so I'll tell you something. I'll make it easy for you.' Ginger looked baffled by this train of thought. Edward leaned forward. He was staring at Ginger, willing him to hold the stare. He lifted the flare a few inches off the chart table with his right hand. 'There's this old nautical saying,' he paused for a moment. 'Only admirals and arseholes stand in the gangway. I think you're an arsehole.'

For the briefest second Ginger's expression registered incomprehension. Edward slammed the base of the flare on the table. There was a dull explosion.

Oh Christ, thought Edward. Not a dud flare.

Ginger's eyes darted towards the flare which Edward now swung towards his face. The flare blazed its fourteen thousand candela of light. Edward closed his eyes and ducked. He was blinded by the brilliance. He heard a shot. Acrid smoke seared his lungs. He heard Ginger scream. He held the flare up and opened his eyes. His retina snatched the image of Ginger's silhouette before he closed his eyes again. He pointed the flare at where Ginger's crouching body had been. He heard Ginger scream again. The flare ripped across the saloon like a flame-thrower. The noise was deafening in the enclosed space of the boat.

Edward had survived. He held the upper hand. He advanced, holding the flare ahead of him. He was filled with anger and rage as he pointed the flare at Ginger's writhing shape. Edward looked behind him and saw the gun lying on the saloon floor. He picked it up and stuffed it in his pocket. He turned, scrambled up the stairs into the cockpit and dropped the flare into the water. It boiled on the surface.

He looked back into the boat. Ginger was curled up, his jacket smouldering. Flames licked at the saloon cushions. Edward pulled the fire extinguisher from the bulkhead and sprayed dry powder over the flames.

Finally there was silence. Except for Ginger's rasping breath. At least he wasn't dead.

'Ginger!' he shouted. 'I want the address.' Ginger didn't react. Edward stood behind him, gun ready in his hand. He grabbed Ginger's jacket collar, and pulled him. Ginger twisted uncomfortably. Edward looked away instinctively. Ginger's hands had been burned raw, and were spread like talons. His hair had gone. His face was no longer identifiable. The features had been cauterised. Edward forced himself to look back.

'Fuck you, Ginger!' he shouted. 'I never wanted this. It was your idea. All I want is the address. Where is Julia?'

Ginger might have been looking at him, but it was hard to tell. The eyelids had taken the full force of the flare. Slowly his head shook from side to side.

'Listen carefully, Ginger. I'm going to get that address from you. I don't care how long it takes.' He walked back to the chart table and pulled out another flare and held it in front of him. Maybe Ginger couldn't see it. 'I have another flare in my hand. I will set it off in a few seconds if you don't tell me the address.'

Edward listened. Ginger's rasps seemed to be coming quicker. He was speaking, but his lips weren't moving.

'I can't hear you,' he said.

'In my pocket. Letters,' said Ginger, with difficulty.

Edward pressed the gun to Ginger's back and felt in the jacket pockets. He withdrew the mobile phone and car keys from one pocket. In the other he found two letters.

'. . . hospital,' Ginger muttered.

Edward ignored him and unfolded the letters. The first was a reminder for insurance renewal. The second was a letter from a solicitor referring to the sale of a Snooker Hall on Kingsland Road.

'Is Julia being held at the Snooker Hall?' asked Edward.

Ginger nodded

'I hope you're not lying to me?'

Ginger shook his head.

'I tell you what I'm going to do. I'm going to release Julia. If I find her, then I'll call an ambulance for you. If not, I'll come back and finish you myself.' Edward hesitated a moment. He passed his hand in front of Ginger's face. There was no reaction. Blinded. Tough shit. 'You sure you're telling me the truth?'

Ginger slowly lowered himself on to his elbows. He rocked in a foetal crouch. Edward slipped the gun into his pocket. He leaned over Ginger and retrieved the heroin; he might still need to bargain. He switched off the fuses on the boat, and climbed into daylight. He shut the cockpit door behind him. It was good to breathe the fresh air.

He ran to the car and started driving. He dialled Ballot's number and Annelies answered. Ballot was not there. He gave Annelies the address of where Julia was being held, and told her to find Andy Ballot.

He didn't like to think what would happen to Julia if Spider didn't hear from Ginger.

He needed to speak to Ballot. It was time to make a deal. Maybe he was at Fetter Lane. He dialled Andy's office number.

# 5

Tate took more precautions than usual when he returned to his basement after the phone call from his source in customs. He felt uneasy. Although the source said there was no need to worry, something warned him that it was time to leave. Of course the customs man didn't want to sound the alarm; he had received two hundred and fifty thousand pounds up front, in Cyprus, and would receive the same again upon completion of the deal. The man was keeping Tate in the picture. Only, Tate didn't like the picture.

Ballot had found out that Sheehan was his alias, but that was all he knew. Well, Sheehan was history now. The radio pager had been dumped. If anyone asked, he'd say he knew Martin Sheehan years ago, but they'd not been in touch for years. The last he heard of Sheehan was that he was running gems out of Kenya or India or some exotic place like that. He could work Sheehan into a very interesting person.

Ginger was too hot to contact. It appeared half the customs force was after him, even though he'd given them the slip. He probably had the heroin. He'd have to market it now. Tate would keep the advance. One day they might meet and settle the accounts. If Ginger was smart he'd put the heroin to sleep somewhere and wait for the heat to blow over. Ballot would pull him and Spider for questioning soon; but they'd had enough practice at being interrogated over the years. They'd say nothing. They valued their lives.

Tate felt the briefest pang of regret for Edward. They'd been close in the old days, but they wouldn't be chatting any more because Edward had made the cardinal mistake. He had spoken to customs. Tate had worked it out; it explained how Ballot knew Julia had disappeared.

It had been Ginger's idea to blow Edward away. Now Julia would join him in the foundations of some concrete building. Edward was a stupid bastard. It could have been resolved so easily.

Tomorrow Tate would slip over to Ireland, then fly from Shannon to the States. He had an appointment to call his customs officer in a month for a debriefing. Things should have cooled down by then. There would be sufficient change to pay him off from the million and a half which Jason was delivering to Oliver. Then they'd plan a new scam. It would be a pity not to make use of all those connections. This was just a hiccup.

Tate pottered around the flat with a garbage bag, cleaning up. He didn't want any science projects lurking in the kitchen when he came back in a few months. He ripped the stained sheets off the bed and put them in the bag. He pulled out some clean laundry. He experienced a moment's revulsion as he thought about the previous night's tart. Sex was a messy business. He hated losing control of himself.

# Chapter 15

## 1

Vince paced the Fetter Lane office. He was nervous. He didn't like it when Andy disappeared, following some lead of his own. It was hard to know what course of action to take when he was kept in the dark.

His phone rang. He pulled it out of his pocket and flipped it open. It was Andy.

'How's it going?'

'We lost them,' said Vince. He didn't have time to explain how Ginger had made surveillance impossible, before Andy was snapping down the line.

'You've fucked it up, Vince. All that work was a waste of time. Those guys were leading us to the evidence. Why didn't you arrest them if you thought you were going to lose them?'

'Do me a favour, Andy, tell me what we were going to charge them with? It was a bit over the top for ten officers to arrest them for driving without due care and attention!'

'Shut up,' said Andy, viciously. 'I suggest you return to Ginger's house and relieve the guys watching it, and pray Ginger reappears.'

'You're wasting your time.'

'In which case you can help me do it,' snapped Andy, and cut him off.

Vince snapped the phone shut, and grinned. He was managing to keep things together. He was taking risks, but that was what he was paid to do.

The surveillance operation on Ginger almost brought the whole scam to an end. Vince congratulated himself on his cunning. It hadn't been easy to ensure Jay spotted the red Ford he was driving. Ginger wouldn't have noticed in a million years. He grinned at Ginger's counter-surveillance tactics; they'd left customs no options but to abort. By now, though, the exchange would be over. He looked at his watch. Ginger had the heroin and Edward Jay was history.

'Venables! I'd like a word with you.'

Vince looked up, surprised. 'Sir!' he said. He rose to his feet. Simon Patterson's expression was serious.

'Where's Ballot?'

'I don't know, sir.'

'This business with Davidson? What's your opinion?'

'Frankly?'

'Yes.'

'Andy doesn't have a leg to stand on. He has no evidence that Davidson was accepting bribes. And a wad of cash doesn't constitute proof.'

'Ballot told me that he was tipped off by Edward Jay.'

Vince felt his heart stop for a moment. His stomach fluttered. 'He's in touch with Jay?' he asked, unable to keep the surprise from his voice.

'Apparently.'

Vince grasped for some adequate response. 'He should have arrested Jay immediately.' Thank God, he hadn't.

'That is just what I was thinking,' said Patterson. 'I've got the Met on my back. They want to set up a meeting with Ballot this afternoon and sort this thing out.'

'I'm not surprised, sir.' Vince's mind was elsewhere. He wondered if Andy was with Jay at the moment. No. He couldn't be. He'd just called. Perhaps they were setting up Ginger. 'There's something I don't understand, sir. Why didn't Andy tell the team? We've been floundering in the dark for a couple of weeks.'

'Jay told him that Tate had a source inside the department.'

Vince's mouth went dry. 'That's ridiculous.'

'Yes. I'm beginning to think so myself.'

'You know what I think, sir? I think these guys are very smart. I think they've invented the cat and thrown it among the pigeons. They're probably laughing their heads off.'

Patterson nodded, slowly. 'This thing has got out of hand. Ballot has taken personal prejudice too far.'

Vince nodded. He should have paid Andy far more attention. Andy was a clever bugger; but he could be discredited. 'Apparently Samuel Tate ran off with Andy's fiancée when they were lads. Andy never got over it.'

Patterson looked up, and blinked with surprise. He looked away, staring out of the window, deep in thought. He sucked at his cheeks. Finally he came to a decision. 'Tell Ballot I want to see him immediately. It's time to call this whole thing off. It's got out of hand.'

'Yes, sir.'

Vince watched the Chief stalk out of the room. He heaved a sigh of relief, and sat down.

Damage limitation. That was the first priority. He would find out what Ballot knew, and then discredit him. That was all very well, so long as Ballot wasn't witnessing the meeting between Jay and Ginger. He had to find Ballot; once the Chief spoke to him, they were all home and dry. And he'd have the second instalment paid into his Swiss account.

Vince stood up and walked to Andy's desk. He looked through the drawers and pulled out the files. He flicked through the papers searching for some unfamiliar lead. He shuffled through the bank statements.

He reached out automatically for the phone and answered it.

'Ballot?' asked the voice.

'No. He's not here.'

'Where can I reach him?'

'Who is this speaking?' asked Vince.

'I need to talk to him urgently.'

'If you leave a message I'll make sure he gets it.' Vince stopped leafing through Andy's papers. This was interesting.

'Who are you?' asked the voice.

'Venables. Andy's second-in-command.'

'Tell Andy that Edward called. Tell him I want to make a deal. Tell him I've located Julia . . .'

Vince listened, numbed. Perhaps it was time to step back and become a customs officer once again. He'd been careful. But not careful enough. Not if Tate was caught. There were too many questions and only Jay could answer them. Jay had found out about the place in Kingsland Road. If Andy spoke to Davidson he'd know that Vince had known about that. Mistakes like that were an embarrassment.

'What about Phillips?' asked Vince.

'Phillips?' asked Jay.

'Ginger.'

'I'll let you know,' answered Jay, enigmatically, before hanging up.

Vince replaced the receiver. It was always a question of being in the right place at the right time. He had intercepted a call which might have brought the whole pack of cards tumbling down.

Instead, Jay was about to enter a cul-de-sac.

# 2

The pain became worse. Ginger turned his head from side to side. He couldn't see. Every time he moved it felt as if his skin was being ripped from his face. He began to distinguish shades of light and dark. He could not work out whether there were shapes, but a panic welled inside him. He was blinded. If he could reach a hospital maybe the doctors could do something. He didn't believe that bastard Jay was coming back. Spider would sort out Jay's shit; he was never coming back. He'd sort the girl too. Spider would be edgy already; he was waiting for the call. Trouble was, Spider didn't know he was stuck in this boat. He had to get out.

He began crawling. He kept knocking into objects. The place was cramped. Every time his hands touched a surface the pain seared through raw nerve endings. He sat down and propelled himself backwards, pushing with his feet. It took an eternity. But he hadn't come this far for it to end on some crappy boat.

His blood pounded in his ears. He nearly fainted and his head lolled sideways, catching on something. The pain jolted him into consciousness. At last he felt the steps against his back. He stood up carefully, each movement making him wince, and with each wince he gasped with pain. He sat on each step, repeating the same searing movements each time. He'd be out soon. He'd call Spider and warn him that Jay was on his way. He'd have Spider deal with Jay slowly. The thought made the pain bearable.

He leaned against the doors on the top step. They weren't locked; he tumbled through, over balancing backwards, and landed on his head in the cockpit. The numbness evaporated in a blinding flash of agony as his head grazed the cockpit grating. The pain stretched towards an ever receding crescendo. He didn't know if he was screaming. It seemed an eternity before silence fell again.

'Help,' he croaked.

There was no answer.

At least he was outside. He could feel the cool wind, and his eyes discerned a diffuse light. He sat for a while trying to gain his bearings. At last he continued the slow journey to the shore. He explored his route, feet stretched ahead. He negotiated the cockpit coamings. He found the lifelines along the side of the boat. He'd soon be ashore. Progress would be quicker then. He would stand up. Someone would see him. Someone would help him. To a telephone. Then the hospital.

He eased himself on to the gangplank, backwards, carefully slipping under the lifelines. He shuffled along, pushing himself backwards, bracing his feet against the hull.

As he was falling he remembered why he had been so nervous when he first stepped on to the boat. The plank had only been resting on the edge of the deck. As he hit the water he gasped, and the first mouthful entered his lungs.

# 3

Julia lay on the bed. She'd spent the past two days huddled in the grey blankets, sleeping and dozing. She tried not to think about her predicament. It was so awful it was absurd. She tried to ignore the musty smell of the dilapidated building. She closed her eyes and thought of being at home. She wove daydreams in which she played with her baby in her warm clean flat, where the windows were open and the sunshine splashed on to the carpet. She realised, without any guilt, that Edward made no appearance in these dreams. He was in her past.

She gently stroked her baby, over and over again. The baby was big and there wasn't enough room to kick any more. She could feel that little life inside her. In some ways she didn't feel resentful about the incarceration. It gave her time to be alone with her child.

Every time she heard the phone ring in the distance it raised her hopes. It held the possibility of contact with the outside world. It broke her equanimity. This time she began crying. She couldn't help it. Her situation was hopeless. 'Help,' she repeated weakly between her sobs, as if it were a prayer. She heard the door open. Spider was holding the telephone. He pushed it roughly towards her mouth and she gripped it with one hand. 'Help,' she muttered, incoherently. Then she heard Edward's voice. He sounded normal. It sounded as if he were in control of the situation. She started to speak. He seemed to have no idea what she was going through. Before she could speak again the connection was broken. 'Edward,' she repeated twice into the dead telephone, before dropping it. He had rung off. Fuck him. She couldn't even count on him.

Spider picked up the telephone. 'Leave me alone,' said Julia.

Spider didn't leave. He sat on the edge of the bed. His presence jolted Julia into awareness. She tensed. She had made this room into her world, and now her privacy had been invaded.

'My sister had a baby,' said Spider. 'They took it away from her.'

'Why?' asked Julia.

'They said she was too young. She was fifteen years old.'

Julia didn't comment. She wasn't going to waste her sympathy on his dysfunctional family.

'Have they shaved you already?'

'What?' exclaimed Julia. Perhaps she had misunderstood.

'They shaved her's. It was like she was a little girl again. She showed me afterwards. When they weren't watching.'

Julia said nothing. She looked at Spider with horror, but he wasn't looking at her. She didn't want to hear this.

'I shouldn't talk to you like this. He told me not to talk to you.'

'Who did?' asked Julia. She realised Spider was barking mad, and she had to humour him. The clock in his head was ticking away.

'The last time they caught me talking to you they hit me.'

'Who hit you?'

'My dad. I used to get into the bed with my sister. It was warm and safe. Then we used to do it. But he didn't like it. My dad thought it was alright for him. Not for me.' Spider stopped talking and looked at her. He wasn't seeing her. He didn't recognise her. She was only a figment of his warped imagination. For the first time she acknowledged that anything could happen to her in that dismal room, and no one would know. 'He's not here now,' Spider said.

'I wouldn't be too sure about that,' said Julia. She was going to scotch any ideas like that. She was getting the hang of this game.

'He's not here, because he's dead.'

'But he might still be watching,' said Julia.

Spider's lazy eye flickered. 'No. When you're dead, you're gone.'

'Not always,' said Julia quickly.

'Yes, he is. That's what they told me. He's never coming back. Now we're together, and I've got to get you ready.'

He stared at her for a long, long time. Slowly he picked up the hem of her dress and pulled it to her thighs. Julia was too shocked to react immediately. She couldn't look at him. She pushed his hands away abruptly. He made her sick. She stared at the wall.

# 4

Andy sat on the sofa in the small reception room, and flipped through a magazine impatiently. Finally the door opened. The girl was pretty. She wasn't more than twenty years old. Andy wondered why she was working as a call girl. Maybe she was supporting a drug habit; but he wouldn't make that his business unless it became necessary.

She wore a black dress, black stockings and high heels. She knew what her punters liked. Her auburn hair was tied back with a simple gold clip. She gave Andy a friendly smile as she walked through Contact International's reception room into Dawn's office. She guessed Andy was a client, although she rarely met them at the office.

'Hello, Jane,' said Dawn. 'The gentleman in reception wants a word with you.'

Andy stood and approached the office as Jane turned in the entrance. The friendly smile had gone. Gentlemen who wanted a word were bad news.

'Thanks, Dawn,' she said sarcastically. 'You could have warned me. I wouldn't have bothered to tart myself up.'

Dawn shrugged her shoulders.

Andy was surprised by Jane's voice. It was cultured, almost plummy. 'I want to ask you a few questions,' he said.

'About what?' she asked curtly.

'He's with the Customs and Excise,' interjected Dawn.

'I'd like to see some proof.' Jane stared at Andy. He reached inside his jacket and produced identification.

'Is there somewhere private we can talk?' asked Andy, turning to Dawn.

Dawn couldn't conceal her disappointment. Her curiosity had got the better of her. 'There's only next door.'

'That's fine,' said Jane. She leaned forward and switched on the radio which sat on the desk. She smiled maliciously knowing that she had prevented Dawn from eavesdropping. She tossed her head and closed Dawn in the office.

'What do you want?' she asked petulantly, sitting on the small sofa. Andy stood awkwardly in front of her. The sofa was far too intimate for the two of them. He stood in the middle of the carpet.

'I want to know about one of your clients. A man called Sheehan.'

'I never remember their names,' Jane said automatically. 'Why should I?'

Andy opened his briefcase and retrieved the photograph of Tate in company with Ginger and Spider. It was still the most recent one he had. He passed it to her, stabbing a finger at Tate. 'How about this man?' he asked.

Jane gave it a cursory glance. 'I've never seen him before.'

Andy stared at her. 'You're sure about that?'

She looked at the photograph again. She tossed it on to the table in front of her and replied, 'Of course I am.'

Andy felt a moment's panic. He couldn't have made a mistake. This couldn't be another dead end. Sheehan and Tate must be one and the same.

Andy realised she wouldn't admit to anything until she was sure she couldn't be incriminated. He wondered whether she was one of Tate's regulars. She might tip him off. Perhaps Tate supplied her habit in return for services. Andy had to take a chance. 'I could make life very difficult for you. I could put the tax people on to you. I could have the police visit you. Right now I could take you in for questioning for seventy-two hours. I could make life intolerable for you.' He paused to let that sink in. Jane stared at him coldly. He had a hunch. 'I could call up your family and tell them to bail you out.' Jane's eyes flickered with doubt for a second. 'They might not like to know what the apple of their eye does for a living.'

Andy offered Jane a cigarette. She refused. He lit one. 'But, I don't have time for all that. If you don't help me now I'll do all those things I mentioned. But I won't stop there. I'll keep coming back because I'll believe you were aiding and abetting this man. Just when you thought I had disappeared I'll turn up, because I'm a vindictive bastard. I'll haunt you, and your past will haunt you for ever.'

Jane pursed her lips. 'I can't help you if I don't know him.'

'Don't give me that shit,' Andy snapped. 'I know you saw him last night.'

Jane didn't flinch. She picked the photograph off the table, and frowned, giving the perfect imitation of someone deep in thought. Her movements were calculated. A smooth liar, this one. 'Yes,' she said at last. 'it could be him. Most of the time he was wearing a mask. He was sick.'

'Can you remember where you met him?'

'Off Holland Park Avenue.'

'Was it a house or a hotel?'

'It was a house. A basement flat.'

'Can you remember the number?' asked Andy eagerly.

'No.'

'Would you remember it if you saw it?'

'What's in it for me?' asked Jane.

'I'll owe you a favour if it's in my power.'

Jane looked at him. She was surprised by the sudden sincerity in his voice. 'Just give me my taxi fares, and forget about me,' Jane answered. She seemed to have come to a sudden decision. 'Sheehan's a nasty piece of work anyway.'

Andy picked up the photograph and as he was about to return it to his briefcase he realised that he didn't know where it had been taken. It wasn't taken outside either Ginger or Spider's homes. They lived in terraced houses. The police photographer had obviously been positioned at a site which they frequented. He looked at the picture carefully. The building in the background looked as if it was a warehouse. He shouldn't have overlooked something as obvious as that.

He dropped the picture into his briefcase. 'Let's go,' he said.

Downstairs Andy hailed a taxi. He sat impatiently as they encountered heavy traffic on Park Lane.

'You said Tate was sick. What did you mean?'

'He's a pervert. Really weird. I hate people like that. Usually I try not to make value judgements. I mean it's a job and all that. If people weren't different I'd probably be out of pocket money. This one wanted to do all kinds of strange stuff. Not just bondage. Usually you tie up some bloke, stick him in the cupboard and have a cup of tea. Maybe talk dirty through the keyhole. Stuff like that. This one, he had a thing about doing it in the bath. He tried to put my head under water when he popped his nuts. I thought he was bloody drowning me.'

'I don't understand,' said Andy. Alarm bells rang in his head. All he could think of was Rosa. She had drowned. Death by misadventure. 'Can you explain that to me again?'

'Yes. First of all we went into the bedroom. He had some champagne and we started drinking. He took my clothes off. I told him the price was for a straightforward job. He said not to worry about that. He'd pay for any extras.' Andy didn't want to listen, but he couldn't help himself. He was imagining events from twenty-five years ago. He imagined it was Rosa talking to him as Jane described in detail the various violations which Samuel had performed on her body.

'You didn't complain?' asked Andy at one point.

'Everything has a price,' said Jane. 'That's what he kept saying. But I stopped in the end. There's some stuff I won't do.'

'Why do you do any of it?' asked Andy.

'I'm paying my way through college,' said Jane bluntly.

'What about the bath?'

'Some people get a kick being suffocated when they come. It's not unusual. Sometimes you get people who take a couple of amyl nitrates which are a real heart stopper. Well, he wanted me to hold his head under water while I fucked him. This was after all the other stuff. I thought he was going to drown. He must have been under for three minutes. Then he said it was my turn. Thank God it wasn't a swimming pool.' She paused. 'Otherwise I would have been drowned.' She looked at Andy. He was staring straight ahead. His lips were curled with anger. 'Why do you want to know? What's it all about then?'

He didn't answer at first. After a moment or two his face relaxed. 'Something from a long way back,' said Andy absently.

'What are you going to do?' asked Jane.

'I'm going to nick him. Then I'm going to throw away the key.'

'Good luck,' said Jane. 'That's where he belongs.'

He looked at her and suddenly felt paternal. 'Are you really doing this to pay your way through college?'

'Yes.'

'What about your parents? Aren't they supporting you?'

'They think it's a waste of time.'

'What are you studying?'

'Film.'

'Give me your address. I might be able to fix some sort of community reward for you out of this.'

'Really?' she almost laughed. 'I don't think so. I'd rather pass on the publicity.'

# 5

Vince drove past the boarded Snooker Hall on Kingsland Road, and sized it up. There was no sign of activity. He might need a few tools to break inside. He had the keys of his trade in the boot. A sledgehammer, jemmy and screwdriver; that was all customs needed when they went on a bust and the suspects didn't open up. There were few feelings to equal that of putting a sledgehammer through someone's door at dawn.

He parked the car down a side street. He needed to be circumspect. It would be disastrous if he were seen in the vicinity. He wished he could speak to Tate, but couldn't risk it in case the number showed on the bill for the mobile phone. It was better to leave Tate out of it. Tate had already been indiscreet once; he had told Jay that he had someone well placed inside customs, and now Ballot knew. There was no knowing what Tate would do if he was caught. Even Tate was turning into a risk; but then, Tate had only been a stepping stone to Akbar, who held the key to the future.

For a moment Vince considered turning his back on the whole conspiracy. He was ahead. He had his nest egg in a Swiss bank. He wondered what had happened to Ginger. Perhaps he had double-crossed them. Perhaps Spider had gone too, and the girl was waiting for Jay to pick her up; but then Jay wouldn't have called Ballot. No, it was wrong to back out. He'd come too far. Now, he only needed to tell Spider that Jay was arriving and then they would have the heroin. If he pulled this off there would be more.

Vince walked to the rear of the building. This was going to be a tricky operation. He knew Spider, but Spider wouldn't recognise him and wasn't likely to answer the door to a stranger. If he was persistent Spider would probably let loose with a shotgun. It was ironic that Spider owed him a favour; if his picture had been forwarded to the Dutch then he'd have been identified as de Groote's killer by Monique. He wondered how Jay's girlfriend was getting on; if the report into the death of Monique was characteristic, Spider was a nasty piece of work.

He stood outside the door and listened. He looked around. A few grimy windows overlooked the courtyard, but there were no signs of life behind them. He noticed that the large padlock was unlocked. He turned the door handle carefully. It was locked from the inside. He felt the top and bottom of the door. There were no bolts. He decided to slip inside and make sure Jay wasn't already there. He could arrest Jay if he found him; then dispose of him one way or another. If Spider was alone he would explain that he had a message from Tate, warn him that Jay was about to turn up, then disappear while Spider took care of him.

He pulled out the flat iron bar from inside his pocket and slipped it into the door jamb. He levered the edge of the door until the screws of the lock groaned free. The door swung open. He stood for a moment, peering into the gloomy interior. He entered silently, closing the door behind him. He moved from room to room. The ground floor was deserted. As he climbed the stairs, he heard a muffled voice.

# 6

This was why Annelies liked the job. Things changed so quickly. For two days she had been incarcerated in Andy's flat waiting for Edward Jay to make contact; and her patience was exhausted. She was sick of the waiting. She was sick of the television, the videos, the flat, the curtains, the carpet and the job. She had been on the verge of doubting Andy.

One phone call changed all that. Andy thought he had found out where Tate was hiding, and she was rattling her way in a taxi to meet Edward. Her instructions were to keep him with her at all costs, and on no account let the department know they were in contact with him.

She wondered if Edward had reached Julia before her. He must already have been on his way when he called. Suddenly it occurred to her that Edward's phone call had not been as straightforward as she thought. Edward was not telling Andy he wanted a meeting, or that Julia had been freed. He was calling for help.

'You sure this is the address you want?' said the taxi driver, pointing at the boarded building.

'Yes. I think so,' said Annelies, scrabbling in her handbag for her purse.

As Annelies looked for an entrance to the building she realised what she was doing was stupid. She had no authority in England, and she should never have been placed in this situation. If anything went wrong it would be her responsibility. She took out the phone and called the office, only to find that Andy had not yet returned. She asked for Vince, but he had disappeared. She decided to find Edward, stall him, and persuade him to wait for Andy.

# Chapter 16

## 1

Andy had done it. He'd finally cracked it. He had found out where Tate lived. In half an hour the basement flat would be under surveillance. The next time Jay called they'd work out a deal; if he called again. He might have done the exchange with Ginger, and if he was lucky then Julia was free.

Even if Jay never surfaced again there was a fighting chance of getting Tate now they knew where he lived. The moment he slipped up, they'd be on to him.

Andy barely made it into the Customs and Excise building before he was told to report to Simon Patterson. He ran up the stairs. He wanted to call Annelies and find out whether Jay had called. He needed to arrange the surveillance on Tate.

Priorities! The Chief was the most important. He had to be kept in the picture, and persuaded to give authorisation for the surveillance.

He knocked on the door, and opened it before waiting for a reply.

'Sir, I've cracked it. I know where Tate is hiding.'

Patterson nodded. 'Sit down, Andy. We need to have a talk,' he said.

'Sir?' questioned Andy, apprehensively.

'We've reached a stalemate on this operation. I have an extremely concerned Deputy Assistant Commissioner of the Metropolitan Police Inspectorate on the phone. He insists you corroborate the allegations about Davidson.'

'I can't do that until I've seen this operation through to the end.'

'You have consistently failed to provide me with any concrete evidence for any of your theories. I have an unpleasant suspicion that your obsession with Tate has allowed you to fall victim to your own imagination.'

'We've discussed this before, sir. We're investigating a massive conspiracy. My informant tells me that Tate has the facility to import over twelve tons a year. That could be cannabis or heroin. He has people inside customs who are helping him.'

'I'm worried about this obsession with Tate. I hear he was romantically involved with one of your girlfriends many years ago, and that you have made this thing personal, so to speak.'

'How did you hear that?' asked Andy, sharply.

'Venables told me.'

Andy's heart stopped. Only one person knew that. Samuel Tate. Now Tate had told Vince.

But Andy knew he couldn't accuse Vince yet. Patterson would sneer at such a convenient suspect. 'That is irrelevant. But I am more certain than ever that Tate has someone inside the department.'

'If that's the case then your informant should make a statement to that effect,' said Patterson.

'Are you prepared to grant him immunity from prosecution?' asked Andy.

'That depends on his role. Our guidelines are quite clear about that. We cannot ignore his crime if he is a principal involved with the planning of the operation. Likewise, if he is trying to seek mitigation it's not going to cut much ice.'

'I will endeavour to obtain a statement from him. If he agrees we will have to consider including him in the witness protection programme.'

'That's all very well. But until you obtain that statement this case is closed.'

'You can't do that, sir. It's a waste of all the resources to date. I've had to take risks in order to get this far. One of them was arresting Davidson.'

'Well, I would say that was irresponsible in itself. I've spoken to Venables, and he agrees the whole operation is a waste of time.'

'He wouldn't know any better,' said Andy, exasperated. 'You're the only one to know the full story.'

'I don't buy it any more. This case is closed until further notice. Furthermore, you will make yourself available at the earliest opportunity to give evidence to the Police Inspectorate.'

Andy stood up. He had to contact Annelies. 'Very well, sir. You'll find me in the office.' He left the room.

# 2

'James Kelly,' the voice echoed down the corridor. It reverberated in Spider's eardrums. He didn't know if the voice was real. His head snapped round. He peered down the corridor. A ghostly figure stood at the end.

'Kelly? I want a word with you.'

The girl had been right after all. Someone had been watching. He took his hand from her neck and stood up. He walked towards the voice.

'We don't have much time,' said the voice. 'You don't know me, but I know you. I've got a message for you from Tate.'

Spider couldn't make sense of the words. They were all the more frightening for that. As he approached the figure he picked out the features. The face was a mask.

He had been caught again; but this time it would be different. He pulled his knife out of his pocket and struck at the mask. It disintegrated. A red film smeared over it.

A scream echoed.

Spider struck again and again.

He stared at the body on the floor and wondered where it came from. He would put it back there. He began dragging it along the floor, then stopped. Perhaps there would be more where this one came from. He wondered how many more there would be.

They were trying to stop him talking to his sister.

# 3

From the front the building looked impenetrable. The windows were boarded and the door was obstructed with balks of timber. Posters were billed over the shuttering. Edward looked suspiciously at the neighbouring buildings in case Ginger had given him the wrong address. He walked round to the back. There were no signs of life. A ruined car stood in a loading bay. He had expected Andy to be there before him. He was surprised by the absence of activity. The back door of the building was ajar. He walked cautiously across the yard to the car which offered some cover. He felt he was being watched from the dark windows of the warehouse behind, which blocked out the light.

He crouched behind the car and took Ginger's Smith and Wesson from his pocket. It looked straightforward. There was a clip. Safety catch. Double action. It was a long time since he'd been in contact with firearms, and then he'd shown little interest. He wished he'd listened more carefully.

He looked at the door. There was still no sign of life. He held the gun beneath his jacket and ran quietly across the yard to the door. He looked behind him and saw someone watching him. It was Annelies. He felt relief that he wasn't alone. He stood to one side of the door and beckoned her to join him.

'Where's Andy?' he whispered.

She shook her head. 'I don't know.'

'Shit!' said Edward.

'I think he has found Samuel Tate,' she offered by way of explanation.

Edward smiled. 'At last!' He hesitated for a moment. He took a deep breath. 'Let's go in,' he said.

'No,' she said. 'We wait for Andy.'

Edward shook his head. He opened the door gently. He exposed the gun, from under his jacket. Annelies stared at it. He ignored her.

Ahead of him there was a short corridor. To the left was a door. He peered inside. The toilets. He reached the swing door at the other end, and peered through the cracked glass in the upper half.

He pushed the door. The spring groaned, echoing in the hall, breaking the silence. For the briefest moment it was quiet. Then he heard running footsteps. He looked, and saw Julia descending the stairs in the corner. She saw him, and hesitated for a moment, before she recognised him. Her dress had been ripped to the waist, and hung in tatters. Her attention was caught by something at the bottom of the stair well. Edward couldn't see. She retreated up the stairs; horror on her face. She looked back at Edward, as if begging him to do something.

Julia turned to run back, and her foot caught the torn hem of her dress, tripping her. She fell awkwardly on the stairs. She rolled down, glancing off the bannisters, arms flailing in an attempt to break her fall.

'Julia!' shouted Edward, starting forward to pick her up. He sensed movement to his right, swung round and saw Spider.

Edward pulled the trigger of the gun wildly, before he had fully raised his arm. He heard the shot, and knew it had missed. He pulled the trigger again. Spider was almost on top of him. He saw the knife. He saw the blood on Spider's sleeve. Whose blood? He shot wildly, ducking away, and falling backwards. He kicked out at Spider who was hurling himself at him, and rolled away.

Edward brought up the gun, elbows on the floor, held it with both hands and pointed it at Spider's head, four feet away.

'No!' he heard Annelies scream.

He pulled the trigger.

The gun kicked.

Then there was silence. He stared at Spider, waiting for him to move again. There was a spasm. He kept aiming at the head, and the bright red hole.

Finally Edward rolled away and stood up. He looked at Julia, but Annelies was quicker than him, and had an arm around her. Julia was gasping for breath, her mouth open in a soundless scream. She was swaying, her legs curled beneath her. Her hands were clutching her unborn child and Edward could see blood seeping between her legs.

'Ambulance!' he shouted at Annelies. 'Get an ambulance.'

'There is a telephone in my bag,' said Annelies calmly.

Edward scrabbled in the bag, found the telephone and dialled. He paced the floor, answering the operator's questions automatically. 'Name.' 'Address.'

He followed the trail of blood around the corner and saw the bloody corpse. He hesitated, peering closely at the face, scared that it might be Andy.

'Caller! Are you there, caller?' The operator caught his attention. 'Nature of injury.' 'Cause of injury.' He tried to sound calm. How much more information did they want? It seemed to take an eternity before the details were recorded.

He switched off the phone, and knelt beside Julia. He looked at Annelies. 'There's a body over there,' he said.

'Who?' asked Annelies.

Edward shrugged. 'I don't know. He's dead.'

Annelies didn't go to look. 'Help me to lay her on her side,' she ordered.

Edward carefully moved Julia's legs from under her, and Annelies gently laid her head on her lap. She stroked Julia's hair.

Edward took Julia's hand. She pulled it away.

'I'm sorry, Julia,' he said.

It was a long time before Julia replied. She answered in a quiet voice. It was quite deliberate, quavering a little from the pain. Her face was ashen, and beginning to glisten. The pool of blood between her legs was growing a deeper red.

'Leave me alone, Edward. It's all over.'

Edward stared at her, startled. He looked at Annelies.

'Now you must call the police, Edward,' said Annelies.

'No. I don't think so,' said Edward. He looked back at Julia, 'I'm sorry, Julia. I didn't know this would happen. I tried my best. But you're safe now.'

'Leave me alone. I never want to see you again,' she said.

Annelies shook her head at Edward.

'Julia—'

Then Julia screamed. A long, loud, piercing scream which cut him out and drowned his words. A scream of frustration and pain.

Edward heard it, closed his eyes, and finally understood. When it ended, Julia buried her head in Annelies' lap and cried; small gasps of pain.

Edward stood up. He looked at Julia, her head buried, her hands grasping Annelies's coat, her knuckles white.

Edward looked at Annelies. She stared at him. Willing him to go. Willing him to stay. Willing the police to come. He saw nothing but his own pain. It was over.

Edward turned, looked with hate at Spider. He picked up the gun, and fired a last shot into the body. It barely moved. He put the gun in his pocket. And Ginger could suffer on the boat for eternity; he dropped the telephone into Annelies' bag.

He walked out of the door.

242

# 4

It was six o'clock. The customs officers in Fetter Lane were still shocked by the news that one of their number had been killed during an investigation. They waited for their instructions. They all felt that Vince's death could as easily have been their own. They did not understand why it was taking so long for orders to be issued. They wanted to be back on the case. They knew that the murder would fall under police jurisdiction; but the case itself was theirs.

In his office Patterson prevaricated. He wanted to keep the lid on the whole affair; but that was the only point on which he agreed with Andy. The case should never have been closed; Andy had vindicated himself, and now he refused to hand it over to the police.

Andy was exasperated. 'You can ignore the fact that Vince knew something about my past which only Tate knew. You can ignore Jay's tip off that Tate had someone placed in the department. You can even ignore the fact that someone leaked the information of de Groote's girlfriend's whereabouts. But you can't ignore that he was heard talking to Kelly by Jay's girlfriend, and that she distinctly believed he was the enemy.' The police could handle the murder. They could handle the abduction. They could go looking for Edward Jay. But Samuel Tate belonged to customs, and to Andy.

'Yes,' said the Chief, 'but we don't know exactly what was said. Venables might have been negotiating her release.'

'I hardly think that's likely. Why didn't he summon assistance when he found out where Julia was being held hostage?'

'It seems somewhat fortuitous that the very officer who cannot defend himself is being accused of corruption,' said Patterson.

'Sir, I'm willing to ignore that issue for the moment. There are more important things at stake. We should make sure no mention of this is leaked to the press,' said Andy. 'If this gets into the news then Tate will be gone. At the moment he has no idea how badly things are going for him.'

'I don't know if the police will accept that,' cautioned Patterson.

'They better,' warned Andy.

The Chief stared at him. He knew what Andy's warning meant; he was threatening to instigate the biggest internal investigation into corruption the department had ever known. It was best for morale if that didn't happen; and it never need happen, because Kelly was dead and he had killed Venables. If Andy was right about the corruption, it was a convenient scenario. 'What about your informant, Edward Jay?' asked Patterson.

'I don't know if he will contact us again. But I do know that the consignment of heroin changed hands, because Jay found out where Julia was being held hostage. That means Phillips must contact Tate at some time in order to pass over the drugs or the money.'

'The police will want to put out an All Ports Warning in case Jay tries to skip the country.'

'Fair enough. Just so long as it isn't plastered across the newspapers. I'd like them to put one out on Tate, alias Sheehan, simultaneously, in case he slips away while we're having this discussion.'

'What's the news on Jay's girlfriend, Julia?'

'Annelies is still with her at the hospital. She's suffering from shock. No interviews are being allowed.'

'What's her condition?'

'She's had an abruption.'

'A what?'

'Apparently she fell. She's pregnant. The afterbirth separated from the wall of the uterus. She's being kept in for observation. They may have to perform a caesarian.'

'The baby?'

'They're hopeful.'

'So the police haven't been able to interview her?'

'Not yet.'

'They might well conclude that Venables was working under cover, and that Kelly found out.'

'They might come to that conclusion,' said Andy, unconvinced.

'And you are sure you can link this whole thing to Tate?' asked Patterson.

'Yes,' said Andy bluntly. 'Unless he's already disappeared.'

'Then go ahead.'

They looked at each other.

'Davidson?' The Chief reminded Andy.

'I think that's the least of our problems at the moment. I'm sure the Deputy Assistant Commissioner will realise that our investigation is not complete.'

Patterson nodded. 'Keep me informed of your progress, day and night.'

'I will, sir,' said Andy. He didn't bother to tell the Chief that he had already posted two officers to watch Tate's flat before news of Vince's murder had broken.

# 5

Edward knew he had lost everything. All he had left was his freedom, and he was not going to lose that. It was time to leave England. It was time to work on his escape plan. There was no way the customs or the police would let him walk away from this scam. He forced himself not to look back; it would only slow him down. He was surprised he was still at liberty, and if he could keep the momentum going he'd survive.

He had options. He still had the van which had once been the start of a legitimate business. He tried not to think about those plans of a new life with Julia; they seemed so long ago. He would contact Jason, and beat Samuel to the money. He needed that money in the future. Samuel wasn't having it. He'd make sure Samuel realised who took it. He only wished he could be there when Samuel realised that his oldest friend had finally ripped him off.

Edward had a friend in Bradford with a trucking company who'd drive him out of England. He'd make his way to Spain where he had contacts who could fit him up with a new identity, and one day when the dust had settled he'd be back in touch. He'd sort out a trust arrangement for his child. He'd make sure his child never had to take the risks he did. Perhaps he'd slip back into England and see Julia again when her scars had healed, and maybe she would realise he was worth another chance.

For the briefest moment he was gripped by a terror that something might have happened to the baby. He suppressed the fear. If he succumbed to the fears, then his freedom was meaningless.

He dumped Ginger's BMW in the garage and picked up his van. It might be a mistake using it, but it wouldn't be for long. When he was out of the country he'd give Ballot a call, and tell him where it was so he could pick up the heroin. But first, he had to make some phone calls.

Edward met Jason in Sainsbury's supermarket on the Cromwell Road at seven. They walked to Jason's car carrying their groceries. It was like old times; the end of another scam.

'You look terrible,' commented Jason.

'I've had problems,' replied Edward. 'I've got to leave the country.'

'They're not on to you?' asked Jason, alarmed.

'No,' Edward lied. 'But I was seen in the wrong company.'

'I was told you were out of the country,' said Jason.

'I changed my plans,' said Edward. He decided it was better not to tell Jason the details after all. 'How did things go with you?'

'Like a dream,' replied Jason. 'No problems at all.'

'I'm sorry Samuel got in touch with you.'

'To tell you the truth, I was pissed off. I thought it was a liberty all round.'

'Did he give you a number where you could call him?' There was always the chance Samuel had slipped up.

'Yeah. A pager number. Anyway, I'm glad you phoned. He had some complicated arrangements for handing over the money to some banker in the City.'

'He never did learn to do things the easy way.' They walked in silence for a moment or two. 'Call the banker and let him know I've picked up the paperwork. You don't want any misunderstandings.'

'Don't worry, I will,' said Jason.

'I won't be working with Samuel again,' said Edward. 'He's too dangerous. Tell the good guys to keep clear of him.'

'Thanks,' said Jason. The warning was unnecessary, and he knew better than to ask any questions.

They got into Jason's car and Edward directed him to where he had parked. Jason opened the boot, took out three cardboard boxes and loaded them into the van. He ostentatiously handed Edward the bag of groceries for the benefit of any onlookers. They were a couple of bachelors doing the weekend shopping after work. 'The money's all there. The final score was nine hundred kilos give or take a few grams at seventeen fifty a kilo. That makes one point five seven five million. Happy counting. It was good to do business, Edward.'

They stood awkwardly for a moment or two. 'Will you do something for me, Jason?'

'What is it?' asked Jason, cautiously.

'Julia is in hospital at the moment. I don't know when she'll be out, but I'd like you to give her something from me.'

'Why don't you—?' he began, but Edward interrupted him.

'We're finished,' Edward said, and looked away. He felt a lump in his throat.

'Of course I'll do it,' said Jason.

Edward pulled out one of the boxes from the van and passed it to Jason. 'Give her that for me. Tell her I still love her.'

Jason nodded.

'Thanks Jason. I'll give you a call sometime. Maybe we should go for that dinner one day.'

Jason nodded. Edward stepped into the van and started the engine.

'Edward!' said Jason. Edward looked at him. 'Good luck,' said Jason quietly.

Edward drove away. It was the first time he had left a meeting before Jason.

As he drove through London towards the A1, Edward amused himself with the thought of how Samuel would react when he found out he had been ripped off. He liked the idea of Samuel catching up with him in the future. Samuel had always been terrified of a rip-off. In all his years of running drugs he'd only experienced a twenty grand theft. Now he was going to know how it felt to lose a million. His worst dream was about to come true.

Edward imagined some future meeting between them in some Bolivian hotel or Spanish bar. He looked forward to that encounter.

Edward hunched over the steering wheel, driving carefully. Only a couple more hours until he dumped the van. Pete was waiting for him in Bradford and then he would be safe. He and Pete had worked together for over ten years. He'd helped Pete set up the trucking operation. Now Pete knew all the customs procedures at Dover. He was known by many of the officers because he did a round trip to the Continent every week. He worked regular hauls with the truck. Most truckers who turned to smuggling were caught because they made stupid mistakes. They came into the country with unprofitable cargoes or empty trailers. No regular haulage company could afford to run an empty trailer. The cowboys set up an operation and bought a cheap truck for a few grand. Pete's rig was worth thirty-five, and it paid for itself legitimately. The others bought trailers and built false bulkheads, and were surprised when customs measured the interior and found the false compartments. Edward had bought the refrigerated trailer, and removed the insulation. There was a tool kit on the Continent with the correct rivets to replace the panels. There were spare doors which could be packed with dope.

They'd brought material into the country in a hundred different ways, and taken the money out. The customs had even asked Pete to report if he noticed anything suspicious about other trucking operations. He had one of the best outfits because he'd set it up with Edward. They'd had it made. They'd even run a small food canning operation at one time, bringing in the dope as tinned tomatoes and peaches.

Samuel had blown it all. Samuel's greed had blown it all. Edward wanted revenge. He suddenly realised he was doing this the wrong way. Samuel had to know who was responsible for his downfall. He wanted vengeance because Samuel had ruined his relationship with Julia. He wasn't going to let Samuel get away with ruining his life. Samuel had to pay for it. Ripping off a million pounds wasn't enough. There were some things money could not buy.

When Julia heard about this, she might give him another chance.

Edward pulled into a service station. He telephoned Pete to change their arrangement. Afterwards, he felt better. He would enjoy taking his revenge on Samuel. When he'd done this, he wouldn't have to look over his shoulder in case Samuel tracked him down. Samuel would be otherwise occupied, locked away in the big house.

# Chapter 17

## 1

It was late evening when Andy collected Annelies from the hospital. She looked tired. She had stayed with Julia until they took her to the operating theatre, then waited until she heard that the caesarian had been successful, and that the baby girl was born.

Annelies had formed a bond with Julia, supporting her through her ordeal, and now that it was over, she felt empty. Andy put his arms around her, and gave her a squeeze. She folded into him for a moment, then felt his resistance, and pulled away. They walked out of the hospital on to the street. It was a clear night and they both savoured the sudden calm after the day's urgency. He told her what had happened, and listened to her story.

'There's nothing more we can do now,' he said, 'except wait.'

She slipped her arm though his as they walked. 'Don't think about it any more,' she said.

'No,' he agreed. 'I'm tired of thinking now. I've wanted Tate for fifteen years. I've given it my best shot.'

They walked in silence for a while. 'I think I'll go home, have a drink and go to bed.' Annelies didn't comment. 'You don't have to come,' he added. 'You've been stuck in the flat for two days. You're probably sick of it.'

'If you want to be alone, maybe I will go for a movie,' said Annelies.

'That's not what I meant. I'd be happy for you to come back.'

Andy waited at a bus stop.

'Why do you not take a taxi?' asked Annelies. 'It is quicker.'

'What would we do with the extra time?' he answered. 'I'd only drink one more glass of vodka before I went to bed.'

Annelies smiled. She liked his dry sense of humour. She liked him after all, despite the bumpy start to their relationship. He took out his cigarettes, and her hand slipped from his arm. She watched him, standing with his back to the wind, face illuminated by the lighter's flickering flame. He was crying out to be loved, but he didn't know it. He kept himself so tightly closed; and she wondered who had hurt him all those years ago.

They sat on the bus. He was conscious of Annelies's warmth beside him, and the absence of her hand on his arm. He hadn't wanted that last cigarette; but he felt her hand invaded his privacy, and now he missed it.

Andy couldn't stop thinking about the case. He wouldn't let Simon Patterson get away with sweeping the truth under the carpet. He wasn't letting Vince get some posthumous award for dying in the course of duty. If the truth spoiled the Chief's chances of receiving a New Year's gong, that was tough; and it would spoil his chances, because shit stuck. The whole department would be smeared.

He wouldn't pull any punches when he wrote his report. He'd point out that caution and a lack of confidence in the officers handling the case were responsible for the failure. He'd find the proof of Vince's involvement with Tate. He'd snout around at Heathrow. Vince had made a number of journeys out there to do with his trip to Cyprus. Maybe one of them would provide the key. Andy would nail the charges to Vince's coffin, and then see who turned up for the funeral. Sod you, Venables. You made a big mistake with your toothy smile and lips like a terrier's arsehole.

'Hey! Relax!' said Annelies. She put her hand on his arm. 'You are so tense. Your body is like electric. I think maybe you need a massage. What is wrong?'

'Nothing,' said Andy. 'I was just thinking.'

Annelies knew he would never open up. Old dogs didn't learn new tricks. He'd lived in that cage for too long. People like him were safe to have as friends. They made no demands in relationships, and never reached inside her. She loaned them the beach but they never swam in the sea.

When they reached the flat Andy poured them both a vodka. Annelies retreated to the sitting room, and sat on the sofa. He took off his jacket and tie, chose a record and put it on.

'Come here,' said Annelies, putting her hand on the sofa next to her. She never knew what made her do some things. It seldom mattered. Life was a series of mysterious turns and there was always some way of getting back home.

Andy sat down awkwardly. 'Come,' said Annelies, and gently removed the glass from his hand. She pulled him towards her and held him in her arms. He relaxed for the briefest of seconds then resisted. She gripped his hair, pulled his face towards her, and kissed him. She parted her lips and slowly felt his tongue explore.

Uncontrollably, Andy's hands began that tentative survey. His fingers slipped beneath her jersey and traversed her back. They found her breasts, and held them for a moment. She yielded. He yielded. For a moment they melted into one another.

'Are you sure this is a good idea?' he whispered in her ear.

'Why not?' she answered, quietly.

'Then shall we go next door?' he asked, unnecessarily.

They made the clumsy journey into the bedroom, and undressed in the darkness. She lay back on the bed, her arms curled under the pillow, her body illuminated by the shaft of light through the half-closed door. He closed his eyes and ran his hands from her thighs to her breasts, experiencing the firmness of her flesh. He pressed his lips on hers.

His body was soft and warm, so unlike the muscular physique of her boyfriend in Holland. Andy was very gentle. She wrapped her arms and legs around him. She pulled him towards her, and felt his hard penis nuzzling against her thighs.

'Please,' she whispered, 'don't come inside me.'

'I'm not that reckless,' he answered.

She laughed.

She stretched her hand down and carefully guided his penis into her. Slowly she moved her hips, drawing him deeper and deeper. Gradually their soft cautious breathing gave way to pants, and their hands' delicate brush strokes turned to grappling. His body thrust between her legs.

'Don't come,' she said. 'Don't come inside me.' She twisted her body and he slipped out of her. She took him in her hand and ran her fingers rhythmically up and down until he came on her stomach. Then she held him tight.

Andy wondered why this had happened. He couldn't make sense of it. He was too tired to think. He felt his eyelids dropping. He would doze for a moment or two. He moved his hand and stroked Annelies's cheek before he sank into sleep.

Annelies listened to Andy's breathing. He was asleep. The first time was never the best, but the novelty of the experience could never be repeated. She had no regrets. She ran her fingers down her body and touched her clitoris.

Andy was still asleep when the doorbell rang. He struggled awake and gently disentangled his limbs from Annelies's body. He looked at his watch as he stumbled into the sitting room. He wondered who was calling at two in the morning: it was probably some drunk at the wrong door. He picked up the entry phone. He recognised the voice on the line immediately, and pressed the button to open the front door.

Andy rushed back to the bedroom. He was wide awake now. 'Annelies!' he said, shaking her gently. 'Wake up!' She moaned. 'Wake up. It's Jay. He's come back. Get dressed.' He pulled on his clothes quickly. He was still buttoning his shirt when he heard the knock on the door.

# 2

Edward had left Bradford. He was committed to the plan now. He'd given the money to Pete to keep for him. 'I may be gone for some time. You'll hear from me. Put this lot away somewhere. Maybe abroad. Definitely abroad. Spread it about the banks. It'll take a year to bank it. Start with small accounts and build them up. You can keep the interest for your trouble.' He never questioned the faith he put in Pete. If he started questioning the few people he trusted, the whole world would come tumbling down.

Pete was big, solid and dependable. He smiled from under his big moustache in response to the instructions. His eyes twinkled as he peered into the boxes. He stroked his bald head with a large palm, smoothing imaginary hair. He whistled when he saw the bundles of notes. 'I thought you were too young to be allowed on the Great Train Robbery.'

'Brinks Mat,' joked Edward.

'It'll be there when you come back,' said Pete, gravely. And Edward knew he meant it.

Pete didn't ask any questions. He was used to Edward's sudden appearances and disappearances. 'Watch yourself,' he said, in farewell.

Then Edward was driving south again, exhausted. He stopped frequently at the service stations for coffee, trying hard to stay awake.

'Hello, Edward,' said Andy. 'I didn't expect to see you again so soon.'

'Have you arrested Samuel yet?' Edward asked, dispensing with the niceties. If they'd picked up Samuel that was the end of it.

'No,' said Andy.

'But you know where he is?'

'Yes,' Andy nodded.

'You've got him under surveillance?'

'Of course.'

Edward relaxed a little. That made things easier. 'Good, because I've done some thinking. You can't prove the case against him unless you catch him with the heroin. And I have the heroin.'

'What happened to Ginger?' asked Andy.

'Samuel ordered him to kill me. He came off worse.' Edward shrugged.

'Did you kill him?' asked Andy.

'No. He was alive when I left him. Not in great shape. But alive.'

'Come into the sitting room,' said Andy. 'You look exhausted. This is going to take some time. I need to know what you did after Ginger gave us the slip.'

Edward told him what happened on the boat, and where it was.

'Any objection if I despatch someone there immediately?' asked Andy.

'No.' Edward shook his head. 'By the way, if you trawl the canal basin around the boat, you'll find the tea chests which contained the consignment.'

Andy picked up the phone and called the duty officer at Fetter Lane.

Annelies emerged from the bedroom. Edward heard the door close. He started. He stood up, defensively, before realising who it was. His nerves were shot.

'Hello, Edward,' said Annelies.

'How is Julia?' he asked.

'She is all right. And you are a father.'

Edward smiled, for a brief second, perplexed at the contradictory emotions. He should have been elated but felt only sadness.

'You have a baby girl,' said Annelies.

Edward nodded. He sat down again. Andy had put down the phone. They were both watching him as if he were dangerous. He began to doubt himself.

'So,' said Andy finally, 'why are you here?'

'I want a deal,' said Edward.

'No deal,' said Andy. But he would deal. He might have to. 'You killed someone. That can't be overlooked.'

'It was self defence.'

253

'I know,' agreed Andy. 'I think you'll get away with that.'

'This is what I propose,' said Edward. 'I will deliver the heroin to Samuel. In return you will bring no charges against me for smuggling, or dealing in hard drugs.'

'You're guilty of smuggling controlled substances,' said Andy.

'I agree. I'm willing to stand trial for smuggling cannabis. I'm willing to take my chances on those charges. After all, it's not so bad, is it? Not when one of our political parties votes to legalise it?'

'I don't want to comment on that,' said Andy. 'But I'm willing to accept your proposition so far.'

'Good,' replied Edward. 'Then let's get on with it, before Samuel makes a break.'

'Why the change of heart?' asked Andy.

'Because of Julia. Samuel ruined the only thing I cared about. All your evidence against Samuel is circumstantial. Even what I've told you about his financial affairs may not help, if he's closed those accounts. They might not have been in his name. They'll lead you to other people, but not necessarily Samuel. This is the only way.' He paused. 'Anyway, I want revenge.'

'You've thought about the consequences?' asked Andy.

'Sure. Samuel is not going to forget this little betrayal. He still has friends. Even if this scam bankrupts him, they owe him favours, and I don't fancy my chances after I've fingered him. Maybe you'll give me a new identity. Lock me up in my own private prison. Section 42. I've thought about it, and it's worth all that.'

Andy said nothing. He didn't know if Edward would qualify for the Witness Protection Programme. He called the duty officer again and told him to send six men to join the four officers who were already watching Tate.

They drove in Andy's car to the garage in Maida Vale and retrieved the heroin from the BMW. Edward sat in the back seat. 'This is how I want to do it,' said Edward. 'I will deliver the heroin. I want a moment alone with Samuel. I want him to know what he has done. When I come out, then you can arrest him. He'll be holding the goods, and you'll have witnessed the transfer.'

'He may refuse to accept the heroin. Especially if you tell him you're shopping him.'

'I won't tell him that. I only want him to know that none of this would have happened if he hadn't betrayed me. I want him to know his organisation was ruined because of his greed. When he's arrested I want him to know I fingered him.'

Andy nodded, although he wasn't sure. There was still plenty which could go wrong. It might be better to arrest them as they met, although Tate could deny he knew what was in the bags.

'Can you open the bags inside his flat, so there's no doubt Tate knows what's in them?'

'I can do that,' said Edward. After a few moments he asked, 'Tell me something. Why do you want Samuel so much?'

'Fifteen years ago I used to work on the fishing boats out of a small place called Brightlingsea. I had a girlfriend called Rosa. Tate killed her.'

There was a stunned silence in the car. Annelies looked at Andy. Things were becoming clearer to her.

'I heard it was an accident,' said Edward.

'No. It wasn't an accident,' said Andy. 'But how do you know about it?' he asked defensively.

'I was there,' said Edward. 'It was the first scam we ever did. We brought in some cannabis from Holland. I can't remember how much now. I turned up pretending to be a mechanic and took the stuff off the boat. I never went back there again. It was quite a long time later I heard someone had been drowned.'

'That was Rosa. Tate's first victim,' said Andy, angrily.

'I'm sorry,' said Edward. 'I'm sorry to hear that.' He paused, then added. 'So let's nail him good. I'm counting on you to put him away for a long, long time.'

Andy surprised himself. He pulled over, turned in his seat and faced Edward. He extended his hand. Edward took it, and they shook. 'You've got a deal,' Andy said, and smiled grimly. He turned back, and drove on.

Men were such strange creatures, thought Annelies. She put a hand on Andy's thigh. She wondered how he really felt. She wondered whether he really believed that Tate's arrest would make him happier. She doubted it could make a difference after all this time. She hoped he didn't have too many expectations. Simply convicting Tate wouldn't change his life; it wasn't like that, not after fifteen years. The habits and defences were too deeply etched in his character.

'We're approaching Tate's place,' said Andy. 'It's the basement flat of number forty-seven. There's a green—'

'I know which one it is,' interrupted Edward. 'He's a clever sod, renting this place all these years.'

Andy turned the next corner, and stopped. Across the road was a dark blue van; the driver raised his hand, acknowledging their arrival. Customs and Excise were ready.

# 3

Edward descended the steps to the basement flat. One thing was certain, if Samuel was dreaming peacefully, he was about to wake up to a nightmare. A security light switched on automatically. He put the bags down, outside the door. His heart began to race. It was curiously apposite that his partnership with Samuel should be ending where they had hatched the first scam all those years ago. He took out a cigarette and lit it. He inhaled deeply. He fingered Ginger's gun in his pocket. For the first time he felt in control of a situation with Samuel.

He had a feeling that he might still be on that ferry at dawn. Customs wouldn't be expecting him to make a break for it. Their attention would be focused on Samuel.

Edward rang the doorbell. He waited patiently. There was no sign of life. Perhaps Samuel had already flown. No! Andy was confident he was still there. He rang the bell a second time. He waited.

Footsteps. The door opened.

'Edward!' said Tate. 'What the fuck are you doing at this time of night? Come in.'

'I'm delivering the drugs, Samuel,' said Edward. 'I've got Julia, no thanks to you. But a deal is a deal.'

Tate looked at the bags suspiciously. 'Bring them in,' he said, holding the door open. Edward lifted the bags and walked through to the sitting room.

Tate closed the door behind Edward, then switched on the light. He had obviously dressed hurriedly before answering the doorbell. Although he was wearing a jacket, he was still tucking his shirt into his trousers as he followed Edward. 'Sit down,' he said, perching on the edge of the sofa.

Tate's brain was whirring into action. A knock on the door in the middle of the night was never good news, but he hadn't expected Edward. How had Edward found out where he was hiding? Someone must have told him, but there was no one who knew. 'How did you find out where I was?' Tate asked, making sure his voice didn't betray his concerns.

'Someone told me,' said Edward.

256

Someone? That someone had to be the customs. They must have found out somehow. It meant Edward was trying to do a deal. But Vince had reported that Edward met Ginger. Something must have gone very wrong. 'Who?'

'Your customs officer, before Spider slit his throat.'

Tate raised his eyebrows. 'Why have you come here?'

'I came to give you the heroin.' Edward leaned forward and unzipped the bags. 'It's all in there.'

'Ah yes. The heroin,' mused Tate. 'You know, I thought you were going to rip me off.'

'Oh, but I have ripped you off, Samuel,' replied Edward. 'I've collected the money from Jason. I'm keeping it for all the trouble you've caused me.'

There were more important things than money at stake now. 'I haven't heard from Ginger or Spider. Do you have any news of them?' asked Tate.

Edward stared at Tate. He looked forward to seeing his reaction. 'Spider's dead. He tried to kill me. So did Ginger. I left him in poor shape.'

Tate raised his eyebrows. 'Oh dear,' he commented. Edward was manifesting an uncharacteristic ruthlessness these days. 'So you managed to resolve things with Julia?'

'This is bullshit, Samuel! You put them up to all that. You were responsible for bringing Julia into this. You've fucked up everything.'

'It's a bit of a worry, Ned.' Tate shook his head. 'You wouldn't be double-crossing me, would you? My old chum?'

Edward looked at Tate, 'I'm off now. We won't be seeing each other again.'

Tate nodded thoughtfully. He stood up and walked to the fireplace and picked up a packet of cigarettes, took one out and put it in his mouth. He patted his pockets looking for a light. He put his hand into his jacket pocket. 'You're playing a dangerous game, Ned. The way I see it, you're the only witness. Without you they don't have much on me.' Tate took the gun Ginger had given him out of his pocket.

He pointed the gun at Edward's head. 'In case you get any heroic ideas, I'm a very good shot. I did a lot of practice in Ahmed Akbar's villa in Pakistan, while I was setting up this deal.'

Edward wondered how long Andy would wait outside before bursting in.

Tate smiled, and kicked the coffee table out of the way. The vase smashed. He pulled Edward to his feet by grabbing his shirt, and ripped it.

'Fuck you, Edward. You've got it wrong again. Your silence is my only insurance policy.' He held the gun under Edward's jaw, pressing it into the bone. His face twisted with hate. 'Fuck you, now. You fucked up the biggest scam of all.' Tate pushed Edward against the mantelpiece, sweeping the ornaments on to the floor. The room was beginning to look like there had been a fight.

Edward held Tate's hand and the gun. He stared into Tate's eyes. 'I have an insurance policy, Samuel.' He put his hand into his coat pocket and felt the gun.

'Yeah?' sneered Tate.

'I've done a deal,' said Edward. 'This is a set-up. There's a Black Maria waiting for you on the street.'

# 4

As Annelies and Andy watched Edward disappear down the steps to Tate's flat, Andy said, 'I think I'm going to get that bastard after all. But I need Jay as well, to be really sure.'

'How do you think the court will find Edward's position?' asked Annelies.

'I'll make sure the judge knows how much he co-operated. He stands a good chance.'

Andy paced up and down the road, looking at his watch. He wondered how long to give Edward. Five minutes, he decided.

Annelies imagined the scene in the flat. She imagined Edward opening the bags of heroin, and wondered how Tate would react. Suddenly she realised what it was which nagged at her. She could have kicked herself. When Edward mentioned revenge, the word had made her uneasy. Now she knew why. Edward still had the gun.

'Andy!' she said, 'Edward still has the gun.'

Andy looked at her nonplussed, at first; then comprehension dawned.

'He said he wanted revenge, but I did not think he meant to kill Tate,' she said unnecessarily. Andy was already speaking into the radio, telling his men to move in. They ran towards the flat.

They heard the shot.

They clattered down the basement steps. Andy banged on the door. 'Customs and Excise! Open up. You are under arrest.' He saw that the windows were covered with bars. He stepped back, and the officer carrying the sledgehammer pushed his way forward. They all stood back as he swung. The sledgehammer drove into the door. The wood splintered. The officer swung again, and again.

# 5

Edward struggled to stay awake. He kept drifting into unconsciousness. He couldn't remember where he was. It had been a long day. He jolted awake from time to time. He woke and he slept, drifting in and out of reality. He couldn't remember how he got on to the articulated truck. It was noisy. All he wanted to do was sleep. It felt as if someone had hit him in the chest with a sledgehammer.

The truck lumbered out of the fog into the bright lights of Dover harbour and stopped. The driver got out and walked into the ticket office. He seemed to be taking a long time. They had some time to kill before the ferry departed. Waiting, always waiting. Waiting for phone calls. Waiting for meetings.

'I never thought I'd be taking you out of here. Is this the end?' asked the driver. Edward didn't recognise the voice. It wasn't Pete after all. It sounded like Samuel. He looked but he couldn't recognise the face. It was fine. Maybe Pete couldn't make it after all. Everything was going according to plan. He was leaving the country. That was the only thing that mattered.

'I don't know,' said Edward. 'I need a rest. Do you want to go on working?'

'It's handy you know. A bit extra from time to time.'

Edward woke when the engine started and the truck pulled forward to Passport Control and the queues for the ferry. Two customs officers waved them down and gestured them to one side.

'What is it?' asked Edward, alarmed.

'Nothing,' said the driver. Edward noticed with surprise that Pete was driving after all. 'They're going to check we're not running on red diesel.'

'Red diesel?'

'It's just routine. Relax. Relax.'

I'll never get away from them thought Edward. He shivered as the cold wind blasted through the door. 'We forgot...' he said. He was supposed to hide in the refrigerated section amongst the frozen carcases.

'It doesn't matter,' said Pete.

A moment later the truck moved forwards. 'With the single market they're not supposed to look at your passport,' said Edward. He tried to move his arm but couldn't.

'Shall I tell them, or do you want to?' Pete stretched out of the window to hand over the passports. Andy Ballot flicked the pages to check that they were in date and passed them back, continuing his conversation with a colleague.

The truck rumbled on and joined the queue for the ferry. This was the point of no return. This was the traditional departure point for British exiles in the old days, but Edward didn't plan to live in Boulogne. He was going South, to the sun and a new life. Dover harbour didn't make him feel remorseful about leaving Britain. There were the grubby cars and the dirty trucks. He knew it all too well. He'd smuggled a few tons through here in his time. The biting wind whistled across the open tarmac, grasping at the dockers' ragged coats and endlessly sorting through the scraps of paper which held a clue. He dozed in the warmth of the cab.

He struggled awake as the truck lurched on to the ferry. He only felt a brief pang of remorse. He found himself standing on the stern of the ship. A girl was standing next to him. It was Julia. He watched the lights of Dover recede into the fog. He wondered if he would ever see England again. He looked down at the cold black water being churned by the ship's propellers. The icy fog swirled in, obscuring the lights, and smothered him. The last sound he heard was a seagull's cry, but it didn't make sense.

# 6

Tate watched Edward reel backwards. The back of his head took off, and sprayed the wall with blood. Samuel fell with Edward as he crumpled on to the carpet. He knelt, quickly wiping the gun with his handkerchief, and pressed it into Edward's hand. He stood back and admired his handiwork.

It looked like there had been a struggle. The blood was messing up his carpet.

Edward's hand was clutching something in his coat pocket. He pulled it out and found another gun. He stared at it with surprise. The devious bastard had planned to shoot him! He looked at Edward's body with disgust. He disentangled Edward's fingers from the gun and carefully picked it up with his handkerchief. He dropped it into one of the bags containing the heroin, and zipped it up.

Tate heard footsteps outside. He reached for the phone and dialled three digits.

'Emergency services,' said the operator. 'Which service do you require?'

'Police!' snapped Tate.

He heard the customs shouting outside. As he walked to the rear of his flat with the cordless phone, he gave his address. He locked himself in the bathroom, and said, 'A man has just been shot in my sitting room in the course of a struggle. I am now barricaded in the bathroom. There are people breaking down the front door, and I think they are going to kill me.'

'Please hold the line.'

Tate waited a moment while the police cars were deployed.

'Can you tell us whether your assailants are likely to have firearms?'

'I should think so,' said Tate. He held the receiver away from his ear. 'It sounds like they're in the house now,' he said. He could hear the bedroom doors being flung open. He held the receiver to the bathroom door. Time for a bit of panic, he thought.

'He's in here,' shouted a voice.

'Stand back!'

The bathroom door flew off its hinges. Tate watched Andy Ballot pick himself off the floor.

'I've got you this time, you bastard!' Ballot hissed. Tate looked at the receiver in his hand. He guessed the police had heard that. He cut the connection.

'I don't think so,' said Tate, contemptuously. 'By the way, the police will be here in a minute. They will want to know why you encouraged an armed criminal to come into my house.'

# Epilogue

'I Samuel William Tate, make this statement of my own free will. At five o'clock on the morning of 2 May, I was woken by my front door bell ringing. When I opened the door Edward Jay, a man I had known for some years, pushed his way into my flat. I had been contacted by him some weeks previously wanting to borrow money for some venture. I refused. He continued to pester me with his requests, asking me to phone him at all hours. I took pity on him and tried to help him in practical ways.

On this occasion Edward Jay appeared distressed. I invited him into the sitting room. He told me that he was involved in some dealings with two men I knew and that he had killed one of them, James Kelly, known as "Spider". I asked him if he had contacted the police but he denied it.

I proceeded to question Edward Jay but his story was confused and I felt he was, for want of better expressions, disturbed and paranoid. He thought that I was responsible for the kidnapping of his girlfriend by Patrick "Ginger" Phillips. In fact, my only dealings with Phillips and Kelly had been to discuss investment in a snooker hall. The intention was to create a leisure empire by expanding out of a greyhound racing enterprise in which I used to have an interest in South London.

I asked Edward Jay what was in the bags he had brought with him and which he placed in the sitting room. He said they contained drugs, and proceeded to open one, from which he produced a gun and threatened to shoot me. It was not clear what he was hoping to achieve. It appeared that his dealings with Phillips and Kelly had gone wrong. I do not know the nature of those dealings. I was extremely frightened and when the opportunity arose I wrestled with Jay for control of the gun. During the struggle the gun discharged itself and unfortunately shot Edward Jay. I panicked when I heard what I assumed to be Jay's associates arriving at the front door. I called the police immediately and hid in the bathroom. I was very shocked by these events. I thought I was going to be killed.

At no time did the men who broke into my flat identify themselves as customs officers, and under the circumstances it is not surprising that I was terrified.

I know nothing of Phillips' and Kelly's other interests. They only approached me as a potential investor in the snooker hall enterprise. I gave my accountant the proposals but he felt that the business was not sound. In addition, I felt dubious about the origins of their wealth.

I had met de Groote in Holland many years ago. He was neither a close friend, nor was I involved, other than personally, with him. I saw him six months ago at his request. It turned out that he too wanted to borrow some money, but I was not able to oblige. I am very sorry to hear from you that he was killed and hope that my inability to make a loan was not in any way responsible for his subsequent death. I assume he was killed by unscrupulous business colleagues.

I saw Edward Jay's girlfriend, Julia, about eight months ago. When I heard that Jay had been imprisoned in Pakistan for ten years I felt that it would be charitable to see if she needed any help or support. I had known her for some years and felt that she should not have been involved with someone as unprincipled as Jay. Julia told me that Jay had won a reprieve and would soon be returning to England. She told me that she intended to end her relationship with him.

I do not have any bank accounts in Switzerland, Luxembourg or any other country outside Great Britain. At present my bank account holds in the region of 800,000 (eight hundred thousand) pounds.

The radio pager belongs to Martin Sheehan. He allowed me to use it because he is abroad. I find the radio pager convenient because I am seldom at home and it is important that people can contact me at any time.

I admit using Martin Sheehan's credit card on occasion for services. There was no intentional deceit involved. The transactions were of a personal and private nature and Martin would have no objection to this. We always settle our accounts at a later date. I do not know where he is at the moment, but I am sure he will substantiate what I have told you in due course.

I do not know anything about the heroin which Edward Jay brought to my house. It is not surprising that he was so disturbed when he visited me if he was involved in such activities. However, Jay had smuggled drugs in the past and I am not surprised to hear that he was involved in further nefarious activities. I am shocked to hear that I was under suspicion of being involved in this conspiracy. It shows how careful one must be in choosing one's business partners, or even acquaintances.

You ask if I have any criminal record. I was found guilty of tax evasion some ten years ago in connection with a property deal. No, I have not and I have never been involved in any dealings with drugs, nor have I been convicted of any such dealings.

*The Scam*

I would certainly not have been interested in any commercial ventures with Phillips and Kelly had I suspected that they were involved in crime.

I would like you to note that this statement is made willingly by me, and that I have not insisted on my solicitor being present. I have answered all your questions both fully and honestly. I would now like to contact my solicitor.'